Scales
AND
Steel

AMY CAMPBELL

To those who refuse to be the story others tell about them.

This is a work of fiction. Names, characters, places, and incidents are the product of the author's imagination or are used fictitiously. Any resemblance to actual persons, living or dead, events, or locales is entirely coincidental.

SCALES AND STEEL

Copyright © 2026 Amy Campbell

All rights reserved. No part of this book may be reproduced or used in any manner without written permission of the copyright owner except for the use of quotations in a book review.

Cover design by Amy Campbell
Map by Amy Campbell
Chapter headings, heading art, and dividers designed by Amy Campbell
First edition: February 2026
www.amycampbell.info

v 113025

What They Don't Tell
You in the Ballads

Once upon a time, there was a prince turned dragon, a knight sent to slay him, and a princess who did not, under any circumstances, want rescuing.

That's the version the minstrels might sing—glorious battles, noble sacrifice, a happily ever after forged in fire and steel.

But that's not this story.

This is the part they don't put in the ballads. The part with broken trust and burning guilt. With aching silences and questions that don't have easy answers. With a knight who isn't sure what he's fighting for, and a dragon who never asked to be one.

Scales and Steel is a fantasy romance, yes—but it's also about grief, survival, and the long, stubborn work of becoming something more than what the world says you are. It's about choosing love even when you don't believe you deserve it.

Below, you'll find content warnings for themes that may be distressing, followed by a list of tropes you can expect along the way. If you like to read with both eyes open—whether for safety or satisfaction—this part is for you.

Thank you for being here.

Content Warnings

THIS BOOK CONTAINS the following themes:

- Grief, survivor's guilt, and PTSD
- Depression and brief suicidal ideation — Chapter 17
- Death of family members (off-page, but deeply felt)
- Emotional trauma and self-blame
- Torture (on-page, emotionally intense) — Chapter 20
- Magical body horror (painful transformation scenes)
- Violence and battle scenes, including dragon combat
- Abuse of power, coercion, and political manipulation
- Reference to war crimes (destruction of a kingdom, targeted purges)
- Internalized shame and fear of hurting others

Tropes

- Enemies to lovers
- Beauty and the Beast, but gayer
- Forced proximity
- Hurt/comfort
- Only one bed (eventually)
- Slow burn with pining so bad it might be contagious

- Angst with teeth
- Found family
- A princess with rock-throwing accuracy and no chill
- Banter as emotional warfare
- Magic gone wrong
- Knight falls for the dragon he was sent to kill
- Protective instincts vs political orders
- The prince no longer wants the throne—but maybe he still deserves it

AVALIS
MORVANE
ISENDRETH
REVENDAR
ISLE OF KELOS
N
AVALIS

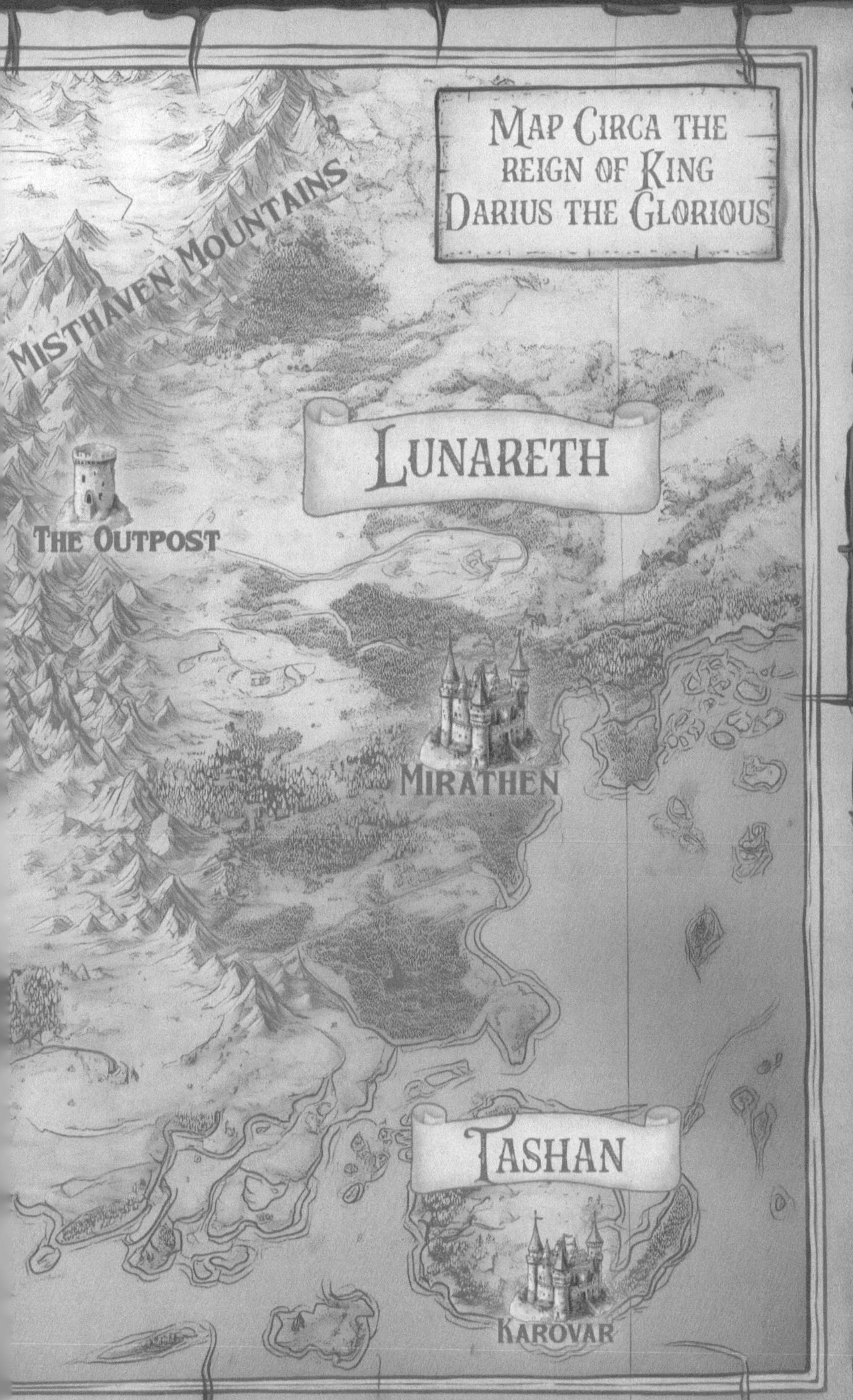

MISTHAVEN MOUNTAINS
MAP CIRCA THE REIGN OF KING DARIUS THE GLORIOUS
LUNARETH
THE OUTPOST
MIRATHEN
TASHAN
KAROVAR

Chapter One

Ten years ago...

Gold ran down Cedric's brow, warm as sunlight, rich with the scent of myrrh. The priest's cool fingers traced an ancient sigil across his forehead, and Cedric inhaled deeply, steadying himself. This was meant to be sacred. A blessing. And it was. A quiet pride stirred in his chest—he had trained for this moment, had prepared for it. He believed in his duty and in the legacy passed down to him. But gods, he had never enjoyed the *staring*. So many eyes—assessing, expectant, waiting for him to stumble.

"Kneel, Prince of Lunareth."

The priest's words echoed through the High Temple of Aurenis. The vast chamber soared above Cedric, its mirrored walls catching slants of sunlight from narrow celestial windows. Sunburst mosaics stretched across the domed ceiling, displaying the history of Lunareth and its rulers in bands of gold and red jasper.

A hush fell over the gathered nobility. His mother and father stood at the very front, positioned just beside the priest. His mother's proud smile was tinged with joy, while his father, ever composed, stood nearby to take part in the ritual when needed. Cedric straightened under their gaze, drawing strength from their presence. But he couldn't see his sister, Gwenna. She was probably off making trouble somewhere, even during a formal ceremony.

The priest dipped his fingers into the sacred oil again, the flecks of gold shimmering as he anointed the backs of Cedric's hands. An acolyte stepped forward, carrying a thin golden circlet upon a velvet cushion.

"This circlet marks you as the kingdom's protector, the heir to Lunareth," the priest intoned. "May you serve with wisdom and strength."

The moment the metal touched Cedric's forehead, a strange sensation rippled through him—like a key turned in the wrong lock. It vanished as quickly as it came, lost beneath the priest's unwavering voice.

"By the will of the gods and the blessing of your ancestors, you are named the Gilded Prince."

King William Cleburne stepped forward, placing a firm hand on Cedric's shoulder. "As you step closer to your future, remember this: power is not measured in conquest, but in kindness. A ruler is judged not by how he commands armies, but by how he protects those who cannot protect themselves."

The words settled into Cedric's bones, heavier than the circlet. He swallowed, throat tight, then lifted his gaze to meet his father's as he spoke the vow he'd memorized. "Before Aurenis and all who bear witness, I swear to guard this kingdom and its people with wisdom and mercy. I swear it upon my name, my blood, and my breath."

The priest gestured, and Darius stepped forward from the line of acolytes, carrying the shallow bowl of polished obsidian—the sacred stone.

Cedric's heart stuttered. He suddenly wished he hadn't

asked his friend to take part in the ceremony. Too much of a distraction.

Darius had always drawn him like that—too familiar to fear, too dangerous to resist. A hand offered in loyalty, a blade hidden just beneath the skin. Cedric trusted him. Needed him. Wanted him more than he should have.

He extended his hand without hesitation.

The priest passed the ceremonial dagger to Darius, its handle wrapped in golden silk. Darius came closer, so close that Cedric caught the scent of him. *Don't think about that right now. Focus.*

"The world will change because of you," Darius murmured, so quietly only Cedric could hear.

Their eyes met, a breath too long. Then Darius reached, taking Cedric's hand in his own as he turned the palm upward. Cedric was so focused on the sensation of Darius's touch that he almost didn't feel the pressure of the dagger's tip.

The blade bit cleanly into Cedric's flesh. A sharp sting bloomed, followed by a slow, pulsing ache. A thin line of crimson welled up, slipping down his fingers. Darius caught the drops in the bowl, tilting the obsidian to hold it—a gleaming crimson pool shining dark against the stone. Cedric clenched his jaw against the pain, unwilling to show weakness before all of those eyes.

Darius flashed a grin at him, then hefted the bowl for all to see. "I bear witness to the bond. Blood given, oath taken, life bound to duty."

The priest nodded to Darius. Cedric watched as he slipped away to join the acolytes of Aurenis. But duty took precedence over longing. He forced himself to let Darius fade into the crowd.

The priest lifted the second ceremonial vessel. A shallow bronze brazier, coals smoldering within. He poured a vial of sacred resin into the embers. A plume of smoke wafted upward, shifting from pale gold to deep amber, the scent rich and heady. The smoke curled in slow, beckoning tendrils, waiting.

Cedric closed his eyes and inhaled.

The warmth filled his lungs, seeping through him like liquid sunlight. For a moment, something stirred deep inside, something half-asleep and waiting—

Then the moment passed, interrupted by the priest's final pronouncement. "By sacred rite and sovereign will, I name you Prince Cedric Cleburne, Gilded Heir of Lunareth."

Applause swelled around him, and Cedric banished all thoughts of the strange sensation. For a moment, he allowed himself to breathe, to absorb the moment—the temple's golden light, the heavy scent of myrrh, the comforting presence of his father beside him. But the solemnity of the ritual had already begun to fade, replaced by the expectant murmurs of the gathered nobility. The ceremony had been the easy part. Now he had to endure the celebration.

His father beamed, clapping a hand on Cedric's shoulder. "You did well, Ced. We're so proud of you."

Mom hurried over, taking his still-bleeding hand in hers. She pressed a handkerchief against it. Warmth bloomed beneath his skin. "This will hold until you can see the royal healer." She winked, voice light, but the magic laced beneath her words was unmistakable. "Go on, get this taken care of. We'll see you in the great hall."

Cedric smiled, holding the handkerchief in place. The soft tingle of his mother's magic danced across the cut. It was unfortunate she couldn't do more, but they were in public. Too many watching eyes. "Thanks, Mom. I'll be there as soon as I'm no longer at risk of bleeding all over the marble."

She kissed his forehead. Then she turned as King

William offered her his arm, and together, they started toward the great hall.

TOO MANY EXPECTATIONS. The thought hissed like steam in Cedric's skull.

The great hall glittered with a thousand watchful eyes. Courtiers swarmed like jeweled beetles, their silks shifting like oil-slicked water, and at the heart of it all, Cassara Marovelle stood among them—a striking figure in dark silver and blue.

The woman who would soon become his betrothed.

The word sat like iron in his stomach. It was meant to be a triumph, a political bond between Lunareth and Revendar, but all he felt was...trapped. Cassara met his gaze briefly, offering him a polite nod, before turning away to speak to a noblewoman draped in furs.

Cedric touched the now-healed scar on his palm, rubbing it as a distraction. He would have to go speak with her soon. It would be rude not to. But still, his gut clenched.

It's what I must do. We both know this alliance isn't for love. No, it was for trade and mutual protection. Already, the Avilisian empire was pounding on Revendar's door. The ever-growing tide of refugees was proof enough that their western neighbor was soon to be in dire straits.

Gwenna's punch to his arm demanded his immediate attention. His sister's frown was a masterpiece of teenage disdain, her cheeks flushed under auburn curls. "You look like you'd rather stab yourself with a dessert fork than be here," she declared.

Ah, Gwenna. Her words cut through the room's syrup, a welcome distraction.

"You're not wrong." He sighed, gaze sliding to a cluster of courtiers preening in silk monstrosities. One man's lace collar could've doubled as a siege weapon. Cedric's own collar chafed. "Where were you?"

Gwenna's eyes widened in her best *what-ever-do-you-mean?* expression.

"I just hope you weren't getting into the temple's wine again." Cedric frowned at her.

"Slander and lies," Gwenna shot back. "That was *one time*."

He snorted. "One time was probably enough to permanently put you on Aurenis's dark side. What were you actually doing?"

Gwenna grinned, eyes glinting with mischief. "If you must know, I was borrowing a map from the war room."

Cedric stiffened. "You what?"

"Relax, I'll put it back later." She grinned at him.

He gave her his best serious look, which had no effect on her. "You realize you're telling that to the Gilded Prince, right?" If anyone found out, there would be questions. Uncomfortable ones. "You could get into real trouble for this, Gwenna."

"I'm telling my *brother* who loves me dearly and wouldn't dare breathe a word of this to anyone." Gwenna's grin broadened. "And hey, this is a celebration! So let's celebrate!" Her lips brushed Cedric's cheek. "Byeeeeee." Her skirts hissed against his boots as she vanished into the crowd, a fox slipping into tall grass.

He sighed, rubbing the back of his neck. This celebration might be in his honor, but somehow, he didn't feel as if he belonged at *all*. Cedric glanced around, noticing the gazes of several nobles land on him, as if judging the perfect opportunity to pounce on their newly minted Gilded Prince.

That was the last thing Cedric wanted to deal with at the moment. Perhaps it was time to seek out his future wife.

Cedric eased through the crowd, nobles slipping out of

his path with respectful bows or curtsies. He nodded to them, smiling at Cassara as he approached.

Dressed in a flowing gown of deep blue with silver piping, Cassara Marovelle stood with the kind of stillness that commanded attention rather than begged for it. Embroidered patterns of stags and ivy gleamed along her sleeves—symbols of Revendar's noble lineage—while a silver circlet rested against her platinum hair, catching the chandelier's glow.

The Revendarian princess broke away from her current conversation to greet him. "Prince Cedric. Or should I say, Gilded Prince? Congratulations."

"Thank you, though it's symbolic more than anything else," he said with a shrug.

Cassara raised a brow. "Symbols have power, Prince Cedric. Does your Gilded Prince ceremony not have roots in tradition?"

He blinked at the question, mind churning as he sought every bit of history he knew about the ceremony. "That's what they say. It's meant to sanctify me as the heir, to... solidify my role."

Cedric stalled as she continued to give him an expectant look, seeking more than the little he'd offered. He cleared his throat. "You'll have to forgive me. I'm..." He hesitated, choosing his words. But if anyone would understand his current state of mind, it would be another royal child. "I'm overwhelmed and can't think straight right now."

His honesty caught her off guard. Cassara's eyes widened, but then her expression softened. "I can't fault you for that. Sometimes...well, this life is more demanding than anyone else knows."

Her voice had become a whisper, the words for his ears alone. Cedric relaxed a fraction. Truth be told, he hadn't been given a moment of time alone with Cassara, to get to know her. To discover if she might be compatible as a friend, if nothing else. Perhaps that might be a possibility. It gave him hope.

"It is," Cedric agreed. But he felt the prickle of eyes on him and knew he couldn't remain with her much longer. The reason for Cassara's presence at court hadn't been announced yet, and he couldn't appear to favor a foreign princess over his own people. He sighed. "I'll speak more with you soon."

Cassara nodded, though her expression was more polite than excited. "I look forward to it."

He stepped away, casting around for a safe place to continue this farce. If Cedric had to remain at this celebration, he was doing it on his own terms. Across the hall, he glimpsed a friendly face. Darius. Heaving out a soft breath, Cedric headed toward him.

As he slipped through the crowd, he caught snippets of conversation:

"...a war brewing, I tell you. The border patrols should be doubled."

"...filthy beggars from Revendar flooding the city. We should shut the gates before we're overrun."

"—His Majesty clings to the idea of alliances, but sentiment won't stop an empire. The boy is of age now. Perhaps it's time Lunareth had a ruler who understands strength."

Cedric clenched his jaw. The voices melted together, whispers and grumblings twisting between the strains of a violin. He exhaled slowly, forcing his hands to unclench. The petitioners in court earlier that week had included a mother and her two sons, their clothes ripped and dirty, bodies gaunt with hunger. His father had ordered they be given food and shelter. Their faces haunted him, and it took Cedric a moment to banish their memory.

Tonight was meant for revelry. Cedric plowed onward. The great hall's vaulted ceiling stifled laughter and torch smoke alike, its soaring arches adorned with garlands of moonflowers already wilting beneath the warmth. By the time he reached the shadow of the banquet table's carved griffins, sweat glued his linen undershirt to the hollow between his shoulder blades.

Darius waited as always, a study in effortless confidence, one boot propped against the column's fluted base. He lifted his tankard in a salute, pulling his tunic taut across shoulders still lean from last summer's growth spurt, but broad enough now to make Cedric's throat dry.

"There you are, my Gilded Prince." The tankard Darius thrust into Cedric's hands sloshed liquid the color of a sunset. "Quite popular tonight, aren't you?" Darius slung an arm around Cedric's shoulders.

"I'd argue the party is more popular than I am," Cedric said, the lie flavored with truth.

Darius smirked, tipping his tankard slightly. "Oh, but where would the fun be without its reluctant guest of honor?" He patted Cedric's shoulder. Then his countenance shifted. "I can't believe the Revendarian princess is still here. Shouldn't she be running home with her tail between her legs?"

Cedric frowned, tapping his index finger against the tankard as he debated how much to tell his friend. Darius's mother was the royal spy mistress, and Cedric knew Lady Valcairn knew why Cassara Marovelle was in attendance. But Darius's comment implied that she hadn't seen fit to enlighten her son, however.

He should know, Cedric decided. If for no other reason than to keep him from saying something that might seed future problems. "She's here for a reason."

"And that is...?" Darius cocked his head.

Cedric pursed his lips. "You're going to have to keep this secret for a few more days. Can you do that?"

His friend grinned. "Oh Cedric, you have *no idea* how good I am at keeping secrets." He eased closer, so close that

Cedric caught a whiff of the fragrant soap Darius favored. "What is it? Are they being annexed to Lunareth, perhaps?"

"We're to be betrothed later this week," Cedric whispered.

Darius's eyes widened. "Truly, Ced? We're *really* going to have a marriage alliance with that kingdom? The one that can't keep a bunch of unshaved barbarians from crossing their borders?"

The tone of disbelief and scorn instantly put Cedric on the defensive. "It would be mutually beneficial."

"It just seems unfair, that's all." Darius shrugged. "You, of all people, stuck with a woman you don't even..." He trailed off, giving Cedric an expectant look.

"My parents didn't love each other at first, either," Cedric reminded him. Though it was really more of a reminder for himself. In his heart, though, he knew he could never truly love Cassara. Not romantically; not the way she probably deserved. "But things have a way of working out."

"Ever the optimist." Darius's expression slipped into a smile. "Well. I suppose I should be congratulating you then, shouldn't I? Let's drink to your future."

Cedric picked at the tankard's pewter handle with his thumbnail, a distraction from Darius's close proximity. He hesitated, then pushed the drink back toward him. "Maybe another time."

But Darius wouldn't be dissuaded. "Ced, come on. This is special, just for your big day!"

Gods, Cedric always had a difficult time telling Darius no. He glanced inside the tankard. "What is it, dishwater?"

Darius laughed, a warm sound that made gooseflesh race across Cedric's arms. "Hardly. It's made of exotic fruits not found in our lands. Have you heard of pineapple?"

"Heard of it, yes. Seen one? No." Cedric eyed the drink.

"Then you're in for a treat. Taste." Darius took a sip of

his own, savoring the flavor with a sigh. "It's one of several fruits. I think you'll find it delightful."

He sniffed the beverage first—a habit born of one too many *festive surprises*—but all he caught was the faintest whiff of citrus and something earthy, like sun-warmed grass.

Against his better judgment, he took a sip. The liquid hit his tongue with a deceptively innocent sweetness, like stolen summer peaches, before the tartness sparked—sharp as a lemon's kiss, lingering just long enough to make his jaw clench. He coughed, blinking at the tankard.

"That's...surprisingly good," he admitted, rolling the taste on his tongue like a thought he wasn't sure he should keep. He turned the cup as if its dull metal might reveal secrets. "Pineapple, you say?"

Darius's grin widened, smug and devastating all at once. "One of several fruits, yes. It's a blend." His voice was smooth, a blade honed to perfection, and his eyes—gods, his beautiful eyes—gleamed with something Cedric couldn't name. Triumph? Amusement? Or something far more dangerous, something that coiled around Cedric's heart like a vice and sent heat licking up the back of his neck.

Cedric swallowed another mouthful quickly, more to busy himself than out of thirst, not trusting himself to meet that gaze for too long.

His gaze flicked downward as Darius lifted his cup. Something glinted in the candlelight. A gold ring. In all his years, Cedric had never seen his friend wear a ring. The metal gleamed against Darius's skin, its ruby centerpiece catching the light like a smoldering coal.

"You wear rings now?" Cedric teased, nudging Darius's hand with his knuckles.

Darius glanced down at it, flexing his fingers with a lazy shrug. "An early birthday gift from my mother," he said, tipping his cup toward a nearby table where Lady Priscilla Valcairn sat, deep in conversation with a nobleman. "She insisted it would suit me." His expression turned wry. "A symbol of responsibility or some such lecture I didn't bother listening to."

Cedric huffed a quiet laugh. "That sounds like her. And you."

Darius tapped the ring absently against his cup. "Doesn't it?" He swirled his drink. "She said it was my father's. He brought it back from Revendar on his last expedition." His tone was light, but Cedric caught the slight edge beneath it. "He passed not long after."

Cedric didn't need the rest of the story. Lord Valcairn had sought out the druids of Revendar for healing, but their magic hadn't saved him. Whether they'd failed or simply refused, Darius had never forgiven them.

Rather than dwell on it, Cedric rolled his eyes, leaning back against the pillar. "Gods help us all when you start listening to your mother's fashion advice."

Darius grinned, knocking his cup lightly against Cedric's. "Oh, Cedric," he murmured. "You wound me."

Cedric's gaze drifted again—always, inevitably, betraying him—to Darius's hair, mahogany strands gilded by lantern light, tousled just enough to seem effortless. A dangerous lie. *Nothing* about Darius was effortless. Every glance, every word, every move was honed for maximum effect. Cedric knew this, had *always* known this.

But still...

He knew the exact curve of Darius's brow when scheming, the way his lips thinned during lectures—but *this?* The softness of his smile now, the quiet, almost disarming warmth behind his eyes? That was a far crueler weapon than any sharp remark or veiled threat. That was the trap Cedric had walked into too many times before.

And would walk into again.

Cedric's pulse stuttered.

Stop. You're drunk on idiocy.

"Did you do this?" Cedric asked, too abruptly. The hall's din swelled around them—lutes twined with laughter, goblets clinking like discordant bells—but Darius's reply cut through cleanly.

"Happy birthday. This will be a night you won't forget." Darius lifted his tankard in a toast. Cedric's cheeks burned, and not from the drink.

Darius refilled his tankard without asking, the drink cascading in a golden stream. Cedric drank anyway, letting the sweetness blur the edges of his wariness. The warmth spread—first in his belly, then his limbs, loose and weightless. He caught his parents' distant conversation, their faces crinkled with pride, and for a heartbeat, the world softened. The tapestries rippled like living things, their embroidered hawks soaring in the candlelit haze. Even the stone floor beneath his boots seemed to sway, as if the castle itself had taken a drunken lurch.

By the time Cedric stumbled into the corridor, the buzz in his skull had sharpened to a hive's roar. Cold air struck his face, a mercy after the hall's suddenly unbearable heat. He braced a palm against the wall. His mind felt like wool soaked in honey.

Somewhere behind him, Darius spun the treasury minister's daughter in a whirl of silk, his laughter trailing like smoke. That sound—rich, smug, *too much*—threaded through Cedric's mind, leaving a strange, aching tightness in its wake.

He blinked, trying to steady himself, but the floor swayed beneath his feet. *I need to sit. Just for a moment.*

When Cedric pushed himself upright, his legs buckled, and the thought shattered. He caught himself awkwardly, the world tilting around him.

He hadn't had that much to drink. Had he?

His chambers loomed ahead, the oak door swimming in and out of focus. He made for it with grim determination, shouldering it open and stumbling inside. The fire had died down to embers, casting the room in dim smudges of charcoal and ash.

He fumbled off his shoes—one disappearing under the bed—and collapsed onto the mattress with a groan. The sheets were cold against his skin, but he barely noticed.

The pillow smelled of lavender. Or maybe that was the drink still twisting his senses. Gods, it was still clinging to him, coating his tongue like a spell meant to muddle his mind. His fingers clenched the fabric beneath him.

Gwenna's grin flitted through his mind. Then his mother's laughter, bright as harp strings. Then...Darius.

His intoxicating, effortless grace. The way his eyes held galaxies of unspoken promise. The heat of his arm slung around Cedric's shoulders. The ghost of his smile, curling like the rim of a goblet, like an invitation Cedric should never, ever take.

You did something to that drink, he thought hazily.

Cedric groaned and dragged the pillow over his stomach, pressing down, as if he could shove the nausea back. As if he could shove Darius back.

And then his gut *heaved*.

He rolled sideways, swallowing bile. The garderobe. He needed the garderobe. But when his feet hit the rug, pain erupted. Not the dull throb of too much drink, but a thousand needles searing through muscle and bone. His legs buckled. Cedric crashed to his knees, a raw, strangled cry tearing free.

His breath hitched. His fingers curled against the floor—except they weren't fingers anymore.

Talons.

Long, curved, gleaming wet in the low light. His nails were gone, peeled away like shed leaves. The bones of his hands cracked, stretched, reshaping as golden scales bloomed across his knuckles, pushing through flesh with a sickening pop.

He pressed his shaking hands—*claws*—against the cold stone floor, as if doing so might somehow halt the impossible changes wracking his body. His gut soured, and for a heartbeat, he thought, *This can't be real. This isn't happening.* But the searing pain crawling up his spine told him otherwise.

He sucked in a desperate, jagged breath. "No..."

The sound that left him was wrong. Too deep. Too monstrous. His hand shot to his throat, but the skin there was already shifting—bubbling, hardening, elongating. A scream tried to claw free, but what tore from his chest was a roar.

A sound he had never made before. One that didn't belong to him.

He was changing. Warping. *Losing himself.*

A sob tore free as he crawled toward the door, clawing at the stone, at himself, at whatever was happening to him. He had to stop it. He had to get *help.*

And then, through the searing haze of his mind, a single thought cut through: *Mom.*

His breath hitched. His hands—claws—dug into the floor. *She always knows what to do. She always helps. She always—*

A sharp pop cracked through his spine. His vision whited out. But he kept moving. Because if he could just get to her... If he could just reach her...

She'd fix this. She'd fix *him.*

Chapter Two

Finn jolted upright, the screams shattering his slumber. Sweat chilled against his skin, sheets twisted around his legs like bindings trying to hold him down. But the screams couldn't be ignored. Danger.

Finn yanked on his trousers, the fabric sticking to his damp skin, then shoved his feet into his new boots—still reeking of the tannery. He fumbled with the laces, urgency tangling his fingers.

The hallway air carried the sharp tang of his mother's nightly tea, bitter in the back of his throat. She stepped from the dimness, her knuckles white where they gripped her robe, her face pale with fear. Finn's own pulse thundered in his ears. *Protect.* The instinct roused in his bones, in his blood—older than his fifteen years, older than reason.

"What is it, Mom?" His voice cracked, thin and frightened. He clenched his jaw, gaze locking onto the armor by the wall. Moonlight crawled over its surface, catching on the runes etched into the steel. It should've been a symbol of strength, a promise of the future he'd trained for. Instead, it mocked him. *Tomorrow's dream, tonight's joke.*

Torchlight bled through the doorway, carving jagged shadows across his mother's face. "Dragon."

What? Finn's knees locked, his grip slipping against the doorframe. *Legends.* But legends didn't reek of smoke and charred stone. Didn't gouge the sky with claws that made the cobblestones tremble beneath his boots. His tongue turned useless, stuck to the roof of his mouth. *Move. Breathe.* He lurched outside and stopped in his tracks.

The knights' families lived in a small cluster of houses at the edge of the palace grounds. A short walk, normally—a piss-and-a-joke distance. Tonight, that stretch of packed dirt might as well have been the ocean. Flames ripped through the sky like rabid wolves.

A huge, winged shape gleamed against the inferno. Finn's gut coiled with nausea, acid burning the back of his throat. Thrill and terror tangled inside him, twisting so tight he couldn't breathe. His fingers twitched, aching for a sword, for something solid to hold onto. *Destined to be a knight.* The words rang empty now, drowned by the thunder of his own pulse.

"I have to do something," Finn muttered. He whirled back inside, skidding across the floorboards to grab his armor. His hands shook as he tried to fasten the buckles. This was the same armor he had admired just hours ago, the same set he'd planned to don with pride in the morning. Now, the straps felt stiff and uncooperative in his clumsy fingers.

His mother rushed to him, eyes damp with tears. "Finnian, no. You can't go," she said, even as her hands—traitorous in their love—helped fix a stubborn buckle. "The knights are already there. The king's guard, your father...they'll handle it. Stay here. Stay *safe*."

He turned to her, torn between reaching for her and running. "Mom, I—" The words stuck. How could he explain the pull in his chest, the grim certainty that if he didn't go, if he didn't try, he'd never forgive himself?

She started to say something else, but he never heard it. His feet were already carrying him out into the smoke-filled street.

The distance to the palace felt like miles. His steps seemed to slow under the pallor of fear and the sting of ash in the air. The roar of the dragon rose over the crackle of fire, peppered with shouted orders from knights and shrieks from fleeing servants. Finn pressed onward, boots pounding against cobblestones.

By the time he reached the outer courtyard, the heat of the flames licked at his face. Stone archways that had once been regal entrances now glowed orange, the tapestries within catching fire. Knights and palace guards dashed about in confusion, some trying to corral terrified courtiers, others aiming crossbows or spears at the dragon as it surged back into the palace.

Finn spotted an opening through the side doors of the great hall. With all the chaos, no one stopped him. He darted past frantic pages and into the billowing smoke. The acrid smell burned his nostrils, forcing him to cough. Sweating beneath his newly donned armor, he pressed a hand to his mouth and nose, desperate to see what was happening.

The remains of the once-opulent hall stretched out before him—columns toppled, tapestries aflame, and rubble strewn across the floor. A man stood in the heart of devastation, sword raised against a monstrous, gold-scaled dragon. A glint of firelight on the knight's armor made Finn's pulse thunder.

"Kavros save us," Finn whispered.

It was his father.

Sir Wesley stood poised, sword in hand. The enchanted steel of his armor glimmered with arcs of reflected flame.

Somehow, despite the swirling sparks of debris, he cut a calm, determined figure. Until he saw Finn.

"Run, Finnian!" Sir Wesley's voice carried across the chaos, panic lacing his tone. "Get out of here! Get to safety!"

Finn froze. Everything inside him wanted to obey his father's command to run—wanted to flee the choking smoke and unrelenting heat. But he couldn't tear his gaze from the dragon.

It hunched beneath a gaping hole in the ceiling, where shattered rafters and splintered stone jutted like broken bones against the night sky. The creature's long, curved horns had tangled with a chandelier, now hanging drunkenly by a single chain. The scattered starlight above mingled with the glow of flames licking around the half-destroyed roof, creating an otherworldly glare on the dragon's golden scales.

Its wings, half-spread, filled the ruined ballroom with a terrible, inescapable presence. Every inch of it was designed to kill. Its talons carved deep gouges in the marble, its powerful tail lashed through the smoke, and its great, golden head moved with the slow deliberation of a predator enjoying the hunt. Watching. Waiting. Deciding.

And its eyes—those merciless, glowing eyes—found Finn.

He wasn't just a stray survivor. He wasn't even a threat. The dragon's gaze pinned him in place, not with curiosity, but with a cold, measuring intent. It wasn't the look of a mindless beast. It was a predator marking its next kill.

Finn's pulse slammed against his ribs. He couldn't move. Couldn't *breathe*.

Then Sir Wesley's battle cry rang out.

His father's sword struck, punching through the layer of thin scales just below the dragon's left wing. The beast shrieked—not just in pain, but in fury, the sound tearing through the crumbling hall like a living thing. It reared back, a violent, bone-rattling quake shaking the walls. Cracks split through the remaining patches of ceiling.

Finn stumbled, shielding his face as shards of stone and plaster rained down. A deep, reverberating groan rippled through the castle, the walls shuddering under the weight of destruction.

The dragon lurched, twisting as it recoiled from the wound. Claws raked deep into the marble, struggling for balance, its tail sweeping in a wide arc. The sheer force of its movement sent a violent tremor through the chamber.

It collided with a crumbling column. The weakened stone gave way instantly, splintering apart in a cascade of rubble.

Finn's stomach lurched as he saw the rubble begin to give way. His father's face turned upward—too late.

Stone collapsed in a deafening avalanche.

Finn's scream tore through the destruction. He ran toward the wreckage, panic hammering through him. His mind was a blur of fire and falling stone, of his father buried beneath crushing weight—until a change in the air sent ice knifing down his spine.

Something shifted. Finn skidded to a halt, breath locking in his throat. The dragon whirled to track him—a deliberate, predatory pivot.

It saw him. It *wanted* him.

Jaws parted, revealing jagged teeth gleaming like a row of daggers. A low, deadly rumble shook the floor, and Finn's stomach plunged as a terrible glow ignited in its throat.

Every knight's tale he'd ever heard about dragonfire burning men to ash slammed through his mind in a paralyzing rush.

He couldn't move. His boots felt nailed to the floor.

Smoke coiled through the shattered room, tinged with the scent of blood and destruction. Finn's father was gone.

The castle was crumbling. His future destroyed in a single breath.

The dragon reared back, its maw luminescent with flame. Finn squeezed his eyes shut, the burn of tears lost to the sting of smoke. There was nowhere to run. Nowhere to hide. The fire was coming.

Present day

FINN BOLTED UPRIGHT, a strangled cry dying on his lips. The echo of it reverberated off the walls of his bedchamber, dampened by the resounding silence that followed. Sweat plastered his nightshirt to his skin, and his heart pounded so violently he half-expected it to make a break for freedom. Frankly, it had the right idea.

For a moment—terrifying and all too familiar—he was that helpless boy again, lost in the smoke and flame. And gods, wasn't he tired of reliving it.

Then reality reasserted itself, his chamber coming into focus in the grey pre-dawn light. The heavy draperies, the polished oak armoire, the small bronze statue of Kavros on the mantel—reminders of his faith and of the man he'd become. Or at least, of the man he was *supposed* to be. Right now, he mostly felt like an idiot who needed more sleep and fewer nightmares.

"It was only a dream," he whispered. *Just a dream. Just my own mind kicking me in the ass again. Truly, a delightful way to start the morning.*

He slid his legs over the edge of the bed, pressing the heels of his palms against his eyes to banish the final, lingering wisps of memory. He could still smell the acrid smoke as Solavere Palace burned. A trembling sigh escaped him. There would be no more sleep now; the first pale streaks of dawn were already creeping through the tall windows that overlooked the capital city of Mirathen.

The city was a bastion of art and architecture—at least the buildings crouched around Solavere Palace were. Over the last decade, the palace itself had undergone extensive restoration, replacing the sections ravaged by dragon attack with fresh masonry and gilded details that glinted in daylight. It was said Lunareth's builders were the finest in the world, and the palace was their crowning jewel—a place meant to inspire awe and drown out the memories of terror.

Finn inhaled slowly, willing his pulse to calm, then set about his morning routine. He poured cold water from a basin into a shallow bowl, splashing it onto his face in a bracing shock that banished the haze of sleep. It also forced the last vestiges of the nightmare to recede—if only for now.

His armor rested on a wooden stand nearby. Finn ran his fingertips over the steel breastplate, feeling the familiar ridges of the etched metal. The etched falcon in flight—the Brightmoor crest—stood proud beneath his touch, a symbol that had once belonged to his father. The armor had been reforged a few years back, but the crest remained, its legacy older than he was. Even now, a slight pang of sorrow surfaced whenever he looked at it.

"Nothing good comes from dragons," he whispered, fingers tracing the falcon's outspread wings.

He shoved the thought aside, jaw tightening as he buckled each piece into place. Next came his sword belt. The blade it carried was an exquisite piece of craftsmanship, forged by a master smith who dedicated each strike of the hammer to Kavros, god of creation, ambition, and destruction.

Drawing it partway free, he caught sight of his reflection in the polished steel. He was no longer that helpless boy trembling among the ruined columns. He was Sir Finnian

Brightmoor now, a man shaped by a decade of relentless training and hardened by a vow to avenge his father's death.

And yet the dreams persisted. If he closed his eyes, he could still see the flames licking at the tapestries, could still hear the thunderous crash of rubble.

A soft knock pulled him from his thoughts. Re-sheathing the sword with a decisive *snick*, he raised his voice. "Enter."

The door creaked open to reveal a wide-eyed page, perhaps thirteen or fourteen years old. "Begging your pardon, Sir Finnian," the boy managed, gaze darting between Finn and the sword, "but His Majesty King Darius the Glorious requests your presence in the throne room immediately."

Finn's eyebrows rose. That was never a good sign. "Did His Majesty say why?"

"No, sir. Only that it was urgent."

"All right. Tell His Majesty I'll be there shortly."

The page bobbed his head and hurried off, leaving Finn to wonder at the summons. If King Darius actually called something *urgent,* it either meant trouble or a very long speech. Possibly both.

He strode from his chambers, down corridors still dim with flickering lanterns. Sunlight was just beginning to peer over the high walls, igniting motes of dust in golden beams. Servants were already bustling about, and guards were shifting stations like clockwork. The palace bore scars if one knew where to look—sections of masonry that had been rebuilt, tapestries newly woven to replace those lost in the fire and ruin of the dragon's attack.

But not all the wounds were from that night. The city had changed in the last few years, shaped by the ongoing war in Revendar. In the lower districts, refugees from the western kingdom still crowded the streets—displaced farmers, outcasts, even those rumored to be druids in hiding. Some had fled their crumbling homeland, driven out by violence that had yet to end. Others had come seeking sanctuary, only to find resentment waiting for them.

Finn had overheard the muttered complaints of merchants more than once. Too many mouths, too few hands willing to work. *Ah, yes. The noble art of blaming the desperate. A time-honored tradition among those who never missed a meal.*

But it wasn't just the usual grumbling anymore. Lately, the whispers had sharpened to accusations.

They brought this on themselves.

The druids of Revendar consorted with dark magic—why else would a dragon slay our royal family?

They should count themselves lucky we let them live at all.

The last thought made Finn's stomach turn.

As he neared the throne room, Finn picked up on a subtle crackle of energy in the air. Courtiers congregated in tight clusters as they headed for breakfast, their voices low but urgent. He caught snatches of conversation:

"...dragon sighting in the mountains..."

"...Princess Gwenna, after all these years..."

"...surely our knights will be sent..."

His pulse raced like a spooked horse. *Dragon.* The word curled in his gut like smoke. His fingers twitched toward his sword's hilt before his mind caught up. This wasn't the ruins of Solavere Palace. He was no longer a powerless boy.

He forced his legs to keep moving. A dragon sighting? And Princess Gwenna—missing for so long—mentioned in the same breath? His thoughts ground against each other like a blade against a whetstone, sparking with possibilities, none of them good.

The great oak doors loomed ahead, flanked by a pair of guards in polished armor. They inclined their heads respectfully as he approached, then pushed open the doors. Finn's breath caught as he stepped inside.

In daylight, the throne room glowed with brilliant color.

The high, vaulted ceiling rose overhead, supported by pristine marble columns. Stained-glass windows, painstakingly replaced after the destruction of years past, cast shifting pools of jewel-toned light across the marble floor.

Impressive. Or at least, meant to be. A kingdom rebuilt in glitter and gold, as if that could erase the past. A painting of King Darius facing down a gold dragon hung on the wall near the entrance.

Finn forced himself to walk forward, ignoring the knot that formed in his throat. He glanced at the dais, where the magnificent throne rose in all its opulent glory—fashioned of gold, inlaid with precious gems. It shone like a beacon, a symbol of the king's power and the kingdom's desire to move beyond tragedy.

And there, lounging with casual grace upon that glittering throne, sat King Darius the Glorious himself.

Finn liked the king. He really did. But sometimes, when King Darius looked at him, it felt less like being seen and more like being...weighed.

His gaze lingered on the king's hazel eyes. There was a calculating coldness there that never quite matched the brightness of that cool smile. Finn had seen sharper steel dull itself behind a pleasant face before. Sometimes he wondered if it was simply the mark of a royal: a mask one had to wear when holding an entire kingdom in one's hands. He couldn't recall if the old king held such a look.

He approached the dais, catching snippets of grave whispers from the cluster of advisors around the throne. Their expressions were grim, underscoring the sense of urgency clinging to the room like a gathering storm.

Finn dropped to one knee, bowing his head. "Your Majesty. You summoned me?"

"Ah, Sir Finnian Brightmoor," King Darius greeted, his voice as smooth as honey. "Rise, my loyal knight. We have matters of importance to discuss."

Finn stood, meeting the king's gaze. The warmth in King Darius's voice was performative, like a merchant flattering a buyer before naming an outrageous price. But beneath the charm lay something sharper, something colder. The shift in the king's tone set Finn's nerves on edge.

King Darius leaned forward. "Tell me, Sir Finnian—what do you recall of the tragedy that befell this castle ten years ago?"

Finn's gut clenched, the question striking harder than a mace to the head. He had just woken from the ruins of that night, and now the king wanted to discuss it over morning court? He swallowed hard, forcing his voice steady. "I...I was here that night, Your Majesty," he managed. "When the dragon came."

The king nodded slowly. "Yes. I recall you lost your father in that attack. Sir Wesley—one of our most loyal knights. He gave his life for the kingdom."

Finn swallowed past the lump in his throat. "He died protecting the royal family."

"Indeed, he did," King Darius said softly. A hint of something—pity, or perhaps curiosity—crossed his features. Then the king straightened, his tone growing crisp. "And it appears we may need that same valor once again."

Finn's pulse quickened. He had spent a decade training, pushing himself to the brink, all to be ready if ever another dragon threatened these lands.

King Darius spread his arms wide, addressing the room at large. "For ten years, we have mourned the loss of my betrothed, Princess Gwenna," he went on, his voice rich with a grief long worn to polished stone. "The night of the dragon's attack changed everything. That night, the land that might have been our ally betrayed us under the guise of a Revendarian princess."

A ripple of agreement passed through the gathered courtiers. Finn caught a few exchanged glances—some smug, others grim, as if this was merely confirmation of what they had long suspected. A few even nodded, murmuring to their neighbors, their expressions dark with certainty.

"For so long, we believed my precious Gwenna dead, or taken away by the very dragon that tore our palace apart. But now," King Darius continued, his voice carrying with it a theatrical flourish, "we believe Princess Gwenna may yet live. The same dragon has been sighted near the Misthaven Mountains, no doubt hoping to slip within our borders for another attack."

A tidal wave of whispers swept through the chamber. Finn's breath hitched. Hope, skepticism, and fear collided in his thoughts. Could it truly be the dragon? After all this time?

King Darius let the crowd buzz for a moment before lifting a hand to silence them. He glanced in Finn's direction, a sharp glint in his hazel eyes. "We have tried to verify these sightings, of course," he said, voice almost conspiratorial. "I have, in fact, already sent a small party of knights to investigate."

Finn's eyes widened. He knew the knightly roster by heart—who had been deployed where and when. He'd heard no rumor of any official expedition to the Misthaven Mountains. Because there hadn't been one. Which meant Darius had done this quietly, and that never boded well.

"Your Majesty," he ventured carefully, "I was unaware any knights had been sent to the mountains. Who—?"

"They were not of our regular forces," King Darius interjected, his voice clipped. "Mercenaries, knighted outside the kingdom's usual ceremonies. I enlisted them quietly, without fanfare. Their mission was to bring the beast back to me. *Alive.*" His mouth curled in distaste. "And they failed."

Finn's stomach dropped. *Alive?* That was madness. "What use is a live dragon?"

Darius exhaled sharply, as if Finn had asked something

tedious. "None, if it refuses to be tamed." His expression darkened. The king waved a hand, pacing a step down from the dais, "Because of their failure, I realized I required a knight I could trust completely. One whose reputation for cunning and skill was unmatched, and whose loyalty to Lunareth is beyond reproach." He turned to Finn, his gaze heavy with expectation. "If the druids of Revendar did unleash this beast upon us, it is only fitting that a knight of Lunareth be the one to end it."

And there it was.

Finn drew a slow breath. "I see. You wish for me to attempt what these...others could not." His words tasted sour as he added, "Capture the dragon?"

The king shook his head. "No, Sir Finnian. If the dragon cannot be controlled, it's of no use to me. Your task is to slay the dragon and rescue Princess Gwenna from its clutches."

Finn glanced around the throne room, fully aware of every courtier watching him—judging him. The pressure of so many gazes unnerved him, but none so heavy as the memory of that night ten years ago.

Finn's pulse hammered. This was the moment he'd imagined a thousand times—though somehow, in those visions, it had felt cleaner. A chance to avenge his father, to prove himself. Not a political spectacle, not this carefully curated drama with King Darius at the helm. But the dragon was real. That part, at least, had not changed.

He straightened his spine, giving King Darius a determined nod. "Your Majesty," he said, voice steadier than he felt, "I accept. By my father's memory, I will see this done. I will not fail."

A surge of applause rippled through the room, punctuated by uneasy murmurs. *Nothing like a bit of fanfare before being sent to fight a dragon who's dispatched every other knight it crossed.* King Darius descended the final step from the throne and clasped Finn's shoulder, leaning in just enough that Finn could catch the faint scent of jasmine and incense that clung to the king's fine clothes.

"I knew you would not disappoint me," King Darius said, low enough that only Finn could hear. There was approval in his voice, but also something akin to a veiled threat. "You have a personal stake in this mission. Let that sharpen your blade...and your wits. The dragon is cunning beyond measure, and none who have gone against it survived to tell the tale. You must not join them."

Finn did not flinch. He'd been fighting for years—against men, against monsters, against ghosts that would not let him sleep. He would fight now, too.

Finn offered a terse nod. "I'll do whatever it takes to succeed."

"See that you do," King Darius replied. "Our kingdom's future—and *yours*—depends on it."

With that, the king stepped back, turning to confer in hushed tones with his advisors. A hundred questions swirled in Finn's mind: how had King Darius discovered this dragon's location? Why keep the mercenary attempts a secret? It was all so...strange.

Still, the heartbeat of excitement refused to be stifled. A mission. A chance for vengeance. An opportunity to save the princess—and perhaps the kingdom. Finn pushed aside the unease roiling under his skin.

He had fought to defend Lunareth's borders, to protect its people. But sometimes, it had been hard to tell who the enemy really was. A farmer with a stolen sword? A mother shielding her starving children? A druid who had done nothing but exist? He had raised his sword against them all.

Now, he was being sent to slay a dragon. At least the beast was a known enemy—one bred for destruction.

Finn strode from the throne room. He couldn't stop replaying the king's words—his urgent tone, the implicit demand. None of the mercenaries had returned. *None.* A bad sign, no matter which way he cut it. A chill slid down Finn's spine at that thought, but he brushed it aside. *Duty first.*

Pausing at a wide, arched window, he took in the sight of Mirathen stretching out below. The early morning sun bathed rooftops and winding streets in soft gold, as if blessing the realm with a fresh start.

Or maybe it was a sign from Kavros, the Shaper of Flame, urging him onward. Finn had always believed the fire god guided any who stood at a forge or took up a blade with honest purpose. If this quest demanded steel and strength, then perhaps he was precisely where he needed to be.

His gaze shifted to the distant, hazy peaks of the Misthaven Mountains. Somewhere in that rugged wilderness, a golden-scaled dragon lurked—and possibly Princess Gwenna, lost to the kingdom for ten long years. He gripped the hilt of his sword, a shiver of grim anticipation curling in his gut. Let it come. He had trained for a decade to face exactly this.

THE CASTLE ARMORY was a buzz of steel and echoing voices, a place that always quickened Finn's blood. Squires darted between racks of weapons while apprentices tested the edges of fresh-forged blades. The air tasted of metal dust and sweat—the scent of honest work. No scheming courtiers here, no carefully veiled orders. Just steel, purpose, and the men who knew how to wield it. And for a moment, Finn felt utterly at home.

A voice boomed above the din. "Sir Finnian!"

Finn turned, already recognizing the rough-edged bark before he saw the man behind it. Only Thorne could make his name sound both like a greeting and a reprimand. The old weaponsmith limped toward him, eyebrows drawn up in curiosity. Thorne had once served with Finn's father, both in the forge and on the field, and Finn trusted him with his life.

"I heard the news," Thorne went on. "You're off to challenge the beast that's been haunting our kingdom?"

Finn gave a wry twist of a smile. "You make it sound like I volunteered."

The blacksmith snorted. "Ah, lad. Kavros grant you strength, because you'll need it."

At the mention of their shared deity, a spark of pride warmed Finn's heart. Many knights prayed to Aurenis for honor or Thalos for cunning, but those with a taste for the forge and creation—men like his father—gave their devotion to Kavros. That faith flowed through the ringing of hammers on steel, every sword a tribute to the god's fiery power.

Master Thorne jerked his head for Finn to follow him deeper into the armory. "This way, boy. I've something that might catch your interest."

They passed rows of breastplates and halberds until they reached a tall, iron-bound cabinet fixed to the wall. Thorne fished out a small key from his apron and slid it into the lock, his gnarled hands surprising in their finesse. The lock clicked open, revealing a sheathed sword resting on a velvet-lined shelf.

"It's special, this one." Thorne's words were full of reverence. He eased the weapon into view, letting the morning light dance along its length. "This here is a longblade. She's a good deal longer than the toothpick you currently use—but one you can wield with one hand or two, depending on the situation. Forged under a prayer to Kavros, during Aurenis's Festival of the High Sun."

"Doesn't get much better than that," Finn said, awestruck.

Thorne grinned, then winked. "Oh, but it does. The blade's metal is hammered with scales from a slain dragon brought to us by a Hunter of Rynvath. This blade here? It's thrice-blessed. It'll do the trick."

Finn whistled. He stepped closer, enchanted by the faint swirling patterns in the steel, like ripples on water. A blade wasn't just a weapon—it was a craftsman's legacy, a warrior's lifeline. The crossguard gleamed, etched with motifs of fire and serpentine scales, and the pommel held a polished ruby that seemed to smolder from within. This was no ordinary sword. This was a work of art.

"It's...incredible," he said softly, sliding his fingers along the flat of the blade.

"Aye," Thorne said, pride and sadness mingling in his tone. "Your father commissioned it. Said he had a feeling it'd be needed one day. 'A sword for the realm,' he called it." The old smith's voice tightened. "I finished forging it just before the attack. Was going to present it to your father officially. Then...you know how that ended."

A lump formed in Finn's throat. He glanced up, meeting Thorne's weathered gaze. "Father never told me." Had never even hinted.

"He wanted it to be a surprise. A gift for you. You have my apologies. I would have presented it sooner, but it was forgotten in those dark days." Thorne offered the blade to him. "Well, now it's yours. May Kavros's fire burn bright in it —and in you."

Finn swallowed hard, his father's memory rising up. There was grief, yes, but also a fierce surge of determination. He wrapped his fingers around the hilt, testing its weight, its balance. "I...thank you. I'll wield it with honor."

Thorne's lips twitched into a begrudging smile. "See that you do, lad. Your father would never forgive me if I let his boy die on my watch." He paused. "He gave it a name, you should know."

At that, Finn's lips quirked. His father had loved to name his weapons, a tradition that made other knights roll their eyes. Finn had always loved it, though. He swallowed, for a moment feeling closer to his father than he had in a decade. "What did he want to call it?"

"Sunwrath."

Finn held the name in his mind, then nodded. It was a good name. A worthy name. He only hoped that he was worthy of it, too.

Finn gently slid the sword into its sheath. He unbuckled the belt holding his own and handed it to Thorne. "Seems I won't need this, at least for now."

Thorne accepted it with a nod, then clapped a heavy hand on Finn's shoulder, the gesture as comforting as any blessing. "Now, off with you. There's a dragon needs slaying, or so I hear."

THE STABLES WERE alive with activity—grooms rushing to tack horses, stable hands ferrying sacks of feed, a few knights preparing for their patrols. The scent of hay and leather hung thick in the air, mingling with the occasional sharp tang of manure.

Ghost, Finn's warhorse, was already saddled, her nearly white coat gleaming in the morning light. The mare snorted as he approached, stamping a hoof against the packed ground. Her way of saying, *What took you so long?*

From behind a nearby bale of hay, a wiry boy emerged—Tom, freckles scattering across his cheeks like spattered paint. "Sir Finnian! You're truly going? To fight a dragon?"

Finn reached over, plucking a stray piece of straw from the boy's mop of hair. "Looks like you've been fighting a hay bale yourself." He tucked the straw behind Tom's ear with mock solemnity. "But yes, I am."

Tom's eyes were wide as saucers. "You'll kill it, won't you? With one swing of your sword, just like in the ballads?"

Finn snorted. "If the ballads were right, knights wouldn't need armor, and dragons would die of embarrassment the moment we arrived." His expression sobered. "A dragon isn't a simple foe, Tom. They don't go down easy."

"But you're the best, sir," Tom insisted, voice brimming with earnest faith. "You'll come back a hero, I just know it!"

Finn exhaled, adjusting his sword belt. Gods, if only it were that simple. But Tom's certainty, his belief—it was a reminder of why Finn fought. "I'll do my best."

He swung into the saddle. Ghost snorted, shifting impatiently beneath him. She was ready to run, always was.

Finn gave the stable hands a nod, then turned Ghost toward the main gate. As he loosened the reins, the mare surged forward into a canter. Finn relaxed. No court, no politics—just the open road ahead.

Passing through Mirathen's winding streets, Finn felt both eyes and murmurs follow him—citizens peeking out of doorways, merchants pausing over wares. A knight on horseback, off to slay a dragon. A perfect story. News traveled quickly, and already rumors crackled in the air like sparks: the princess, the dragon, the king's shining knight off to save them all. He heard whispers of hope and fear, well-wishes, and even a few prayers to Aurenis or Kavros for victory.

Though he held his head high, shoulders square, a thousand questions churned. Why the secrecy? If Princess Gwenna had been alive all this time, why was there never a trace? And how had the same dragon that killed his father eluded every Hunter of Rynvath for a decade? A beast that size couldn't just vanish—unless someone wanted it to.

Before long, the city gates rose before him. Guards stepped aside, saluting as Finn passed beneath the great stone arch. The last threshold between duty and the unknown. He guided Ghost onto the open road that wound through rolling farmland, the hills eventually giving way to deep forests and, in time, the looming silhouette of the Misthaven range.

He paused atop a gentle rise, letting his gaze sweep back over Mirathen. Solavere Palace's spires glinted in the sunshine, a kingdom standing tall, as if it had never burned. Here at the edge of the wild, the wind rustled tall grasses at the roadside, carrying with it the scent of pine from a nearby grove.

For the briefest moment, Finn closed his eyes and breathed in, centering himself. No applause here. No whispers. Just wind and steel and purpose.

"Father," he whispered under his breath, "I'm doing this for you. For your memory. For the realm you loved." His hand drifted to Sunwrath at his side. The sword his father left him. "May Kavros guide my blade as surely as you once guided me."

Then, without looking back again, he urged Ghost into a brisk trot. The city receded behind him, and the mountains beckoned.

Finnian Brightmoor was no longer the frightened boy who cowered in the embers of a ruined ballroom. He was a knight blessed by Kavros's flame, a warrior armed with the deadliest sword the realm offered. A man with nothing left to fear—except failure.

And he did not intend to fail.

Chapter Three

Cedric had always loved the thrill of flying—perhaps the only part of this cursed form he did not resent. The wind curled beneath his wings, lifting him higher.

As he banked low over the rolling treetops, the world below blurred into a vast expanse of green, the morning light setting the leaves aglow. No walls, no expectations—just open sky and the rush of crisp air in his lungs. Here, above it all, he felt almost...alive. Or, at least, more alive than he ever did with his feet on the ground.

Back when he'd prayed to Aurenis, he used to imagine the god of the sky welcoming him into the endless blue. But that was before the transformation. Before he realized how hollow his old faith felt now that his wings were real and his prayers unanswered.

These days, he sent a silent word of thanks—or maybe defiance—to Thalos, the god of change and chaos, whose dominion seemed to resonate with the unpredictability of a man who occasionally became a massive gold-scaled dragon.

He adjusted his wings, mindful of the precious cargo clutched in his foreclaw: a small basket half-filled with freshly gathered strawberries.

Hunting for game had been the plan, but the sweet scent of ripened berries had lured him. They'd always been one of his favorites. It had taken exquisite control to pluck the fruit without crushing them under his talons. *Another day's small victory*, he thought wryly.

Ahead, the canopy thinned just enough to reveal a lookout tower rising from the forest. Its top poked above the tall pines, marking the old outpost that he and Gwenna called home. Morning mist still clung to the mountains beyond, like pale veils draped across the peaks.

The outpost had once been a military station, but an avalanche sealed off the valley years ago, cutting it off from supply routes. Cedric found solace in its half-wild, half-domesticated sprawl—a place where a monster like him might hide from prying eyes.

He backwinged to slow his descent, slipping through the gap in the branches. Landing jarred him, but he took pride in how deftly he managed it these days. Only a few paces away, a brown and white goat bleated in greeting. *Clarence*, Cedric thought with an inward sigh. *Sent by Thalos to keep me humble.*

It took mere heartbeats for the nimble goat to thrust its muzzle into the basket and steal a strawberry. Cedric snorted a hot breath in protest, but Clarence bounded off, berry juice staining his white muzzle in triumph. One day, that goat would push his luck too far. Cedric gave a half-hearted thought to letting the forest predators solve his Clarence problem, but of course, none dared lurk with a dragon nearby. Besides, the goat was a terror, but he and Gwenna had grown oddly fond of the beast. Despite himself, Cedric felt a faint tug of amusement.

Hobbling forward on three legs, he kept the basket clutched tight in his free claw. His heightened dragon senses prickled with each step—he could hear Gwenna's footsteps, the gentle clucking of the hens in their coop, the rush of a nearby stream winding through thick undergrowth. When he turned the corner around the outpost's storage shed, Gwenna was there, rich red hair catching the morning sun.

"Strawberries again?" she teased, peering into his basket. "You said you were going hunting."

He released a low huff and gave a roll of his golden eyes, pointedly glancing at the half-full basket. If only he could say, *It's not as easy as it sounds.* But he was trapped in silence—a monstrous shape with no ability to speak, not unless he shifted back to his human form, which wasn't possible until the sun vanished beyond the horizon.

Gwenna grinned as if she understood his unspoken complaint. "Yes, yes, I know—picking berries with talons is probably more challenging than actual hunting. I'll stop teasing." She gave his scaled shoulder a friendly bump of her fist.

Even after ten years, Cedric marveled at her casual closeness. She never looked afraid. She never hesitated to touch him, as if he were still her older brother in human form. Sometimes he could almost believe he was.

A sudden bleat from the bushes drew their attention. Clarence materialized for a second raid on the berries. Gwenna hissed in exasperation. "Clarence! You menace!" She rescued the basket just in time, though the goat managed to steal another berry. He trotted off, tail wagging in smug victory.

"You're lucky we don't roast you over a spit," Gwenna muttered after him, only half-joking. Cedric rumbled deep in his chest, echoing the sentiment. With a wry shake of her head, Gwenna turned back to him. "How about I make some breakfast? I'll bring it out when it's ready."

Cedric nodded, watching as she turned with her dual burden of strawberries and eggs, striding into the area of the outpost that served as living quarters and kitchen. After all these years, he should be used to the barriers in his life, but they still stung. Ten years since he had fled the only home he'd ever known, clad in the unfamiliar scales of a dragon. Ten long years since he'd slain his own parents and lost everything in his world.

Everything except Gwenna.

He shook off the ache that threatened to sink its claws into him and ambled toward the enclosure where they tried to keep the goats corralled. *Tried* being the operative word. The fence had clearly been tested overnight—bent boards, gaps where curious muzzles might have pushed through.

Clarence, the head troublemaker, stood proudly on a small rock, as though daring Cedric to fix the boundary. He eyed the dragon's approach with a haughty bleat—just loud enough to be irritating, but not quite the full-throated shriek Cedric had learned to recognize as actual warning. For all his faults, the beast had good instincts.

Cedric rumbled, lowering his head until their gazes were nearly level. He wished he could snarl an ultimatum: *Steal one more thing, and it's a spit for you.* But the goat merely flicked an ear, unimpressed by the beast towering over him.

A resigned sigh of hot breath escaped Cedric's throat. He scanned the fence, making mental notes of what needed repairing. Yes, in his human form he'd be able to patch it up —maybe with a bit more wood from that fallen oak near the eastern wall. The knowledge that he could fix it gave him a glimmer of satisfaction. He still had use, even in this cursed life.

"Being bested by goats again?" Gwenna called, hands on her hips as Cedric slunk away from the goat pen.

Cedric lashed his tail once, partly in annoyance at the goat, partly in embarrassment. After a final, warning glare at the shaggy menace, he lumbered toward his sister. Gwenna laughed, clearly not impressed by his draconic scowl, either.

She jerked her thumb toward the old stables. "I've got breakfast ready, if you're hungry."

Hungry was an understatement. Cedric felt the roar of it

deep in his gut, the morning shift always stirring a ravenous heat that gnawed at him from within. In his earliest days of this curse, an almost bloodthirsty need for food had consumed him. He'd since fought to wrestle control from the beast inside, careful never to let hunger turn to frenzy. Gwenna complained he ate too little, that he should feed himself properly—but Cedric had grown wary of indulging anything that smacked of draconic instinct.

He ducked his head beneath the stable's doorway, stepping inside with careful grace to avoid scraping the timbers. Their makeshift "dragon quarters" were as homey as a barn could be, mostly because Gwenna insisted on it. He cast a fond glance at the floral tapestry she'd hung on the far wall— a bright bit of color that always lifted his spirits. Initially, he'd scoffed at her effort, but privately, he enjoyed having something pretty that was just...for him.

His sister had set a simple meal on a sturdy wooden table: a bowl of porridge and eggs for herself, and a generous plate of bacon and fried eggs for him. He padded over, lowering his great head so he could reach. The aroma of crisp bacon made his nostrils flare. At once, his stomach snarled a demand, and he gratefully tore into the food.

"So," Gwenna said around a spoonful of porridge, "any sign of trouble on your flight?"

Cedric shook his head, a quick side-to-side motion. He was careful to pick up a slice of bacon with his scaly dragon lips instead of snapping up the entire plate—an exercise in finesse he'd mastered over the years.

"Good," Gwenna murmured, though there was a furrow between her brows. "That's good."

That slight hitch in her voice set Cedric on alert. Something bothered her. He huffed softly, dipping his head until they were at eye level. She seemed reluctant to speak, her gaze sliding away.

After a moment, she sighed. "Sorry. I've just been

thinking a lot. Your birthday is coming up." She paused, swirling her spoon in the porridge. "Hard to believe it's been this long since..."

Since I transformed. Since I tore our lives apart. The bacon turned to ash on his tongue. Memories unspooled in his mind: the bright glare of dragonfire, the screams, the horrifying realization that his own body had caused such devastation.

That *he* had done those things.

Gwenna stood, coming around the table to place a warm hand on his shoulder. Her palm felt small against his scales, but no less comforting. "I don't regret it," she said fiercely, voice trembling with conviction. "None of it."

But how could she not, when it was his own monstrous form that had brought about their parents' deaths? He blinked, lowering his gaze to the freshly swept floor. He'd never forget the sight of blood on the palace marble or how it had felt to flee into the night, leaving everything behind. How was she so forgiving?

Gwenna's hand slid in small circles over his scales. "Ced, we've been over this a thousand times. It's not your fault."

It wasn't. The problem was, they didn't know what had brought on his transformation. Maybe if they'd been back at Mirathen, they could have consulted the great library there. Consulted with scholars and wizards. But they didn't have any of that, not here. They only had their wits and each other.

He exhaled a gusty, unhappy breath. She had sacrificed so much to be with him. To help her brother through the worst years of his life.

Gwenna pinned him with a familiar, exasperated look. "Enough. I can see those gears turning in that thick skull of yours." She offered him a small smile. "I know you, Ced. You can't keep blaming yourself for what happened."

He gave a low rumble, something halfway between a sigh

and a growl. If only letting go of guilt was as simple as Gwenna's words. Still, he was grateful for her love; he'd have lost himself in despair long ago if she hadn't been by his side.

They returned to their meal in relative silence until Gwenna cleared her throat. "We're running low on supplies again: flour, thread...the usual. One of us will need to head to town soon."

Cedric nodded, swallowing the last bite of egg. He reached out carefully with one foreclaw, pointing toward the door that led to his wood shop. Gwenna's face brightened at once.

"You've finished some new carvings?" she guessed. "Wooden dragons, I presume?"

He huffed, nodding. It was ironic, making miniature versions of the creature he'd become. But the carvings sold well enough, and children adored them. If it helped them survive, he'd keep carving dragons, knights, even silly goats if it came to that.

"Perfect," Gwenna said, her earlier somber mood lifting a fraction. "We'll trade them in town for what we need."

Cedric had delicately lipped up another piece of bacon when a commanding bleat broke their peace. He and Gwenna exchanged tense looks. Clarence might be a handful, but they'd only heard that particular tone on occasions when danger lurked in the woods.

And not just *any* danger. Knights on the hunt.

Gwenna set down her spoon, wetting her lips and appearing to be more composed than Cedric knew she was. "Well, it seems like we have visitors. Ced, you should probably stay put in here for now."

Cedric snorted, shaking his head to show his disdain for her idea. Even though he knew it was the most logical, at least for now. If he tried to fly away, they'd see him. And if he flew off, Gwenna would be vulnerable.

She sighed, patting his shoulder. "I know. But I'll stay

hidden while I see what's going on." Gwenna cracked a grin. "Besides, this'll be a good chance to see if my new defenses work. We agreed it's better to scare them off rather than... well, you know."

True enough. Cedric had enough blood on his claws. They'd gone a few blessed weeks without invaders, and Gwenna had put her very un-princesslike hobby of tinkering to good use. Wouldn't it be worthwhile if it scared away their foes before Cedric and Gwenna had no choice?

Finally, he nodded, though he made a grumpy noise to make it clear he didn't like it.

"Be back soon!" Gwenna headed out of the stable, shutting the door securely behind her.

How many times had she insisted on shielding him from danger? If things went sideways, she might be the one snared by danger. The thought turned his stomach.

Cedric forced a deep breath. He curled his tail around his hind legs, trying not to pace like a caged animal. *You are not merely a dragon,* he told himself fiercely. *You are Cedric Cleburne, son of King William, rightful heir to the throne. The Gilded Prince of Lunareth. You won't let fear—or hunger—dictate your actions.*

Chapter Four

Finn guided Ghost toward the yawning mouth of the cave. A chill draft hissed from the darkness beyond, carrying with it a faint metallic tang that made the hairs on his neck prickle. Blood. Old, but distinct. This tunnel, he had learned from locals, was the only viable route into the hidden valley where an abandoned military outpost supposedly lay.

He reined Ghost to a stop at the threshold, leaning forward in the saddle to peer into the gloom. "Well, that looks inviting."

Ghost's ears twitched, her muscles bunching under the saddle. *Smart girl.* Finn couldn't blame her; the entrance was littered with bones picked clean, some still draped in tattered scraps of armor.

Glinting steel caught his eye—gauntlets, sword hilts, and dented breastplates scattered like discarded relics of a lost battle. No familiar crests, no insignias tying them to Lunareth. Just scraps of mercenary colors, some unmarked, others bearing symbols of companies Finn only vaguely recognized. But one piece made him pause.

A torn scrap of fabric, half-buried in the dirt, its color

muddied by blood and dust. Deep crimson, with the faintest outline of a black sunburst at its frayed edge.

Finn frowned. Avalisian.

Not unheard of—sellswords came from all corners of the world, and plenty of ex-Avalisian soldiers had turned to mercenary work when their empire had no further use for them. Some even sought work in Lunareth, taking coin from whoever would pay.

That had to be the case here. King Darius had hired mercenaries for this mission, after all—this one must have been among them. Nothing strange about that.

And yet... Finn couldn't shake the feeling that something was off. The Avalisian Empire had no love for Lunareth. Why would one of its men be out here, hunting a dragon for a Lunarethen king?

"Focusing on the wrong thing, Finn," he muttered to himself.

No, better to take in the tableau as a whole. This wasn't a simple warning. It was a *display*. A deliberate message, like a raider staking heads on pikes outside a conquered city. Whoever—or whatever—dwelled beyond this cave didn't just kill. It wanted its victims to be *seen*.

Finn swallowed hard. "Kavros's forge," he muttered, lips pressing into a grim line. There were better places to die. More dignified ones, at least.

He slid off Ghost's back, stepping carefully around the skeletal debris. A knight's half-collapsed skull grinned up at him from beneath a battered helm, and Finn's breath caught. *That could have been me,* he thought. *Might still be, if I'm not careful.*

He glanced at Ghost, patting her reassuringly. "Want to turn back?" he murmured. "Because I wouldn't hold it against you."

She blew out a loud snort, shifting her weight but not moving. Loyal, even when she had more sense than he did.

Finn exhaled, steeling himself. "I guess you're right. We've come too far, and it would be a pity not to see what the fuss is all about."

Grasping the reins, he led her inside. Pointed stalactites jutted from the vaulted ceiling like the teeth of some ancient beast, waiting to swallow them whole. The narrow path forced them into single file, Ghost's hooves clattering against the stone in staccato echoes. The outside light faded, but a fuzzy lichen clinging to the walls emitted a glow that was enough for Finn to make his way—barely.

Several tense minutes passed as they navigated the twisting passage. Then, ahead, the faint glow of the exit. Finn's shoulders sagged with relief at the promise of open air. And preferably fewer bones.

The moment they stepped outside, the dense embrace of the forest met them. Finn paused, scanning the area. No skeletal warning signs. But there was also no princess waiting to be rescued with a gift basket in hand. Shaking his head, Finn climbed back into the saddle.

He rode deeper into the woods, unease prickling anew at the eerie hush. Too quiet. No birdsong, no chittering squirrels—nothing. Even the wind hardly stirred the leaves. The Misthaven Mountains loomed ahead, their rugged peaks fading into a tangle of mist and pine. Somewhere up there, hidden in the wilderness, the dragon waited.

The journey from the capital had been long but uneventful—too uneventful, perhaps. Finn had pushed hard, stopping only when necessary to rest Ghost and replenish supplies. Now, with each surefooted step she took, tension twisted in his gut.

This was it. He was close.

And that meant confronting the very creature that haunted his nightmares. Or, more accurately, the thing he'd spent years preparing to kill.

A twig snapped beneath Ghost's hoof, obnoxiously loud

in the quiet. Reflexively, Finn's hand dropped to Sunwrath's hilt, thumb brushing over the ruby in its pommel. Overreacting wouldn't help if something was watching. Wouldn't stop a blade, either.

They pressed on, the branches overhead weaving a patchwork of shifting shadows. Twice, Finn caught himself craning his neck to search the dim spaces between trees, certain he'd glimpsed gold scales reflecting the sunlight. A trick of the light? Or a trick of the mind? Either way, when he looked again, there was nothing but wind-stirred leaves.

"Easy, girl," he murmured, patting Ghost's neck. Not that she needed the reassurance—her ears flicked back, unimpressed. If anything, the words were more for himself than the stalwart mare. She snorted, tossing her head as though to say, *We've been through worse.*

The dense forest tightened around them, branches twisting overhead so thickly that sunlight had to fight its way through, casting speckled patterns across the mossy ground. A fragile silence had settled again, which only heightened Finn's unease.

A sharp prickling sensation crawled over the back of his neck. Finn drew Ghost to a halt, hand dropping to Sunwrath's hilt as his gaze swept the underbrush. Something was here. Watching.

Then, movement. A flicker at the edges of his vision. Then another, and another. A slow dread settled in his chest when he realized shapes—at least half a dozen—were shifting in the undergrowth, silently encircling him.

Finn swallowed, the dryness in his throat at odds with the clammy chill creeping down his spine. *Brilliant. Nothing like eerie silence and invisible enemies to keep things interesting.*

"Show yourselves!" he called, aiming for commanding and confident rather than on edge and vaguely annoyed.

The only response was a stillness thicker than fog. Even Ghost seemed tense, ears pinned back, muscles taut beneath him. She had good instincts. He trusted them almost more than his own.

Sunwrath whispered free of its sheath, the ruby set in the pommel flashing. Finn scanned left to right. *How could so many approach without a sound? No footfalls, no voices, no clank of armor.*

He nudged Ghost forward a step, then another. The shapes at the edges of his vision swayed but did not advance. Ambush? Or something worse? Sweat trickled down his temple.

Then Finn got a clearer view of his mysterious foes. His breath stilled as he realized they were wooden silhouettes, mounted on hidden hinges. Painted shapes, nothing more.

Finn heaved out a long breath, half relieved, half irritated. The crude cutouts stood frozen in mock battle poses, arrayed like sentries. Some resembled knights in armor, swords raised; others were monstrous things with crooked horns and reptilian tails. They creaked in the breeze, shifting just enough to trick the mind into believing they moved.

"Clever." Finn sheathed Sunwrath once more. "Someone has a flair for theatrics."

Ghost snorted, her tension easing now that she sensed no real danger. Finn nudged her closer to one of the silhouettes, eyes narrowing. Even crude as they were, they had *worked.*

The artistry was rough, but the design? Alarmingly effective. Not just meant to deceive—meant to unnerve. To make intruders question themselves. Second-guess their own senses.

He reached out, tapping a knight-shaped cutout with two fingers. It rocked on its hinge. A scare tactic. Like scarecrows intended to keep crows from a field, though in this case they were meant to...what? Keep rescuers away from a captive princess?

Finn continued on, carefully weaving between the

wooden figures, his mind working through the possibilities. Who set these up, and why?

The dragon? Unlikely.

The princess's captors? Or perhaps...someone else entirely?

Finn advanced only a short distance before a thunderous clamor exploded overhead and all around—a symphony of chaos that sounded like a kitchen had just declared war on itself.

Pots, pans, and assorted scrap rattled violently, their clang echoing off the trees and seeming to come from everywhere at once.

Finn startled, instinctively ducking as he yelped at the unexpected sound. Ghost, by contrast, didn't so much as flinch. The warhorse merely paused, ears flicking in what could only be described as mild irritation.

Finn straightened, shaking his head. "Nice of you to pretend to care," he muttered, brushing off the adrenaline surge.

Ghost twitched an ear back at him. *Get on with it.*

He squinted at the dangling pots and pans. Finn spotted wires and ropes strung among the trees, nearly invisible behind tangled vines. Another trap, or alarm. Set it off, and the entire contraption turned into a percussion ensemble from hell.

Effective. Even knowing it wasn't a real attack, his pulse still hadn't quite settled.

Ghost sighed, hooves shifting in the dirt as though unimpressed by his delayed realization.

Finn gave her a look. "I see you're taking this very seriously."

She swished her tail in what he was fairly sure was a gesture of profound indifference.

Fine. Moving on. He swung down from the saddle and knelt beside a cluster of cords looped around a low branch.

Whoever had built this contraption was cunning, resource-ful, and—judging by the sheer amount of noise—determined to scare intruders off rather than fight them outright.

They don't want open combat. Maybe they were too few or simply trying to avoid bloodshed.

But that didn't make sense, not with the skeletal remains left outside the cave. Finn wiped a bead of sweat from his brow. *Focus. There's a puzzle here. Solve it.*

Before he could trace the ropes further, Finn glimpsed a flash of movement in his periphery. He froze.

Auburn hair caught the light as a slender figure slipped between the trees. Finn's breath stalled in his throat. Princess Gwenna?

He'd seen the official portrait hanging in Solavere Palace —a bright-eyed royal girl with that same distinctive shade of hair. Could it truly be her?

Finn was off and moving before his brain fully caught up.

"Princess Gwenna!" he shouted to be heard over the racket, breaking into a run. "Wait! I'm here to help!"

Branches clawed at him as he pushed forward, but she was already slipping away, vanishing between trees like a ghost in the mist.

Finn skidded to a halt near a gnarled oak, torn between chasing blindly or returning to Ghost. *Was that really her?*

He glanced back, gauging the risk of leaving Ghost alone. She stood exactly where he left her, unbothered. Her dark gaze tracked him with mild patience, like she was waiting for him to be done with whatever nonsense he was about to run into.

"Stay here, girl," Finn called.

Ghost flicked an ear. Possibly acknowledgment. Possibly boredom. Either way, she wasn't moving.

Finn turned back toward the tangled undergrowth ahead. Too thick for a horse, but not for someone on foot. He didn't waste time hesitating. Finn plunged forward, brambles raking across his armor, branches snapping in his wake. He ducked under a low limb, boots slipping slightly in the damp earth as he pushed harder.

The trees thinned.

Ahead, a stone watchtower loomed, draped in ivy. A weed-choked courtyard stretched before him—an abandoned military outpost, just as he'd been told.

This was it.

His gaze swept the area, searching for any sign of movement—a flash of auburn hair, a flicker of gold.

"Princess Gwenna!" he called, wincing at the roughness in his throat. "It's safe now. I'm here to rescue you!"

Silence answered him. The wind stirred the ivy across the walls, and in the distance he could just make out the faint noise of birds returning to the forest canopy.

Then, from within the tower, a voice crackled with outrage: "Piss off, you armored twat!"

For a beat, his brain simply refused to process the words. Princesses were supposed to beg for rescue, not curse out their would-be saviors.

That's...not what I expected. He had pictured so many things on this ride. A trapped princess, lonely and afraid. A woman desperate for help. Maybe even a tearful reunion with civilization after ten years of solitude.

This?

This was not in the script.

Finn exhaled slowly, resetting his expectations in real time. Straightening, he called back, keeping his voice even despite the whiplash in tone. "Your Highness," he said, "I understand you've endured something terrible here. I promise, I mean you no harm."

A pause. Finn tilted his head, waiting for a response. None came.

He cleared his throat. "King Darius sent me to rescue you."

For a moment, all was still again.

Then, the same defiant voice, brimming with frustration. "I said *piss off!* I don't need rescuing, and I'm *certainly* not going anywhere with you!"

Finn blinked. *Well,* that *was emphatic.*

He gritted his teeth, confusion tangling with irritation. This was *not* how rescues were supposed to go. What was going on?

Was she brainwashed? Doubtful. She sounded far too coherent for that. Possessed? Also unlikely. Unless possession made you really, *really* annoyed.

Which left the most plausible option—this is what a decade of captivity does to a person. Especially a princess who once lived in a gilded palace and now, apparently, lived in a ruin full of trap-rigged cookware. But Finn had seen no sign of Gwenna's potential captors, or of the dragon, so this was his best opportunity to free the princess.

He forced a calming breath. Fine. She wanted defiant? He could work with defiant.

"I'm coming in, Your Highness," he announced, picking his way across the courtyard toward the door. Finn heroically avoided tripping over a good-sized rock shrouded by the weeds.

His free hand hovered near Sunwrath's hilt while the other reached for the door handle. Because if she wasn't alone, he'd rather not go inside unarmed.

Finn barely had time to test the tower's door before a resounding roar ripped through the clearing. The sound vibrated through him, rattling his bones, snapping him into high alert. His body reacted from sheer instinct and training. Sunwrath flashed free of its sheath, Finn's stance low and braced for defense or attack.

A massive, golden reptilian shape emerged from behind the tower. The dragon's scales caught the sunlight, dazzling in arcs of molten brilliance. Finn's stomach plummeted, fear and adrenaline boiling together in a white-hot surge.

The same dragon that killed my father. The one that ruined my life.

Jaws parted in a low, rolling growl of challenge as the dragon prowled closer. Its wings half-unfurled, casting an intimidating silhouette. Finn couldn't help but note the dark intelligence in its gold-flecked eyes. This was no mindless creature—there was a keen awareness there.

His pulse thundered in his ears, but he held his ground, Sunwrath raised. His grip tightened, feet shifting back as the dragon prowled closer.

Another step forward for the dragon, another back for Finn. No, he couldn't retreat. Not when the beast that caused so much heartbreak stood before him. Jaw clenched, Finn hefted the longblade, assessing the dragon. *Go for the soft point of the throat or wing joint.* That was his best chance.

A sudden cry shattered Finn's concentration. "No! Stop!"

Princess Gwenna burst from the tower, red hair tumbling over her shoulders, eyes burning with something fierce. Not fear. Not desperation. Anger.

And why in all the hells was she running *toward* the dragon?

His breath caught—because she wasn't just standing near the dragon. No, she was *in front of it*. Shielding it. Finn staggered, mind scrambling to make sense of what he was seeing.

The dragon made a low rumble—not quite a threat, not quite amusement.

Finn remained in his defensive stance. "Princess Gwenna," he tried again, steady, but urgent, "that dragon is dangerous."

Gwenna didn't move. "And you're not?" she challenged.

He took a cautious step closer. "It killed your family."

Gwenna's expression darkened. Before Finn could read

more of her expression, the ground trembled beneath his boots.

The dragon had shifted—not to attack, but to place itself between them. A deep growl rolled from its chest like distant thunder. But something about the beast's posture seemed...hesitant. Its talons flexed in the earth, but its jaws remained closed, the lethal fangs hidden.

Finn's anger surged. *Hesitant or not, this monster is the reason my father died. He* didn't hesitate.

Years of training and vengeance burned through him, fueling the lunge. Sunwrath flashed in a tight arc, angled for the vulnerable spot between head and neck—where armor thinned, where a clean strike could end it.

The dragon recoiled, wings mantling in a sweeping dodge. Finn braced for a counterattack—a gout of flame, a clawed strike, *something*.

It didn't come. The dragon retreated, but still blocked Gwenna. The princess stood behind the beast, arms crossed.

Finn took a step backward, sucking in a breath to help his mind focus as he tried to figure out what the hell was going on. A stolen princess who didn't want rescue. A dragon that didn't attack on sight.

It didn't matter, though. He'd made a vow.

"You must see reason!" he shouted, his voice raw. Finn tried another lunge, but the dragon sidestepped again. It let out a warning snarl, but still no attack. "I'm not your enemy, Princess Gwenna! I came to save you—"

"Save me from what?" she yelled back, eyes flashing. "My own independence? *Leave*, you fool!"

His thoughts snagged on that. *Independence?*

Damn it all.

If Gwenna wouldn't come willingly, then—fine. He'd force her hand. Get her away from the dragon *first*, argue later.

The beast growled, tail lashing like an agitated cat, but

still held back. Finn's mind raced. *No claws. No fire. No real fight. It's holding back. Why?*

Did it matter? Not really. Not when this was the dragon he'd dreamed of killing for so long. Its hesitation gave him an opening.

He feinted left, sword slicing through the air. The dragon dodged, wings flaring as if shielding Gwenna.

That was exactly what Finn wanted.

He lunged, driving the beast back a few paces. Gwenna edged aside to avoid the dragon's retreating claws, ducking beneath an outstretched wing.

There's my opening. He slammed Sunwrath into its sheath mid-motion, sprinting for the princess.

Grab her and run. That's the only way. Deal with the dragon later.

He was almost there when the dragon's tail came out of nowhere. It caught Finn's legs, and he lost his footing entirely.

The world tilted—sky, trees, dirt, all blurring together. He tumbled end over end, slamming through the underbrush with bone-jarring force, though his enchanted armor absorbed the worst of it. Pain blazed in his side as he rolled to a stop, body screaming in protest. For a moment, white spots swarmed across his vision, and he tasted blood at the corner of his mouth.

Finn struggled into a sitting position. He forced a ragged breath, gulping air into his throbbing lungs. Beyond the tangle of branches, he glimpsed the dragon, still standing guard in front of Princess Gwenna. It hadn't chased him. It hadn't tried to finish him off. Instead, it regarded him with narrowed, golden eyes, as though daring him to try again.

Finn clenched his teeth, humiliation burning hotter than the pain lacing his ribs. The princess was watching, her expression difficult to read. Not fear or the desperation of someone longing for rescue, of that he was certain. If anything, she looked furious with him for intruding.

He pushed to his knees, swallowing a groan as pain licked up his side. *Damn it.* The thought came unbidden, thick with guilt and grief. *I failed.*

His fingers twitched for his sword—only to spot it several feet away, half-buried in the dirt. The distance might as well have been a mile.

Swallowing the coppery taste in his mouth, Finn staggered upright. His balance wavered, but he steadied himself with a sharp inhale. It took far too much effort to reclaim his sword. He wasn't fighting this battle again today. The dragon's unwavering glare promised that a second charge would end far worse. Finn's soldier instincts cut through the haze of anger: *Withdraw. Regroup. Live to fight another day.*

With a muffled curse, he stumbled toward the treeline, one hand clasped tight over his ribs. Leaves and brambles snagged at his legs, as if the entire damned forest wanted him gone. He pushed forward anyway.

He shot one last look over his shoulder. The princess had stepped beside the dragon again, her posture less defensive, more...resigned. Finn's stomach twisted as he caught the relief on her face. Relief that *he* was leaving.

His jaw locked. *That thing killed her parents. Burned their palace. Took everything. And she's standing beside it like a trusted ally?*

Finn's hands curled into fists, frustration and confusion churning hot in his mind. *Fine.* He was in no shape to keep fighting today. But he'd be back.

He had to find Ghost, tend to his wounds, and—most importantly—figure out how to break the dragon's hold over the princess. Because whatever had happened to her in these ten long years, whatever the beast had done to twist her mind...

Finn *refused* to leave her here.

Chapter Five

Cedric exhaled a weary groan as the final traces of gold shimmered off his skin, the dragon's scales receding into soft, human flesh. The transformation left his muscles throbbing in protest, as though they hadn't quite forgiven him for forcing them into such a monumental shift. Even after all these years, the process felt painfully surreal, as if his bones never fully welcomed their old shape.

He rested a hand against the stable wall, catching his breath. Cedric donned the set of clothing he'd laid out in the early morning hours before his forced shift.

The sun's last rays had dipped below the horizon moments ago, plunging the clearing into indigo twilight. The outpost courtyard stood silent, the faint rustle of night birds in the distant trees the only sound. A relief after the day's near disaster.

"Ced?" Gwenna's voice drifted through the open doorway. She stepped out into the courtyard with a lantern in hand, its glow haloing her auburn hair. Concern etched lines across her face. "How are you feeling?"

He managed a tight smile, straightening. "Like someone

punched me in every bone simultaneously," he replied, voice tinged with weary humor. "So...the usual."

Gwenna sighed. "I've got some liniment you can use, if you need. But did you see that knight's livery?"

Her swift change of subject caught him off balance for a moment, but Cedric refocused quickly. It hadn't been something they could discuss after they had chased the knight off. "Lunareth."

She nodded. "Come on. Dinner's ready and we need to talk."

Together, they made their way into the old kitchen. Cedric had patched the roof when they'd first come here. Lanterns hung from the beams overhead, bathing the area in warm light.

Cedric lowered himself onto a wooden bench, mindful of his still-protesting muscles. Gwenna hovered nearby, setting a small kettle on the fire. The flicker of flames danced over her face, illuminating the worry in her eyes. Neither spoke for a while, the tension from today's encounter still hanging thick between them.

"That's the first Lunarethen knight we've seen." Gwenna shoved a plate toward him already laden with roasted rabbit haunch, hard cheese, and flatbread.

The aromas made Cedric's stomach growl in appreciation, and it took all of his willpower not to pick up the haunch and greedily rip the meat from bones. He used a fork and knife, like the royal he had once been. "If he comes back, we can't kill a Lunarethen knight."

Gwenna chewed a hunk of bread, aiming the tines of her fork at him. "Oh, we certainly *can*."

Cedric rolled his eyes. "We shouldn't." He tore off a piece of bread. "Not when that knight is one of our own." That was the part that unsettled him the most. For ten years, no one had come. No search parties, no royal decrees. But now, suddenly, a Lunarethen knight had been sent. *Why?*

"Not ours anymore," Gwenna groused. "We can't keep doing this."

Cedric grimaced. "He's not the first knight to come nosing around, Gwen."

"It only takes one to be the last," she pointed out, her tone soft but cutting. "And did you hear him? He wants to *rescue me*." Gwenna rolled her eyes, the gesture as unprincesslike as possible.

That, at least, was a source of amusement. Cedric chuckled. "As if you need rescuing."

"Exactly." She speared a piece of meat. "But that means he'll probably come back. Or if not him, someone else. I... we've had more intruders in these last few months than in the first nine years combined."

Cedric stared at the triangle of hard cheese as if it held the answers he sought. "So you think it's time we left?" The question tasted bitter on his tongue. The outpost had been their sanctuary—battered, overgrown, but still theirs. He couldn't imagine finding another place so remote or so easily defensible.

Gwenna's lips pressed into a thin line. "I don't know. Where could we possibly go that would be safer? Lunareth's knights are hunting dragons and rogue princesses, and evidently we're on their list. If we move closer to any town, we risk even more trouble."

He let out a heavy breath, studying the lantern's glow. "Then what do we do?" The day's events flashed in his mind —his protective fury at seeing the knight reach Gwenna, his confusion that the man hadn't struck a killing blow when he could have. Was it because Cedric hadn't been on the attack? "We've done everything to keep them out. And yet they keep coming."

"Maybe..." Gwenna frowned, hugging her knees. "We redouble the traps. Or expand the perimeter. I could salvage more metal scraps from the old armory and rig new defenses."

Cedric managed a half-smile. "If anyone can turn scrap into a near-death experience for unwelcome visitors, it's you."

She snorted, though her eyes remained worried. "We can keep them out for a while, but how long?"

His jaw tightened. As much as Cedric disliked it, his sister had a point. They couldn't keep this up. "Then we make a plan," Cedric said quietly. "If we can't hold them off forever, maybe we *do* need to find somewhere else. I'm just not sure where."

They fell silent for a moment, the crackle of the fire filling the gap. An evening breeze rattled the nearby windows. Cedric's eyes flicked to the darkness beyond, a pang of longing tugging at him. He couldn't fly again until dawn, but part of him wanted to soar far away from this entire cursed situation.

Gwenna's voice cut through his thoughts. "Tomorrow night," she ventured, "once you're human again, maybe we can go gather more supplies? We'll need them if we stay. And if we leave...we still need them."

Cedric shook his head. "Not *we*. Me."

She glared at him. "Why leave me behind?"

Cedric sighed. "Because people are actively looking for you. They want the lost princess. No one's searching for a dead prince."

Gwenna pursed her lips. "But you can only go at night. It's dangerous."

He rolled his shoulders. "I'll be fine. I can fly part of the way as a dragon." It was the easiest way to navigate the cave, certainly. Why go through when one could go over?

His sister huffed out an unhappy breath. "Fine. But for the record, I hate being left behind, you know. I'm not a fragile flower!"

Cedric chuckled. "No, you're certainly not." He smiled. "I promise to be careful. And I'll be back before dawn."

They lapsed into a companionable silence for a time. Despite the stress twisting in Cedric's gut, he felt a deep well of gratitude for this worn-out outpost—at least here, no courtiers or advisors policed every moment of their lives. And, more importantly, Gwenna was safe.

He rubbed at his still-aching ribs, wishing the transformation didn't leave him feeling so damaged. "We'll figure this out," he murmured at last, as much to himself as to Gwenna. "Somehow."

She looked at him, determination burning in her violet eyes. "We always do."

The night deepened around them, crickets humming beyond the walls. Cedric let the warmth of the small fire soak into his bones, all the while wondering how many more nights they could spend here before another knight—or worse—appeared at their doorstep. But for now, he had Gwenna's company and a tentative plan. *I can't ask for more than that.*

And as the darkness pressed close, he silently vowed that, no matter what the future held, he wouldn't let their sanctuary crumble without a fight.

But a part of him wondered if they'd already lost.

Chapter Six

Finn shifted in the saddle, half-tempted to yank off the tangle of twigs still clinging to his battered armor. But every time he raised an arm, his ribs stabbed with pain.

He guided Ghost through the gates of Duskridge, forcing himself to keep his chin high. The tall silhouettes of the watchtowers cast long shadows over the village square.

The village was thriving. More so than Finn imagined it might, so close to the Revendarian border.

Duskridge had always been a quiet place, its stone cottages battered by northern winds. Merchants hawked bright Revendarian cloth, their voices rich with the lilt of their homeland. A woman in simple wool robes stirred a pot outside a cookhouse, the scent of spiced lamb curling into the crisp air—not a Lunarethan recipe, but one passed down through generations. Here, in the shadow of the border, they did not try to blend in. They carried their culture openly, woven into the fabric of their new lives.

That should have been a comfort. Instead, unease curled in Finn's gut.

Maybe the Misthaven Mountains shielded them from

conflict. Maybe the war had simply moved on without them. Or maybe they had stopped seeing Lunareth as their salvation.

He shook away the thoughts. Those were none of his concern at the moment.

Surviving his current embarrassment was.

Farmers and tradesfolk paused in their daily routines to whisper behind calloused hands as he rode by. Finn caught snippets—hushed exclamations about the blood on his cheek, or the weary slump of his shoulders.

Let them stare, he told himself. He'd fought a dragon—sort of—and all he had to show for it was bruised ribs and a shredded ego. Not exactly the stuff of ballads.

They see me as a failure, he thought, glaring at a trio of gawking children. One of them pointed, mouth agape, until an embarrassed mother shooed the child back. "Mama, why does the knight look so sad?" the boy asked, voice carrying. Finn clenched his jaw, wishing he could melt into the ground.

The reality stung. He'd come so close to rescuing Princess Gwenna. The memory of the outpost and her furious eyes still burned in his mind, tangled with the image of that perplexing dragon. Neither creature—princess nor beast—had acted the way he'd expected. *Or wanted them to act,* he admitted to himself, wincing as he shifted in the saddle.

A weather-beaten man beckoned him from the roadside, snapping him out of his thoughts. "You look like you could use a drink, son," the old-timer said, voice rasping, "and The Drunken Dragon's got the best ale 'round." The sign overhead depicted a frothy mug swaying gently in the late afternoon breeze.

A bitter laugh escaped Finn's lips. *The Drunken Dragon. Perfect.* Perhaps it was Thalos and his chaos mocking him.

Still, the prospect of a stiff drink tempted him more than he cared to admit. After stabling Ghost in a nearby livery—murmuring apologies to the mare for the hurried brush-down—he forced his aching legs into the tavern.

Inside, the air hung thick with the scent of spiced ale and roasting meat. Timber rafters enclosed the space, giving it a cozy, if somewhat stifling, atmosphere. Conversations stuttered and quieted as Finn entered, and he was glad he'd pulled out the worst of the twigs at the stable. He felt a dozen sets of eyes track him as he limped toward the bar.

A barmaid—Marla, by the stitching on her blouse—approached with a motherly sort of concern crinkling the corners of her eyes. "You look a sight, Sir Knight. Anything I can get for you?"

"Ale," Finn said, easing onto a stool and hissing when his bruised ribs pinched. "And...information, if you're willing."

Marla handed him a tankard brimming with dark ale. "Drink's a copper. The rest might cost you more," she teased gently, but her gaze held genuine sympathy.

He took a long gulp, the cool bitterness a welcome balm for his tattered nerves. When he set the mug down, he leaned forward, voice lowered. "I'm seeking information about a dragon." The last word came out strained.

A hush rippled through the tavern. A wheezing old man at the far end erupted into laughter. "Oho! The dragon, he says! Well, let me tell you about the dragon, lad. Meanest, ugliest beast you ever did see. Breathes fire hot enough to melt steel, they say. Why, I saw it myself, just the other day. Came swooping down over the village, screeching like a banshee—"

"That was your mother-in-law, you old fool!" someone called out, eliciting a round of laughter.

Finn's cheeks burned. *This is no joke.* His gut clenched, remembering how the golden scales gleamed in the sunlight —and how easily the beast had knocked him aside.

"I saw it," he insisted, voice sharpening. "Out in the forest, near that abandoned outpost. It—" *It protected the princess,* he wanted to say, but he couldn't quite force the words out. He tried to steady himself with the reminder that he was duty-bound to uncover the truth.

The laughter died, replaced by tight silence and sidelong glances. Marla's face turned serious. She leaned in, her whisper hardly audible over the crackle of the hearth. "We do not speak of the dragon with outsiders."

Finn blinked, pulse picking up. "But I'm a knight of Lunareth." *Surely that counts for something.*

She inclined her head, but her expression remained guarded. "Exactly. And that's why I'll tell you this: *there is no dragon.*"

Finn's breath caught in his throat. For a second, Marla's words rattled around in his head, colliding with his certain knowledge of what he'd seen at the outpost. *That damned dragon was real.* He could still feel its tail smashing into him. The blow to his pride stung almost as much as the bruises. Yet the villagers of Duskridge insisted otherwise.

"What?" he blurted, face heating with a mix of confusion and exasperation. "Had you not heard me say I'd *seen* it? I know what I saw."

Marla's stance hardened, as though preparing to shield her entire village with nothing more than her apron.

"Yes," she allowed, her tone carrying an edge of caution, "and you *didn't* see it, Sir Knight. Because you see, ever since that dragon *didn't* appear here—" she placed pointed emphasis on the denial, "—our farmers have flourished. No predators attack their herds. By Sylvara, not even crows harass the crops."

A murmur of agreement stirred among the villagers nearby. One man—a broad-shouldered blacksmith with a Revendarian accent—lifted his mug. "Aye, and for that, we're grateful."

Finn blinked. He hadn't expected the villagers to rise to the dragon's defense, much less feel *gratitude*.

The man met his gaze, unflinching. "Many of us were given no choice but to run, Sir Knight. War took our homes, took our lands. You know this." His expression darkened. "But here, we're safe. The dragon—" he cut a glance at Marla, then exhaled sharply. "The *storm* has never turned on us."

Finn ground his teeth. On one hand, their words confirmed the villagers had knowledge of the beast. On the other, Marla and her cronies were contradicting themselves —claiming it both existed and did not. But it wasn't just their words that twisted his gut.

It was the way they looked at him. The way the blacksmith's gaze lingered. The way no one else in the tavern rushed to explain themselves, as if daring him to argue. The hush that settled over the room wasn't fear—it was something heavier. Something closer to defiance.

They weren't afraid of the dragon.

And they sure as hell weren't afraid of *him*.

"That dragon is a monster," he spat.

Marla snorted, unimpressed by his hostility. "Easy for you to say, when you don't live off the land," she said flatly, meeting his gaze with a challenge of her own.

Finn's stomach churned with frustration. He sensed he could argue until he was blue in the face, but it would get him nowhere. *They've clearly made peace with the beast—and the princess, for all I know.* Yet how could they ignore the dragon had once slain the royal family? *None of this makes sense.*

He cleared his throat, swallowing hard. Time for another approach. "I, uh... came across an old outpost in the forest," he ventured, moderating his tone. "Any idea who might live there?"

Marla seemed to relax fractionally, though her stance remained guarded. "You've been out where Gwen lives?" she asked, pouring him another splash of ale. She said the name so casually it jarred Finn from his brooding.

He blinked. "Gwen? You mean Princess Gwenna?"

She gave a baffled laugh. "Princess? No, just Gwen. Odd girl, but kind enough. Lives up at that old outpost with someone else—we're not sure if he's her husband or kin. They come down from time to time to trade supplies."

Finn's pulse spiked. *So she and this 'someone else' do come here.* The memory of the princess—vehement, fiery, yelling at him to leave—tangled with Marla's depiction of "Gwen." For a moment, he tried to reconcile the two images. *Could the princess have chosen to live in the forest with the man who rigged those traps?*

"Tell me more about them," Finn pressed, keeping his voice level. "The woman—Gwen—and this man she lives with."

Marla shrugged, wiping a stray drop of ale from the bar. "Not much to say, Sir Knight. They arrived a few years back, set up in that tower. Gwen's a miracle worker with tinkering. The other one's some kind of woodcarver. His pieces sell like hotcakes. They carve out a quiet life up there, I suppose."

Finn swallowed, thoughts spinning at breakneck speed. *If Gwen truly is the missing princess, why hide? And who is this woodcarver?* He nodded his thanks to Marla, fumbling a few coins onto the bar for the ale and her reluctant answers. "Is there somewhere I can stay for the night?" he asked, muscles still throbbing from the day's—and the dragon's—punishments.

Marla gestured to a narrow staircase at the back of the tavern. "We've a couple of rooms upstairs for travelers. For a few silvers, you can have one."

Finn dug into the leather pouch at his waist and deposited five shiny silver coins on the bar.

Marla grinned and swiped them up, exchanging them for a key. "Rest well, Sir Knight."

Finn wound his way up the tavern's creaking stairs, a single candle sputtering in the hallway. He slipped into the cramped room, little more than a cot with a thin blanket, and set his bag on the floor.

After stripping off his armor piece by piece—wincing at every bruised spot—he finally collapsed onto the bed. Lumpy as it was, it felt like a damn throne after the day he'd had.

His dreams that night were merciless. Golden scales flashed behind his eyelids, tangled with angry violet eyes and the memory of his father's death. He jolted awake more than once, heart pounding.

He rose the next day with a stiff back and a resolve to dig deeper. Gwen, the woodcarver, and that thrice-damned dragon—somehow, all of it formed a puzzle he intended to crack.

THE NEXT EVENING, Duskridge's market square blazed with torchlight. Colored lanterns hung from the wooden eaves overhead, painting the scene in cheerful hues. Despite the late hour, merchants hawked their wares, cloth-swathed stalls lining the streets. The mingled scents of roast spices, freshly baked bread, and orchard fruits filled Finn's nostrils.

The voices around him were a mix of Lunarethan and Revendarian, their cadences blending in a way that might have once seemed strange, but here, it felt comfortable. Normal.

He passed a stall selling woven charms shaped like tiny leaves—druidic symbols for protection, though they were a rarity Lunareth. The vendor, an older woman with weathered hands, caught his gaze and quickly tucked the charms behind a basket, as if expecting trouble. Finn frowned. For years, the kingdom had hunted druids to extinction—or so it was said. And yet, here she was, selling their symbols in plain sight.

Finn shook his head and continued on. He wasn't here to search for Revendarian druids.

He was about to turn a corner when something stopped him dead in his tracks: a beautifully carved wooden dragon statue perched on a crate in front of a modest stall. Lantern light shimmered across the intricately rendered scales, bringing each ridge and talon to life with striking detail. Its wings were poised for flight, carved with loving care. *Such craftsmanship...* A strange recognition tugged at Finn. *This looks so much like the dragon I fought.*

"Beautiful, isn't it?" a soft voice said at his elbow. He whipped around to see a middle-aged villager in a simple tunic, a knowing smile creasing his lined features.

Finn tore his gaze from the statue. "It's...remarkable," he admitted, voice betraying genuine awe. He reached out, hesitant, and ran a fingertip along the dragon's snout. "Who made this?"

The man's smile deepened. "Cedric. He's got a genuine gift, that one. Not from here, but he fits well enough."

Something in Finn's stomach swooped—half anticipation, half trepidation. Marla had mentioned Gwen lived with a woodcarver. If this was the same man, then he was likely the one who'd set those traps. And if Gwen truly *was* Princess Gwenna, then Cedric might have answers—about her past, about the dragon, about *everything*.

The villager scratched his chin, shifting when Finn didn't respond. "I could introduce you, if you like. He's not here often, but he's here tonight."

Finn squared his shoulders, ignoring the persistent throb in his ribs. "Yes," he said, forcing a calm into his voice he didn't quite feel. "I'd like that."

Finn followed the villager through the bustling market, his gaze flicking across the lively stalls. The tempting scent of spiced apples and roasting meat made his stomach rumble. *Food later. Answers first.*

Ahead, the villager angled toward a quieter corner, where torchlight struggled to reach. Finn spotted two figures near a table lined with carvings much like the dragon he'd seen. But he hardly spared them a glance. His focus was on the men.

One of them, a burly figure with a thick beard and arms like tree trunks, gestured animatedly as he spoke with the other man. His heavy fur-lined cloak and the dusting of sawdust across his tunic fit every expectation Finn had of a mountain craftsman. That had to be Cedric.

The man laughed at something, throwing back his head with an uproarious howl. Finn braced himself, already preparing for a clash of wills.

The villager halted nearby, clearly hesitant to interrupt. Before Finn could step forward, the burly man clapped the other on the shoulder, then turned away.

"Cedric," the villager called. "This knight was admiring your dragon statue. He wanted to meet you."

The larger man didn't twitch or turn. But the other man —the one Finn had immediately dismissed—lifted his head.

Finn pursed his lips. *That can't be Cedric.*

He had pictured a shaggy mountain man—someone weathered, broad-shouldered, all rough edges and practicality. The kind of man who belonged in the wilderness.

But Cedric...wasn't that.

He stood at his stall like a wolf surveying its territory, lean and poised. His golden hair caught the torchlight, loose waves falling across his brow. Finn's gaze traced the sharp angles of his face—the sculpted lines of his cheekbones, the curve of his mouth. His well-worn clothes carried subtle embroidery at the seams, and he wore a vest that fit too well to be secondhand. A silver chain glinted at his throat, a detail that snared Finn's attention longer than it should have.

A slow, uncertain heat curled in his gut, unwelcome and undeniable.

The villager muttered a quick farewell and disappeared into the crowd, leaving Finn standing there, still trying to reconcile this poised, golden-haired artisan with the rugged trap-setter he'd imagined.

Maybe it was the way Cedric watched him—assessing, amused, like a predator indulging a curiosity rather than a man meeting a stranger. Finn should have been wary. Instead, something about that gaze sent an inconvenient thrill down his spine.

Then Cedric spoke, voice warm despite the guarded gleam in his eyes. "Always a pleasure to meet an admirer of my work." His lips quirked with amusement. "Though I must say, it's not often I get knights interested in my carvings." A slight pause, a tilted head. "What is your name?"

Finn blinked. The villager had mentioned Cedric wasn't originally local, and Finn had assumed he was Revendarian. But there was no trace of the accent. No rolling vowels, no clipped consonants. Either he'd lived here long enough to smooth his speech—or he was hiding where he came from.

Then Finn realized Cedric was waiting for an answer.

"I'm Sir Finnian Brightmoor, but you can call me Finn." That was too familiar, damn it. *I'm not here to flirt, and more's the pity*. He cleared his throat, forcing himself back on course. "I appreciate fine craftsmanship when I see it. Your dragon...it's unlike anything I've ever seen."

For the briefest moment, something unreadable flickered across Cedric's face—gone too quickly for Finn to pin down. Then he inclined his head, speaking softly. "Thank you. I find dragons...fascinating creatures. So often misunderstood."

Finn's instincts bristled. Not alarm bells—not quite. *Misunderstood?*

He thought of golden scales flashing in the forest. Of the

sheer force behind that tail strike, sending him flying. *Misunderstood* wasn't the word *he'd* use.

He should walk away. Keep his distance. Stick to the mission.

Instead, his traitorous mouth had other plans. "I'd love to hear more about your work."

Kavros hammer me into scrap metal. That was far too earnest. Too eager. *Gods, what is wrong with me?*

Cedric's gaze flicked over him. Finn had the distinct, unnerving sensation of being picked apart, layer by layer.

Desperate to salvage his dignity, he straightened. "Perhaps over a meal?" *Gods,* he still sounded too open. He forced a casual nod. "I'm new in town and could use the company."

Cedric's gaze darted around the lantern-lit square, as though he half-expected, or rather, *desperately* hoped, for someone to appear and whisk him away. After a pause, Cedric sighed as if he'd just been asked to do something particularly exhausting. "I suppose I could spare some time," he allowed. "The Drunken Dragon has decent food."

Finn stiffened involuntarily, memory flashing to the tavern's raucous laughter and the moment he'd been dismissed over talk of the dragon. He cleared his throat, hesitant. "I was hoping to enjoy the night air," he said, nodding toward a stall where skewers of meat sizzled invitingly over an open flame. "Would you be opposed to finding a place to sit outside?"

Cedric followed his line of sight to the food stall, then gave a small, tight nod. "There's a bench across the square that's not claimed."

Finn's tension eased into a grin, encouraged by this tentative truce. "Go have a seat and save it for us. I'll get dinner. Something good to look at." Damn it. Inwardly, Finn winced. "*Eat.* I meant good to eat."

Cedric's brow arched, his expression full of dry amusement. "I should hope so." The woodcarver turned away, though not before Finn caught his expression. His lips twitched, like he was fighting back either a smirk or a sigh of exasperation. "I'll go see about that bench."

Then Cedric wove through the crowd. Finn found his gaze lingering longer than necessary, watching the way Cedric moved. There was a grace to him that was at odds with the hermit woodcarver facade he showed the world. Like this was not where he belonged.

Finn exhaled softly. *He's...interesting.* Not just because he was attractive, though there was certainly that. No, it was something else.

He had faced warlords and assassins, had stared a dragon in the eye without flinching. And yet here he was, thrown off-kilter by a damn woodcarver.

Gods, he needed to keep his head clear. There was a princess to save—or figure out—and a dragon to slay, or at least neutralize. And this Cedric? He was likely an enemy. *Stay focused, Finn.*

But as he made his way to purchase the skewers, his mind kept returning to those gold-flecked eyes. A memory of how Cedric had looked at him—assessing, guarded, but warm at the edges—left Finn's pulse a fraction quicker than before.

Answers first. He forced his attention back to the vendor and ordered two hearty servings of roasted vegetables, lean cuts of meat, and the vendor's seasoned sauce. The savory aroma set his mouth watering. If nothing else, the promise of a shared meal might open a door to more information— about Gwen, the outpost, and the dragon carvings.

And that was the only reason he was looking forward to this conversation.

Definitely the only reason.

Absolutely, unequivocally, *not* at all related to Cedric's eyes or the way his voice made Finn want to curl up and purr like a cat.

Balancing the skewers in hand, Finn navigated back through the swirl of color and torchlight. He spotted Cedric seated on a simple wooden bench at the square's perimeter, lanterns shimmering above like a cluster of fallen stars. A faint breeze stirred, carrying the scents of spiced wine and sweet pastries. From a distance, Cedric's profile was all sharp lines and quiet tension, his posture betraying the caution Finn recognized in seasoned soldiers. *Why is he so on edge?*

Steeling his nerves, Finn approached, struggling to ignore the low flutter in his stomach. He told himself it was only the prospect of answers that made his pulse thrash—*not* the calm intensity of Cedric's gaze or the faint smile that teased the corners of his mouth.

"Dinner," Finn announced, extending one skewer. "And, maybe, a conversation worth our while."

Cedric accepted the skewer with a slight tilt of his head, his fingers brushing Finn's for the briefest moment—just long enough to be *annoyingly* noticeable.

Finn sat beside him, a respectable distance apart. But between the warmth of the lantern light, the scent of sizzling meat, and the easy way Cedric had settled into their impromptu meal, that respectable distance suddenly felt like a chasm.

Finn bit into his food, the heady mix of smoke and seasoning momentarily distracting him from the questions swirling in his mind. Or at least, that was what he told himself. Because somehow, all he truly registered was the quiet presence of this frustratingly charming woodcarver.

Stop it, Finn. You need answers, not the growing, deeply irritating realization that you find this man attractive. But his pulse wouldn't settle, and he found himself acutely aware of every small sound Cedric made as he ate.

At last, the silence became too charged to endure. "So, Cedric," Finn ventured, trying to keep his tone conversational, "how long have you lived in this village?"

Cedric took a sip of the cider he'd brought, his gaze thoughtful. "I don't live in the village, but near enough. It's been a few years now. Duskridge is a peaceful place, for the most part. Though we do get the occasional excitement." His lips curved slightly, as if at a private joke. "Like battered knights stumbling in asking about dragons."

Finn groaned, letting his head tip back against the bench. "Ah. You heard about that."

"Word travels fast in a small village," Cedric said, far too pleased with himself. He popped a piece of meat into his mouth, chewing thoughtfully before adding, "Though I have to say, 'knight wanders into town ranting about dragons' isn't the usual fare for local gossip."

"I was not ranting," Finn muttered into his skewer, glaring at it like it had betrayed him.

Cedric scoffed, entirely unconvinced. "Oh, of course not. Just making an impassioned speech in the middle of the tavern, voice raised, perhaps a dramatic gesture or two—"

Finn shot him a look. "You weren't even there."

"I didn't have to be." Cedric's grin was bright with good humor. "I have a vivid imagination."

Finn huffed, trying (and failing) not to find Cedric's amusement ridiculously distracting. He was supposed to be getting information, not charmed out of his wits.

"I hope you won't take offense," Cedric continued, his gaze colored with something just on the edge of serious, "but may I ask why you're so interested in dragons?"

The question, asked so politely, set an uneasy tremor through Finn. *Just how much does he already know?* He swallowed a chunk of roasted pepper and wrestled with how much truth to reveal. Something about Cedric—his calm confidence, his quietly intense gaze—made Finn want to confess more than he intended. Which was *ridiculous*. He hardly knew this man.

"It's...complicated," he said finally, lowering his voice as though the details might be overheard. "I was sent here on a mission." A lump rose in his throat when he thought of Princess Gwenna scowling at him from the outpost. "To slay a dragon."

Cedric turned, fixing him with a look that was far too intense for someone who carved wood for a living. "Why do you want to slay this dragon?"

It was a simple question, but there was something off about the way he asked it. Too careful. Too calm. And was that...a hint of *irritation?*

Finn shifted on the bench, suddenly feeling as if he was the one under scrutiny. "The dragon is holding the person I'm here to rescue hostage. It's a monster," he said, almost like he was convincing himself. *It took my father.*

For a long moment, Cedric was silent. He ran a fingertip through the condensation on his mug, drawing aimless patterns. When he finally spoke, his voice was subdued, laced with a hint of sorrow. "Perhaps the real monsters are not the ones we expect to find in dark caves, but the ones hiding behind polite smiles and noble causes."

Finn stiffened, a spark of indignation flaring in his chest. *Does he mean me?* He pinned Cedric with a sharp look. "What exactly are you implying?"

Cedric met his gaze head-on, and *damn him*, he didn't flinch—not even a little. The intensity in those molten-gold eyes made Finn's breath catch, which only annoyed him further.

"Good and evil, heroes and monsters...these are comforting labels, but they often fall short of the truth." He took a slow sip of cider, as if he hadn't just upended everything Finn had been taught about right and wrong. "In my experience, most beings—human or otherwise—are capable of both great kindness and terrible cruelty. It's our choices that define us, not our nature."

Finn stared at him, stomach tightening. There was a

weight behind those words, a personal knowledge that Finn couldn't quite place—but felt.

And worse? It left him at a loss for a good retort. So instead, he scoffed, chewing another piece of meat with unnecessary force. "You talk like a philosopher."

Cedric's mouth twitched. "And you argue like a man who thinks he already has all the answers."

Finn shot him a narrow look. "I get the feeling that was an insult."

Cedric took another bite from his skewer, chewing with an infuriating slowness. "Was it?"

Oh, this man was going to drive him insane.

Finn exhaled sharply, rubbing at a sore spot on his wrist. "I'm doing what duty dictates," he said at last. The words felt flimsy.

"Duty," Cedric echoed softly, as though tasting the word. He let out a humorless laugh. "I know a thing or two about duty."

Intrigued despite himself, Finn leaned back, bracing his arms on the bench. "And what has duty taught you?"

Cedric's lips curled in something that wasn't quite a smile. "That it can be both a shield and a cage. It can protect us from our darkest impulses, but it can also blind us to greater truths." His gaze flicked to Finn, eyes simmering with what could only be described as righteousness. "Tell me, Sir Knight, have you ever questioned the orders you've been given?"

Finn stiffened, indignation flaring. Of course he'd questioned orders before—hadn't he? *But it wasn't his place to—No.* He pushed the thought aside. That wasn't the point. "My orders come from those wiser than myself. It's not my place to question them."

Cedric huffed a quiet breath, somewhere between amusement and pity. "Isn't it?" He leaned in, and Finn caught the faint scent of pine and something wilder, something that sent his pulse careening off course. His voice was a murmur, dark velvet over steel. "If you're the one swinging the sword, doesn't that make you responsible for the consequences? Otherwise, you're just a very well-dressed weapon."

Finn opened his mouth—whether to argue or say something scathing, he wasn't sure—but his thoughts locked up. Because they were too close now. Close enough that he could see the fine freckles across Cedric's nose, the way the torchlight reflected in his gold-flecked irises, the twist of his mouth like he already knew exactly how much he was getting under Finn's skin.

Finn's heart slammed against his ribs, a bewildering mix of anger and something far more dangerous prickling beneath his skin. *Kavros, help me keep it together.*

"You speak as if you know more about my mission than you're letting on," Finn accused, his voice rough.

Cedric's eyes flicked briefly to Finn's mouth.

Then he pulled back, just enough to seem like a deliberate retreat, and Finn hated how it left him feeling oddly bereft.

"Perhaps I do," Cedric murmured. "Or perhaps I simply know what it's like to be trapped by expectations." A trace of something—*grief? Regret?*—shadowed his features. "Be careful, Sir Knight. The path you're on may lead you places you never intended to go."

Finn's hand instinctively dropped toward his hip, where Sunwrath should have been. He'd left it in his room above the tavern, but the motion was reflexive. "Is that a threat?" He wasn't entirely sure if he meant it—or if he just needed something to fill the charged silence.

Cedric stood, and there was no triumph in his expression, only a deep, aching sadness. "No," he said, voice soft as velvet. "It's a warning. For your sake, as much as anyone else's." His gaze flicked across the crowd, then back to Finn.

"I should be going. It's late, and I have a good distance to travel."

Then, just like that, he turned on his heel and slipped away, weaving through the villagers like mist dissolving in the morning sun. Finn sat there, stunned, the taste of roasted meat still lingering on his tongue, his pulse refusing to settle.

What the hell just happened?

Chapter Seven

Of all the people who could have walked up to me tonight, it had to be him. Cedric's breath formed faint clouds in the cool night air as he made his way from Duskridge, a small lantern clutched in one hand and a sack of supplies balanced on his shoulder.

The moon hung low and bright in the sky, painting the world in silver and shadow. He didn't really need the lantern—his night vision was sharper than most thanks to his draconic curse—but it gave him an excuse to pretend he needed light. It was comforting, too, in its own way. A tether to humanity when the beast within him was never far from the surface.

As soon as the knight had spoken, Cedric recognized the voice. He'd never seen his face—Finn had worn a helmet during the attack—but the voice was unmistakable. The same one that had assured Gwenna he had come to her rescue, who had insisted Cedric was the real threat.

And even as he'd hidden his fear at being discovered behind a mask of amusement and indifference, he'd found the knight *far* too interesting.

The town receded behind him, market lights flickering

until they became little more than a speck against the darkness. He tried to focus on the road. Cedric gritted his teeth, shifting the weight of the sack on his shoulder. *Finn.* The name lodged in his mind like a thorn. Their conversation in the market still played over and over—his attempt to project calm, Finn's intense stare, the heat in the knight's eyes that Cedric couldn't quite dismiss as simple anger.

The *flirting.* The knight had most definitely been flirting...hadn't he? Cedric huffed out a frustrated breath. Truth be told, he was out of practice when it came to basic social interactions.

And I found him handsome. Rather enjoyed the conversation. Aurenis grant me common sense! He's a knight.

More than once tonight, he'd replayed their argument—faces inches apart, heat sparking in a way he had no right to feel for a man who wanted him dead.

He forced a slow exhale, trying to calm his pulse. But the memory persisted, surfacing like a wave he couldn't quell. *He's just another knight, a fanatic for duty—someone who'd see me dead if he knew the truth.* The cold air smelled faintly of pine and damp bark, laced with the earthy musk of the undergrowth. His draconic senses picked out every subtle shift in the breeze. He almost wished a predator would skulk out of the shadows, just to give him a concrete enemy.

Because the real threat, the one that tweaked his nerves, was intangible. The knight's determination. *He won't be dissuaded. Not easily.* Even Gwenna's furious rejection hadn't changed his mind, apparently. *If only he'd just turn around and leave before things escalate.*

Moonlight caught on the narrow deer trail beneath his boots. The forest pressed in on either side—gnarled trunks looming like silent sentinels. It was a place that once might've frightened him, but after ten years, Cedric felt safer here than he ever had in the corridors of Solavere Palace. Here, at least, the shadows didn't judge him.

Cedric squeezed his eyes shut for a moment, letting the night wind brush against his cheeks. What would he do if Finn came back? If he came at night, Cedric could speak with him...but what were the odds of that?

He rounded a bend in the path, and the silhouette of the old outpost came into view, half-hidden by twisting vines and encroaching trees. Home. And yet, tonight, it felt less like a refuge and more like a tenuous fortress against the tides of the past.

He paused at the edge of the clearing, letting his gaze flick to the sky. The moon's silver glow revealed roosting birds on skeletal branches, their eyes reflecting tiny pinpricks of light. *Is the knight out there now, planning a return?* A shiver of unease slid down Cedric's spine.

Finn wasn't dangerous because of his skill or stubbornness. It was the way he looked at Cedric—not like a monster, not like an enemy. But something *infinitely* more dangerous. Like he wanted to *understand* him.

Gods help him, but a traitorous part of Cedric *desperately* hoped the knight came back.

Enough. He shoved the thought aside and kept walking. Gwenna was likely waiting for him, and he had a thousand questions to parse before dawn demanded the inevitable shift.

I might have to leave this place, he realized bitterly. *All because of him.* The forest had become a haven, a quiet pocket of wilderness where he and Gwenna could exist without constant fear.

He swallowed the lump of frustration in his throat. Could they really uproot themselves again? Gwenna deserved better. She'd built a life here—her tinkering, her goats, her quiet contentment. *And I dragged her into it.* Anger flared, a familiar self-loathing that had never quite left him.

But I won't kill another knight for no reason, he vowed silently, the wind biting at his cheeks. *If Finn forces my hand...*

I'll find another way. The very notion churned his stomach. Fighting Finn—somehow the idea bothered him more than any other mercenary or bounty hunter who'd ever come calling. Was it because Cedric had learned his name, had spoken to him in a way that made him human and not a cruel enemy? Or perhaps it was because he'd glimpsed the shadow of doubt in the knight's eyes.

Or maybe it was the way Finn had looked at him just before Cedric left. *More personal...more dangerous.*

He paused in the courtyard, scanning the silent ruins. Night insects buzzed, and for an instant, he let the stillness envelop him. *This is home,* he reminded himself, heart heavy. *I just hope it stays that way.*

He clutched the sack of supplies—flour, salt, new threads for Gwenna's sewing. Simple things that made their life a little more comfortable.

A soft sigh escaped him as his gaze drifted toward the treetops. If Finn came back, he wasn't sure what scared him more—the fight he'd have to win, or the truths he wouldn't be able to avoid.

Chapter Eight

Finn dozed fitfully on the uncomfortable bed at the tavern. Cedric's words kept looping through his mind, a quiet echo that eroded his certainty: *Be careful, Sir Knight. The path you're on may lead you places you never intended to go.*

By the time the first grey light of dawn filtered through the window's warped shutters, Finn had made up his mind—he had to return to the outpost, observe, and try to glean the truth behind its residents.

He left Ghost stabled in town—stealth was paramount, and weaving through the dense forest on foot seemed wiser than drawing attention with a horse. The fresh morning air nipped at his cheeks as he slipped out of Duskridge. The sun remained just below the horizon, spilling pale light over the rolling hills. Every so often, a distant rooster's crow punctuated the calm.

An hour later, the forests thickened, branches forming a woven canopy overhead. Here, the breeze whispered secrets through the leaves, and shadows stretched long across the mossy ground. Finn moved cautiously, checking each step for tripwires or hidden snares. Gwen—*Princess Gwenna*, he corrected—was clearly adept at tinkering. The barmaid had said as much. So it stood to reason that she'd built the traps.

Or had she? He frowned, recalling the woodcarver's deft hands. Traps were more of a craftsman's work than a tinker-er's, weren't they? And Cedric...Cedric seemed capable. Too capable.

Finn touched Sunwrath's hilt as he stepped over a tangle of roots, scanning the path ahead. Either way, someone here was *very* good at keeping people out.

Eventually, Finn reached the spot that had given him chills on his first approach: a grim tableau of bones and battered armor, arranged like a macabre warning at the mouth of the narrow cave. Morning light caught the corroded edges of breastplates, and empty eye sockets glared in silent rebuke. His stomach tightened at the sight.

He tried to swallow the unease creeping up his spine. Finn ducked into the mouth of the cave, its cold gloom seeping into his bones. Here, the air smelled damp and somewhat metallic, the echo of dripping water magnified by the enclosed space.

The cave seemed longer this time, his heart pounding at each corner as though he expected a dragon to burst from the shadows. *Calm down,* he told himself. *You faced that crea-ture already, and it didn't kill you.*

Finally, the narrow tunnel opened onto a sliver of forested valley. Sunlight beamed through the foliage, and Finn allowed himself a determined breath. *I'm back.*

Finn pressed on, branches snagging at his surcoat, a few catching the edge of his gorget beneath his helmet. Once he spotted the watchtower rising above the treetops, he slowed his pace, moving with the stealth of a hunter.

A thick patch of bushes offered a decent vantage point with minimal risk. Settling in behind them, he was grateful for the protection his enchanted armor provided.

Hours stretched, the sun climbing higher. Finn's muscles

cramped, and he shifted carefully to avoid drawing attention. No movement. No sign of Cedric—or the princess. Twice, he nearly gave up, imagining how Gwenna might have already been taken elsewhere. But then a door creaked, and his pulse quickened.

Gwenna emerged, chestnut hair glinting in the midmorning sun. She carried an empty basket and wore practical, earth-stained clothes—hardly the finery of a royal. Finn watched as she ambled toward a small garden plot near the base of the tower. She knelt without hesitation, plunging her hands into the soil to harvest a row of root vegetables. *Carrots, maybe?* He tilted his head, wishing he had a better angle.

"Clarence!" The exasperation in Gwenna's voice rang through the clearing. "Get out of those beans right now, you gluttonous beast!"

Finn bit back a chuckle as a shaggy goat trotted into view, chewing with unwavering audacity. Gwenna squared her shoulders, glaring at the creature. "I swear, one of these days I'm going to turn you into a fine roast," she huffed, though her tone brimmed with fondness.

A small smile tugged at Finn's lips. This was no fragile princess caged by fear. She was independent and unafraid, scolding goats and tending gardens as though this life were completely hers.

Confusion swarmed in his mind. *Does she really need—or want—saving?* But the memory of her lineage loomed: her family slain, the golden dragon spiriting her away. *Maybe the dragon enthralled her, robbing her of her past.* The thought left a bitter tang in his mouth.

Suddenly, a swift shadow darted across the clearing, and Finn ducked out of habit. When he dared to glance up, the sight made his blood run cold. The golden dragon—its scales ablaze with reflected sunlight—circled overhead in a wide arc. Finn's pulse hammered, fingers brushing the hilt of his sword. *Not yet. Observe first.*

With powerful strokes of its wings, the beast navigated a gap in the treetops, landing in the clearing with surprising grace. Clouds of dust and stray leaves swirled around, but there was no roar, no flicker of flame. Instead, it folded its wings, a low rumble in its throat—less a threat, more a greeting?

Finn tensed, expecting Gwenna to recoil in terror or run for cover. To his astonishment, she lit up like someone greeting a dear friend. "There you are!" she called, relief coloring her voice. "I was beginning to think you'd gotten lost."

Finn swallowed hard, gaze darting between Gwenna and the dragon. She closed the distance, fearless, that same fondness she'd shown the goat now directed at the towering reptile. *This can't be normal.* His hand settled on Sunwrath's pommel.

Finn stared, incredulous, as the dragon bowed its head and extended sharp claws—only to deposit a woven basket at Princess Gwenna's feet like an offering. *It didn't attack—it's giving her...supplies?* Every instinct he possessed screamed that this was impossible, that dragons were mindless beasts of fire and fury. Yet here it was, behaving almost...*helpfully*.

Princess Gwenna crouched, a gleeful grin lighting her face as she peered inside. "Oh, excellent! These mushrooms will be perfect for tonight's stew. Though I'm not sure we'll have any beans left, thanks to a certain four-legged menace." She shot a wry glare at the goat, Clarence, who sauntered nearer, more curious than afraid.

Finn's jaw tightened. *In all the stories I've heard, goats should be terrified of dragons—yet here we have a goat with more courage than sense.*

His mind reeled, each new detail more bizarre than the last. *A dragon hunting mushrooms for stew? Is that what I'm seeing?* Gooseflesh raced along his arms, and he had to remind himself to breathe. *This is so wrong.*

"You got back late last night," Princess Gwenna continued, her tone almost scolding as she peered at the dragon with genuine concern. "I was worried."

The dragon snorted in response, a rolling rumble that vibrated in Finn's chest even from a distance. Princess Gwenna nodded as though she understood every nuance of the creature's low grunt.

"Of course you didn't want to wake me," she said, attempting a mock-stern look that dissolved into affectionate exasperation. "And then this morning you fly off before I can check on you!"

Finn's breath caught as he watched them—this casual closeness, a language all their own. It belied everything he'd been taught: that dragons were apex predators, incapable of empathy. They were acting more like...family. *Has she truly befriended her captor?*

He swallowed the knot in his throat, but his thoughts slipped away like a greased pig when something tugged at his waist. He jerked away and nearly toppled over, arms flailing to keep his balance. *What the—?*

The goat. Its hungry eyes were fixed on the leather pouch dangling from his belt. "Shoo!" Finn hissed, trying to keep his voice low. "Go on, get away!"

It bleated at him—an alarmed, annoyed sound—and then, as if offended by his refusal to share, the goat bounded off. Straight toward Princess Gwenna and the dragon.

Rynvath's hairy balls, Finn cursed under his breath. The princess and dragon whirled in unison toward the goat's bleating. *They're going to see me.*

His heart hammered in his ears. *This is it.* If Princess Gwenna truly was enthralled, he had to act. If the dragon was controlling her, or at least conditioning her to stay, he owed it to her—and to the memory of his father—to set her free.

He exploded from the bushes with a roar that shredded his throat raw. The dragon's gaze—those cursed, molten eyes—snapped to him. "Princess! Stand back!"

The beast reared, wings flaring into a fortress of sinew and scale around Gwenna. Finn charged, Sunwrath screaming toward the vulnerable spot beneath its jaw. But the dragon twisted, serpent-smooth, and his blade carved only air.

"*Nivara take you!*" Finn snarled. He feinted left, then swung right, aiming for the delicate wing membrane. Claws met steel in a screech that crackled up his arms. The dragon's warm breath billowed over him. Still no fire. No claws raking his guts. Just those damnable talons, deflecting, always deflecting, as if he were a dull whetstone to polish them on.

"Stop!" Gwenna's cry frayed at the edges. Finn barely heard, too focused, too driven to get through the dragon.

Another thrust met with a parry. Finn's sword skidded off scales, spraying sparks. He swung at the dragon's neck. The beast slid aside. He jabbed at its belly. A talon flicked the strike away. Muscle and scale, moving like water over stone. His arms trembled.

"Fight me, you spineless worm!" Finn's spittle struck the dragon's snout. It didn't flinch. Its tail curled around Gwenna, like a mother hen protecting a chick. The wrongness of it seared Finn's nerves. How *dare* it pretend to care!

He lunged, blade screaming upward in a killing arc. The dragon leaned back and Sunwrath grazed a single scale. A chip no bigger than a fingernail clinked to the moss. *Useless. Worthless.* Finn's boot crushed the fragment as he spun, slashing wildly at its legs. Talons caught each strike. *Clang. Clang. Clang.*

Breath sawed in his lungs. Reason guttered—the distant

voice urging strategy drowned under a tidal roar of *hate*. He didn't want strategy. He wanted to feel scales split. Wanted the dragon's dying shriek to shake the trees.

Finn feinted toward its heart, then pivoted, the blade plunging for the joint of its hind leg.

The dragon sidestepped, tail brushing Finn's thighs—not a strike, just a nudge. It could have sent him flying, could have crushed him beneath one massive claw, but it didn't. It was holding back. Even *now*. Even as Finn swung for its throat.

Rage drowned reason. *It's mocking me. It's toying with me.* A snarl ripped from his throat as he surged forward, blind to anything but the need to see this beast fall.

His foot snagged. Root or talon, he'd never know. Finn bounded up, attempting to recover his footing. A shadow blurred—not the dragon's bulk, but something smaller. Faster. With auburn hair.

Crack.

Pain ricocheted inside his skull, the blow sending a shockwave through his helm. His vision split, tilting sideways as his ears rang. Darkness swallowed the dragon's silhouette.

Chapter Nine

Cedric sighed, closing his eyes to brace against the familiar agony that heralded the return of his human form.

When it was over, he slumped forward, breathing hard. The cool night air brushed against his bare skin, straw poking at his knees and elbows. Sweat gathered at his temples. *Still better than being trapped in scales,* he told himself.

A single lantern hung from a post nearby, casting weak light on the stable's rough-hewn walls. Shadows jumped and twisted with each sway of the flame, and for a moment, Cedric just watched, trying to calm his erratic heart. *Another day survived,* he thought grimly. But the next instant, the memory of the unconscious knight flooded his mind. *We haven't survived yet.*

He forced himself upright, wincing at the lingering stiffness in his limbs. The clothes he'd hung over the stall door that morning still waited for him—loose trousers and a simple linen shirt, well-worn boots that had seen too many miles. He pulled them on quickly, fingers clumsy in his rush. Each tug at the laces only reminded him of the knight's steel-grey eyes, brimming with conviction and...hatred.

It was that hatred that had wounded Cedric the most. *That look...as if he despises everything I am.*

The wooden door to the stable creaked on its hinges as Cedric pushed it open. Outside, the night was calm—a faint breeze carried the scent of pine, mingled with the smoke and herbs drifting from the old tower's kitchen. The outpost felt oddly tense in the cool moonlight, the usual sense of peace overshadowed by the knowledge that an armed knight lay inside.

Hopefully still alive.

He paused at the threshold, inhaling slowly, then stepped across the courtyard to the tower's entrance. Gwenna stood in the far corner of the kitchen, arms crossed over her chest, fury sparking in her violet eyes.

"Well?" she demanded, voice edged with impatience. "What are we going to do with him?"

Cedric's gaze followed hers, drawn to the prone figure on the kitchen floor. Even now, lying helpless, the knight seemed formidable. His dented armor reflected the lantern light in dull glints. The same Revendarian steel armor Cedric had seen every knight of Lunarath wear. His helmet had been pulled off and now rested on the table.

"You just left him here?" Cedric asked, unable to mask his surprise. He'd imagined she might have at least dragged him into an unused storeroom, if only for privacy's sake.

Gwenna's lips thinned. "What else did you expect? Besides, we can't keep him here. It's too dangerous. We should—"

"Should *what?*" Cedric cut in, his voice sharp. "Kill him? Dump his body in the forest and hope no one comes looking?"

Gwenna's jaw clenched, and her glare held firm. "If that's what it takes to keep us safe, then yes."

A chill rippled through Cedric. Once, the thought of taking a life had horrified Gwenna. But ten years of running and hiding, coupled with the inevitability of violence, had changed them both.

He knelt beside Finn, gingerly touching the knight's shoulder. "No," he said softly. "We can't keep doing that, Gwen. Not anymore. He's a knight of Lunareth." Something in his chest twisted at the words. *Wouldn't he have been sworn to protect me under different circumstances?* He cleared his throat, glancing up at Gwenna. "Besides, I spoke with him in the village. He's misguided, but not evil."

"You *what?*" Gwenna snapped, her eyes narrowing to annoyed slits. "When were you planning on sharing *that* little detail?"

He raked a hand through his disheveled golden-brown hair, wincing at the tangles from his recent shift. "I was going to tell you, but then...everything happened so fast." He gestured at the unconscious knight. "I met him in the market. He was asking questions about dragons, and I wanted to know why he was so determined to kill me."

Gwenna's indignation wavered. "And?" she prompted, voice quieter now.

"And he truly believes he's on some grand, righteous quest," Cedric answered, a hollow pang forming in his chest. "He thinks I abducted you, that I've been holding you captive all this time. In his mind, he's the hero—coming to rescue you from a monster."

"He's in for a rude awakening when he comes to," Gwenna muttered, snorting in disbelief.

Despite the tension in the room, a weary, humorless smile tugged at Cedric's lips. He stared at the knight's face, smudged with dirt and blood. A shallow cut marred his forehead, the scrape already scabbing over. He recalled the flash of determination—and yes, hatred—written there only hours ago.

A pang shot through Cedric as he remembered the humor in the knight's voice at the village, the curiosity in those steely eyes. *He hates me because he thinks I'm a monster—and I can't blame him.*

Finnian stirred, and a low groan slipped from his lips. Cedric's heart jolted—some mixture of relief and apprehension—at seeing the knight regain a semblance of consciousness. Cedric leaned in, mindful of the tender swelling behind Finn's ear.

"He's got a nasty bump," Cedric muttered, probing delicately at the bruise. *Good thing I came in now*, he thought grimly. Another few hours without tending and the knight could have ended up with a worse injury than a sore head.

"What *exactly* did you hit him with?" he asked, glancing at Gwenna with mild incredulity.

She offered a tight shrug. "A rock. It was the first thing I could grab."

Cedric shook his head, though a hint of amusement curled at the corners of his mouth. "Remind me never to get on your bad side."

His attention drifted back to Finn, who was seemingly oblivious to their discussion. The sharp determination that had defined him in battle was gone. His features were slack, breath ragged, dark lashes stark against too-pale skin. He looked impossibly young like this—too human, too breakable.

And Cedric hated how he noticed. Hated the way his gaze lingered a beat too long, the way unspoken emotion twisted in his heart. He couldn't allow his mind to drift there. It was an impossibility.

"We should treat this before it gets worse," he said, "and get him somewhere more comfortable than the kitchen floor." His gaze slid to Gwenna.

She let out a dramatic sigh, rolling her eyes. "Sure, I could have dragged him up the stairs and bumped him against every step on the way. Didn't seem wise."

Cedric had to admit, she had a point. She might be

strong, but carrying an armored knight up a narrow stair-case was no small feat. "All right, fair enough." He stooped, bracing one arm behind Finn's shoulders. "Give me a hand?"

Between the two of them, they hoisted Finn into a carry across Cedric's shoulders. The knight wasn't a lightweight—heavier than Cedric expected, but nothing he couldn't handle. *Sometimes I forget how my strength changed along with my curse,* he thought, pushing back the guilt that always followed that realization.

"If you're so determined to take care of him," Gwenna said, the reluctance in her tone undeniable, "I'll bring that yarrow salve I made last week."

"That would be great," Cedric replied, gripping Finn's legs more securely. Part of him wanted to reassure her, to promise they'd handle this mess. But Gwenna's set jaw warned him she wanted no more comforting words right now.

He ascended the narrow stone steps with care, mindful not to let Finn's legs or arms—and especially his head—bump against the walls.

The spare bed was little more than a wooden cot with a thin straw mattress, tucked into a corner room that had once belonged to an outpost officer. But it would serve. Kneeling, Cedric carefully lowered Finn onto the cot, adjusting his limbs so they wouldn't dangle off the edge. *At least it's better than the floor.*

He frowned at the knight's armor. It was scuffed and dented, straps caked with dirt. The pieces had clearly seen better days. Days that didn't involve Gwenna and Cedric. *He can't heal properly wearing this,* Cedric thought. *And it can't be comfortable.*

Cedric leaned over the immobile man, hands hovering for a beat, as if asking permission the knight couldn't grant. With a resigned sigh, he eased open the buckles running along Finn's side. The straps creaked in protest as Cedric slid them free of their loops.

Calm down, Ced. You're only doing this out of necessity.

Certainly not because it had been so long since he'd touched anyone else, much less someone as handsome as Finn.

When he lifted the first panel, a subtle glow clung to the armor, remnants of the enchantment that powered its resilience. Cedric marveled at the faint shimmer. It had been ages since he'd seen the magically enchanted armor worn by a knight of Lunareth. He shut his eyes for a moment, imagining happier times.

Standing on a balcony, peering down as a knight rode out on a mission, their armor gleaming as Lunareth's crimson and gold flags fluttered overhead.

Cedric allowed himself a sad smile at the memory. The arm guards came next, buckled tight around Finn's biceps. The straps gave under Cedric's careful tug, revealing sweaty linen sleeves beneath. Cedric's gaze caught on the flex of muscle, the warm skin underneath—*too close, too intimate.* He swallowed hard, forcing his focus back to the task at hand. Cedric moved on to the thigh guards, which didn't really help the whole proximity issue he was currently battling.

For Aurenis's sake. One handsome knight ends up in front of you, and he's all you can think about. Your brain is not below the belt, Ced.

The final step was freeing the chest piece fully, lifting it away from Finn's torso. A purple bruise bloomed on the knight's chest, but it was the pale scars that drew Cedric's attention. His fingers hovered, a sudden awareness of how close they were—how exposed Finn seemed, and how easily Cedric could trace those scars with a touch.

He pulled back, shaking off the thought. *Gods, this is going to be a problem.*

Soft footsteps in the hallway announced Gwenna's

return. She stepped into the room, a small clay jar in one hand and a bowl of water and cloth in the other. Without ceremony, she thrust them at Cedric. "Here," she said, curtly. "This is all you. I need to go find...something."

Cedric took the proffered items, but raised a brow. "What?"

She crossed her arms, eyeing Finn with a mix of exasperation and guarded concern. "I need to find where he got the *audacity*," she grumbled under her breath, as though it were a serious errand.

A startled laugh escaped Cedric. The sound of his amusement seemed to thaw some of Gwenna's tension, though she maintained a tight-lipped scowl for show. Instead of leaving, she stepped back, leaning against the wall where she could watch but remain out of the way.

Cedric sat at the edge of the cot. He dipped the cloth into the bowl of water Gwenna had brought and wrung it out, then carefully blotted the crusted wound on the knight's forehead. Finn didn't stir, but the crease between his brows deepened.

"Relax," Cedric murmured, though he suspected Finn couldn't hear him. "Just cleaning you up." He gently wiped away the worst of the grime.

The cloth came away tinged with dried blood and dirt. Cedric set it aside and popped open the jar of salve. A pungent, earthy aroma wafted up, reminding him of the times Gwenna's homemade remedies had soothed him after a day spent hauling timber or scouring the forest for fresh game.

"Let's hope this helps," he muttered, dabbing his fingers into the salve and spreading it along the swelling.

Cedric's gaze settled on Finn's face, where unconsciousness had done little to soften the strong planes and defined angles. The lantern light skimmed over his features—the proud cut of his jaw, the high cheekbones, the faint crease between his brows, as if even now, he resisted surrender.

Dark lashes rested against sun-bronzed skin, their depth accentuating the symmetry of his face. A thin scar marked his jawline, a remnant of past battles. It suited him, somehow, adding to the undeniable presence he carried, even now, stripped of his armor and vulnerability laid bare.

Gods, he's exquisite.

The thought hit like a stray ember, burning at the edges of his restraint. It wasn't some startling revelation—he'd noticed Finn's handsomeness the moment they met. But here, in the quiet, with his guard lowered and his life quite literally in Cedric's hands, it felt...different.

Not the time, he scolded himself, jaw tightening.

He forced himself to concentrate on his task, smoothing the salve gently around the base of Finn's skull and across the cut. The knight let out a faint groan but didn't stir further.

Gwenna stepped over to assess the knight, no longer glowering quite so fiercely. "Those are some nasty bruises on his chest."

Cedric's shoulders tensed. *I put them there.* His gut clenched at the memory of his tail connecting with the knight, sending him spinning into the underbrush. Cedric bit down on his lower lip. He'd seen bruises before—hell, he'd had similar bruises like this himself from not paying attention around horses in the royal stables. This was no different.

Only it was.

"Ced?" Gwenna prompted. "Something wrong?"

He swallowed. "Nothing."

She frowned, disbelieving. "You have that look about you."

Gwenna didn't need to expand what she meant. He knew.

They both knew his tendency to go too deeply into his own head, to let his own regrets and guilt overshadow everything.

Cedric cleared his throat. He would think about something else, then. "Really, I'm fine." He dipped his fingers into the salve, returning to his original task.

His gaze fell on Finn, and suddenly, all his dour thoughts fell away as he took in the knight's contours beneath the mottled bruising. *Right. I can do this. You're just taking care of someone who needs help, Ced. That's all.*

He worked carefully, spreading the salve over the worst of the bruising. He traced the map of old scars and the firm muscles beneath. Finn let out a quiet sigh, his body shifting under Cedric's touch.

Cedric froze, momentary panic flaring. He yanked his hand away.

But after a beat, Finn went slack again. Cedric relaxed. His hands lingered longer than they should have, fingertips ghosting over the deep purple blooming along Finn's ribs.

Cedric exhaled sharply, trying to shake the feeling creeping under his skin. This was ridiculous. *He* was ridiculous. Why was he so damn aware of this man? *I'm supposed to be tending an injury, not cataloging the angles of a knight's collarbones like some love-struck fool.*

He needed a distraction—anything that wasn't Finn or the treacherous pull of his own thoughts. His mind grasped for an escape, reaching frantically, like a drowning man lunging for a rope. *Something else. Anything else.* He dredged up old memories, latching onto one before Gwenna could notice his reaction.

"Do you remember," he asked, "that summer when Father took us to the seaside? You were determined to catch a mermaid with your bare hands."

"You told me they only appeared at night, so I snuck out of our rooms. I was convinced I'd lure one ashore with left-over bread crusts." Gwenna let out a small laugh, the tension draining from her posture.

Cedric managed a small smile. "Father nearly had a heart attack when he discovered you were missing at dawn. And Darius and I—" He stopped short, the name catching in his throat like a hot coal at the mention of his former friend. His sister's betrothed.

Gwenna's lips pursed, and she shook her head, as if to banish Darius's name. "If only the mermaids had dragged *him* under. He was a bad influence, anyway."

Cedric nodded. She wasn't wrong, but now he couldn't dismiss his old friend so easily. Not when Darius had stepped forward after Cedric's supposed death, claiming the crown and announcing a secret betrothal to Gwenna.

He tried to shake away the anger and suspicion, but it refused to fade. Cedric picked up the cloth he'd used to clean Finn, wiping the salve from his hands.

Finnian's eyes fluttered open, unfocused and confused. He blinked sluggishly, as if struggling to piece together where he was. His brow furrowed, a flicker of recognition in his grey depths—but before he could speak, a faint grimace twisted his face. His eyelids fluttered, his body tensed slightly as if bracing against nausea, and then he slipped into unconsciousness once more.

Gwenna folded her arms, her expression grim. "Cedric, we can't keep him here. Even if we don't...dispose of him, we can't risk him waking up and seeing you. What if he puts it together? What if he realizes you're the dragon?"

Cedric pressed his lips into a thin line, pacing from one corner of the small room to the other. The lantern light flickered, illuminating cracks in the walls, the worn tapestries from the outpost's military era.

"I know," he muttered, pushing aside an old wooden stool with one foot to make more space. "But we can't just let him go, either. He'll run straight to Mirathen, bring an army to our doorstep." He let out a shaky breath.

"What do you intend to do? Keep him as a pet?" Gwenna asked, eyebrows raised.

"As much fun as a dragon keeping a knight as a pet sounds, we're probably better off with our goats and chickens." Satisfaction shot through Cedric at Gwenna's amused snort. "Maybe we...we tell him the truth. Or part of it, anyway. He's not a brute. Maybe he'll leave us alone if he realizes we're just living our lives, not hurting anyone." He took a deep breath. "I'll talk to him—like this, as a man. We'll make sure he never even sees the dragon side of me."

"But he already *saw* the dragon," Gwenna pointed out, eyes narrowing. "*Twice*. You're not exactly forgettable."

Cedric winced, recalling how Finnian had lunged at him in the clearing, sword flashing like a brand of righteous fury. "We'll just say...the dragon's a pet. It's gone hunting or something." He grimaced at the feeble lie. *Thalos, how gullible must we hope he is?* Still, it was better than murdering a knight of Lunareth. "I'm sure his memory of it is hazy anyway, especially after that knock to the head."

"You always were the optimist in the family," she said, voice dry. Then, after a beat, she frowned. "But you're putting a lot of faith in someone who just tried to kill you."

Cedric gave her a rueful smile. "I know."

Gwenna's arms tightened over her chest. "And if you're wrong?" she challenged. "If he wakes up, realizes you're the dragon, and we have to fight him all over again?"

Cedric hesitated. That was a reality he hoped never happened. "Then I'll handle it."

That answer clearly didn't satisfy Gwenna, but she sighed and raked a hand through her hair. "Fine. But I swear, if he so much as twitches wrong, I'm throwing another rock at his head."

"Fair enough." A weary smile tugged at Cedric's lips. He glanced toward the narrow window—a half-broken shutter letting in a chilly breeze. Something to be repaired. The sky outside had deepened to inky black, dotted with scattered stars.

"You should sleep," Cedric told Gwenna, forcing gentle authority into his voice. "I'll keep watch tonight. You can relieve me in the morning."

Her lips pressed into a tight line. "And when will you sleep, Ced?"

He shrugged, avoiding her gaze. *My human hours are short enough; I can't waste them asleep.* "I'll doze during the day...as a dragon," he said, voice flat. "Just make sure he stays out of the stables, all right?"

She studied him for a moment, her expression wavering between concern and acquiescence. Then she nodded. "Fine. But wake me if anything changes." With that, she moved to the door, pausing only to level him with a final, searching glance. Then she slipped out, leaving Cedric alone with Finnian.

Cedric exhaled, dragging the stool closer to the knight's bedside. The small flame of the lantern danced across the walls, illuminating the soft contours of Finnian's face. *Gods, he looks young,* Cedric thought, brushing aside the curtain of black hair from Finn's forehead to check the bruise.

Cedric rested an elbow on one knee as he watched the slow rise and fall of Finnian's chest. His mind drifted back to their brief conversation in the market: the fervor in the knight's voice as he spoke of duty, the unwavering sense of purpose that Cedric had once admired in the men and women who served the crown.

In another life—if Darius hadn't twisted everything, if Cedric hadn't been cursed—things could have been different. *Could we have been friends?*

The idea made Cedric's heart clench with longing. But the memory of Finn's fervor refused to be dismissed.

He shivered, scolding himself for such pointless daydreams. "Stop it. He's here to kill you, remember?"

Still, he caught himself wishing that he could trust Finn, that he could show the knight who he really was without fear. But that path was littered with uncertainties—and the certain knowledge that if Finn recognized Cedric as the dragon, there would be steel in his hand before Cedric could utter a word.

Leaning back against the wall, Cedric folded his arms across his chest. Outside, the wind whispered around the tower's crumbling stones, a lonely sound that echoed his own unease. *Finn's arrival,* he thought, *has set something into motion—something we might not be able to stop.* Whether that meant redemption or ruin for him and Gwenna, he couldn't begin to guess.

Chapter Ten

Consciousness hauled Finnian back by the collar. His skull pulsed like iron struck by a blacksmith's hammer. The sour taste of bile coated his tongue.

When he finally cracked his eyelids, the room bucked beneath him. Finn gritted his teeth against the vertigo, fingers digging into sweat-damp sheets. Rough linen chafed his palms.

The air smelled of yarrow poultices and wood smoke, undercut by the metallic tang of blood—his own, he guessed, from the crusted stiffness at his temple. His probing touch found a bandage, the lump beneath it throbbing in time with his heartbeat. *Rynvath's teeth.* Whatever the princess had clobbered him with, she'd put her royal spine into the swing.

He lay in a narrow bed. Sunlight spilled through a single shuttered window on the far wall. The modest room was sparsely furnished—just a small table, a creaky wooden chair, and a footlocker near the door. *Better than a dungeon cell,* Finn thought, though the distance between him and his armor—he spotted it on a table across the room—felt like a mile. His sword, his dagger, even his boots were well beyond reach. *So much for a quick escape.*

Slowly, he swung his legs over the side of the bed. The instant he moved, a lance of pain shot through his skull. The room tilted sickeningly, shadows sliding in his periphery like waterlogged ink. Finn clenched his jaw, gripping the edge of the mattress in a white-knuckled grip until the nausea faded to a bearable churn.

Each breath sent dull reverberations through his skull. Even so, he forced himself upright, jaw locked against the wave of dizziness that turned the floor into a rolling ship deck. *The window. Focus on the window.*

The jagged ache receded enough for him to see outside: an expanse of lush forest spread out below—green treetops swaying in a gentle breeze. A pang of disquiet clenched his gut. The golden dragon could be anywhere out there, free to roam.

The door's screech nearly sent him crashing. Finn braced against the wall, knuckles whitening on cold stone as the world lurched sideways. Pain lanced through his skull—a hot poker behind the eyes. He'd pay good coin to never hear another hinge creak again.

"You shouldn't be up."

He knew that voice. Honeyed steel, sharp enough to draw blood.

Gwenna stood framed in the doorway, sunlight catching the silver threads in her woolen overdress. No damsel's silks here—this was practical garb, sleeves rolled up to reveal muscular forearms. She carried a tray like a soldier bearing a shield, steam curling from a clay bowl. Finn's stomach rolled at the smell of stew.

"You hit me." Finn glared, though the effect was undercut by the fact he had to lean against the wall for support. "With a rock."

Her lips twitched. Not a smile—a dagger being drawn an inch from its sheath. "You were trying to kill my...pet. What did you expect me to do, curtsy?"

He opened his mouth to retort, only to realize *she's right*. He'd come here expecting a helpless victim. Instead, he found a woman who had decked him with a rock and now regarded him with a mix of annoyance and genuine concern. Gwenna might wear no crown, no fancy attire, yet she carried herself with more authority than some nobles he'd encountered.

"But...the dragon," he started, voice faltering under her pointed stare.

"Is not the topic of discussion at the moment," she replied, finality ringing in her tone. Her gaze flicked to the bed. "Sit down. You can hardly stand, and I'd rather not haul you off the floor a second time."

Pride flared in Finn's chest, warring with the throbbing in his skull. Part of him wanted to argue, but his vision still blurred at the edges, and he feared losing what little dignity he had left. Reluctantly, he sank onto the bed. A faint wave of relief washed over him as the room stopped spinning.

Gwenna settled onto a nearby chair, angling it so she could keep a close eye on him. She shoved a bowl of stew toward him. "Eat," she commanded, voice brisk. "We'll deal with your bandage after you've got something in your stomach."

Finn stared at the murky broth. His stomach growled despite his suspicion, but paranoia still whispered in his ear. *Could she have poisoned it?* He shot her a wary glance.

Gwenna's eyes flashed with annoyance. "If I wanted you dead, I wouldn't have bothered patching you up. Now eat."

She had a point. Finn's stomach clenched hard enough to grind stone, a hollow ache radiating up his ribs. He snatched the spoon, wolfing down stew so fast the heat scorched his tongue—greasy rabbit, overcooked carrots turning his mouth to glue. He didn't care. His hands shook as he scraped the bowl clean, the *scrape-scrape-scrape* of metal on clay echoing louder than his pride.

While he ate, Gwenna shifted her attention to the makeshift medical station she'd set up on the small side table. Clean bandages, a jar of pungent salve, and an assortment of cloth scraps were neatly laid out. Finn pretended not to watch too closely, but in truth, he couldn't help comparing this confident, no-nonsense woman to the fairy-tale vision of a captive princess he'd carried in his head.

"Why are you here?" he blurted at last, setting aside the now-empty bowl. His stomach felt less hollow, but his mind still churned with questions. "If you're not a prisoner, why stay in this tower?"

Gwenna froze, but then she resumed reorganizing the bandages. "It's complicated," she said softly, eyes downcast. "This place...it's home now. It's safe."

Safe. The word rang oddly in Finn's ears. He frowned. "Safe from what?"

Her eyes flicked up. For a split second, he saw it: pupils dilating like a spooked mare's. Then gone. "There are worse things in this world than dragons, Sir Finnian."

He blinked. *Sir Finnian*. She used his name—and title—like she'd known it all along. "How do you—"

"You talk in your sleep." Gwenna cut in. "Now relax."

He stiffened as her fingers brushed his scalp. The salve burned icy, then numbed. A strand of hair slipped over her shoulder, tickling his cheek. His jaw locked. Relaxing was a surrender.

"It's healing well," she observed, more to herself than to him. "The swelling's gone down considerably."

He scarcely heard her, lost in the rush of confusion swirling in his head. *This woman—this princess? Tending my wounds? Nothing about this situation makes sense.* His memories of the previous day blurred together—the dragon's reluctance to fully fight, the unexpected care he'd received while half-conscious, and the presence of another figure...

A face. Golden-brown eyes. *Cedric.* The name fell from his lips before he realized he'd spoken it aloud.

Gwenna's thumb pressed too hard on the bandage and Finn hissed. She offered no apology. "My brother," she explained. "He's the one who looked after you last night."

Brother. Finn's brow knit. A fleeting memory tugged at the edges of his mind: someone with concern etched into his expression, a soothing voice amid Finn's pain. "I...I think I remember him."

Gwenna nodded, stepping back once she'd finished re-bandaging his head. "You woke up for a moment," she said, placing the salve aside. "He was worried the knock to your skull did more than just bruise you."

Finn tried to recall more details—the quiet of night, the dance of lantern light, the gentle but firm touch of hands on his skin. His thoughts kept snagging on the idea that none of them acted like the villains—or victims—he'd expected. "Where is he now?"

"Out," Gwenna answered, her tone vague. "He's often away during the day."

Finn couldn't quite put his finger on it, but something felt guarded in her voice. A memory nudged him—there was a Prince Cedric once, rumored dead at the claws of the golden dragon. *Could it really be...?*

"Your brother," he drawled, trying to keep the tremor out of his voice. "He wouldn't happen to be *Prince* Cedric Cleburne, would he? The one who was supposedly killed by the dragon?"

Gwenna's expression shifted—a crack in the cool confidence she wore like armor. But then it was gone, smoothed into neutrality. "My brother is Cedric," she said, too carefully. "As for whether he's a prince...titles don't mean much out here in the forest."

Finn narrowed his eyes. "That's not a no."

She huffed, shoving a strand of auburn hair behind her ear. "It's not a yes, either."

The reality she refused to confirm left him reeling. If Prince Cedric was alive, and Gwenna too, that meant so much of what he'd been told back in Mirathen was wrong—or twisted. *Protected by a dragon?*

"What really happened?" he asked, voice dropping to a low intensity. "Why are you both here? What are you hiding from?"

Gwenna's expression hardened. "That's not a story I'm willing to share with someone who came here to kill my friend and drag me back to a life I left behind."

Finn winced, the accusation lancing through him. His jaw tightened, teeth grinding against the sour tang of guilt on his tongue. "I came here to rescue you," he protested, the words rougher than he intended, his calloused palm flattening against the sweat-damp linen on his thigh. "To fulfill my duty as a knight of the realm."

"And who gave you that duty?" Gwenna challenged, her voice sharp enough to carve stone. "Who sent you on this *noble* quest?"

"King Darius," Finn answered automatically. He stilled, tracking the blood draining from Gwenna's face, the faint tremor in her throat as she swallowed. Fear. Anger.

"*Darius*," Gwenna spat, the name curdling the air between them. "*Of course* it was Darius."

A nervous chill crept along Finn's spine. The king had ordered him to come, but he hadn't given many details about Princess Gwenna's condition—only that she was a captive of a monstrous dragon. Now, seeing Gwenna stand here unshackled and fiercely protective of the beast... *Were we all lied to?*

"What does King Darius have to do with this?" he asked, and he couldn't keep the edge from his voice. A faint part of him cringed at the disrespect—King Darius wasn't known for forgiveness when it came to slights.

Gwenna shook her head, her silhouette a blade of shadow against the window. "That's none of your business."

Finn exhaled slowly. *No matter how vital it might be to me.* Clearly, she wasn't going to volunteer the truth. He forced himself to stand, ignoring the swirl of dizziness that made the walls tilt. Pain surged in protest, but he refused to let it show. "Then let me speak to Prince Cedric," he demanded. "Let me understand what's going on here—why you'd choose to stay in an abandoned tower with a dragon for company."

Gwenna glanced at the window, sunlight gilding the tension in her shoulders. "He'll be back soon. When night falls." Her nose wrinkled, a hint of defiance. "And he's just Cedric." Something in her tone suggested this was more than a matter of practicality—she was determined to shed the burden of royalty.

Finn nodded slowly, mulling that over. He was starting to grasp how important secrecy was to them, though the full reason still eluded him. *So Prince Cedric is alive.* The revelation battered at Finn's sense of duty—if Prince Cedric and Princess Gwenna truly lived, that meant the line of succession hadn't ended the way King Darius had always implied.

Finn's pulse thudded in his ears, a war drum drowning out the lie. He flexed his fingers, wishing he had Sunwrath close at hand. "What do you plan to do with me?"

The erstwhile princess arched a brow. "We're still deciding."

A leaden weight settled in Finn's stomach at those words. *They could dispose of me any time.* He cleared his throat, forcing himself to keep eye contact. "Can I make a request?"

Gwenna cocked her head, sunlight catching the steel in her gaze. "Sure. Whether I'll grant it is another thing."

"It's about my horse." The words loosened something in his chest. Finn inhaled, the memory of Ghost's warm leather-and-hay scent momentarily overriding the room's mustiness. "I have her stabled in town, but only left enough coin to cover two days of boarding." He paused, not missing the way her shoulders relaxed. "Some livery stables are quick to sell off steeds whose riders haven't paid for their keep. And Ghost is special to me."

He saw the brief conflict in her expression—reluctance warred with a genuine softness he hadn't seen before. She let out a sigh. "I don't think you'll be in shape to hike down there anytime soon. But I can go myself in the morning, bring her back here."

A surge of relief flooded Finn's chest, and he smiled for the first time since he woke in this tower. "Thank you," he murmured. It was a small concession, but it felt like a life-line. *At least Ghost will be safe.* The mare's comforting presence already braced him—a phantom nudge against his shoulder.

Then, a dull thump from somewhere below made them both tense, followed by the bleat of a goat. It was either a door—maybe the barn door—or the goats were up to no good.

"And that would be Cedric," Gwenna said, heading for the door. "We'll have dinner, and then no doubt he'll want to come up to check on you himself."

Finn nodded, a fresh jolt of nerves sparking. *So I'm finally going to meet him—Prince Cedric, or just Cedric, as she insists.* He eased himself back onto the bed, the day's exertion stealing what remained of his energy. Everything still throbbed—his head, his pride—but at least he could rest a little before facing the tower's other occupant.

Chapter Eleven

Cedric hissed against the molten pain of the transformation. His wings crumpled inward with a sound like tearing parchment, golden scales dissolving into sweat-damp flesh. He staggered as his talons shrank to toes, the stable's hay prickling his newly human soles. Flexing his fingers—*fingers*, gods, the relief of joints that bent instead of hooked—he inhaled deeply.

A faint gust of night air curled into the stable, carrying the aroma of Gwenna's cooking and reminding him of his very human hunger. Cedric ran a hand through his hair, still feeling the phantom weight of horns that were no longer there, and quickly dressed in his worn tunic and breeches. He tugged on his boots—scuffed from countless forays into the forest—then pushed open the stable door.

The goats in the adjacent pen stirred at the sound, shifting in the twilight. Lilac, the smallest of the herd, flicked her ears but remained curled in her favorite corner, unimpressed by the disruption. Clarence sprang over to the fence and greeted Cedric with a sharp, demanding bleat before unceremoniously dropping goat pellets in the hay.

One of the younger goats skittered away from the mess with an offended snort.

"Goodnight to you too," Cedric chuckled. At least Clarence was consistent, in his own mischievous way.

He made his way across the moonlit courtyard to the tower's entrance, heart tightening a little at the thought of what awaited him within. Gwenna was at the hearth, stirring a pot that gave off the savory aroma of her signature rabbit stew. The small kitchen glowed in the firelight, and seeing his sister framed by that warmth made Cedric sigh in relief.

"There you are," Gwenna said, her voice pointed but edged with relief. "I was beginning to think you'd flown off and left me to deal with our...guest all by myself."

Cedric winced. He could hear the tension beneath her words, and he hated that she felt so on edge. "You know I wouldn't do that," he said softly. Stepping around to help set the table, he kept one ear tuned to her mood. "How is he?"

"Awake. Asking questions. Being entirely too perceptive for my liking." Gwenna's words bit like a winter wind.

An uneasy current rippled through Cedric. *Of course Finn would be perceptive.* That keen intelligence had sparked in every word the knight spoke during their brief interaction in the market square. "It's only natural he'd have questions," Cedric offered quietly. *If I were in his position, I'd be brimming with them, too.*

Gwenna met his logic with stubborn silence, the same silence she wielded whenever she thought he was being willfully stupid. And maybe he was.

But her frustration wasn't just about the knight—it was about *him*. Because in her eyes, Cedric had the luxury of believing things could change. That words could fix what swords had broken.

Gwenna was willing to kill a Lunarethen knight to keep them safe. And while Cedric understood her reasoning, he couldn't let himself cross that line. Maybe he was too idealistic. Maybe talking to Finn was pointless. But *gods*, he was tired. Tired of hiding. Tired of killing when there was no other choice.

They ate in silence, each lost in troubled thoughts. The stew was as delicious as ever, but Cedric barely tasted it. Every spoonful felt like a countdown, reminding him that time was running out before Finn learned too much. When Gwenna finished, she stood to clear the bowls, but Cedric lifted his hand.

"I'll handle them," he said, standing. "You've had a long day."

She eyed him doubtfully. "You hate doing the dishes."

A tired laugh escaped him. "I still do, but it's the least I can do after you spent the day shepherding a suspicious knight." Heat pricked behind his eyes, guilt for all the ways Gwenna had carried burdens he couldn't while trapped in dragon form each day. "You've earned a bit of rest."

Gwenna's lips parted, as if she might protest, but then she slumped a little. "All right," she conceded. "I am bushed. Just...promise me you'll be careful?"

Cedric snorted. He'd been groomed to rule a kingdom. And while that training was more than a decade old, he was no slouch with simple tasks at the outpost. "I'm fine. Everything is fine. Totally fine."

"You realize that's not at all convincing, right?" Gwenna asked cheerfully. But she came over and gave him a hug anyway. "If you need me, come wake me."

"I won't be doing that," Cedric said immediately. Gwenna was never in a good mood when woken prematurely. If people thought *he* was scary as a dragon, they had never beheld a sleep-deprived Gwenna. His sister laughed, then headed for her room.

Cedric allowed himself a smile as she left, then returned to the task at hand. He washed and dried the dishes, then straightened the kitchen area. There wasn't much to do, though, and Cedric was just delaying what he knew must come. Finn was here—was hurt—because of him.

He made his way back up the stairs, pausing outside Finn's door. Taking a deep breath to bolster himself, he knocked softly before entering. There was no answer, so Cedric gently shoved the door open. Gwenna had fed their guest earlier, though he'd brought along a bowl of stew covered with a towel to keep it warm, just in case the knight was hungry again. Cedric moved to set the bowl on the small table, then placed the lantern he carried beside it.

The moment metal touched wood, Finn startled awake, eyes snapping open. Cedric's pulse picked up, but he schooled his face into a calm expression.

"You," Finn said, voice rough with residual pain or grogginess. There was no immediate hostility, just watchfulness.

"Me," Cedric agreed, attempting a reassuring smile as he dragged a chair closer to the bed. The lantern illuminated the caution in Finn's grey eyes. *Not anger, at least. Small victories.* "You're looking much better than you were last night."

Finn carefully pushed himself upright, wincing at the effort. His intense gaze stayed locked onto Cedric's face, searching for...what, exactly? Answers? Reassurance? Weakness?

"I remember you," Finn said softly. "From the market."

Those words hit Cedric with a spike of relief and tension both. *So he recalls.* He forced a tight smile. "Yes, that was me." A man living a lie, hoping the knight wouldn't see through it. *Life's complicated.*

"You didn't mention you were a prince." Finn's tone was cautious, but there was no immediate accusation in it.

Cedric's stomach twisted. *Of course, that would come up first.* He scoffed, jaw tightening. "I'm not," he said curtly. "Not anymore."

Finn's eyes lit with something Cedric couldn't quite

figure out. "Right," he said slowly. "Because you're supposed to be dead."

So that's how it's going to be. Cedric shook his head. This was *not* a conversation he intended to have. "You shouldn't be moving around so quickly," he deflected instead, eager to change the subject. "Nice and slow, or you'll end up dizzy on the floor again."

Finn's expression shifted, becoming unbearably stubborn. "The knight's physician would have me walking by now."

Cedric snorted. "The knight's physician isn't here, is he?" He crossed his arms, leaning back just enough to be irritating. At least, that was Gwenna's observation about this pose. "Unless you want to take it up with Gwenna, who—need I remind you—put you in this condition in the first place."

Finn scowled, muttering something under his breath that Cedric was fairly certain wasn't *thank you for your concern.*

Shaking his head and allowing himself a small chuckle, Cedric stood and moved closer, pulse quickening at the prospect of touching the knight again. "May I?" he asked, gesturing to Finn's head.

Finn hesitated only a moment before nodding.

Cedric reached out, fingers skimming carefully around the bandage. "It looks much improved," he murmured, half to himself, keeping his voice neutral. "How's your vision? Any dizziness?"

Finn gingerly rubbed his forehead. "Better," he admitted. "A bit fuzzy around the edges, but it's not spinning like before."

Satisfied, Cedric stepped back, settling into the chair. He tried, and failed, to come up with a conversational topic. Finn, despite the blow to his head, was faster.

"You were a prince. The one who was supposedly killed by the dragon." The knight's gaze almost pinned him in place.

Great, back to my favorite topic again. Cedric drew a slow breath, schooling his features. "If I were dead, I wouldn't be having this conversation, now would I?"

Finn's brow lifted. "That's not really an answer."

Cedric narrowed his eyes. "If it soothes your conscience, then consider me a very convincing impostor." He followed it up with a single-shoulder shrug, as if the whole thing had been a matter of theatrics and not a big, scaly curse.

Finn scoffed. "You're being impossible. *Why? Why* fake your own death? Why hide away in this tower?"

Something in Cedric cracked. *Fake.* The word sat wrong, heavier than Finn probably meant it. *If only it had been that simple.* His bravado thinned, like fabric worn too threadbare to hold. "It's... not like that." He rubbed the back of his neck, debating how much to reveal. "There are things about that night—about everything—that you might not understand."

Finn let out a slow exhale and, despite the obvious ache in his head, leaned forward. "You'd be surprised what I can understand."

Cedric swallowed hard, torn between the instinct to protect himself (and Gwenna) and the bizarre, magnetic pull of this knight, who—gods help him—was just stubborn enough to make Cedric want to talk.

For a moment, Cedric sat there, mouth half-open, the urge to speak burning like a smoldering coal in his chest. The thought of finally sharing his secret with someone besides Gwenna was almost intoxicating.

But he couldn't.

Not when the cost of that confession would be too high for them all.

His gaze dropped to Finn's hand resting in his lap. "I'm sorry," he said quietly. "I can't."

Finn's shoulders sagged, disappointment shadowing his eyes. "I understand." He cleared his throat. "Can you at least tell me about the dragon? The one that's supposed to be guarding this tower?"

Cedric's heart clenched. *Dangerous territory.* No matter how carefully he stepped, he risked revealing more than he could afford. "What about it?"

Finn's brow creased as he tried to order his thoughts. "Your sister called it a pet," he said at last, voice edged with skepticism. "But it looked exactly like the one that attacked the royal family. This one was strange, though. It didn't attack me. It seemed almost...reluctant."

Cedric swallowed hard, remembering that moment. The way Finn had looked, standing there in his gleaming armor, sword raised. *Righteous fury burning in his eyes, ready to skewer me without hesitation.*

He should have fought the knight. Should have killed him. But Cedric hadn't. Not just because he liked Finn—not that he was ready to unpack *that* mess—but because if he had, if he'd let himself become the monster Finn already believed him to be...

Cedric feared that he'd never find his way back.

"The dragon is..." Cedric paused, searching for the least incriminating words. "Not what you think. It's not a monster. It's...a protector."

Finn leaned forward, wincing a little. Cedric almost reached out to brace him, but stopped himself. A dangerous habit, this urge to touch Finn.

"A protector?" the knight repeated. "Of what?"

"Of us," Cedric said simply, forcing himself to hold Finn's gaze. "Of this place. Of our freedom."

For a moment, Finn said nothing. Then confusion and some hint of realization warred in his expression. "You talk about it like it's intelligent. Like it's..."

Cedric's pulse spiked. *He's putting it together.*

But after a beat, Finn sighed, running a hand over his

face. "Never mind. I must still be more addled than I thought."

A soft, tremulous sigh escaped Cedric. *Thank Nivara, Keeper of Secrets.* "You should rest," he advised, standing and putting some much-needed distance between them—both to hide the relief washing over his face and to stop himself from doing something reckless. Like letting this conversation continue. "Your body needs time to heal."

He turned to leave, but before he could take a single step, Finn's hand shot out, fingers curling around Cedric's wrist in a firm grip. The warmth of that touch jolted Cedric more than any blow could have, and he froze, meeting Finn's gaze.

"Thank you," Finn said, voice hushed. "For helping me. For...not killing me when you had the chance."

Cedric's throat constricted at the gratitude in Finn's eyes. *If only he knew.* If only he understood just how close he had come to dying in that clearing—how Cedric's instincts had screamed for him to fight, to end the threat before it could end him. How much of a battle it had been, not just to spare Finn's life, but to preserve the last scraps of his own humanity.

"I could never..." Cedric started, then faltered, the words catching like thorns in his throat. *Gods, why was this so difficult?*

Finn's grip was warm and entirely too distracting.

Cedric swallowed, exhaling sharply before gently pulling free. He masked the turmoil twisting in his mind with a carefully neutral expression, though he wasn't entirely sure he pulled it off. "You're welcome," he finally managed.

Finn arched a brow. "That sounded painful."

Cedric rolled his eyes. "I'm not used to thanking people for making my life more complicated."

Finn smirked, utterly unfazed. "Oh, I can promise you— it's only going to get worse."

Cedric scoffed, stepping back before he did something stupid. "Wonderful. I can't wait."

And Finn—the infuriating man—actually winked.

Gods, I should have let Gwenna hit him twice. Cedric huffed out a breath and pivoted away.

As he reached the door, a sudden commotion from outside shattered the moment—bleating followed by a clatter of something heavy tipping over. Cedric pinched the bridge of his nose.

Finn tensed, still every inch the knight ready for battle. "What was that?"

Cedric didn't even have to guess. "Clarence," he groaned. "He's probably broken out of his pen again. No doubt leading another goat uprising."

Finn's eyebrows rose un understanding. "I know that goat," he said with a rueful note that bordered on humor.

Cedric let slip a small smile. *If nothing else, we share a mutual nemesis in Clarence.* "Yes, well...that's my princely duty," he joked, forcing lightness into his tone. "To quell goat rebellions."

Finn actually smirked a little, eyes dancing with good humor. "Isn't that what your knights are for?"

Cedric snorted softly, heat rising unbidden to his cheeks. *Did I really just say princely duties?* "Not my injured knights," he parried, an odd warmth lighting his heart. He swallowed, pushing that feeling down. "You're charged with staying here and healing," he added, more seriously.

Amusement danced across Finn's face, and Cedric's heart gave a quick, treacherous flutter. *He truly looks better when he's not scowling at me.*

Cedric tore his gaze away, fixing it on the door instead. "I'll check on you again soon," he promised, voice soft. *Gods, why did it come out like that?* Without waiting for a reply, he turned on his heel and hurried out.

He shut the door quickly. Too quickly.

Cedric pressed his back against it, exhaling a slow, ragged breath.

The soft click of the latch was the only sound in the corridor, but his mind refused to quiet. The way Finn had looked at him, the way his fingers had curled around Cedric's wrist. How had such a simple touch left him rattled?

He swallowed hard. It didn't matter. It *couldn't* matter.

Pushing off from the door, he took the stairs two at a time. *Focus on the goat. Focus on anything else.* But even as he reached the ground floor, the cool night air rushing in through the open archway, his heart was still beating far too fast.

"Cedric!" Gwenna's exasperated shout rang across the courtyard. "If you don't get out here and deal with this blasted goat, *I swear—*"

Clarence bleated in triumph.

Perfect. A disaster he could actually deal with. *Anything* to take his mind off the knight inside the tower.

Chapter Twelve

Finn crept down the narrow wooden stairs. He tensed, breath catching in his throat, as if expecting the entire tower to rouse at his intrusion. *Just how lightly do they sleep here?* he wondered, pausing a moment to strain his ears. But no voices or hurried footsteps answered. Only silence, broken by the distant chirp of morning birds outside.

Relieved, he continued downward, emerging in the tower's main room. Dawn's first light streamed through the windows, painting everything in gentle shades of gold and grey. On a small kitchen table sat a simple meal—bread, cheese, ripe fruit—and next to it, a folded note. Curiosity pricked at Finn as he opened it and read:

Finn,
Gone to the village to fetch your horse.
Should be back before midday. Help yourself to
breakfast.
-Gwenna

He exhaled, the knot of tension in his chest loosening. *She's bringing Ghost.* Relief warred with the uneasy reminder that he was still a guest—perhaps even a prisoner—amid uncertain allies. A quick glance out the window confirmed the sun had only just cleared the treetops. Gwenna, it seemed, was an early riser. His gaze drifted back to the spread on the table, and his stomach reminded him that healing knights required sustenance.

"Right," he murmured, setting the note aside. "No point starving."

He settled into a chair, grabbing a hunk of bread and a slice of cheese. The flavors were fresh, comfortingly simple. As he ate, his mind roiled with the events of the past day. He couldn't stop replaying that conversation with Cedric in the dead of night. The man's revelations—a once-prince, a faked death, a dragon-guardian—were the stuff of half-remembered legends, not something to be encountered in a modest tower hidden in a remote forest.

And yet, none of it felt contrived. Cedric's quiet resolve and the skittishness in his eyes suggested hard truths. Finn found himself uncomfortably drawn to the lost prince's aura of calm strength. *Calm, until he touched me.*

A flush warmed Finn's cheeks at the memory—the spark that leapt when Cedric laid a gentle hand on his wound, the soft intensity in those golden-brown eyes.

Gods, I'm in trouble. As a knight, duty should trump all else. But his usual clarity was muddied by the intrigue swirling around Cedric and Gwenna. Finn grimaced. *Stay focused.* He forced himself to finish the last piece of fruit, though each bite felt overshadowed by the question of what he was supposed to do now. *The so-called missing princess isn't missing at all, and I can't just force her to return. Not unless I want to end up with another lump on my head.*

Finished with his breakfast, he stood, crossing the main room in slow steps. With Gwenna gone, he could snoop around. *But would Cedric see that as a betrayal?* A pang of guilt tightened his gut. The recollection of Cedric's guarded expression made him pause. *He's not a threat, so long as I don't threaten him.* That, at least, was how Finn felt. So far, neither Cedric nor Gwenna had truly harmed him, aside from that singular rock to the skull.

Still, curiosity tugged, and he gave in. He drifted toward an alcove in the corner, where shelves crammed with books and scrolls lined the stone walls. The place smelled of old parchment and a faint whiff of herb satchels—maybe to keep pests away. He traced his fingertips along the spines, lips moving as he silently read the titles: herbal compendiums, bestiaries, and—surprisingly—a row of fairy-tale collections. He plucked one of the latter off the shelf, the leather binding cracked from heavy use, the pages yellowed and dog-eared.

Knights and dragons. Princes and princesses. The faintly colored illustrations showed valiant warriors in shining armor, triumphant over monstrous beasts. Something about these stories felt closer to reality now—like stepping into a reflection of his own predicament. He frowned, flipping to a well-worn page depicting a proud prince standing beside a dragon.

His gaze rested on the prince—the sharp cut of his features, the grace in his stance, the way he held himself with quiet authority even in the presence of a beast. The orange dragon loomed beside him, but Finn didn't spare it a glance. It was the prince who held his attention.

Is that so different from Cedric? The thought sent a shiver through him. He swallowed hard, then forced himself to snap the book shut. Sliding it back into place, he stepped away, as if that could put distance between himself and the prince who occupied far too much of his mind.

A rhythmic *clip-clop* of hooves outside jolted his attention away from the shelves. *Horse.* His heart leapt—Ghost.

Without hesitation, Finn hurried to the window. Sure enough, Gwenna emerged from the tree line astride his beloved grey mare. Relief surged in him like a warm tide, and before he quite registered the motion, he was dashing to the tower door.

"Ghost!" he called, grinning ear to ear as he pushed the door open. His horse nickered in response, ears pricking at the sight of Finn. "Gods, I've missed you," he murmured, resting a hand against the mare's neck. He inhaled the familiar scent of horse sweat and hay.

The princess—though she'd deny the title, apparently—slid down from the saddle and gave him a small, tired smile. "Good morning, Finn. I see you're up and about."

"Thanks to you and your brother," he said, stroking Ghost's velvety nose. The mare snorted, nudging him in greeting. Her welcome felt like a heartening reminder that some things, at least, were straightforward. "It's good to see you too, Ghost."

Gwenna's smile widened, traces of fatigue lingering at its corners. "She's a good horse," she said fondly. "Came from quality stock, I can tell." She patted Ghost's shoulder. "Didn't even spook when a rabbit bolted in front of us. I knew I was in good hands...or I guess, hooves." A teasing gleam lit her eye.

It was a simple remark, but Finn frowned all the same. *She really went alone? What if something had happened—bandits, or worse?* He kept his voice casual, feigning mere curiosity. "Did Cedric not come with you?"

Gwenna's posture stiffened. "No," she said after a beat. "He was up late wrangling a rogue goat."

Finn blinked. "I...see." He cleared his throat, shifting awkwardly. "But thanks again for bringing Ghost. I hope it wasn't too much trouble."

Waving off his gratitude, Gwenna turned toward the stable door. "Not at all. Let's get her settled, shall we?"

Finn nodded, leading Ghost alongside Gwenna. The heavy wooden door groaned in protest as Gwenna pushed it open, allowing bright shafts of morning sunlight to fall across the stable's straw-strewn floor. The stable was tidy—but with a curious emptiness to it, as though some of the stalls had been removed. Why?

His gaze snagged on a pallet in the far corner—a makeshift bed of straw with a pillow and a folded blanket. A simple shirt and trousers lay neatly beside it. Confusion rippled through him.

"Is someone sleeping in the stables?" he blurted, glancing at Gwenna.

She followed his line of sight, and a rueful smile tugged at her lips. "Ah, yes. Cedric. Sometimes he has trouble sleeping indoors. He prefers it out here."

A prince sleeping in a barn? Finn's brow furrowed, trying to reconcile this new image of the lost prince—sleeping on a bed of straw, like some farmhand. "Wouldn't he be more comfortable in, you know, a real bed?" he asked carefully.

Gwenna just shrugged. "Cedric's always been…unconventional." But there was a flash of something in her eyes—fondness, perhaps, or gentle exasperation—that Finn couldn't quite decipher. He recognized that look; it reminded him of the way siblings spoke of well-meaning but troublesome brothers.

He nodded, not pressing further. Part of him *wanted* to pry, to unravel the intricacies of Cedric's life. Another part, the chivalrous knight in him, insisted he respect boundaries in this place, where he remained a trespasser. Gwenna showed him where to stable Ghost and fetch fresh water.

"I'm going to put together some lunch," Gwenna said, once Ghost was munching contentedly. She dusted her hands off on her tunic. "I figure we could all use a meal after such an early morning."

Finn nodded, offering a small smile. "I'll be right in. I just want to give Ghost a good grooming and pick her hooves."

With a confirming nod, Gwenna left. As soon as the stable door swung shut, silence settled again, broken only by the soothing munch of hay as Ghost ate. Finn exhaled, leaning into his task. With each stroke of the currycomb, his gaze strayed to that straw pallet in the corner. He couldn't banish the image of Cedric curled up there, hair likely tousled with bits of hay clinging to it. *Why on earth would he—?*

And *why* did he care so much? Was it simply because, after being missing for so long, the prince was an enigma? Or was it something deeper—like the quickening of his heart at Cedric's touch, the soft hush of his voice, the way he looked with that haunted sorrow beneath the surface?

A sigh escaped him. *I hardly know him.*

Finn set the brush aside and pulled out the hoof pick, focusing on cleaning Ghost's hooves. When Ghost was in pristine shape, he latched the stall door, gave her one last affectionate pat, and headed for the outpost's kitchen. The aroma of simmering broth and herbs drew him in like a beacon.

"Smells incredible," he said, voice echoing in the stone-walled room. Gwenna stirred a pot while humming a snatch of some tune. She turned at the sound of his voice.

"Thanks! It's just a simple vegetable stew," she replied. "We have some decent bread left over, too."

"Reminds me of one my mother used to make," Finn commented, inhaling the earthy scent of carrots, onions, and thyme. In truth, it sparked memories of simpler days before tragedy sank its claws into his life. "I haven't seen your brother today. I wanted to thank him for letting me stay."

Finn paused, arms folded across his chest, watching Gwenna's hesitation on the carrot she was chopping. She looked up at him, her expression cautious, almost defensive.

"Cedric...works at night." Gwenna returned her attention to the carrot, chopping it with a concerning amount of pressure. "He's asleep right now."

Finn arched a brow in curiosity. "Works? Doing what?" Then he paused. "Oh, do you mean the wood carving?"

"The wood carving," she agreed with careful phrasing. "Among other things."

Wood carving at night, in a tower with minimal light, struck him as peculiar. *But then again, everything about this situation is strange.* The prince sleeping in a barn, Gwenna's refusal to dwell on the past, the protective dragon that roamed the forest.

Wait...sleeping in the barn? When he and Gwenna had stabled Ghost, the pallet had been empty. For a moment, Finn considered pressing her—why wasn't Cedric on the pallet in the barn? Or was he sleeping in the outpost somewhere? The watchful look on Gwenna's face cautioned him to tread lightly.

They settled into lunch. Gwenna steered the conversation toward safe topics—small anecdotes about the local wildlife, a passing reference to the village trade. Finn listened intently, occasionally asking polite questions. He gathered bits of insight into how they lived here: Gwenna's tinkering, some garden harvests, and occasionally venturing to town. Yet that was the extent of what she'd share. *She's wary,* he reminded himself. *I'm still an outsider.*

After lunch, Finn insisted on cleaning up. He felt restless, wanting to do *something* useful, so Gwenna relented with a teasing threat that he not overexert himself. Washing bowls and spoons provided a comforting rhythm, temporarily pushing aside the morass of larger questions— about Cedric's midnight woodworking, Gwenna's suspicion, and the dragon that haunted his mission.

He spent much of the afternoon with Ghost. Gwenna

suggested allowing Ghost a chance to graze, so he led the mare toward the goat pen.

The goats trotted over to investigate the newcomer in their midst, bleating curiously as Ghost snatched up a mouthful of grass. Most of the goats cautiously sniffed at the mare before losing interest. Clarence, however, was another matter entirely. The troublemaker eyed Ghost with clear suspicion before letting out a challenging bleat and attempting to headbutt her shoulder. Ghost flicked an ear, completely unbothered, and simply stepped aside, leaving Clarence to huff indignantly.

Finn chuckled, shaking his head at the goat's antics. "You're lucky she doesn't see you as a threat."

Eventually, the mare wandered to a shady corner of the pen, settling in with contented flicks of her tail. Finn remained by the fence for a few more minutes, watching the easy rhythm of the animals before his curiosity drew him back inside.

He drifted toward the library alcove again, scanning the spines of the books for one that might help pass the time. The day wore on, and he fell into a light doze in a chair by the bookshelf. By the time he stirred, the sunlight had shifted, painting the stone walls in long, golden beams. He could hear Gwenna moving about, the telltale sounds of clattering pots and pans signaling the start of the evening meal.

Finn descended to find Gwenna preparing yet another savory dish—something involving roasted meat that made his stomach rumble just from the smell. His mind flicked to Cedric again: *He was resting, presumably. Will he finally make an appearance?*

Gwenna filled two cups with water from a jug. They chatted as she continued the meal preparation, with Finn chipping in—mostly about Finn's horse and the goats, interspersed with the occasional dry remark about how she hadn't expected to be hosting a knight-errant in their tower.

Finn tried to laugh it off, focusing on the casual banter, but his thoughts inevitably circled back to Cedric's absence.

"Will Cedric be joining us?" he ventured at last, pitching his voice as evenly as he could manage. Something about the question felt loaded, like he was asking permission to see the man again.

Gwenna glanced at the window, likely checking the sun's position. "Yes, he should be here shortly. He never misses dinner."

Finn let out a quiet exhale. *Good,* he thought, forcing an untroubled nod. "I can't say I'd blame him. This smells delicious." He gestured to the haunch of meat Gwenna was fussing over, juices sizzling in a shallow pan. His mouth practically watered just at the sight.

Before they could continue, the patter of hooves and a sudden, high-pitched bleat from outside broke the moment. Gwenna froze, spoon still in hand, then groaned, rolling her eyes heavenward. "That has to be Clarence again! Gods above, that goat is insufferable."

Finn laughed—an involuntary reaction to her exasperation. He pushed back from the table, ignoring the faint twinge in his healing injuries. "I'll go check on him," he said impulsively. Perhaps it was a chance to prove he wasn't completely helpless.

Gwenna lifted an amused brow. "Sure you're up for it? You might want a battalion of knights at your back."

He smirked, heading for the door. "How bad can a single goat be? I'll bring him back, just you wait."

Stepping outside, Finn found himself bathed in the dying light of the day. Gold and rose hues streaked the sky, illuminating the courtyard and the goat pen. Ghost lifted her head from an evening graze, ears flicking as Finn approached. Around the mare, several goats milled about. Except Clarence, who was conspicuously absent.

Sure enough, the fence on the far side looked compromised—warped boards and splintered edges hinted at the goat's latest escapade. Finn sighed, bracing himself for the hunt. *All right, troublemaker, where did you run off to?*

He scanned the tree line. The woods beyond stood in dappled twilight. If Clarence had bolted there, Finn might be in for a chase. He winced. *Well, I volunteered,* he reminded himself, forging onward.

An imperious bleat split the air. Finn spun on his heel. Clarence stood at the edge of the clearing like some smug minor king surveying his dominion. The goat flicked his tail, chewing leisurely on a mouthful of grass as if daring Finn to try.

Finn sighed, rolling his shoulders as he slowly advanced. "All right, you rascal. Let's get you back where you belong."

Clarence, of course, had other plans.

Before Finn could react, the goat lunged—a blur of matted fur and curved horns. The impact punched into Finn's stomach like a battering ram, driving the air from his lungs in a ragged gasp. He hit the ground hard, making Finn regret his lack of enchanted armor as his shoulder blades struck knotted tree roots. Pain radiated up his spine. He wheezed, fingers clawing at dirt as he fought to suck in a breath that wouldn't come.

He had faced armed opponents, wild beasts, even the claws of a dragon—but apparently, it was a damned goat that would best him.

Footsteps pounded nearby. Finn blinked through watering eyes as Cedric's face swam into view—sharp features drawn tight with concern. "Finn!" The prince dropped to one knee. Strong fingers skimmed Finn's arm, checking for injuries. "What happened? Are you hurt?"

Finn grimaced, his pride nursing a deeper wound than his body. He shoved himself upright, wincing at the throbbing ache blooming across his torso. "Just got taken out by a goat." He swiped a hand across his mouth, tasting soil and humiliation. "Clarence seems to have picked a fight I wasn't ready for."

A warm chuckle escaped Cedric, but his golden-brown eyes still swept over Finn, lingering on the grass stains streaking his borrowed clothing. Finn swore he could feel those eyes like a touch.

When their gazes met, Finn's pulse thundered. Not from the fall.

"You sure you're all right?" Cedric extended a hand, dirt smudging his knuckles.

Finn grasped it without thinking. *Bad idea.* The contact sent an inexplicable jolt through him—the prince's firm grip, the kind of touch that made Finn's heartbeat trip over itself in a way he did *not* appreciate. Cedric hauled him upright, boots slipping on loose dirt before Finn found his footing.

"It just knocked the wind out of me," he managed, quickly letting go before he could register the warmth lingering in Cedric's palm. "Though maybe I should avoid challenging goats in the future."

Cedric's lips quirked. "That may be wise." Amusement danced in his eyes, brighter than the stars above. "Maybe stick with dragons."

Dragons. Finn's throat went dry as old memories sprang to life.

He cleared his throat, the motion tugging at his bruised muscles. "I'll leave goat wrangling to you for now." The words came out stilted. When his eyes met Cedric's again, the dragon memory dissolved like smoke. There was only the flecked amber of the prince's gaze, the faint lines at their corners from too many stifled smiles. Kavros help him, but Finn could lose himself in those eyes if he wasn't careful.

Gwenna's voice cracked through the moment like a whip. "What in Sylvara's name is taking so long?" She stood framed in the kitchen doorway, flour dusting her apron. "Are you out there wrestling with the goat?"

Finn tore his gaze from Cedric, suddenly all too aware of how ridiculous he must look, covered in dust with his dignity lying somewhere in the dirt behind him. "Just, uh, giving Clarence a refresher on respect." His ears burned.

Gwenna gave him a once-over and arched a knowing brow. "Looks to me like you're the one who got the lesson." She waved a hand toward the door. "Come on in. Dinner's ready."

Finn risked a glance at Cedric. Twilight deepened the hollows of his cheekbones, gilding his long hair like a crown. Unfair, really, how the fading light seemed to conspire in making him look every bit the prince he claimed *not* to be.

For a heartbeat, Finn wondered how those strands would feel between his fingers. The thought struck out of nowhere, slipping past his defenses before he could shove it aside.

"Let's get inside, shall we?" Cedric's voice broke his thoughts, light as sun through storm clouds. But as they turned toward the tower, his sleeve brushed Finn's arm—an absent touch, a whisper of contact that burned through layers of linen like a brand.

Finn nodded, falling into step beside him.

The night stretched before them, full of unknowns, full of truths left unsaid. And for the first time since setting foot on this journey, Finn wondered if this quest was leading him somewhere entirely different than he'd ever expected.

Chapter Thirteen

Finn was not about to let a goat have the last word.

Clarence had bested him once today, but Finn still had his dignity. (Well, *some* of it.) Which was why, after dinner, he pushed back from the table and stretched, giving Cedric a pointed look. "I'll help you fix the fence."

Cedric quirked a brow, clearly amused. "Will you?"

"Yes," Finn said, already standing. "Consider it a matter of knightly honor."

From across the table, Gwenna snorted. "You mean your wounded pride."

"Same thing." Finn waved a hand dismissively. "Either way, that fence needs fixing, and I'm not letting Cedric do it alone."

Cedric heaved a put-upon sigh, but didn't argue. "All right, if you're so determined." He stood, pushing his chair in neatly, and gestured for Finn to follow.

The evening air was crisp, carrying the scent of hay and damp earth. Finn rolled his shoulders, trying to shake off the stiffness still lingering from the pre-dinner *incident*. Clarence, thankfully, was nowhere in sight. He was probably lurking, waiting to strike again.

"Honestly," Finn began as they approached the fence, "I don't know that you and Gwenna even need a dragon for protection with that goat around."

To his surprise, Cedric laughed. It was a sound that Finn hoped to hear much more frequently. The prince grinned. "Now that you mention it, I think you're on to something." Cedric led him to a small shed near the goat pen and retrieved a hammer and some nails.

"Speaking of protection...what *did* happen to all those adventurers who supposedly came looking for a dragon?" Finn raised an inquisitive brow.

Cedric didn't even glance up as he selected a nail. "Clarence."

Finn blinked. "...Come again?"

Now Cedric did look at him, *utterly* deadpan. "They crossed Clarence. They did not return."

Finn stared. He was mostly sure Cedric was joking. Probably. Maybe. "...You're messing with me."

Cedric only smiled. "Am I?"

Finn squinted. "Yes?"

No answer. Just the faintest curve of Cedric's lips as he turned back to work.

And now Finn was *less* sure.

"But really," Finn said, tone shifting. "They all came after Gwenna and the dragon." He spoke it as a fact, since King Darius had already confirmed as much. His lips pressed together as he mulled it over. *None* of them had made it back.

Which meant the king had a vague idea of where Cedric and Gwenna were. But not a precise location.

"They were mercenaries." Cedric's tone was even as he trudged toward the goat pen. "You're a knight of Lunareth, but I assume you've encountered merc knights before?"

Finn nodded. "Their loyalty is bought by the highest bidder. Their honor is...transactional."

The prince was tight-lipped, but nodded. "Yes. And if any of them had gotten through, who knows what they would have done to Gwenna before returning her to Mira-then?" When phrased that way, Finn couldn't say he blamed their defensive approach.

Finn's mind wandered back to the grisly display. So many insignias he didn't recognize, except for the lone Avilisian one. Finn couldn't put a finger on why that troubled him.

Cedric glanced over his shoulder. "Can you hold a board in place?" His question made Finn forget all about unusual mercenary trappings.

Finn scowled. "I can use my hands for things besides swinging a sword."

Cedric grinned, handing him a plank of wood. "We'll see."

Finn took the board, gripping it with mock indignation. "What do you think I am, some kind of reckless brute who only knows how to solve problems with violence?"

Cedric just gave him a look.

Finn sighed. "Okay, *sometimes*. But I know how to hold a board, Cedric."

"We'll still see."

Finn muttered under his breath, but held the board in place, anyway. "So, perhaps this isn't a question I should pose as you wield a hammer, but why let me live?" He raised his brows. "Was it my good looks?"

Cedric didn't even pause mid-swing. "And people say *royalty* have egos," he commented, though a smile tugged at his lips. The hammer came down, driving the nail in with a satisfying *thunk*. He paused, meeting Finn's gaze. "No, it's because you're one of ours. You're of Lunareth."

Finn blinked, thrown by the simple certainty in Cedric's tone. *You're one of ours.*

His fingers flexed against the board, gripping it a little tighter. It wasn't what he'd expected.

"Right," Finn said, slower this time. "I suppose that means I owe you, then."

Cedric raised his brows, reaching for another nail. "If you're offering..." His tone was light, but something in his eyes made Finn's stomach twist in a way that had nothing to do with nerves.

Finn smirked. "Depends on what you're asking." Then his expression shifted. "How did you learn how to do all this? You're a prince. Not exactly the practical sort."

"Hold the board straight." Cedric shot him a look. "And just because border diplomacy seldom involves planks and nails doesn't mean it's something we can't learn."

Finn winced. He hadn't meant to offend. "I just imagine...most nobles couldn't do this. *Wouldn't* do this."

"We had no choice, Finn. Our options were die of exposure or figure out how to survive." Cedric shrugged, driving another nail home. "You can see which we chose."

Finn absorbed that, his smirk fading. He looked down at the rough wood beneath his hands. Cedric wasn't just good at this—he *needed* to be. He hesitated, turning the next plank over in his hands. "You and Gwenna have been out here for a decade." The words felt strange now—too big, too real. "Meanwhile, things in Lunareth have...changed."

"Things *everywhere* have changed," Cedric corrected, though something akin to pain briefly crossed his face. "Revendar is a husk of what it once was, thanks to the Avilisian Empire and their schemes."

"So the recluse prince keeps up with news?" Finn asked, unable to keep the note of challenge from his voice.

"Since knowledge of current events helps keep me alive, yes." Then Cedric's voice became little more than a whisper. "And I may be a ghost as far as Lunareth is concerned, but I still care."

Finn's gut lurched at that soft admission. *Then why don't you go back? Challenge King Darius the Glorious?* But he sensed that was a question best left for another time. Maybe he could tease that out in a roundabout way.

"Being a knight the past few years hasn't been easy," Finn said as Cedric pulled another nail from the pouch at his belt. "I thought I was protecting my kingdom. That I was fighting for my people."

His words drew Cedric's interest. "But?"

Got you. Finn smiled. "But I've been wondering who I was meant to protect. Those within the kingdom, solely because they had the fortune to be born here? And use my sword to turn away those who come here to seek mercy?"

The prince went very, very still. "You would do as your king commands." It was spoken in the most neutral manner as possible, but Finn still felt the tension thrumming below the surface.

"Someone once told me that makes me a well-dressed weapon." Finn winked at him, hoping the flirty gesture might further throw Cedric off balance.

In response, Cedric snorted. "Sounds familiar, like I know this person."

Finn chuckled. "Perhaps so. Anyway, those words made me think. Especially in Duskridge. Those people, those former refugees...they're not the enemy, no matter what King Darius says." Was it his imagination, or had Cedric nearly startled at the king's name? Finn pretended he hadn't noticed.

Cedric made a noncommittal sound. "We're almost done. You holding that board or not?"

Finn squinted at Cedric as the prince focused a little too intently on hammering in the next board. *Well, I've already poked at every other uncomfortable subject. What's one more?*

"You were friends with King Darius," Finn observed.

Cedric's hammer paused mid-swing. He let out a slow breath. "What passes for friends, I suppose." His tone was uncertain. He sighed, finally driving the nail into place.

"Darius was one of those people where you never quite knew where you stood." There was something unspoken in his voice, but before Finn could press, Cedric straightened. "What made you want to be a knight?"

Finn let the shift in topic slide. "You know, the usual. Heroic tales, a deep sense of duty, an innate desire to put myself in mortal peril for questionable leadership."

Cedric chuckled. "So, not the cloaks and fancy armor, then?"

Finn grinned. "Oh, no, that was a factor. Have you seen how dashing we look?"

Cedric rolled his eyes but didn't argue.

Finn hesitated, then gave the simplest truth. "My father was a knight." He paused, then added, "We have a lot in common, you know. My father died the night of the dragon attack, like your parents."

Cedric stilled. The tension in his shoulders returned, subtle but noticeable. He didn't say anything.

Finn swallowed. He could see it—*feel* it—how much that affected Cedric. That had been the wrong feint to make. *Time to correct it.*

He smirked, trying to lighten the mood. "Of course, I thought knights were all about grand battles and noble quests. Didn't realize most of the job was standing guard at doors while nobles gossiped."

Cedric raised his brows. "Disillusioned?"

"A bit." Finn leaned against the post. "But lately, I've been realizing something. Knights are always needed. By the crown, by their kingdom. But being wanted...that's different."

"Aren't those the *same*?" Cedric asked. "Fairly certain the crown wants to have an ample roster of knights."

"Not the way I mean it," Finn said, watching the prince intently.

Cedric held his gaze for a beat. Then he looked away,

hammering in the last nail with more force than necessary. "There." His voice was quieter now. "That should hold."

They stood shoulder to shoulder, the warmth of Cedric's body a whisper against Finn's arm. The air between them felt charged, heavy with something invisible but undeniable.

Finn exhaled slowly, but it did nothing to steady him. His skin prickled, hyperaware of every breath Cedric took, of the faint scent of cedar and sawdust lingering on his clothes. As if drawn by an invisible force, they turned toward each other.

For a moment, neither of them moved.

Finn's pulse thundered in his ears. Cedric's gaze dipped to his mouth. Finn's fingers clenched the fencepost, his grip so tight the rough wood bit into his palm. He needed the anchor because every inch of him wanted to close the space between them.

To lean in. To find out if Cedric would stop him.

Or let it happen.

Then an obnoxious bleat rang out from the shadows. Clarence.

The spell shattered. Finn groaned, throwing his head back. "I swear, that goat is possessed."

Cedric laughed—warm, unguarded, *real*. Finn would suffer a thousand Clarence-related humiliations to hear that sound again. "Come on." Cedric bumped Finn's shoulder lightly. "Let's get inside before he claims another victim."

Finn sighed, but followed him.

As they walked back toward the tower, Finn couldn't shake the feeling that tonight had changed something. The distance between them was smaller now. The silences felt less like something to be afraid of.

He didn't entirely mind getting humbled by a goat. Especially if it meant Cedric laughing like that again.

Chapter Fourteen

Cedric's talons dug into the cliff face, rough granite yielding beneath their razor-edged curve. The stone radiated heat like a living thing, soaking into the golden plates of his underbelly. His tongue flicked out, tasting pine resin and distant rain on the wind. Below, the forest stretched in a rumpled green blanket; the river glinting like a dropped sword between the trees. His slit-pupiled eyes tracked a hawk's spiraling descent. Then his focus returned to the outpost far below.

Finn was down there.

A soft puff of smoke drifted from his nostrils. He hadn't meant to let his thoughts drift to the knight so easily, but it was becoming harder to stop himself. The memory of the previous night burned in his mind—Finn on the ground, winded from his encounter with Clarence, and Cedric reaching down to help him.

His tail lashed, sending a shower of pebbles clattering down the cliff side. *Stupid. Reckless.* His secondary eyelids slid shut, but it didn't block the afterimage: Finn's storm-cloud eyes widening, a lock of ebony hair falling across his brow as Cedric hauled him upright.

He exhaled sharply through flared nostrils. A brisk gust of wind rattled the leaves below, and Cedric finally tore his gaze from the outpost, forcing his thoughts back into order. The sun was sinking lower. It was nearly time.

The dying rays gilded the western peaks when he finally pushed off, wings snapping taut to catch the late afternoon thermals. The cool air rippled over his scales, carrying the scents of the land below as he dove toward his usual landing spot.

Cedric touched down in the meadow a mile from the tower, his claws sinking into the damp earth. The grass here was tall, golden from the waning season, and it rustled softly as he made his way toward the hollow tree where he kept his clothing. With Finn at the outpost, he could no longer safely transform there. But Cedric was adaptable.

The sun slipped lower.

The moment the last light of day faded, the transformation began.

Cedric sucked in a breath as the first wave of it hit. He gritted his teeth, staggering as his body forced itself back into its natural form. It never got easier. The shift left him gasping, his muscles trembling from the agonizing change from his draconic form.

Transformation always left him raw. Tonight, his shoulders and collarbone burned where wings had melted back into muscle, the ghost of talons itching beneath his fingernails. He pressed his forehead against the oak's gnarled bark, waiting for the world to stop tilting. Stable straw would've smelled sweeter than this leaf mold, but at least here, no one witnessed his shaking hands.

Cold air nipped at his bare skin, raising goosebumps along his arms. He reached for his clothes, pulling on his shirt and trousers with hurried, clumsy fingers. His boots followed, laced with hands still unsteady from the aftershocks of transformation. When he finally stood upright again, fully dressed, he rolled his shoulders, trying to dispel the lingering ache of realigned bones.

Cedric took a deep breath, steadying himself. Then he started down the narrow trail leading home.

By the time he reached the goat pen, moonlight had leached color from the world. His enhanced vision painted everything in icy blues and searing silvers. The latest goat pen repair held—the new planks stood pale against weather-beaten wood. The warhorse mare's warm breath fogged his sleeve as he checked the latch.

The simple motion stirred something old in him.

He missed horses.

It wasn't just a pastime he missed. It was a part of *himself*. Sunset had been *his*—a proud, fiery mare who had carried him through his years as a prince, a constant. Was she still alive? Had Darius's men claimed her after he vanished? The thought made his stomach churn.

It was easier not to think about what he'd lost.

"Don't get stuck in the past," he muttered to himself, the words grinding between his teeth.

Cedric lifted his chin, squaring his shoulders as he strode toward the tower, forcing himself to be present in the here and now. Through the warped glass of the window, he glimpsed Finn and Gwenna setting the table. Cedric slowed, watching unnoticed from the shadows. Gwenna said something, her tone teasing, and Finn laughed—a sound so unguarded, so full, that it sent an unexpected jolt through Cedric. The knight's smile burned brighter than the last flare of sunset. Cedric's throat closed around a breath gone sharp as broken glass.

He couldn't just stand here staring. As he pushed the door open, Cedric called out, "Evening."

Finn turned, his grin widening until it carved dimples into his cheeks. "Cedric! Just in time for dinner."

"Wouldn't miss it." Cedric's answering smile felt brittle as he moved to help Gwenna.

They sat to eat, the fire crackling in the hearth, filling the room with an easy warmth. Cedric focused on his food, forcing himself to sink into the familiar dance of conversation—Gwenna's sharp banter, Finn's dry wit, the way their words wove through the evening like threads in a tapestry.

Then Finn turned to him, and Cedric knew he was doomed.

"So, how's the wood carving been going?" Finn asked, leaning toward him, resting his elbow on the table. "I'd love to see your work sometime."

Cedric's throat betrayed him, constricting around a half-chewed bite of bread. *Haven't touched a chisel or carving knife in days*, he thought, the admission curdling in his gut. He forced himself to swallow—the bread, the guilt, *all* of it.

"It's, uh, been going well," he managed. Then, before he could think better of it, his tongue ran ahead of his caution. "Would you like to come see my workshop after dinner?"

Finn's grin widened immediately, bright as firelight. "I'd love to."

Regret. *Immediate,* tangible regret. Cedric barely had time to process it before Gwenna let out a dramatic, suffering groan. "Gods, please, I beg of you—flirt *less* at the dinner table." She paused, then added, "And maybe not at all."

Cedric scowled. "We are *not* flirting."

Finn, entirely unfazed, speared a piece of roasted meat with his fork and shrugged. "I don't know, *Prince* Cedric. Inviting a knight to your private quarters? People might talk."

Cedric scoffed at the use of his former title, well aware of Gwenna's warning glance. "No one would talk."

Gwenna *thunk*ed her cup down on the table, eyes narrowing. "*I* might talk."

Cedric rolled his eyes so hard he nearly saw the back of his own skull. "It's a *workshop*, not a secret rendezvous."

Finn raised his eyebrows. "Could be both."

Gwenna leaned forward, fixing Finn with a look that was a little too sharp. "And why, exactly, would a knight be interested in my brother's workshop?"

Finn, for once, hesitated—only slightly, but Cedric caught the flicker. Then, smooth as ever, he smiled. "Because I admire fine craftsmanship."

Gwenna arched a brow. "Uh-huh. That admiration better stay strictly *professional*."

"If the gods have any mercy, they'll strike me down *right now*." Cedric rubbed his temples. But when the knight's expression softened—just a fraction, just enough—something loosened in Cedric's chest. A dangerous warmth, curling around his heart like ivy.

After dinner, they cleaned up together, though Cedric hardly registered the task. His mind was already in his workshop, already bracing for what it would mean to be alone with Finn again.

The outbuilding smelled of sawdust and cedar. Lantern light danced along the rough edges of unfinished carvings and half-whittled pieces. Finn stepped inside, his gaze sweeping over the array of tools and figures scattered across the workbenches.

"Wow," he whispered, reaching toward a half-carved raven mid-flight. Cedric tensed, anticipating the inevitable recoil when Finn noticed the dragon figurine lurking behind it, but the knight only lifted a small stag, marveling at its carved antlers.

"These are *incredible*, Cedric."

Pride surged through Cedric's veins. "Thank you. It's just a way to make ends meet, really."

Finn snorted, giving him a dry look. "Hardly. Anyone can look at this and see the passion you put into it."

Before Cedric could muster a response, Finn touched the dragon. His thumb traced the sculpture's articulated tail, the delicate ridges along its back.

Cedric felt that touch like a shock to his spine.

Finn turned the carving over in his hands, his grip light, not like a knight inspecting a weapon, but like someone who actually *cared* about the craftsmanship.

"The detail is amazing," Finn whispered. He glanced at Cedric, brow furrowing, like he was working through something. "How do you do it?"

Cedric exhaled, tension easing just a fraction. "Patience. And a lot of mistakes."

Finn chuckled. "That makes sense. Just...wouldn't have expected this from you."

Cedric arched a brow. "And *this* meaning...?"

Finn grinned, setting the dragon back down with exaggerated care. "Oh, nothing. Just that most princes I've heard about spend their time debating politics, studying diplomacy, and perfecting their waltz—not carving stags out of cedar."

Cedric crossed his arms. "I did study diplomacy." He wet his lips. "A skill which I'm employing at the moment, in fact." Cedric glanced at the tools on his nearby workbench. "If you want, I could show you how it's done."

Finn went still for half a second—just long enough that Cedric felt it. Then, softer the knight said, "I'd like that."

Cedric swallowed. *Too late to take it back now.* "Here, let me show you," he said before he could second-guess himself. He reached for a fresh piece of wood and a carving knife, gesturing for Finn to take a seat on the wooden bench.

Their shoulders brushed as he settled beside Finn, handing over the wood and carving knife. "Hold it like this," Cedric murmured, reaching to adjust Finn's grip. His fingers skimmed over rough, calloused hands—hands made for wielding a sword, not the small carving knife. Finn let Cedric guide his hold without resistance.

Cedric cleared his throat. "The trick is control. You're not hacking at it like a training dummy."

Finn glanced at him, eyebrows lifted high. "That a dig at my technique?"

Cedric sucked in a breath, adjusting Finn's fingers around the hilt of the knife. "No, *this* is a dig at your technique." He gave Finn's wrist a light slap. "Relax. You're gripping it like you're about to duel the wood."

Finn huffed, loosening his hold just a little. "Better?"

Cedric tilted his head in assessment. "Marginally."

He demonstrated, angling the blade against the grain, letting the knife whisper over the wood. "You start with the basic shape. You don't need to press too hard—just enough to get the first layers off." He turned the block in his hands, showing Finn how the blade should glide through the grain, not fight against it.

Then, after only a moment of hesitation, he covered Finn's hand with his own. *Bad idea. Terrible idea.* But necessary.

"The pressure has to be firm, but controlled," Cedric continued, his voice coming out steadier than he felt. He guided Finn, directing his first cut. The knife bit cleanly into the wood, releasing a fine curl of pale cedar that fluttered down onto Finn's thigh. "Not bad." Cedric's breath caught when Finn turned his head—*far* too close—grinning like a rogue.

"Look at that," Finn mused, clearly enjoying himself. "I'm an *artist*."

Cedric scoffed. "Let's not get ahead of ourselves."

Finn made another slow pass with the knife, his brow furrowing in concentration. The lantern light cast warm gold across his cheekbones, tracing the line of his jaw.

Cedric needed to *stop* noticing these things.

The knife's rhythmic *scritch-scritch* filled the silence, but Cedric's attention fractured—fixing on the sweat-damp hairs at Finn's nape, the way his lower lip caught between his teeth in concentration. Finn's breathing was soft, unshaken, as if their closeness was nothing at all. But Cedric? He was unraveling.

Focus on the wood, Cedric commanded himself, even as his traitorous mind whispered how easily Finn could pin him against the workbench, how the knife might clatter forgotten to the floor. His blade slipped, nicking the cedar.

Finn glanced up, brows lifting. "Thought you said this was about control."

Cedric forced himself to exhale, willing the warmth in his face to subside. "Even the best make mistakes."

Finn leaned in, his grin teasing but not unkind. "Good to know you're not *too* perfect."

"Only mostly." Cedric shot him a dry look. "Are you going to carve or talk all night?"

Finn chuckled, returning his attention to the wood. But Cedric had the distinct feeling he wasn't the only one fighting distraction.

Finn turned his head slightly, catching Cedric's gaze. Their faces were suddenly inches apart.

Time stalled.

Cedric's pulse raced as Finn's gaze flickered lower. To his mouth. He could see the way Finn's pupils dilated, the silent pull between them like gravity shifting, dragging them closer.

Every instinct screamed at him to move, to break the moment before it swallowed him whole.

But he didn't.

For a brief, breathless moment, Cedric thought Finn might close the distance. Might kiss him.

And worse—a reckless, aching part of him wanted it.

Then reason sliced through him. *Dangerous.* This was dangerous. He was getting in too deep.

Clearing his throat, he jerked back, breaking the spell. "So, uh, that's the basics," he said, voice rasping in his throat, utterly unconvincing. "With practice, you'll get better at the details."

Finn blinked, as if shaking off the same daze. He straightened, fingers closing around the knife, though he didn't carve. "Right, yeah. Thanks for showing me."

Silence pooled between them, thick as smoke, stretching like a taut rope between two points.

Cedric busied himself tidying the workspace. Ridiculous. It wasn't as if Finn had actually—

No. Don't even think it.

And yet, he could still feel it—the phantom warmth of their near-touch, the way Finn had looked at him.

Finn cleared his throat. "Cedric."

Cedric tensed. "Mm?"

Finn hesitated, shifting his weight. "Can I ask you something?"

No. Absolutely not. "Of course," Cedric said instead, already bracing for impact. Whatever Finn asked, Cedric already knew his answer would likely be a lie.

Finn paused, something thoughtful—or suspicious—in his gaze. "Why do you only work at night? And where do you go during the day?"

Cedric's stomach dropped.

"I saw the pallet in the stables," Finn added.

Shit.

This was his fault. He had gotten too comfortable. Of course Finn had noticed the gaps, the inconsistencies—a perceptive knight would see right through flimsy excuses. Cedric turned away, pretending to adjust some tools. Anything to hide his panic.

"I, uh..." He forced himself to sound casual, rolling his

shoulders as if Finn's questions were nothing more than idle curiosity. "I've always been a bit of a night owl." The words came out thin. Weak. Even to his own ears. "And during the day, I..." He grabbed a chisel, flipping it absently in his palm. "...Patrol the area. To make sure we're safe."

Pathetic. He sounded like a child explaining the absence of a plate of cookies while crumbs covered their face.

Finn arched a brow. "Right," he said slowly. Too slowly. "It's just...I never see you leave or come back."

Cedric gave a half-hearted shrug, still not meeting Finn's gaze.

Finn tilted his head. "And when do you sleep?"

Cedric's mind raced, scrambling for a plausible explanation. Of course, he should have considered that he'd need sleep as a part of his excuse. Amateur mistake. He could almost hear Gwenna's voice in his head: *You should've stuck to flirting.*

Swallowing hard, he turned back around, keeping his expression carefully neutral. *Think. Quickly.*

"I sleep mostly during the day," he said at last. True enough—for now. "And I'm quiet about it. Otherwise, Clarence would start screaming at me every time I moved." He forced a small chuckle, hoping to steer the conversation somewhere lighter.

Finn didn't laugh.

Instead, he studied Cedric with those sharp, stormy eyes, searching. The scrutiny made Cedric's skin feel too tight. He needed to redirect this conversation *now*.

"Hey," Cedric said suddenly, his voice overly bright, "it's a clear night. I should show you something Gwenna and I have been working on."

The knight's eyebrows rose at the abrupt change in subject. "What?"

"Come on." Cedric jerked his head toward the door. "We have to go to the roof of the tower, though."

Finn hesitated, clearly weighing whether to let Cedric slip out of answering his questions. Then, with a sigh, he relented. "All right, but if this is an excuse to throw me off the roof, you're going to have to try harder than Clarence."

Cedric huffed a quiet laugh, relieved by the reprieve. "Tempting," he quipped, "but no."

He led Finn up the winding spiral staircase, the wooden steps creaking beneath their boots. The climb was steep, and Finn slowed halfway up, rolling his shoulders with a wince. Cedric immediately regretted bringing him up here so soon after his injury.

"Sorry. Maybe I shouldn't drag you to the roof when you're still recovering," Cedric said apologetically.

"I'll be fine. You can drag me anywhere." Finn grinned at him as they reached another landing. "I'm not as fragile as that blow to the head would have you believe."

Cedric blinked, trying and failing to shove down the ridiculous warmth rising in his chest.

He turned away quickly, pretending to focus on unlatching the final door. The last thing he needed was Finn saying things like that, looking at him like that, when Cedric's mind was still tangled from their moment in the workshop.

When they reached the rooftop, the night stretched out endlessly. The stars burned against the velvet-dark sky, the moon casting a pale glow over the stone battlements.

But Cedric's focus was elsewhere.

Near the edge of the roof, their telescope gleamed in the moonlight, crafted from polished brass and dark wood. Gwenna's masterpiece. He had helped where he could, carving and assembling the wooden parts, but the real genius was hers.

Finn's brow furrowed, though his eyes lit with interest.

"This is it," Cedric said, resting his hand on the scope. He felt a swell of pride, not just in the craftsmanship but in the countless hours they had spent working on it. "Mostly Gwenna's work. I helped with a few things, but she's the brains behind it."

Finn cocked his head. "What is it?"

Cedric blinked, momentarily caught in the way the moonlight traced over the sharp angles of Finn's face. Then he remembered—of course, Finn had no idea what he was looking at. "It's called a telescope," Cedric explained, giving the polished wood a light tap. "It lets you see the stars more clearly. We saw a shooting star a few weeks ago."

The knight's brows rose. "Really? Can I try it?"

A grin tugged at Cedric's lips. Finn's enthusiasm was surprisingly endearing. "Of course."

He crouched beside the telescope, adjusting the small brass gears at the base, aligning it with the sky. "Gwenna wanted a better way to study the stars. We've been working on it for months. It's not perfect yet, but..." He peered through the eyepiece, made a minor adjustment, then stepped back. "Go ahead. Take a look."

Finn slipped past him, moving in close as he eased down to the eyepiece. A breath of silence—then an audible gasp. "Is that...the moon?"

Cedric chuckled, folding his arms across his chest as he watched Finn take in the sight. "It is."

Finn continued to study the moon, brow furrowed in quiet concentration. "I knew it had splotches on it. But I never knew they looked like that."

"Craters," Cedric said softly. "Those are called craters."

Finn pulled back to look at him, eyes glinting with something between curiosity and admiration. "How do you know all this?"

Cedric cleared his throat. "Gwenna and I have been studying the sky for years. And that's not all." He gestured toward the telescope. "Before you came here, we were tracking some of the nearby planets. Did you know they have moons, too?"

Finn blinked, clearly caught off guard. "I thought everything up there was just...stars."

Cedric grinned, shaking his head. "There's so much more than meets the eye."

He sat down on the low wall that lined the top of the tower, cool stone pressing into his palms. A quiet thrill rippled through him when Finn stepped away from the telescope and sat down nearby.

For a time, they simply sat there, the silence between them comfortable rather than strained. The sky stretched above them, glittering with a thousand tiny lights, as if the universe itself was listening.

Then Finn spoke, his voice quieter now. "Speaking of more than meets the eye..." Cedric tensed. "Can I ask you something else?"

Cedric exhaled slowly, forcing himself to nod. "Go ahead."

Finn hesitated, as if carefully choosing his words. "Why did you give up being a prince? I mean, I know you said it was to protect Gwenna, but...was there more to it?"

Cedric stilled.

He could lie. He'd done it before. But for some reason, tonight, he wanted to offer a small truth.

A long pause stretched between them before Cedric finally said, "Part of it was for Gwenna, yes." His voice was even, which said more about his spectacular ability to suppress his emotions than anything else. "But...there was another reason."

He swallowed. A truth too long buried fought its way to the surface. Cedric half expected Finn to cut in with a barb, but the knight only watched him, really *listening*. "When everything fell apart, my parents were preparing to announce my betrothal to Princess Cassara Marovelle."

"She's Revendarian, right?" Finn asked.

Cedric took a slow, calming breath. "Yes. It was supposed to strengthen our alliance with Revendar, to keep the Avalisians from creeping in at their borders. And more than that, it would have secured access to their Revendarian steel."

The knight cocked his head. "That would have been a huge benefit for us."

"Yes," Cedric agreed, then cleared his throat before continuing. "But after the attack...everything changed. And when the people wanted someone to blame, they looked to Revendar. My marriage—our peace—burned to the ground with my parents. If I had stayed, they might have forced it anyway, but it wouldn't have mattered."

By the furrow of Finn's brow, he understood the connection immediately. "Ah. I've done my fair share of time at the border. Not right to marry you off to a kingdom half the realm thinks is the enemy, anyway."

Cedric's jaw clenched. He wanted to blurt, *I think Revendar is innocent*, but that would lead to *far* too many questions. So instead, he sidestepped to another aspect of the issue. "Even without that, I wasn't looking forward to such a marriage. Even if the treaty had held, it wouldn't have been right—to her or to me. I'm not interested in princesses. Or any women, for that matter."

He braced himself for Finn's reaction. He glanced at the knight's face. And what he saw wasn't judgment. Wasn't surprise. Just...understanding.

"I see," Finn said simply. Then, after a beat, he added, "I'm attracted to both men and women myself."

Cedric hadn't expected that. He blinked, searching Finn's expression for any hint of jest, but there was none—just quiet honesty.

"...Oh." *Brilliant. Absolutely brilliant response, Cedric.*

Finn chuckled, shaking his head. "You look like I just told you I've got three heads."

Cedric let out a small breath, something like a chuckle caught at the edges. "No, I...just didn't expect you to say that."

Finn leaned back, arms resting on the stone ledge. "Well, I don't exactly announce it in every tavern I visit. But...I figured you should know."

Cedric wasn't sure what to say about that. Did he want to know? Yes. Did it complicate things? Also yes.

The star-dappled sky stretched wide and endless, but Finn was *right there*. Close enough that Cedric could feel his warmth, even with space between them.

He should look away. He should say *something*. Something safe, something neutral.

Instead, he looked at Finn.

Really looked at him.

The way the moonlight softened the sharp angles of his face. The quiet steadiness in his eyes, like he wasn't expecting anything—but he wasn't running from this either.

"...Thank you," Cedric murmured. The words felt too small for what he meant, but they were all he had.

Finn's gaze searched his, as if trying to read between the lines. "For what?"

For telling me. For trusting me. For making me feel—gods, I don't even know what I'm feeling. But all Cedric said was, "For being here."

The wind whispered around them, cool against Cedric's flushed skin. Finn's lips parted slightly. The quiet between them wasn't empty—it was heavy and charged.

Finn was so close now. Close enough that Cedric could see the way his breath slowed, the way his pupils dilated, the way his hand—resting so casually on the ledge—clenched, as if resisting the urge to move.

It would be so easy. Too easy. And yet, the thought of closing that distance didn't feel reckless. It didn't feel like a mistake.

It felt inevitable.

Before Cedric could overthink it, he swooped in. His hand came up to cup Finn's jaw, the knight's stubble rough against his palm. Their lips met in a tentative brush that quickly turned into more when Finn responded.

He leaned in, deepening the kiss, and Cedric felt as if he might catch fire from the inside out. The world narrowed, the cold night air vanishing beneath the searing heat blazing through him.

Finn's hand came up, fingers tangling in Cedric's long hair. He memorized the way Finn tasted, the way he breathed against him, the way every worry, every wall, every carefully kept secret momentarily melted away into nothingness.

For the first time in years, Cedric allowed himself to *forget*. To *want*. To simply *feel*.

The warmth of Finn's lips still burned against Cedric's own when reality returned, as sudden as a kick to the head.

He jerked back, air punching from his lungs. His back hit the cold stone, hands splayed as if to brace against the world tilting beneath him. His breath came hard, ragged, like he'd been running.

Idiot.

Cedric's pulse roared in his ears, drowning out the sounds of the night. "I'm sorry," he choked out, the words like ash on his tongue. *What have I done?*

Finn's hand caught his. "Don't apologize." Finn's voice was gravel wrapped in velvet, low enough to make Cedric's traitorous heart lurch. "I wanted that, too."

Cedric's heart *soared* at those words—and promptly plummeted, torn between impossible hope and crushing dread. The unshaken look in Finn's eyes carved through him, deep and aching. Cedric wanted to believe it. *Gods*, he *wanted*.

He wanted to pull Finn in again, to drown in the warmth

of him, to forget for just one more moment that he was a monster. But his mind screamed at him to stop. To protect them both.

"Finn, I..." His voice fractured. The confession tore at him—*dragon, curse, monster*—but fear sealed his lips, cold as iron shackles. "There's so much you don't know about me."

"Then tell me." Finn's thumb traced the curve of Cedric's palm. "Whatever it is, you can trust me."

Tell him how your bones snap and reshape at dawn. How the very tower we stand on blurs into clouds beneath your wings.

How you scorched your own parents to cinders.

Cedric's golden-brown hair clung to his damp temples as he shook his head, hard, too hard, like he could shake off the truth itself. A loose strand caught on his lashes. He swiped it away, voice little more than a whisper. "I can't."

He wrenched his hand free. The sudden absence of contact felt like a bruise.

Finn's face fell. Not anger. Not rejection. Just...hurt. A flinch, quick as a spark before resolve hardened his features. "Whatever you're hiding...whatever you're afraid of...it doesn't change how I feel about you."

Cedric's throat closed. *How I feel about you.*

The words were a lance through Cedric's chest. He lurched away, boots scraping against grit-strewn flagstones.

You'd drive a sword through my heart if you knew.

His laugh came out brittle, edged with hysteria. "You don't know what you're saying." Cedric turned away, wishing in that moment to sprout his dragon wings so he could fly far away. "You don't know me. Not really."

"Then *let* me know you—" The knight stepped forward, the plea in his voice almost undoing Cedric completely. "Cedric, please..."

But Cedric was already backing away, shaking his head, his breath coming too fast, too ragged. "I'm sorry, Finn. I truly am. But this...whatever this is between us...it can't happen."

It was a mercy, he told himself. A clean cut, before Finn could get any closer. Before he could figure out the truth.

Before Cedric ruined *everything*.

Finn's expression twisted, as if he wanted to argue, but Cedric didn't wait to hear what he had to say. He pivoted, his boots thudding against the stone floor as he fled down the spiral staircase.

By the time he pushed through the tower's door and into the night, he didn't know where to go. The stars spun overhead, sharp and cold against the dark sky. He was suffocating. His skin itched with the reminder that morning would come all too soon, that the transformation would rip through him once more, shattering the fragile pieces of his humanity.

The stables.

Without thinking, he stumbled inside, pressing himself against the rough wooden wall as a strangled sound escaped his throat—half a sob, half a breath he couldn't quite catch. *Stupid. Stupid.* He had let himself hope. Let himself believe, just for a moment, that there was a future where Finn could see him—*all of him*—and not turn away in disgust.

He pressed the heels of his hands against his eyes, as if he could scrub away the memory of Finn's warmth, the way his lips had felt *right*, like something Cedric had been missing his entire life.

What a fool he had been.

Because there was no future.

Not for him. Not for *them*.

Cedric had been lying to himself, and worse, he had strung Finn along with him, letting him believe this could be something real. But it wasn't. It couldn't be.

Maybe it would have been easier if Finn had killed the dragon, just as he was meant to.

Chapter Fifteen

Two days. Two agonizing days had passed since that moment on the tower roof. Finn paced the narrow length of his small room, his mind replaying the events for what felt like the thousandth time. Cedric's breath hitching against his lips, the faint tremor in the prince's fingers where they'd brushed Finn's collarbone. The memory of Cedric's hair slipping through his grip haunted him, silken strands dissolving into empty air.

Finn dragged a hand through his own tangled hair. His frustration twisted tighter with each passing moment. He'd hardly seen Cedric since that night. The other man had become a ghost, appearing only for brief moments at mealtimes before vanishing again, as elusive as mist in the morning sun. Even when they occupied the same space, Cedric refused to meet his gaze, responding to Finn's attempts at conversation with clipped, one-word answers.

It was *maddening*.

Even now, the ghost of that kiss burned. *There's so much you don't know.* Cedric's voice echoed, hoarse and frayed at the edges, as it had that night. Finn's gut twisted. What was he hiding? A past lover? A forced vow? A debt owed in blood? His mind chased possibilities, each one more ridiculous than the last. An illness? A threat hanging over his head? Gods, was he a spy, playing some long game Finn hadn't even begun to understand?

Finn scoffed at himself. That last thought was ridiculous, but the frustration remained. He couldn't keep going in circles, trapped in this limbo of uncertainty and unspoken feelings. He needed answers, and he was going to get them, even if he had to drag them out of Cedric himself.

With renewed determination, Finn strode out of his room. He checked the main living area first, where he found only Gwenna, bent over an odd contraption of brass and glass that looked suspiciously like the telescope Cedric had shown him. Tools and bits of parchment cluttered the table in front of her, gears and tiny mechanisms scattered like puzzle pieces. She looked up as he entered, her sharp gaze assessing him immediately.

"Have you seen Cedric?" Finn asked, forgoing pleasantries entirely.

Gwenna sighed, setting aside a tool that looked like it belonged in a blacksmith's forge rather than a former princess's hands. "Finn, I don't think—"

"For the love of the gods, Gwenna, just let me talk to him," Finn interrupted.

She straightened, crossing her arms, and something about the way she studied him set Finn on edge. "What happened?" she asked.

Finn stiffened. *Too perceptive.* "Nothing."

Gwenna's lips pressed into a thin line. "You're a terrible liar."

Finn grimaced, dragging a hand through his hair. "Tell me something I don't already know," he muttered, more to himself than her. He didn't meet her gaze, focusing instead on the scuffed floor. "Look, it doesn't matter. I just need to find him."

She studied him, clearly debating her response. Then she set her tool aside with a *clank* against the table. "He's in his workshop. But Finn..." She hesitated, something shadowed behind her eyes. "There are things you don't understand."

"Then maybe someone should start explaining," he snapped, unable to curb his frustration.

Gwenna's expression didn't change, but she sighed, shaking her head. "If Cedric hasn't told you, then it's not my place."

Finn's jaw clenched. Another wall. Another locked door. "Thanks for the help," he said, not quite meaning it.

"Finn," Gwenna called after him.

He stopped, exhaling sharply before glancing back.

She held his gaze, her arms still crossed. Still wary. "Be careful with him," she said finally. "If you hurt my brother..."

He raised his brows. "You'll hit me in the head with another rock?"

Gwenna aimed a pleasant smile at him. "I'll make that feel like a love tap." She winked, then went back to her tinkering.

"Understood." Though hurting Cedric...that was the last thing he wanted to do.

The walk to Cedric's workshop felt both interminable and far too short. With every step, his thoughts raced ahead of him. *What if Cedric refuses to talk? What if the answers I get aren't the ones I want?* A part of him feared what lay at the heart of all this secrecy, but fear wasn't enough to stop him.

Before he could second-guess himself, Finn reached the workshop door. He took a fortifying breath, clenching his fists at his sides for a moment before knocking.

A pause. Then Cedric's voice, soft through the thick wooden door: "Go away, Finn."

Finn swallowed and squared his shoulders. Not the answer he wanted, but it was a start. "How did you know it was me?"

"Because Gwenna and Clarence don't knock," came the muffled response.

Cocking his head, Finn considered barging in. But something about that didn't feel right. He wanted Cedric to make that choice. "You know, I could take that as an invitation to stop knocking altogether."

Another pause—longer this time. A beat of hesitation so thick Finn could feel it pressing against the door. Then, finally, the latch clicked, and the door creaked open.

Cedric stood silhouetted against the warm lamplight, the sharp planes of his face cast in soft shadow. Finn's breath caught. He looked tired. Not just exhausted, but worn through, like fabric stretched too thin—dark circles under his golden-brown eyes, hair disheveled.

"Sir Finnian," Cedric said, his voice crisp, the formality deliberate. Finn could hear the careful distance in it, the way Cedric wielded his title like a shield. "Now's not a good time."

Finn's jaw clenched. "It's never going to be a good time if you keep avoiding me," he shot back, pushing past Cedric into the workshop. The scent of sawdust and oil filled the space, mingling with something faintly smoky. Finn turned to face him, arms crossing over his chest, determined to hold his ground. "We need to talk about what happened."

Behind him, Cedric sighed, the sound heavy, edged with something dangerously close to defeat. The door clicked shut, and when Finn glanced back, Cedric was leaning against it, arms braced as if physically holding himself in place. Like if he let go, he might do something reckless. Like if he let go, he might come *closer.* After a moment, he retreated from the door, giving Finn a wide berth as he moved closer to his workbench.

"There's nothing to talk about." Cedric's voice was flat, controlled—except for the tiniest waver, a hairline fracture in its icy composure.

"Nothing to talk about?" Finn repeated, incredulous. "Cedric, you *kissed* me. *We* kissed. And then you ran away like the place was on fire and have been avoiding me ever since. I think that warrants at least a *conversation*."

Cedric turned away, silent, though Finn caught a tremor in his shoulders.

"Is it because you're a prince and I'm just a knight?" Finn challenged.

Cedric's head snapped up, startled. "*What?* No, of course not."

"Then *what is it?*" Finn stepped closer. "What are you so afraid of?"

"I'm *not* afraid," Cedric whispered, but his voice trembled, betraying the lie.

Finn seized on it, stepping into Cedric's space. "Then *why?*" His voice softened, insistent but laced with something dangerously close to hope. "Why push me away if you're not afraid?"

Something inside Cedric *snapped*. With a frustrated growl, he shoved past Finn, the sudden movement forcing Finn to catch himself against the workbench.

"Cedric—"

But Cedric was already storming out of the workshop, as if sheer distance might rid him of the conversation entirely.

Oh, no. Finn narrowed his eyes. He wasn't about to let him go that easily.

Finn was on Cedric's heels instantly. And gods, Cedric was *fast* when he wanted to be, even at a walk. Finn almost had to jog to keep up as the prince beat a retreat toward the stable. Cedric shoved the door open.

Finn followed without thinking, slipping inside just as Cedric spun to face him again. The lantern light caught in

Cedric's hair, turning it molten gold. His face was a storm of emotions.

"Can't you take a hint?" Cedric ground out.

Finn exhaled sharply, then shrugged, his lips quirking just enough to be infuriating. "I did. That's why I kissed you back."

Cedric froze.

The air between them stilled.

For a moment, the only sounds were the sleepy shuffle of Ghost in her stall, the occasional creak of wood settling around them. Cedric's chest rose and fell like a man who'd run for his life. His hands twitched into fists at his sides, tension coiling through every muscle.

Finn held his ground, resisting the urge to close the space between them. He had already pushed enough. This choice had to be Cedric's.

For a heartbeat, he thought Cedric might run again.

Then...a single step. A hint of hesitation. And finally...a decision.

Cedric lunged forward, and Finn barely had time to suck in a breath before the prince's mouth was on him, fierce and unrelenting. Cedric's hands fisted in Finn's shirt, pushing him backward. Finn's back hit the stable wall, rough wood snagging his shirt as Cedric pressed against him, their bodies maddeningly close.

This kiss was nothing like the one atop the tower. That had been hesitant, uncertain—a question neither of them had dared to answer. But this? This was raw, undeniable. Cedric's tongue swept into Finn's mouth, hot and demanding, claiming him with a hunger that left Finn's knees weak. Finn's hands found Cedric's waist, fingers digging into the fabric of his tunic, pulling him closer.

Finn's lungs burned, air forgotten, as Cedric's breath whispered against him. A salty tear droplet slid between their pressed lips—Finn didn't know if it was his own or Cedric's, only that it tasted like grief. When they finally broke apart, gasping, Finn didn't let go. He rested his forehead against Cedric's. The prince trembled.

"I should...we should stop."

"Why stop now?" Finn whispered back, a teasing lilt in his tone that couldn't quite mask the desperation beneath. He offered a lopsided grin, a silent plea for Cedric to hold on as tightly as Finn was holding on to him. His thumb traced Cedric's lower lip, still wet and reddened from their kiss.

Cedric made a soft, frustrated huff. "Even if it leads us both into trouble?"

Finn's grin didn't waver. "*Especially* then. I'm adventurous." His laughter faded quickly, replaced by a vulnerability that stripped away the bravado. "Please, Cedric. Don't push me away again. I can't stand the thought of going back to that distance between us."

Cedric's lashes lifted, revealing eyes glassy with tears, gold-flecked irises churning like storm-wrecked seas. "Finn, I...I *can't*," Cedric choked out, his voice hoarse, cracking like something breaking apart inside him.

"Yes, you can," Finn insisted, his hands coming up to cup Cedric's face, thumbs brushing over damp skin. He held him there, refusing to let him retreat into himself again. "Whatever it is you're afraid of, whatever secret you're keeping...we can face it *together*. Just *let me in*."

Cedric's breath shuddered against Finn's lips. Finn had never seen him look so vulnerable—his eyes wide with fear, desire, raw need that begged to be spoken.

"You don't know what you're asking," Cedric whispered, his voice barely audible.

"Then *tell* me," Finn urged. He could feel the slight tremor in Cedric's body, the tension thrumming beneath his skin. "Whatever it is, it can't be worse than this. This limbo, this—" He swallowed, his grip tightening. "This thing where you keep running from me like you don't *want* this."

Cedric flinched, his shoulders drawing in as if to make himself smaller. His lips parted, hesitation warring with the truth, clawing to escape. "I want to tell you," he admitted, so softly it was nearly lost to the night. His gaze found Finn's, filled with a haunting sadness that stole the air from Finn's lungs. "I *really* do."

Finn stilled, waiting.

"I just...I need time," Cedric whispered. "To think about it."

Time. Finn could work with that. It wasn't rejection—it wasn't another door slammed between them. It wasn't Cedric disappearing into the dark and pretending none of this had ever happened. Time meant there was still a chance.

"I'll give you all the time you need," Finn whispered. "But tonight, just *be with me.* No secrets, no shadows—just you and me."

A long pause. Then Cedric sighed, running a hand through his hair, his fingers tangling briefly in the strands. "You make it sound so simple."

"It *is* simple." Finn loosened his grip, giving him the space to leave—but Cedric didn't pull away.

He waited, heart pounding, watching the war flicker behind Cedric's eyes. A choice balanced on a knife's edge.

"Finn." The name was spoken like a decision. Or maybe a plea.

Finn's pulse jumped. "Yeah?"

Cedric swallowed, his hand resting against Finn's chest, thumb grazing his collarbone in a touch so light it sent a shiver through him. "It's been a while since I've been with anyone. Too long."

Before Finn could respond, Cedric's shoulders eased, a quiet surrender, like giving up a battle he never wanted to fight. "I want this." His voice was steadier now, though his fingers still rested where they had landed, as if waiting for permission. "I want *you*."

A rush of desire shot through Finn at the words. "Then let's make up for lost time."

A TINY VOICE in the back of Cedric's head screamed a warning, even as he closed the distance between himself and the knight. This was *dangerous*. Cedric knew it all the way to his marrows. But it had been so long since someone had looked at him the way Finn did. Since someone wanted him —not the prince he once was, not the monster he sometimes became, but *him*.

And gods help him, Cedric *deserved* this, didn't he? *I've hidden away in these woods for years with only my sister and goats for company. I shouldn't feel wrong to want...more.*

This time, he didn't hesitate.

Cedric yanked his tunic over his head. His pulse hammered in his throat as the cool night air kissed his exposed skin. Every nerve ending felt alive, hypersensitive after years of denying himself this kind of vulnerability. The warning voice in his head tried to speak again—*what if he sees the golden scales that sometimes shimmer beneath your skin, what if he knows what you are*—but Cedric silenced it.

He tossed the tunic aside, and with it, another excuse to hide. Cedric swallowed, meeting Finn's gaze. There was steel in his eyes, and gods...so much desire. It nearly took Cedric's breath away.

He came to kill you, that insidious voice deep within whispered again. *That hasn't changed. Nothing will ever change that. Not even this.*

"Gods, you're beautiful," Finn whispered, as if he were examining a masterpiece and not Cedric.

The reverence in his words was enough to shove the

voice in Cedric's head down for good. He closed the gap between them.

CEDRIC HEAVED A SHAKY BREATH, hand trailing up Finn's back in a slow, lazy drag. An unfamiliar warmth filled him, a contentedness he hadn't felt in years. Not just from the intimacy, but from the safety of the knight's arms. The wanting and acceptance. Cedric hadn't known how much he needed that.

For several minutes, only the soft hitch of them catching their breath broke the quiet. They lay tangled in the afterglow, satisfied.

Then Cedric gave a soft sigh. "Told you."

Finn let out a soft chuckle, lifting his head to meet Cedric's gaze. "Told me what?"

Cedric's fingers traced idle patterns against Finn's sweat-damp skin. "That you're mine."

Finn grinned. "Damn right, I am."

The possessive ferocity in the knight's voice made something inside Cedric squeeze in all the best ways. He tucked himself closer to Finn, to the comfort of his warmth. No more words. Just closeness. Just *this*.

Sleep had almost claimed him when Cedric heard Finn's voice, soft as a prayer. "Goodnight, my prince."

FINN STIRRED, wakefulness returning in fragments—the prickling straw beneath his side, the dull ache blooming along his ribs. Perhaps a night of passion while recovering from his injuries wasn't advisable, but he had no regrets.

Sunlight slithered through the thin slats of the stable walls, gilding motes of dust that danced above him. He stretched, relishing the slow burn of spent pleasure, the ghost of Cedric's smile still vivid in his mind.

But when he curled closer to the space where Cedric should have been...he wasn't there.

Finn rubbed a hand over his face. "Cedric?" he called. Surely he hadn't gone far.

A deep, ragged gasp came in answer. No, a *whimper*. Finn bolted upright, his breath hitching, hay needling his scalp as his head snapped toward the source.

Light caught on gold. A massive shape shuddered in the open area of the stable, muscles seizing, limbs trembling with the effort of supporting its own weight. Finn knew what he was looking at. But his mind refused to accept it.

Not possible. Not real. It couldn't be.

A dragon—no, not just *a* dragon. *THE* dragon. The monster Finn had sworn to kill.

The creature scrambled unsteadily to its feet, its wingtips dragging against the stable floor. Finn's body locked up, every muscle frozen, every nerve screaming at him to move, to fight, to run—but he couldn't.

Because those *eyes*. Cedric's eyes. Gold-flecked, raw with emotion. Haunted. *Familiar*.

Finn's stomach twisted, nausea rising. *This is Cedric.*

No. This is a *lie*.

He staggered to his feet, almost tripping on the pile of discarded clothing. Finn's clothing. Cedric's clothing.

Finn had kissed Cedric. Had let himself fall for him. Had let himself believe... And the whole time, Cedric had been the very thing Finn had sworn to destroy.

Finn reeled, his breath shattering from his lungs. A betrayal so vast it stole the air from the room. "You *lied* to me." The accusation ripped from his throat, splintering like bone.

The dragon—*Cedric*—made a keening, grieving noise that didn't belong in the throat of a monster. A raw, searing ache tore through Finn. He had *trusted* Cedric. He had loved him, or at least—he had let himself begin to.

"I let myself be yours," Finn choked out. The words dripped acid, searing his tongue. His throat burned. "I thought we—"

He stopped himself, biting down on the words before he could say something even more damning, even more foolish.

Cedric took a step backward, tail tip bumping the stable wall. His head was low, wings bunched, the posture of a creature feeling shame and regret. Cedric refused to meet his gaze. He made a soft rumble, then spun, shoving the stable doors open with a foreclaw.

A part of Finn wanted to stop him. To demand answers. To make Cedric stay and *face* what he had done. But the hurt was too fresh, the wound too raw. Finn couldn't think, couldn't breathe, couldn't do *anything* except watch in helpless agony as Cedric scrambled away from him.

Finn stumbled after him, as if he might bodily stop the dragon, dressed as he was in absolutely nothing—because why stop making bad choices now? Golden scales rippled as Cedric pivoted, and the thunderclap of his wings almost knocked Finn off his feet.

Cedric soared into the sky, his golden form shrinking against the dawn. Finn stood there, his heart shattering to bits as he watched Cedric disappear into the light.

His father was dead because of that dragon. Because of *Cedric.*

The images flickered in his mind like cruel flashes of memory—Cedric laughing beside him at dinner. Cedric's lips against his own in the dark. Cedric's hands guiding his as they carved wood together.

Then—Cedric's golden wings. His massive claws. His fanged maw.

Finn's father crushed beneath rubble.

A broken sound escaped Finn's lips as his entire world crumbled beneath him.

Betrayal.

Confusion.

Rage.

And worst of all, a deep, aching sorrow that he didn't know what to do with. Because even now, even after all of it —he still wanted Cedric. And he hated himself for it.

Chapter Sixteen

Finn trembled as he saddled Ghost, his fingers clumsy, betraying the turmoil raging inside him. The stable, which had been a place of warmth and whispered confessions mere hours ago, now felt suffocating, its walls closing in around him. Every shadow in the dim morning light twisted into the shape of golden scales, every rustle of straw an echo of wings unfurling.

I have to get out of here.

His breath came unevenly as he tugged the girth tighter than necessary, and Ghost shifted beneath him with a disgruntled snort, ears flicking back in protest. Finn forced himself to pause, dragging in a shaky breath as he loosened the girth a notch. He couldn't afford to fall apart now. He needed to leave—needed distance, space to think, to *breathe.*

But no matter how far he rode, the name tangled in his thoughts like roots too deep to tear free:

Cedric.

The thought of him sent another violent pang through Finn. He squeezed his eyes shut, willing it away, but the images came unbidden—the press of Cedric's lips, the

178

warmth of his body, the quiet, stolen moments between them. Moments Finn had thought were *real*.

And yet...

The same Cedric, wings spread wide in the morning sun, golden and terrible. The same Cedric, fleeing into the sky, leaving nothing behind but shattered trust.

A hollow ache spread through Finn, a weight settling in his chest that no amount of deep breathing could dislodge.

Ghost shifted again, sensing his unrest, and Finn forced his hands to still, smoothing a palm down the mare's neck. "Easy, girl," he murmured, though it was himself he was trying to soothe. "We just need to go."

He had already retrieved his things from inside the tower—his pack slung over his shoulder, filled with what little he had brought on this mission. His enchanted armor, his coin purse, a few supplies. And most importantly, Sunwrath. The sword's presence was reassuring against his back, but now Finn felt like a traitor, unable to wield the sword as he'd vowed. He imagined swinging the blade at Cedric-as-dragon. Would he dance away as before, parry the incoming attack? Or would he take the blow and end the agony between them?

Finn swallowed hard, shoving the thought away.

With a final check of the saddle, he led Ghost out into the courtyard.

The sun had fully risen now, casting long shadows across the ground, and the light—*gods, the light*—caught on the stones with a golden hue that mirrored Cedric's scales too perfectly. Finn gritted his teeth and tore his gaze away, forcing himself to focus on the task at hand.

His muscles remembered the motions even as his mind spiraled.

As Ghost moved out, Finn couldn't stop himself from glancing back at the tower, his gut twisting. The windows were dark, offering no sign of life. No Cedric waiting in the doorway with regret in his eyes. No Gwenna storming out, demanding answers.

Maybe she was still asleep.

Or maybe—maybe she *knew*.

Finn exhaled sharply, willing the thought away. It didn't matter. He didn't have time to face Gwenna, to ferret out her part in this tangled mess. Not now.

He nudged Ghost forward. As they passed through into the trees, Finn looked over his shoulder one last time. He wasn't just leaving the tower behind. Finn was leaving behind every foolish, naïve part of himself that had dared to believe there could be something more.

The only sounds were the rhythmic thud of Ghost's hooves against the dirt, the distant birdsong, and the occasional whisper of leaves shifting in the breeze. Finn should have found solace in the quiet. But his thoughts refused to settle. They looped back, again and again, forcing him to relive everything he believed—everything Cedric had shattered.

The first time he had seen Cedric, standing in the market, quiet and wary. Had he *known* then who Finn was? What he had come to do?

The tentative trust that had grown between them, now tainted beyond recognition.

How much of it had been real? And how much had been a carefully crafted deception?

Finn wanted to believe in the moments that had felt unguarded—the way Cedric had looked at him, the way he had *touched* him. But then he remembered the attack on Solavere Palace. The fire, the screams.

A fresh wave of nausea surged through him. His grip tightened on the reins. *How do I reconcile this?*

Because the dragon that had killed his father, the dragon Finn had sworn to destroy, should not have been the same man who had kissed him with such aching tenderness. It didn't make *sense*.

Finn couldn't shake the image of Cedric's dragon form in the stable, *hunched* and *miserable*, golden eyes filled with sorrow and something dangerously close to fear. That wasn't the posture of a mindless, bloodthirsty beast.

Finn stared at Ghost's wind-tousled mane. His mind was still churning when he looked up and realized the road ahead had split. To the left—the path back to Lunareth's capital. To the right—the road curved back toward the village, toward the abandoned outpost, toward answers he wasn't sure he was ready to face.

Finn hesitated, his heart urging him to turn back, to demand answers from Cedric. But what good would it do? The truth had been laid bare in the stable, gleaming in the morning light. Cedric had lied to him. Not just a small lie, not something forgivable—this had been a deception so vast, so unthinkable, that Finn could scarcely wrap his mind around it.

He blew out a soft breath, willing the shaking in his hands to subside. He needed to focus on his duty. That was all that mattered now. He was a knight of the realm, sworn to protect his people, sworn to serve the king. He had been given a task, and he had failed.

Finn had *failed*.

The depth of that failure squeezed the air from his lungs. He was going to have to face the consequences.

With a heavy heart, Finn guided Ghost to the left. The mare obeyed without hesitation, carrying him farther and farther from the place that had so briefly felt like something more than a mission.

As they continued down the path to the capital, Finn's mind turned to the task ahead. He had to report to King Darius, to inform him that Princess Gwenna had been found, and that she was safe. But what of Cedric?

Finn's stomach churned at the thought of revealing Cedric's secret. The idea felt wrong, like a betrayal, but wasn't it his duty? Hadn't he sworn an oath to his kingdom? He had been sent to slay a dragon, and instead, he had...

Finn clenched his jaw.

He couldn't even put it into words.

And if he told the king? If he dared to speak the truth *aloud?*

Finn could already picture the reaction. The king's fury. The mobilization of an army. Hunters, wizards, knights— every resource thrown toward eradicating the golden beast.

A fresh wave of nausea swept over Finn.

No.

He couldn't do it. Not yet. Not until he knew more. Not until he understood why Cedric had attacked Solavere Palace. He needed the truth—the *real* truth, not the stories traded in taverns or the fearful whispers of courtiers. And he would find it.

But first, he had to explain himself.

How was he supposed to justify returning empty-handed? How would he make the king understand Gwenna wasn't some lost damsel in need of rescue? That she had carved out a life for herself, one she had no desire to leave behind? Finn wasn't sure how he would frame the truth, but he knew one thing: King Darius would not be pleased.

These thoughts plagued him as he rode. The forest thinned, giving way to rolling hills and scattered farmsteads, but Finn barely registered the changing scenery. His thoughts remained a tangled mess.

By the time the sun dipped toward the horizon, exhaustion had settled deep in his bones. His limbs ached, his head throbbed, and the gnawing emptiness in his stomach had become impossible to ignore. When he spotted a small inn nestled at the foot of a hill, relief swept over him like a wave.

He guided Ghost toward it, dismounting with stiff limbs.

The scent of roasting meat drifted to him. It should have been comforting. Instead, it made his stomach twist, dredging up memories of the last meal he'd shared with Cedric and Gwenna—the warmth of their laughter, the way Cedric's eyes had lingered on him when he thought Finn wasn't looking.

Finn swallowed hard and pushed the thought away.

The innkeeper, a broad-shouldered man with a bushy mustache and a well-worn apron, glanced up from wiping down the counter. His eyes flicked to Finn's sword and enchanted armor, and his brows lifted with interest. "Well now, you're a long way from the capital," he said, setting the rag aside. "Not often we get knights passing through."

Finn forced a weary smile. "I don't need any fanfare, just a place to rest for the night. Do you have a room available?"

The innkeeper gave a knowing chuckle. "A bed and four walls? That I can do. The hayloft's open, if you're feeling nostalgic for hard travel. But I'm guessing a real mattress is more to your liking?"

Finn exhaled, the hint of amusement tugging at his exhaustion. "A mattress would be preferable."

"Good choice," the man said, already reaching under the counter for a key. "And your horse? We've got a sturdy stable out back, fresh hay, and my daughter's been fussing over the animals all evening—your steed will be spoiled rotten before sunrise." He slid the key across the counter. "Supper's still hot if you're hungry. Bread's fresh, stew's decent. Drink's extra, unless you look pitiful enough, in which case my wife will probably take pity and pour you one anyway."

Finn nodded, feeling like little more than an actor reciting lines. "Yes, please. Whatever you have will be fine."

After settling Ghost in the stable with fresh oats and water, Finn made his way into the inn's common room. The warmth from the hearth wrapped around him, the scent of stew thick in the air. A few farmers sat in the corner nursing their tankards, speaking in low, familiar tones, utterly unaware of the storm raging inside him.

He dropped into a chair near the fire, grateful for its heat, but the flames did little to chase away the cold that had settled in his heart.

Moments later, a kindly woman with greying hair approached, placing a steaming bowl of stew and a thick slice of crusty bread in front of him. Her gaze softened as she studied him. "Eat up, dear," she said gently. "You look like you could use a good meal."

Finn thanked her, digging into the stew with more enthusiasm than he'd expected. The first bite was rich and savory, the warmth spreading through him, but the simple pleasure of food couldn't drive away the burning ache in his heart.

The fire crackled, its glow casting flickering shadows along the stone walls. A low buzz of conversation drifted from the other patrons, a quiet murmur of lives unburdened by impossible choices. The food sat heavy in his stomach.

He hadn't realized he'd stopped eating until a voice cut through his thoughts.

"You all right there, lad?"

Finn looked up, startled from his reverie. The innkeeper was watching him from across the bar, a cleaning rag in his hand, his brow furrowed in concern. "You seem troubled."

Finn hesitated, clutching the spoon like it was his sword. Then he sighed, rubbing a hand over his face. "Just... wrestling with a hard decision."

The innkeeper nodded sagely. "Ah, those are the worst kind." He leaned on the bar, as if offering wisdom were as natural as serving ale. "But you know what my old pa used to say? 'When your head and your heart don't agree, listen to your gut.'"

Finn huffed a quiet laugh. "And what if your gut is as confused as the rest of you?"

The innkeeper shrugged, offering a knowing smile.

"Then you're in for a rough night, I'm afraid. But morning always brings clarity, or so they say."

Finn didn't reply. He wasn't sure there was anything to say. The old man meant well, but Finn wasn't convinced that dawn would bring anything other than more doubt, more questions with no straightforward answers. More heartbreak.

With that bit of homespun wisdom, the innkeeper moved on, leaving Finn alone with his thoughts once more. His duty pulled him one way, his emotions another.

He knew what he was supposed to do. Duty wasn't meant to waver. Oaths weren't *supposed* to bend for golden eyes and quiet smiles, for hands that had traced his skin like he was something precious instead of something doomed.

His head told him the answer was simple—return to the capital, give his report, warn them all. But his *heart*—his heart ached with an unrelenting agony he had no right to feel. Not for a man he was supposed to call his enemy.

Finn had spent years believing that the dragon was a mindless monster, a scourge that needed to be eradicated for the safety of the realm. But Cedric was not mindless. He was not a beast driven only by hunger and destruction. He was a man—a man who had bled and suffered, who had loved and lost, who had looked at Finn with such raw vulnerability that it left him breathless.

Finn didn't know what to do with that knowledge.

As he made his way up to his rented room, the wooden stairs creaking beneath his boots, he longed for simpler days —days when his path had been clear, when he had known without doubt what was right. But Cedric had pulled Finn into something far more complicated than he had ever imagined.

Lying in bed, staring at the ceiling, sleep remained elusive despite his exhaustion. He could still feel the ghost of Cedric's touch, the way his lips had lingered on Finn's, as though torn between wanting and restraint. The warmth of his body, the hesitant way his fingers had traced along Finn's skin.

And then—*fear*.

Cedric had been afraid. Finn hadn't understood it at the time, but now...*now* he did.

Finn had been wrong. He had been so very, *terribly* wrong.

A lump rose in his throat as he swallowed against the truth clawing its way to the surface. Cedric had every *right* to be afraid.

Finn had been sent to *kill* him.

A shuddering breath escaped him, and he dragged a hand over his face, his mind racing in circles.

He had to return to Mirathen, yes. That much hadn't changed. He needed to speak to the king. But he wouldn't reveal Cedric's secret. He couldn't.

Instead, he would tell King Darius that Princess Gwenna was safe, but that she wasn't ready to return to court. It wasn't a lie—at least, not entirely. It would buy him time. Time to go back to the tower. Time to demand the truth from Cedric.

Time to understand.

Because despite everything—despite the lies, despite the betrayal, despite the firestorm raging in his mind—Finn knew one thing with certainty.

He *needed* to see Cedric.

Dragon or man, it didn't matter.

With that determined thought, Finn finally closed his eyes. Though sleep, when it came, brought little peace. His dreams were a chaotic swirl of golden scales and whispered names, of firelight kisses and the unbearable burden of an unsaid truth.

THE NEXT MORNING dawned clear and bright, the sunlight cutting through the haze of exhaustion clinging to him. Finn sat up slowly, rubbing the sleep from his eyes, his resolve crystallizing.

He dressed quickly, strapping Sunwrath back into place at his side. Downstairs, the scent of freshly baked bread and frying eggs filled the air. The innkeeper's wife offered him a warm smile as she placed a plate of eggs and toast before him. Finn managed a small nod of thanks, but his mind was already miles away.

He ate quickly, shoving food into his mouth without tasting it, then settled his tab and stepped outside. The crisp morning air bit at his skin, chasing away the last dregs of fatigue.

He mounted Ghost, feeling the mare shift beneath him, eager to move.

"Safe travels!" the innkeeper called from the doorway.

Finn gave a final nod, then spurred Ghost forward.

The miles passed in silence, the drum of hooves matching the racing tempo of his thoughts. He rehearsed his explanations. He had never been good at deception, but this time, he had no choice.

The familiar spires of Lunareth's capital loomed in the distance, the sun glinting off their stone facades. It should have felt like home. It should have brought him relief.

Instead, his stomach churned with unease.

Because, for the first time in his life, Finn wasn't sure where he truly belonged.

Chapter Seventeen

The forest canopy blurred beneath Cedric as he soared, his golden wings catching the last dying rays of the setting sun. The world below was a darkening sea of tree-tops, shifting in and out of focus as he pushed himself harder, faster, his wings carving through the cool air. He'd been flying for hours, tracing the jagged spine of the mountains in reckless, aimless patterns, chasing an escape that refused to come.

It was useless. No matter how far or fast he flew, he couldn't outrun the memory of Finn's face—the raw betrayal that had shattered the quiet intimacy of the night before. The shock, the hurt, the way Finn had stumbled back as though Cedric had struck him. And, gods, maybe he had. Maybe the truth had been more of a wound than claws ever could be.

The wind roared past him, whipping along the membranes of his wings, howling in his ears like a taunt. *You should have told him.*

He had known this moment would come. Had tried to push Finn away, had thrown up every barrier he could to prevent the inevitable.

And yet, in that stable, with Finn's warmth pressed against him, with the taste of his kiss still lingering like something sacred—Cedric had allowed himself to hope. *To believe.* To think that, just maybe, he could carve out something for himself in this life that wasn't loneliness or regret.

How utterly *foolish* he had been.

As the sun dipped beyond the horizon, Cedric knew he couldn't delay his return much longer. His naked human form would be too vulnerable at this altitude in the mountains.

Maybe he deserved it. He had misled Finn. Without a doubt, the knight would come back for his blood—no matter what whispered promises he'd made in the dark of night. Cedric glanced down at the snow-covered ridge. Maybe it would be a kindness to die of exposure.

But then Gwenna would be alone. And that knowledge, for all these years, had been the only thing that kept him clinging to this tortured life. His sister didn't know how many times he'd considered his own end. How many times the singular thought of Gwenna's hurt at his loss had stayed his hand.

He sucked in a rumbling breath. Gwenna was his anchor. If he returned for anyone, it was her.

With a heavy heart, Cedric angled downward, gliding toward a clearing close to the tower. His landing was far from graceful—his back legs hit first, claws digging deep furrows into the soft earth before his momentum carried him forward. His body pitched, wings flaring at the last moment to balance him. He trembled. His chest heaved with the effort, and every muscle in his body screamed in protest.

Then, before he could second-guess himself, the transformation took him.

Pain. It struck like lightning through every fiber of his being. Bones cracked and reformed, sinew pulling tight, limbs shrinking, reshaping. His scales melted into flesh, tail wisping into little more than golden effervescence. Cedric clenched his jaw, refusing to cry out, but his entire body convulsed as the last remnants of his dragon form vanished.

He deserved this pain.

When it was over, he lay curled on his side in the dirt, naked and shivering. His breath came in ragged gasps, his lungs burning. The cold surrounded him, but he made no effort to move. For a long moment, he simply lay there, face half-buried in the damp earth, listening to the rustle of the wind through the trees.

Maybe it would be easier to just stay here. Let the forest claim him. Maybe the earth would swallow him whole, and the pain would finally stop.

"Cedric?" The sound of his sister's voice shattered the quiet. Footsteps—running. "Oh, thank Rynvath's hunters! I've been worried sick!"

He belatedly registered Gwenna dropping to her knees beside him, her hands warm as they pressed against his bare skin, checking for injuries. The concern in her voice cut deeper than he wanted to admit.

Cedric forced his eyes open. Gwenna's face hovered above him, her expression a mixture of relief and frustration. She wasted no time in draping a cloak over his shaking shoulders.

"Can you stand?" she asked, her voice softer now, no less urgent. "I brought clothes."

Cedric swallowed, forcing himself to nod. The movement alone made his head spin. His limbs felt like waterlogged planks as Gwenna helped him into a sitting position. The simple act of pulling the linen shirt over his head was an ordeal.

But Gwenna's hands were sure as she guided him, her frustration a silent undercurrent beneath her movements. *She's angry.*

She was right to be.

The moment he was dressed, she straightened, crossing her arms over her chest. "Where is he?" she asked, voice tight with restrained emotion.

Cedric exhaled shakily, barely more than a whisper. "Gone."

Gwenna stiffened. "Gone?"

"He left at dawn." The words tasted bitter.

Gwenna's jaw clenched, her eyes flashing. "I'll kill him," she muttered under her breath. "I told you we couldn't trust him. I *knew* he'd—"

"No." Cedric cut her off, shaking his head. The motion made him sway, and he had to grip her arm to keep himself upright as they began the slow walk back to the tower. "It's not his fault." His voice was hoarse, raw with self-loathing. "I...I should have told him sooner."

Gwenna let out a sharp, humorless laugh. "Told him *what?* That you're the very creature he was sent to destroy so he could carry me off? Oh yes, I'm sure that would have gone over splendidly."

Cedric flinched, but he had no strength left to argue. What was there to say?

They moved in silence after that, the short walk to the tower feeling endless. Cedric's body ached with every step, but it was nothing compared to the gaping wound in his heart.

Inside, Gwenna guided him to a chair by the fire. His limbs felt boneless, heavy with exhaustion. He watched as Gwenna busied herself making a tincture, the clinking of cups and saucers filling the tense silence.

Cedric stared into the fire, his vision unfocused, the flames blurring into shapes that weren't there. Finn's face flashed in his mind—his grey eyes wide with shock, his voice shaking with betrayal. The warmth of his body, the way he had held Cedric close only hours before, like he *belonged* there. A fresh wave of nausea rolled through him.

"Here." Gwenna pressed a steaming cup into his hands. "Drink this. Then you're going to tell me exactly what happened."

Cedric wrapped his fingers around the drink, letting the heat seep into his frozen hands. He took a sip, but the warmth of the tincture didn't reach the chill inside him. He swallowed hard, the words tangled in his throat.

"We were in the stables," he began, his voice a ragged whisper. It felt foreign, like it belonged to someone else. "We...we were..." His jaw clenched, and he shut his eyes, as if that would block out the memory. "I let him into my heart and my arms."

Gwenna's eyebrows shot up, but, to her credit, she didn't interrupt.

Cedric took another shuddering breath. "Afterward, I must have fallen asleep. When I woke, the sun was rising, and I—" He broke off, his grip tightening around the cup. He didn't need to say the rest. The horror of that moment, of feeling his body shifting against his will, the sickening realization that he was too late and there was no way to slip away without Finn noticing. "Finn saw me."

"And then he *ran*," Gwenna finished, her tone flat with ill-concealed bitterness.

Cedric shook his head, the motion sluggish, his entire body resisting the movement. "No. *I* did." The confession was hardly audible. He exhaled shakily, his fingers white-knuckled around the cup. "I saw the look on his face and I... I couldn't bear it. I flew away."

He didn't even mention the things Finn had said. *You lied to me. I trusted you.* The words had lodged in his mind, poisoning him from the inside out.

Silence stretched between them. Gwenna's gaze was heavy on him, unyielding. Finally, she spoke. "So you slept with him, revealed your secret, and then left him to deal with the aftermath alone?"

Put like that, it sounded even worse. *Because it* was *worse.* Cedric flinched as if struck.

"I panicked," he admitted. "I didn't know what else to do. And I can't—" His voice faltered. He swallowed the knot rising in his throat, staring down into the depths of his tincture. "I can't speak as a dragon. I had no way to make him understand."

Gwenna scoffed, throwing up her hands. "*I was here*. You could have gotten me!" She shot to her feet, pacing in tight, angry strides across the small room. "This is a disaster. He could be on his way here right now with an army at his back. We need to leave, Cedric. Now, before it's too late."

Leave? Cedric's pulse stuttered. A cold, creeping fear crawled up his spine, desperation clawing at his throat.

What if Finn came back?

What if he wanted answers? What if—against all reason—he still wanted *Cedric?*

"We can't just run," Cedric said, his voice rough. "This is our home. And Finn...he might not tell anyone."

Gwenna whirled to face him, eyes flashing with disbelief. "Are you *mad?* Of *course* he'll tell someone! It's his *duty*, Cedric. You can't honestly believe he'd choose you over his loyalty to the kingdom?"

Cedric recoiled. Because he *did* believe it. Or at least...he wanted to.

"You didn't see his face, Gwenna." His voice cracked on the words. "Before he saw me change...there was something there between us. Something *real.*"

A muscle ticked in Gwenna's jaw. Her anger bled out, replaced by something softer—something infinitely worse. *Pity.*

"Oh, Cedric," she whispered. She knelt before him, taking his hands in hers. "I know you care for him. But you have to face reality. He's a *knight* of Lunareth. His entire purpose for coming here was to *slay you*. One night of passion doesn't change that."

Cedric wanted to argue. He wanted to *believe*—believe that Finn was different, that the man who had kissed him wasn't the same knight who had set out to slay a dragon.

But doubt plagued him. What if Gwenna was right?

What if he'd been fooling himself all along, seeing what he wanted to see in Finn's eyes?

"I don't know what to do," Cedric admitted, his voice breaking under the weight of it all. His shoulders curled inward, as if trying to make himself smaller. "I've ruined everything."

Gwenna squeezed his hands. "No, you haven't. We're still here, we're still free. That's what matters." She sighed, her grip tightening as if she could anchor him with just that touch. "Look, we don't have to leave immediately. But we need to be prepared. I'll start packing essentials, just in case."

Cedric couldn't bring himself to respond.

"You should rest," Gwenna continued. Her voice had softened, the anger fading into something quieter, more resolute. "You look like you haven't slept."

Cedric nodded, too drained to argue, too wrung out to do anything but accept Gwenna's words. She was right—of course she was. He *should* have slept during the day, should have given his body the reprieve it so desperately needed, but he hadn't been able to. The weight of it all—the grief, the self-loathing, the loss—had become a smoldering ache that sleep couldn't fix. So he had stayed awake, let exhaustion punish him in the only way he could control.

As Gwenna moved through the tower, gathering supplies, Cedric let his mind wander. He thought of Finn, somewhere out in the world beyond this tower. Was he already back in Mirathen, kneeling before the king, speaking Cedric's fate into existence? Had he told them everything? Had they mobilized an army? Or was Finn still out there, riding alone, as torn and uncertain as Cedric himself?

The memory of their night together drifted through Cedric's mind like a specter. He remembered the warmth of Finn's skin, the strength of his hands, the way he had held Cedric as if he were something precious. The way their bodies had fit together, moving in time like they had been made for it. It had felt so *real*, so terrifyingly *right*.

"You're mine tonight," Finn had whispered, his voice full of desire.

"No," Cedric murmured aloud to himself, "I'm not." His eyes burned with tears that wouldn't fall.

Eventually, exhaustion dragged him under, pulling him into a restless sleep where his body sagged into the chair, arms crossed tightly as if to hold himself together. But even in sleep, there was no peace.

He dreamed of a knight riding a grey warhorse, his dark hair whipping in the wind as he rode away, never looking back.

In the middle of the night, Cedric stirred, his skin prickling with awareness at the lightest touch against his forehead. His breath hitched. For one fractured second, his sleep-fogged mind thought it was Finn. But when he forced his eyes open, it was Gwenna kneeling beside him, her face drawn tight with worry.

"You should sleep," he grated, his voice like gravel.

Gwenna exhaled sharply and waved a hand. "I can't. Not when I'm worried about you."

Cedric blinked blearily at her. "Why are you worried about me?"

Her face contorted in the lantern light, her exasperation plain as day. "I would think that's *painfully obvious*. You just had your heart broken, and your *life* is in danger."

He frowned at that, looking away. He didn't want to

think about *either* of those things. Didn't want his sister to worry about him, not when she had already given up so much for him. But what was there to say? He couldn't reassure her—not when he couldn't even reassure *himself*.

The unrelenting silence stretched between them. Finally, unable to sit still, Cedric rose from the chair on trembling legs. Gwenna sucked in a breath, likely preparing to scold him, but he ignored her and walked to the nearest window. He pressed his palms against the sill, bracing himself as he stared out at the darkened forest below.

The trees were still, their branches unmoving in the crisp night air. And yet Cedric couldn't shake the feeling that something was coming. He half-expected to see the glow of torches between the trunks, soldiers emerging like specters to drag him from this fragile life he had built.

But there was only darkness.

"Gwenna." He hated how broken his voice sounded. "What if...what if I'm wrong about him?"

She scoffed, but moved to stand beside him, anyway. "I know you want to believe the best of him." Her tone was softer now, edged with something that might have been sympathy. "But we can't take that risk. Our safety has to come first. *Your* safety most of all."

Cedric nodded absently, still gazing into the woods, searching for something he wasn't even sure was there. But... "I just wish I could explain," he admitted, his voice nearly lost to the night. "Make him understand."

Gwenna didn't respond immediately. Instead, she wrapped an arm around his shoulders, drawing him close.

"I know," she murmured, her breath warm against his temple. "But sometimes, there are no explanations that can bridge the gap between what people expect and what *is*."

They stood there for a long time, staring into the inky blackness of the forest, listening to the quiet hum of the night. Even Clarence was quiet, his usual mischief absent.

Cedric's mind raced with possibilities, with all the things he wished he had said to Finn. How could he have explained? *How do you tell someone that the thing they have spent their life hating is the very thing you are?*

The curse. The years of isolation. The fear that had settled so deeply in his bones it had become a part of him, as real as his scales. How could Finn *ever* understand?

As exhaustion overtook him, Cedric allowed Gwenna to guide him to bed. But even as he lay down, he knew sleep would be elusive. Every time he closed his eyes, Finn was there.

In the night's quiet, as the embers in the hearth dimmed, Cedric made a decision. He *wouldn't* run. Not yet.

He would give Finn a chance to return. To seek answers. And if he did...

Cedric would tell him *everything.* The whole truth, no matter how painful.

It was a small hope, perhaps a foolish one. But it was all Cedric had left to cling to as he drifted into an uneasy sleep, dreams of raven-haired knights and golden dragons chasing each other through his mind.

Chapter Eighteen

It should have felt like a homecoming.

The banners of Mirathen snapped high above the streets, crimson and gold against a sky edged with the last warmth of afternoon. Sunlight caught on the stone walls, glinting off the regal architecture, the winding streets thrumming with life. Merchants called their wares, children wove through the crowd, laughter bubbling as they chased one another in the dust.

Finn rode through the gates, back among his people. But relief did not come.

He kept his head high, his expression composed, his bearing that of a knight of the realm. The children at the roadside beamed at him, wide-eyed with admiration, whispering his name like a legend. He gave them a small wave, as was expected. But inside, there was nothing.

Madness. This was *madness.*

Finn gritted his teeth, his jaw locked tight as he fixed his gaze on the road ahead. He couldn't afford to stumble now. Couldn't let thoughts of *him*—of golden eyes shadowed with pain, of warmth that still lingered on his skin—hobble him when duty remained unfinished.

He had a report to give. A kingdom to answer to.

And then, maybe, he could step away. Breathe. Figure out what to do with the feral prince and princess he had left behind. Figure out what to do with *himself*.

Ghost needed no direction. She carried Finn through the city's familiar streets, her gait sure even as his mind wandered. The bustling market square blurred past—the bright chatter of merchants, the scent of fresh bread wafting from a bakery's hearth, the glint of the palace spires lancing the sky. It all felt unreal, as if he were riding through a dream.

He hardly registered when Ghost slowed of her own accord. Only the sudden lack of movement told him they had arrived.

Tom the stable hand darted forward, his excitement barely contained as he seized Ghost's reins. "You're back! And without a scratch!" His gaze swept over Finn, eager— until it wasn't. His smile faltered. "But...you didn't bring back the dragon's head."

Finn's breath hitched. *The dragon's head.*

The words crashed over him like a breaking wave, dragging behind them a vision that threatened to gut him: a golden skull mounted on a stake, Cedric's eyes vacant, his body broken and still. Bile rose and he swallowed hard, forcing it down.

He managed a smile. "No. I didn't." The words were stones in his mouth, heavy and final. He had no explanation to offer the boy, no justification for why the beast he had been sent to kill still lived.

Boots scraped against stone, announcing a new arrival and a chance for Finn to avoid more questions, at least for the moment.

Finn turned as a palace guard strode toward him, moving with the crisp authority of a man who had no patience for others. The stable hand let out a startled squeak and ducked his head, hastily leading Ghost away.

Finn patted Ghost's flank as she passed. Then he straightened and faced the guard.

"Sir Finnian." The guard's tone was impassive. "His Majesty requests your immediate presence in the throne room."

The summons wasn't a surprise—of course he had expected it—but the urgency was worrisome. He had thought there would be time. A brief reprieve to bathe, to scrub away the exhaustion of the road, to don clean clothing before standing before the king.

Apparently not.

He forced his shoulders back, locking the weariness away. "Of course," he said, projecting as much confidence as he could. "Lead the way."

As they walked, Finn caught the hushed murmur of two passing courtiers. He couldn't make out the words, but the way their voices clipped short as he neared set his nerves on edge.

The tension was thick enough to taste, and Finn felt his unease deepen. *What is going on?*

Ahead, the throne room doors loomed. The guard at his side rapped twice, the heavy sound echoing through the corridor. Silence followed—ten long beats of Finn's heart—before the doors groaned open.

King Darius sat upon the gilded throne, his expression carved from stone, fingers drumming idly against the armrest. The *tap, tap, tap* of his nails against gold was the only sound in the vast chamber, save for the shifting of armor—the King's Guard flanking him.

Finn kept his head high as he approached.

"Ah, Sir Finnian," Darius drawled, his voice deceptively calm. "How kind of you to grace us with your presence *at last.*"

Finn dropped to one knee, bowing his head. "Your

Majesty, I apologize for my delay in returning. I came as swiftly as I could once my mission was complete."

Darius leaned forward, his dark eyes narrowing. "And what of your mission, Sir Finnian? I trust you have good news for me?"

Finn's pulse pounded in his ears. He chose his words carefully. "I have located Princess Gwenna, Your Majesty. She is safe and well."

"Excellent. And where is she now? I assume you've brought her back to where she belongs?" Darius studied him like a cat with a mouse beneath his paw.

Here it was. The moment Finn had been dreading. He inhaled slowly, bolstering himself before he spoke.

"Your Majesty, Princess Gwenna does not wish to return. She assured me she is safe and content—"

"*Content?*" The word cracked through the chamber like a whip. Finn flinched. Darius rose, his fury barely leashed. "She is the *princess of Lunareth!* Her place is *here*, not gallivanting about the countryside on some foolish whim!"

Finn risked a glance up and immediately regretted it. The king's face twisted with rage, his fingers white-knuckled where they gripped the throne's gilded arms. But beneath the anger, something brewed.

Desperation? Fear?

And what had he said? *Gallivanting about the countryside.*

A slow, uneasy chill crept through Finn. When Darius had sent him on this mission, he had painted Gwenna as a captive. A stolen princess in need of rescue. But now...with his fury and choice of words...had he *known?* Had he always known she was there of her own accord?

Or was this simply another of the king's temper-fueled outbursts?

Finn had no time to examine the thought before Darius's seething gaze snapped back to him.

"Your Majesty," Finn tried again, choosing his words as

carefully as he might select a weapon. Only this time, he had no idea what kind of blade the moment required. "I assure you, I did my utmost to persuade her—"

"Clearly, your *utmost* was not enough." Darius's long robes swept across the stone floor as he began pacing, a caged predator scenting blood. The throne room had never felt so small.

Finn braced himself.

"Tell me, Sir Finnian," Darius continued, his voice now frighteningly calm. "Did you at least fulfill the *other* part of your mission? *Did you slay the dragon?*"

Finn's fingers twitched at his sides, his throat going dry. He couldn't betray Cedric. But neither could he bring himself to lie to his king—not outright. He had to choose his words *very* carefully.

"Your Majesty," he said, keeping his tone even but respectful, "there was no dragon threat during my search for the princess."

Darius froze. Then, ever so slowly, he turned. His hazel eyes locked onto Finn's, more dangerous than Cedric's eyes had ever been as a dragon.

"No dragon?" The words were quiet. Too quiet. "Are you telling me that not only did you fail to bring back Gwenna, but you also failed to eliminate the *beast* that has plagued our kingdom? I do believe you're lying to your king, Sir Finnian."

Shit. Finn's mind raced. He could feel the noose tightening. "I found no evidence of any dragon attacks, Your Majesty," he said carefully. "The village I came across, Duskridge, was prosperous. Perhaps the rumors were exaggerated—"

"*Enough.*" Darius's voice cracked through the chamber like a thunderclap. Finn flinched before he could stop himself, his instincts screaming at him to drop his hand to his sword hilt— no. *No.*

He forced himself still, spine rigid, though every muscle was strung tight.

Darius stepped forward. One step. Then another. And another.

"I want the *exact* location of Princess Gwenna and the dragon," he said, each word cutting through the air like steel. "And I want it *now*. No more excuses, no more half-truths. *Where is she?*"

Finn's heart pounded. He was trapped. He *could not* betray Gwenna. And he *would not* betray Cedric.

But to openly refuse the king's command...

He swallowed hard. But Darius wasn't really the king, was he? Cedric should be the one on the throne. Dragon or not, it was suddenly alarmingly clear that he was less of a monster than the current king.

"No."

The throne room fell into a silence so deep Finn could hear his own heartbeat.

Darius stared at him, his expression unreadable, his chest rising and falling with controlled breaths. The stillness stretched into something stifling, a moment balanced on the knife's edge between fury and calculation.

Then the king let out a quiet, humorless breath. "No?" He said it almost delicately, as if testing the weight of the word. Then he took a step forward.

Clearly not a word this man is used to hearing. Finn lifted his chin. "It means I'm not telling you where Princess Gwenna is."

Darius was so still and quiet that Finn hoped for a moment he'd turned into a statue from shock. But then the king spoke, his voice like ice cracking over dark water. "Very well, Sir Finnian. If that is your choice, then you leave me no alternative." He raised his voice, ringing with the power of authority. *"Guards!"*

The sound of steel rasping against leather filled the

chamber as the King's Guard stepped forward, their hands already on the hilts of their swords. At the same time, the great doors of the throne room burst open, and a flood of palace guards poured inside, boots striking hard against the stone.

Finn stiffened, barely keeping himself from reaching for Sunwrath. *Damn it.*

The king's voice was like the crack of a whip. "Sir Finnian Brightmoor, I hereby charge you with *treason* against the crown. You will be taken to the dungeons to await justice for your crimes."

Finn's breath hitched. His thoughts reeled, grasping for sense, for a way to pull this back from the brink. He had given everything to Lunareth—his service, his loyalty, his very life. And now? Now he was branded a *traitor?*

The guards yanked Finn back, dragging him toward the doors. His boots scraped against the polished marble, but he refused to let them force his head down. He kept his gaze locked onto Darius until the last possible moment, searching for any hint of hesitation, any sign of reason.

There was none.

The king merely watched him go, calm now, as if everything had fallen neatly into place.

As Finn reached the threshold, Darius spoke one last time, his voice echoing like a death sentence.

"Sir Finnian, your stay in the dungeons can be very short or very long." A pause, deliberate. Calculated. "It all depends on how quickly you decide to cooperate."

The heavy doors slammed shut, cutting off Finn's view of the king's cold, satisfied smile.

THE DESCENT into the dungeons blurred into a hollow, nightmarish haze.

Finn moved as if untethered from himself, his body a vessel stripped of will, reduced to a *thing* being led. A thing being discarded.

The guards marched him down a spiraling, torch-lit staircase, deeper and deeper beneath the castle. With each step, the air thickened—damp, cloying, laced with the bite of mildew and rusting iron. Every breath tasted like decay. Water dripped somewhere in the dark, a slow, haunting beat, counting down the moments of his ruin.

How had it come to this?

He had known Darius would be displeased. But this was something else. The fury in the king's voice, the vehemence of the accusations—it went beyond wrath, beyond punishment. *Treason.* Had he miscalculated that badly? Had Darius always been this unhinged, or had Finn simply been too blind to see it?

Boots scuffed against uneven stone as they reached the corridor, a narrow gauntlet of iron-barred cells, yawning dark mouths waiting to swallow him whole. A guard wrenched open one of the heavy doors, the screech of metal on stone cutting through the silence like a death knell.

"Inside, *traitor.*" The word hit harder than the shove that followed.

Finn stumbled forward, catching himself against the damp, unyielding wall. The door crashed shut behind him with a brutal thud.

The lock turned.

And just like that, Sir Finnian, once one of Lunareth's most trusted knights, was no one.

FINN SLUMPED against the damp stone wall, his breath coming slow. His body still thrummed with the aftershocks of adrenaline, the phantom pulse of a battle already lost. Cold seeped through his shirt, slithering against his skin.

His mind would not still. He had *failed*.

Failed his mission. Failed his duty. Failed his king. And now...now he had failed Cedric and Gwenna as well.

How long before Darius sent others? How long before the king hunted them down, loosed his wolves upon them?

Finn clenched his fists. *I should have seen this coming.*

He had been too careful. Too restrained. He had thought he was choosing his words wisely, treading carefully through the storm of Darius's rage. But he had miscalculated. If he had pressed harder, questioned more, he might have seen the truth buried beneath the king's fury.

This was never about Gwenna.

It was about power. About control. About the *dragon*.

Cedric's face flashed through his mind—not as a beast, but as a man. His golden-brown eyes warm with laughter. His lips parting in a breathless sigh.

A softness that Finn had not been meant to witness. A truth he had never been meant to hold.

His throat tightened. He shut his eyes against the ache hollowing out his heart, but it did nothing to dull it.

Hours bled past, marked only by the distant shuffle of boots, the slow, rhythmic drip of water. The cold deepened, burrowing into his bones. His muscles locked against the unyielding stone.

Still, his mind refused to be silent.

This will not be the end.

Finn's jaw tightened. Somehow, some way, he would find a way out of this dungeon.

He had to. Because Gwenna and Cedric were in danger. And he *would not* let them face it alone.

Chapter Nineteen

The shrill ring of a contraption beside the bed jolted Gwenna awake, her heart lurching into her throat. She swore under her breath, scrubbing a hand down her face. Every single time. You'd *think* she'd get used to her own blasted invention by now, but no—it still startled her like a war horn at dawn.

With a groan, she swung her legs over the side of the bed, shaking off the remnants of uneasy dreams. The images clung to her mind, sticky as cobwebs: Cedric, trapped in his dragon form, surrounded by soldiers, their blades glinting in torchlight. She had screamed for him, fought to reach him, but her limbs had been made of lead, her voice swallowed by the night. And then...

She shook her head violently. *No.* It was just a dream. But the unease remained, burrowing deep in her gut like the embers of a dying fire.

Gwenna lit the bedside lantern, the golden glow spilling across the stone walls of her room. How many days had it been since Finn left? Five? Six? Each morning, she awoke wondering if today would be the day soldiers stormed the tower, swords drawn, ready to drag them back to the life she had no intention of returning to.

And Cedric—he was falling to pieces. She knew the signs too well, remembered the way he had withdrawn when they had first fled to the outpost, how he had moved through the world like a ghost of the man he had been.

This was *worse.* He was listless, his presence muted, as though his body remained while his mind drifted somewhere he couldn't escape. He went through the motions—eating, speaking, existing—but the light in him had dimmed, smothered beneath guilt and something deeper, something heavier. And if he thought she was going to sit back and let him sink, then her idiot brother had clearly forgotten who he was dealing with.

Rolling her shoulders, Gwenna dressed swiftly. A soft wool blouse, a sturdy skirt that wouldn't tangle at her knees, and her well-worn boots laced tight. She wrapped a thick shawl around her shoulders, tucking it close against the morning chill.

The aroma of bread greeted her as she descended. Her stomach tightened—not with hunger, but with worry.

In the kitchen, Cedric stood by the hearth, slicing a loaf of bread with slow, methodical movements, as if the simple act of cutting was the only thing anchoring him to the present. A tremor ran through his grip, slight but telling, before he tightened his hold.

The fire cast shifting light across his face, deepening the hollows beneath his eyes. He looked up as she entered, his expression carefully composed, a rehearsed smile curving his lips—but it was empty, a mask stretched over a broken man.

Cedric must have realized he wasn't fooling anyone, because his gaze quickly drifted back to the bread. "Good morning. I thought something warm might help."

Gwenna dropped into a chair and snagged a slice of

bread. "Warm is good. Eating is better. You planning to remember that part today?"

A flicker—barely there—passed over his face. Not quite amusement, not quite annoyance, something halfway between that reminded her he was still in there. It was more reaction than she'd gotten from him the past few days. "I'll try."

She let the moment sit, then circled back to his greeting. "Anyway. Good morning. I'm thinking of heading into Duskridge."

Cedric hesitated mid-slice. "Why?"

"Because sitting here like anxious hens won't do us any good," she said, reaching for a slice of bread and a jar of jelly. "We need information, Cedric. We don't know what's happening in Mirathen, or if Finn made it back in one piece, or if there's a bounty out for our heads yet. We can't afford to be ignorant."

Cedric's lips pressed into a thin line, his posture tensing as though the mere mention of Finn shattered him all over again. He said nothing at first, his gaze unfocused. Gwenna watched his throat work as he swallowed whatever thoughts were clawing their way up, but the words never came.

She leaned forward, softening her tone just a fraction. "Cedric, I know you're worried, but—"

"I have *reason* to be worried," he muttered, finally looking at her, his expression weary. "If something happens—if someone recognizes you—"

"I'll be *careful*," she cut in, leveling him with a look before he could spiral further. "I always am. No one in Duskridge knows who I really am. As far as they're concerned, I'm just a traveling trader."

He tightened his grip on the knife again. "Gwenna—"

She saw it then—the shadow of something close to fear, but deeper, more desperate. Not fear for himself. Fear of being left behind. Fear of losing her. She was all he had left.

He exhaled, slow and resigned. His resistance crumbled like ash in the wind. "Fine," he groused. "But be quick. And cautious."

Gwenna flashed him a smirk. "You *do* know who you're talking to, right?"

Cedric blinked slowly, like it took effort to pull himself back to the present. His answer was delayed, and when it came, it was little more than a whisper. "Right."

Cedric was sluggish as he placed a plate of toast and eggs in front of her. Gwenna dug in, but her gaze kept drifting to him. He sat across from her, food untouched, eyes fixed on the wood grain of the table. He was here physically, but his mind had already drifted again, slipping into the same place it had been for days—somewhere she couldn't reach.

By the time she finished eating, Cedric had withdrawn completely. His shoulders slumped, his hands resting in his lap like he'd forgotten what to do with them. The bleak emptiness in his eyes made her fingers twitch with the urge to shake him, *wake him up*, but she knew better. He would only retreat further.

Gwenna sighed, pushing back from the table. "I'll be back before sunset. Try not to mope yourself into an early grave while I'm gone."

Cedric didn't respond.

She didn't expect him to.

Brushing crumbs from her skirt, Gwenna grabbed a satchel and began packing it with supplies: a few coins, some herbs she could trade, and a selection of Cedric's wooden carvings.

"It's time." Cedric watched as Gwenna hefted the pack onto her back.

She knew he didn't mean her departure. With a soft sigh, Gwenna wrapped her arms around him, and for a moment, he didn't react at all.

Then, slowly, his arms came up, hesitant, uncertain—like

he wasn't sure how to hold on. But he did. His fingers curled into the fabric of her shawl, gripping too tightly, as if the moment he let go, something in him might come apart completely.

"Be safe," he whispered.

"You, too," she murmured. "Try not to wallow too hard while I'm gone. Your handsome, brooding prince act at least needs an audience."

Cedric huffed a soft laugh, shaking his head, but the shadows in his expression didn't lift. Without another word, he turned and strode toward the barn, fingers already working at the buttons of his shirt.

Gwenna lingered in the doorway, watching as he disappeared inside. Then she waited. The first noise came—a muffled, bitten-off sound that barely slipped past the stable walls, but it made something in Gwenna flinch. Then the next: a sharp, broken inhale, the scrape of claws on straw, the unmistakable, awful sound of shifting bone.

Her stomach twisted. Gods, *how* did he bear it?

Twice a day, *every day*. Bones breaking and reshaping. Skin stretching, muscles twisting into something monstrous. She'd heard village women gossip before, laughing about how their husbands couldn't function with a sniffle while they soldiered through fevers and monthlies without complaint.

If only they knew what Cedric endured.

There was no room for weakness, no luxury of rest. No one to tend to him, no one to ease the pain. He just bore it. *Alone*.

Moments later, a golden head emerged from the stable, Cedric's slit-pupiled eyes fixing on her with a comfortingly annoyed look.

"Sorry," Gwenna called, lifting a hand. "Wanted to make sure you were okay. I'm off now!" She waved, flashing a grin before turning toward the trees. She knew he hated when she overheard his transformation, but too bad. If he thought she was going to stop worrying about him just because he'd perfected the art of suffering in silence, he was sorely mistaken.

The forest was damp and quiet, dewdrops clinging to the edges of leaves and spiderwebs. The morning fog curled lazily through the trees, making the air thick and cool. Gwenna kept her pace light but purposeful, weaving through the underbrush with a route she had walked a hundred times. She never took a direct path. Habit, caution, and paranoia all dictated that she move like a shadow, slipping between the trees in a way that would be difficult to track if anyone ever bothered to try.

Which was stupid. No one was looking for them.

Or, at least, that *had* been true before.

She swallowed hard, shoving the thought down. It sat like a stone in her stomach anyway.

The cave entrance loomed ahead, a jagged mouth in the hillside, half-choked with creeping ivy and moss. The air grew cooler as Gwenna approached, damp with the breath of stone and shadow.

She stepped inside without hesitation.

The darkness swallowed her whole. Water dripped from unseen crevices, the steady *plink, plink* echoing against the cave walls. Beneath her boots, the ground sloped unevenly, slick with condensation. She moved with confidence. She had made this journey before.

The cave twisted and narrowed, then widened again, the faint gleam of daylight teasing ahead. She followed it, emerging on the other side to a world transformed—not by nature, but by *death*.

The bones remained where she had left them.

Mercenary knights, now nothing but brittle skeletons in rusted armor. Some still clutched weapons in their bony fingers—swords crusted with rust, bows snapped and tangled among the undergrowth.

They had come for her. For *Cedric*.

They had come believing themselves the hunters.

And now, they were the warning.

Gwenna stepped past them, unbothered, the same way she had every time since the first incursion. There was no guilt. Not anymore. Only the cold understanding that had settled in her bones these past few months.

If she hadn't killed them, they would have taken her. Would have killed Cedric and carried his head back as a trophy.

She had simply corrected the mistake of their arrogance.

Their rusting armor, their rotting bones, their useless swords still clutched in skeletal hands—*they* were a message now. A silent promise to anyone else who thought they could come for them.

Gwenna did not look back. Let the dead rot where they fell.

The living had far bigger problems.

By the time the village came into view, the sun had burned away most of the fog, casting warm light over the cluster of thatched roofs nestled in the valley. The rhythmic clang of a blacksmith's hammer echoed from the far side of the square, accompanied by the occasional burst of laughter from the tavern, where early risers had already settled in with their tankards.

Gwenna took a calming breath, forcing herself into the role she had crafted over years of careful deception. A trader. A nobody. Just another face passing through.

She entered the village with the easy stride of someone who belonged, nodding to the occasional merchant she recognized. Her ears remained sharp, sifting through the buzz of conversation for anything of use.

At first, it was all the usual prattle—weather and crop yields, the neighbor's no-good son sneaking out at night, the latest engagement between two families whose grand-mothers had feuded for years.

As Gwenna arranged her wares in the market square, she paid little attention to the chatter around her—until something made her stomach lurch.

"...heard it straight from my cousin in the capital," a merchant gossiped nearby, his voice low but urgent. "King Darius is offering a fortune for anyone who brings him the lost princess."

Gwenna froze, her fingers tightening around a wooden carving she had just handed to a customer.

"The *princess?*" the other scoffed, rolling his eyes. "Wasn't she kidnapped years ago? Probably long dead by now."

The older woman across from Gwenna clicked her tongue. "Terrible business," she muttered, accepting the wrapped fox carving without noticing the way Gwenna's hands had stiffened. "You'd think the king would have given up by now."

But the first man shook his head. "No, no. Word is she's alive. The king's desperate to get her back. The reward..." He let out a low whistle. "Enough to set a man up for life."

For half a second, the world tilted.

Gwenna forced herself to move, to keep her hands steady as she tied the twine on the package. She nodded at whatever meaningless words the woman was saying, forcing a polite smile. She couldn't afford to falter.

A reward.

For *her*.

Why now?

She exhaled through her nose. *This isn't the time to panic.* She needed more information—how much did Darius know? How much had Finn told him? Had Cedric's secret been exposed, or was this just about her?

A hundred thoughts tangled in her mind, but only one thing was clear.

She had to get ahead of this.

As the day wore on, she kept her ears open for any scraps of useful information. The rumor of the king's reward was spreading like wildfire, excitement crackling through the air with every whispered conversation.

"I heard she might be in this very region," a young man was telling his friends, his voice alight with the giddy thrill that came from thinking himself at the heart of something important. "Can you imagine? We could walk past a princess every day and not even know it!"

You are right now, idiot. But then he held something up—a sheet of paper, edges curled from handling.

Gwenna shifted closer, careful not to look too interested. The inked lines were crude, the details rough—but there was no mistaking it. A woodcut portrait of her face, printed for all the world to see.

The artist had clearly worked from an old royal painting, back when she'd been forced to sit still for hours while some court fool tried to capture her likeness. The carving hadn't been kind. The nose was wrong, the eyes too large —but the shape of her face, the set of her jaw? Unmistakable.

This is bad.

She edged backward, heart pounding as though she had already been spotted. Her fingers itched to tear the poster from the boy's hands and stomp it to tatters beneath her heel. Instead, she ducked her head, turned, and quickened her pace. *Calm. Stay calm. You're just another trader, just another face in the crowd.*

She needed to get back to Cedric. She needed to warn him.

But as she turned, she collided with something solid— *someone* solid. Gwenna nearly lost her balance, breath hitching as soft hands caught her arms. *Too close. Too close.*

"Oh, I'm so sorry!" a breathy voice exclaimed.

Gwenna looked up into the round, weathered face of the innkeeper's wife. Her gut clenched.

The woman peered at her, kindness laced with curiosity. "No harm done, dear?"

Gwenna forced a smile, stepping back, but the woman's grip on her arms remained firm.

"Are you all right?" the innkeeper's wife asked, eyes narrowing. "You look pale as a ghost."

Gwenna swallowed, shaking her head. "I'm fine, truly. Just a bit tired, that's all."

The woman frowned. "You know... now that I get a proper look at you, you *do* seem familiar. Have we met before?"

A bolt of panic lanced through Gwenna. She forced a breathless little laugh, the kind meant to brush things off, to make people *stop looking*. "Oh, maybe. I come to the village now and then, but I don't live here. Probably just one of those familiar faces."

The innkeeper's wife didn't look convinced.

"No, I *know* I've seen you before," she mused, her gaze sharpening. Then, her attention drifted toward the young men still gawking at the wanted poster.

Gwenna's heart slammed against her ribs. *No, no, no, you are not about to put this together right in front of me.*

She needed to end this. *Now.*

"I'm sorry," she said, layering her voice with feigned embarrassment. "But I really must be going. My husband will wonder where I am."

Before the woman could respond, Gwenna twisted free, slipping into the crowd. Her heart thundered as she forced herself not to *run*. Running drew attention. Running made people chase.

She was nearly at the edge of the village when another problem presented itself. She hadn't eaten.

Gwenna could push through on sheer willpower, sure,

but collapsing from hunger halfway back to the outpost was *not* a risk she was willing to take.

The market was too exposed now. Too bright. Too many people who might glance between her and that damned woodcut and start putting things together. But the tavern...

A slow, cunning smile curled at her lips. *The tavern is always dim.*

She spun on her heel and made for the squat wooden building.

Inside, the air was thick with the scent of ale, roasting meat, and unwashed laborers taking their midday meal. Gwenna found a seat in a shadowed corner, ordering a bread bowl of beef stew. She kept her head down, ears open, letting the flow of conversation wash over her.

And then...

"...heard there's trouble in the capital," a gruff voice muttered nearby. "Some knight locked up for treason, if you can believe it."

Gwenna stilled. She nodded thanks as the server dropped off her meal, gripping the spoon so hard it bit into her fingers.

"Treason?" another voice asked. "What'd he do?"

"Don't rightly know," the first man replied. "But word is, it's got something to do with the princess. You know, the one there's a reward for now."

A chill crawled up Gwenna's spine. A *knight*. Imprisoned. For *treason*. It couldn't be a coincidence.

"You don't think..." a third voice lowered to a conspiratorial whisper. "You don't think it could be that knight who came through here recently? The one asking all those questions?"

"Might be," the first man mused. "Come to think of it, we haven't seen hide nor hair of him since then."

Gwenna's hand clenched under the table. *Finn.* They had

to be talking about *Finn*. Her stomach soured, the rich scent of stew suddenly sickening.

The conversation shifted, meandering to idle speculation about the reward, about whether the princess might truly be nearby. Then—*worse*—whether she might be hiding in the forests surrounding the village.

Gwenna forced down her food, even as their words coiled around her like a noose.

She rose, slipping toward the exit. The moment she was outside, she turned toward the trees, her mind already racing ahead.

She had the necessary information. She needed to get back to Cedric. *Now*.

The journey back to the tower seemed to take an eternity. Gwenna's legs burned from the relentless pace she set, but she didn't dare slow down. Every rustling leaf, every snapping twig sent her heart hammering, paranoia clamping around her like an iron vice. She kept glancing over her shoulder, half-expecting to see torches bobbing through the trees, soldiers emerging from the mist.

By the time she reached the clearing, she was breathless and trembling.

"*Cedric!*" she shouted, voice raw with urgency. "Cedric, where are you?"

A deep rumble answered her. Gwenna silently cursed herself. *The sun's still up*. Damn it. She clenched her jaw and stormed toward the stables, hardly sparing a glance for Clarence as the goat trotted after her. Judging by the scattered hay and the way the fence gate hung ajar, he'd orchestrated another mutiny among the goats. *Typical*. Another disaster for an already disastrous day.

Gwenna ignored him and slipped inside the stable. *Another quarter hour before sunset,* she estimated, wiping sweat from her brow.

Cedric lay curled on the stable floor. He cracked one eye open at her entrance, but didn't bother moving. Didn't even lift his head. He looked as if he hadn't left the stables all day. A fresh pang of worry lanced through her. *He's getting worse.*

She took a step closer, rubbing her forehead. "We don't have time for this."

His other eye opened. She was demanding, yes, but that was nothing new. Gwenna's bluntness rarely startled him. But urgency—*that* did.

With a low, reluctant sigh, Cedric heaved himself upright. The tips of his wings and horns brushed against the stable ceiling as he adjusted.

"It's worse than we thought, Ced."

A sharp, inquisitive growl rumbled from his chest, his tail flicking against the straw. *Explain.*

Gwenna swallowed her fear. "We have to leave. *Now.* And...and we have to help Finn."

His scaled brow furrowed deeply. His head tilted, the ridges above his eyes tightening.

Cedric bumped her lightly with his snout—urging her to slow down and tell him *everything.*

So she did.

She recounted *all* of it. The village. The wanted posters. The whispered rumors of a knight imprisoned for treason. Cedric listened in total silence, motionless save for the occasional fidget of his claws. But as she spoke, she noted the change in his expression, in the way his breathing grew heavier. Shock gave way to grim understanding. Then his entire frame tensed, talons digging into the ground. His nostrils flared, his pupils constricting to narrow slits. She *knew* that look.

"Thalos drown me, of course it's *that time*," Gwenna muttered, already retreating.

The change was coming.

She yanked Clarence by the horn and dragged the stubborn goat outside with her, ignoring his indignant bleats. "You're the *worst* emotional support animal," she grumbled, shoving him toward the pen.

To distract herself from the sounds of cracking bones and shifting scales inside the stable, Gwenna busied herself—refilling the water trough in the goat pen and tossing extra feed for the chickens. But her mind wasn't on the chores. It was on *Finn. What is Darius doing to him right now? How much longer before he breaks?*

The stable door flew open.

Cedric strode out, barefoot and sweat-slicked, his breathing labored. His shirt clung to him, damp from the shift, his blonde hair disheveled. "What do you *mean* Finn is imprisoned?"

Gwenna turned. "I mean exactly what those words sound like," she snapped. "Unless Darius found a reason to lock up *another* knight. But Finn—"

"—is the only knight who *failed* to return with a princess *and* slay an evil dragon," Cedric finished grimly. He took a step back, running a hand through his unruly hair. Then another step. Then he pivoted on his heel and paced. "This is my fault."

Gwenna's jaw clenched. *Gods, not this again.*

She marched after him and clamped her hands onto his shoulders, forcing him to stop. "No, Ced. This *isn't* your fault. It's *Darius*. It's *always* been Darius."

His muscles twitched beneath her grip. He gave a sharp nod, but his expression twisted into something darker. "Darius imprisoned Finn because... because Finn protected us."

That was the same conclusion Gwenna had reached. It was increasingly possible that her brother was correct about the knight's character. And now he would pay for that. She swallowed, peering into Cedric's face. "Darius isn't a good man."

Cedric's shoulders sagged. His head dipped in silent agreement.

They had both *wanted* to believe Darius was good. It had been easier, once. He was charming when he wanted to be, clever, even kind. Gwenna and Cedric had both fallen for it.

"Finn knows. And now Darius will do anything to get that knowledge from him." Cedric stared up at the darkening sky as if it held answers.

Darius didn't bluff. He didn't make empty threats. And he *would* break Finn. He *would* rip that knowledge from him piece by piece, no matter what it took. Once he had what he wanted...

Gwenna refused to let that thought fully form.

Cedric whispered, "We can't abandon him."

She sighed. A large, very loud part of her wished they could. This was *Finn's* mess, after all. He had played both sides. The knight had chosen to betray his duty. He had *chosen* to kiss Cedric, to break his heart, to *leave*.

But for a moment, Cedric had been *happy*. Or as close to happy as he could get. If Finn died because of this, because of *them*, Cedric would never forgive himself. And that kind of guilt—the deep kind that rooted itself in the marrow of your bones—was the sort that destroyed people.

Gwenna rubbed the bridge of her nose. "You'd have to go home."

Cedric flinched. *Home*. The place where everything had gone wrong. Where he had lost himself. Where his life had changed forever.

A sad, knowing smile pulled at his lips. "But I won't be alone."

"No, big brother," Gwenna murmured, voice quieter now. "You won't." She sucked in a breath. "And maybe it's time for things to change. We've been hiding for so long. Maybe it's time we faced our past and took control of our future."

Cedric's eyes burned with new determination. "Sounds like we have some packing to do," he said.

Clarence let out a bleat of agreement.

Chapter Twenty

Finn's world shrank to the walls of his stifling cell. Time blurred, the endless dark broken only by the taunting glow of torchlight bleeding in from the corridor.

He no longer knew how long he had been here—days, maybe weeks.

The stone beneath him was unforgiving, digging into his muscles until even the smallest shift sent pain lancing through his stiff limbs. Hunger plagued him constantly, a dull ache that only deepened with each passing hour. The meager rations they tossed at him were hardly enough to keep him breathing.

At first, he had tried to mark the hours, counting the footsteps that echoed through the corridors. Now, he simply existed.

The silence was unrelenting. It sank into his bones, turned his own thoughts against him. He combed through every second of his confrontation with King Darius, every word exchanged, searching for some other path he could have taken. Some way he could have won.

But there was none.

He had made the only choice he could live with.

And then...*Cedric*. Always Cedric. His memories cut through the dark like a shaft of moonlight on a starless night.

Cedric's warm chuckle when Finn had fumbled with a carving knife. The warmth of his fingers over Finn's own, guiding him. The way his voice had cracked when he'd said he needed time.

And then there were the memories Cedric hadn't meant to leave behind. The quiet, unguarded moments. The way his body had trembled against Finn's that night—breath hitching, fingers curling into him, like he wasn't sure how to hold on but couldn't bear to let go. And the soft, pleased sound he'd made when Finn had pressed a kiss to the corner of his mouth.

Finn clenched his jaw, dragging the memories closer, holding onto them with everything he had. Because if he let go—if he let the darkness swallow him whole—he didn't know if he'd find his way back.

Because if Cedric was out there, *alive*, then Finn had to survive. Somewhere beyond these walls, Cedric was waiting for him.

And Finn refused to let this dungeon become his grave.

A grating scrape jolted him from his haze. The cell door.

Finn forced himself upright, every muscle screaming in protest. His head spun, and the world lurched around him.

A guard stepped inside, carrying a battered tray with a chunk of stale bread and a tin cup of water that sloshed dangerously with every step.

"Here's your feast, *traitor*," the man sneered, shoving the tray forward. It hit the ground hard. The cup toppled, spilling most of its precious contents across the filthy stone.

Finn swallowed against the painful dryness in his throat. He kept his expression neutral.

"Enjoying your new accommodations?" The guard

smirked, his voice thick with mockery. "Quite a step down from the knights' quarters, eh?"

Finn said nothing. He wouldn't give the bastard the satisfaction.

He reached for the bread, ignoring the tremor in his fingers.

The guard chuckled, watching. "Look at you now. The mighty Sir Finnian, brought low. Was it worth it? Betraying your king for *what?*" Then, with a wicked grin, he added, "They say you claimed the princess for yourself before throwing away your honor."

Finn's stomach twisted. Bile burned his throat. "What?" His voice came hoarse, cracking from disuse.

The guard's smirk widened. "Oh? Touched a nerve, have I?"

Finn clenched his jaw, refusing to rise to the bait.

The guard laughed. "Well, enjoy your meal. It might be your last if you don't start talking soon."

He kicked the empty cup, sending it clattering against the far wall. Then, with one final smug glance, he turned and strode out, the clang of the cell door slamming shut behind him.

Silence returned.

Finn stared at the scraps before him, his stomach twisting. Hunger and revulsion warred inside him, but weakness would not serve him here. He forced himself to swallow every dry, tasteless crumb. When the last of the moisture clung to the tin cup, he licked it clean.

Shame burned in his mind, even as his body savored the meager relief.

Then came more footsteps. Not just one set. *Several.*

The sound echoed through the dungeon like the toll of a funeral bell. *Something's different.* Finn tensed, instincts kicking in despite his exhaustion.

The cell door groaned open, iron grinding against stone. Finn's breath caught.

King Darius stood in the doorway. Flanked by a pair of Kings Guard, the monarch stepped inside, surveying the tiny cell with thinly veiled distaste. His nose wrinkled at the filth in the corners, but when his gaze landed on Finn, his mouth curved into something almost amused.

"Ah, Sir Finnian," Darius drawled, stepping forward. "I trust you're finding your accommodations...motivating."

Finn pushed himself upright. His legs trembled beneath him, but he stood.

He would *not* kneel before this man. Never again.

He met Darius's gaze. "Your Majesty. To what do I owe the honor?"

Darius tilted his head, amusement gleaming in his dark eyes. "Come now, Sir Finnian. Surely you know why I'm here." His tone was light, almost jovial. "I've given you ample time to reconsider your position," Darius continued, studying him like a piece of bruised fruit. "Are you ready to tell me what I want to know?"

Finn held his ground. "You sound desperate, Your Majesty." He lifted his chin. Defiant. Unbroken.

Darius stilled.

For a moment, just a breath, his mask slipped—his expression tightening, something ugly flashing behind his eyes.

His smile returned, stretched too thin. *Forced.* "You speak of treason," he said, but the words lacked the lazy amusement from before. His voice was colder now, brittle with barely restrained fury.

He stepped forward, faster this time, closing the space between them with a suddenness that sent Finn's instincts flaring. "Listen to me *very* carefully, Finnian," he murmured, low and lethal. "I am offering you *one last chance.*"

A pause. A beat where all the warmth in his expression drained away.

"Tell me where Gwenna is. Tell me about the dragon. And *all* will be forgiven." He spread his arms wide—too wide, too performative, a show of control that rang hollow. "You can return to your life. You will be restored. Your name will be cleared." He tilted his head, his smile widening like a fissure in glass. "Isn't that what you want?"

For one agonizing moment, Finn let himself imagine it. The cool sheets of his quarters. His polished armor awaiting him. Sunwrath at his hip. The ease of slipping back into a life where his only duty was to serve, to belong.

No questions. No betrayals. No impossible choices.

But then...Cedric.

Finn gritted his teeth. "You keep asking, like I'll suddenly grow a conscience that matches yours." He shook his head. "Not happening."

Darius's smile thinned, the edges brittle. "You mistake defiance for integrity, Finnian. But when you break—*and you will*—it won't be integrity that remains. Only regret." Darius lifted a hand and snapped his fingers. "Guards."

Heavy boots thundered through the chamber as two armored men strode forward, their faces impassive.

"Take him below," Darius ordered.

A muscle in Finn's jaw tensed, but he did not resist as the guards seized his arms with grips like iron.

He had expected this. He had known, the moment he spoke, that this path led only to suffering.

But he wouldn't change a single word. His father hadn't raised him to become a dog trotting at Darius's heels.

Darius stepped closer, lowering his voice so only Finn could hear. "You will tell me, eventually," he murmured, his breath warm and venomous against Finn's ear. "They all do."

Finn said nothing.

The guards marched Finn out into the corridor. As they

headed down, the air grew colder, the torchlight casting long, shifting shadows against the damp walls.

The lower cells came and went, but the guards did not stop. No, they were taking him beyond the dungeons, to the place where stone swallowed screams. The scent of mildew gave way to something worse: old blood, scorched iron, the acrid sting of burned flesh. It clung to the air like a memory, thick and impossible to ignore.

A final iron-bound door loomed ahead. The guard at Finn's left stepped forward and lifted the latch. The door groaned open.

A figure garbed in all black awaited them.

The royal torturer stood motionless, hands clasped before him. A heavy hood concealed most of his face, leaving only his mouth visible—a thin, bloodless line, expressionless as a stone.

Finn's gut churned, but he willed himself not to react.

Chains hung from the walls, rusted dark with old blood. A brazier glowed in the corner, embers pulsing like fireflies, their light licking across a long wooden table lined with knives, pincers, rods—tools of pain honed by experience.

And at the center of it all stood a chair, its wood and iron stained just like the chains.

Darius stepped in behind them. He heaved a long, satisfied breath, surveying the chamber with the enthusiasm of a man admiring fine craftsmanship.

"Ah," he sighed, "there's something so very...humbling about a place like this, don't you think?"

Finn considered keeping his mouth shut. That would be the smart thing to do. But Finn was too angry to do the smart thing. "Isn't Lunareth known for artistry and architecture?" He lifted a brow. "I expected more from the royal suite of suffering. It's so monotone."

Darius's jaw tightened.

Finn bit back a smirk. A tiny surge of pride warmed his

heart. He might be stripped of his sword, but he could still fight.

Darius strode forward, trailing a hand over the interrogation chair's wooden frame. "This is your last chance, Finnian," he said, sounding almost bored. "Tell me where Gwenna is. Tell me about the dragon. And all of this?" He gestured lazily to the waiting instruments of torment. "All of this becomes unnecessary."

Finn's fists clenched. "I'd rather chew off my arm than give you a single scrap of information," he said, voice unwavering. "I've already given you my answer."

Darius smiled. "So you have." He turned to the hooded figure. "Proceed."

The torturer stepped forward.

The guards wrenched Finn toward the chair, shoving him into the seat. Thick restraints were yanked into place, buckling tight across his wrists, chest, and his legs. Trapped. As helpless as an animal on a butcher's block.

Panic brewed in his gut. He forced himself to smother it. Anger. Defiance. Anything but fear.

"I don't usually let anyone strap me down until the third date," Finn muttered, rolling his shoulders against the restraints. "But I suppose I can make an exception."

The torturer scoffed.

Finn sighed. "Least you could do is buy me dinner first."

The leather yanked tighter. Finn hissed through his teeth as the straps dug into his skin, cutting off any illusion of movement. The room shrank around him, strangling him with the knowledge of impending agony.

Darius watched, his gaze glinting, his expression full of assessment—like an artist appraising his canvas.

"You see, Finnian," he said, his voice smooth, "this doesn't *have* to be your end. It can be a beginning—one where you are hailed as a hero rather than reviled as a traitor. All you have to do is cooperate."

Finn exhaled slowly, forcing his pulse to steady. He met Darius's gaze with something close to hatred. "The only new beginning I'm interested in is the one where you're no longer king."

Darius's expression flickered—just for a moment. Proof that once again, Finn's verbal thrust had landed.

He's insecure. Extremely *insecure.* That was useful information—if Finn lived long enough to use it.

Darius's jaw tightened. Annoyance bled into his features, bitter as acid. "Let's begin," he said, masking frustration with cruelty. He gestured to the black-clad torturer—who Finn now mentally named the Duke of Poor Life Choices.

The Duke considered his options before plucking a slender rod from the brazier. The metal gleamed wickedly in the dancing firelight, its surface cherry-red and hissing with heat.

Finn's breath hitched.

His body knew what was coming, even before it touched his skin. The searing heat warped the air, making it shimmer like a mirage. His pulse hammered, his muscles tense.

"The *dragon*," Darius prompted, his tone almost pleasant. "Tell me, and this can all stop."

The rod inched closer. Finn gritted his teeth, forcing the words past his lips. "There...is no dragon." A lie that would cost him. But in his heart, it was true. There was no dragon. Only Cedric.

"Liar!" Darius snapped, turning to glare at the torturer.

The rod met flesh. The world shattered.

Pain exploded through Finn's nerves, a white-hot brand that tore through muscle and bone alike. A jagged breath escaped him, more hiss than scream.

Every instinct shrieked *move, fight, stop this!* But there was nowhere to go, no escape from the agony tunneling deep, lighting up every raw, exposed nerve.

The stink of burning flesh hit his nose. His flesh.

He would not scream.

Finn bit down on his lip hard enough to taste blood, copper flooding his mouth, mixing with the taste of his own fear.

When the rod finally lifted, his vision swam, spots bursting like dying stars before his eyes. But he was still here. Still breathing. And he still hadn't given them a damn thing.

Darius leaned in, his voice little more than a whisper. "You're a fool, Finnian. Throwing away everything for what? A beast and a traitor?"

Finn's breath shuddered. His skin still burned, pain throbbing deep, a searing ache that refused to fade. His muscles spasmed against the restraints, but there was no escaping the agony.

Don't answer. Don't engage.

But the words tore out before he could call them back, ragged between clenched teeth. "Not...a beast," he ground out. "Cedric...is a good man."

Darius went still. Too still. Then, slowly, his head tilted. *"Cedric?"*

Finn's stomach plummeted.

Darius's lips curved, slow and satisfied, like a predator that had just scented fresh blood. "You know his name."

Shit. The mistake crashed through him like a hammer strike. Too much. He had said too much.

Darius crouched, seizing Finn's hair in a brutal grip, yanking his head back until his vision swam. "So, the monster told you his name," Darius whispered, his breath warm against Finn's sweat-slicked skin. "Tell me, Finnian, did he also tell you about the innocents he slaughtered? Wasn't your father among their number?"

The room tilted around him. Pain and exhaustion blurred the edges of his thoughts, but the words hit their mark. Finn's father. His jaw clenched, desperate to cling to certainty, to what he knew. "Cedric would never—" But then his voice faltered. Because he had been there. Had seen it.

Darius chuckled, a bitter, knowing sound. "Oh, he would. And he did. It's clear he used his magic to ensorcel you."

No.

But the seed had been planted. Cedric *was* powerful. *What if...?*

The thought sliced through him, cold as steel, but then... Cedric had tried to turn him away. Had tried to stop him.

And even when Finn had attacked him, *Cedric hadn't fought back.*

No. He *knew* Cedric. And no spell could make love feel like *that*.

The torturer returned the branding rod to the brazier, leaving it to smolder in the dying embers. Then, without pause, he selected something new.

A wooden mallet.

Darius released Finn's hair, rising to his full height, his expression dark with amusement.

"You see, Finnian, Cedric is not the benevolent creature you believe him to be," he said smoothly. "He's a monster. He has a history, a past filled with death and destruction. And you, my dear knight, have been played for a fool."

Finn's heart thudded painfully against his ribs. He wasn't wrong about Cedric. He *couldn't* be. But the pain made things slippery, made certainty feel distant.

"He's not the monster," he muttered, partly to himself, partly for Darius's benefit.

He tasted blood on his tongue. *Darius.* Darius was the monster.

The Duke of Poor Life Choices tested the weight of the mallet in his palm, rolling his wrist, appraising the weapon with idle familiarity.

Finn's stomach clenched.

Then the torturer reached for Finn's right hand. Instinct

screamed, but the leather straps held fast. His fingers flexed. *My sword hand, gods, no—*

A sharp crack split the air as the mallet slammed down against Finn's index finger.

Pain detonated.

Finn's vision flared white, his body arching violently against the chair as agony tore through him, lightning bright, nerve-deep. He felt the sickening give beneath the strike— not just a bruise, not just pain, but something shattering.

His breath left him in a strangled gasp, a sound he didn't recognize as his own.

The next blow landed on his middle finger. Another snap, another fiery wave of agony, a scream locked behind gritted teeth. He clenched his jaw so tightly his teeth might crack.

The torturer adjusted his grip, shifting Finn's pinned hand slightly, angling it. He wasn't rushing. No, he was taking his time, drawing it out.

The ring finger next.

Finn's whole body convulsed as the mallet came down again, a ragged, broken noise escaping before he could swallow it down. He couldn't move, couldn't fight back, only endure. The damage was permanent now. A knight's fingers were everything—grip, control, precision.

He was losing all of it.

Darius watched him intently, eyes gleaming with sick fascination. Like a man admiring a caged beast, waiting to see if it would snap or submit. "Cedric is a monster. A threat." His voice was almost coaxing now, almost patient. "Stop protecting him. Why are you even doing this? Enduring this? Some misguided sense of honor?"

Finn gasped through the agony, his vision swimming, dark blotches bursting at the edges. He wanted to pass out. His body screamed for it. But his pride refused.

His breath rasped through his teeth. The words scraped

against his fractured mind. He was in too much pain to think, too raw to lie. The truth slipped free before he could stop it.

"For *love*," he mumbled.

Darius stilled, his lips parting slightly, as if tasting the words. Then his expression hardened, and he gave a curt nod to the torturer.

The next blow came fast. Finn felt rather than heard his pinky break, the bone splintering like dry kindling.

This time, he screamed.

Darius let it happen. Let the agony rip through Finn's lungs, let it fill the chamber, only to be swallowed by the stone walls.

He must have blacked out. When he came back to himself, Darius was still there. Still watching. And now, disgust twisted his face.

"*Love?*" The word dripped with scorn, but it felt like a cover for...what? Contempt? No. *Fear*. "You *fool*. You know *nothing* about him. About either of them." Darius reached, gripping Finn's ruined right hand, studying it. Finn bit his cheek hard enough to draw blood. "You think love will save *you?* That it will save *him?*" Darius's smile was all teeth. "Love is the first thing I break."

His hand wasn't gone, but his mind was pretending it was. If he could trick himself into believing that, maybe he wouldn't lose himself entirely. Finn wanted to curl in on himself, to escape any way he could. But the straps held fast.

And for a fleeting, wretched moment, he thought about it. Thought about telling Darius everything. Just to make it stop.

Just to be free of this agony.

But then... *No*. The idea sickened him more than the pain ever could.

He forced himself to lift his head. Every nerve screamed. But he still met Darius's gaze.

"I know *enough*." His tongue felt thick, like a lump of bloodied meat in his mouth. Had he been biting it? He swallowed the iron taste down. "I know Cedric isn't the monster you claim him to be."

And then, because he was already damned, he was going to carve his own epitaph. Finn spat blood onto the king's pristine boots.

"Cedric is the *rightful king*." His voice should have broken, but it didn't. "And I swear my life, my sword, and my soul to *him*."

Darius's face twisted. Pure, unbridled rage. "Enough!" he roared, the sound reverberating off the stone walls.

Finn hardly had time to savor the victory before the king turned to the torturer, his fury bleeding into something colder.

"Make him talk. I don't care what it takes." Darius paused, eyeing him. "Break him if you must—but don't kill him." His voice lowered, edged with something calculating. "This errant knight may still be of use to me."

Finn exhaled slowly, teeth bared in a feral, bloodied smile. "Go on, then." His voice was hoarse. "See who breaks first."

Chapter Twenty-One

Cedric always looked forward to dusk. It was the moment his body became his own again, however brief. But today, he obsessively tracked the sun's slow descent, his thoughts tangled in restless loops. It was unnecessary—he *knew* when it would set. The curse had bound that knowledge into his very bones. He could feel it now, buzzing beneath his skin like a living thing, counting down the last moments before he regained his humanity.

When the first jolt of magic struck, Cedric lurched toward the stables, his instincts overriding all else. He had just yanked the stable door shut with his tail when the pain hit full force. He tried to breathe through it, to *control* it, but the magic had other plans. It ripped him apart cell by cell, grinding his body into something unmade before forcing it back together again.

Cedric bit back a scream, his nails clawing at the dirt floor. It felt like drowning in fire. And then, just as suddenly, it was over.

He slumped forward, gasping, sweat cooling on his bare skin. His eyes squeezed shut for a moment as he gathered himself. Couldn't just lay here. Had to get up. Slowly, he forced himself upright. His limbs trembled, weak from the ordeal, but he reached for the clothes he had left folded nearby, dressing as quickly as he could.

Gwenna was already outside, waiting for him. She stood by the goat pen, a pack slung over her shoulders, the other leaning against the fence. Clarence, ever the menace, was attempting to chew through one of the leather straps. Gwenna swatted at him, scowling. "I *will* turn you into boot leather if you keep it up, you infernal beast."

The goat remained unimpressed.

The door creaked as Cedric stepped out, rolling his shoulders against the ache in his muscles. Gwenna caught his eye and lifted a brow. "Ready?"

He exhaled, reaching for his pack. "As ready as I'll ever be." But as he adjusted the weight on his back, his gaze drifted toward the tower. Their *home*. The only home they had known for so long. "Are you *sure* about this?" His voice was quieter now, almost reluctant. "Once we leave, there's no turning back."

Her expression hardened, resolve flashing in her dark eyes. "I'm sure. Your knight isn't the only one guided by duty and honor."

Cedric's stomach twisted at the words. *Your knight.* It was foolish, but something about the phrasing pleased him. Still, he shook his head. "He's not my knight," he muttered, though the words tasted false even to him.

Gwenna smirked but didn't argue. Instead, she swung the lantern off its hook, illuminating the narrow path ahead. Cedric took the lead. The night stretched around them, but he had no trouble seeing. The shadows held no fear for him.

He was the monster lurking in the dark, after all.

As they walked, his mind drifted ahead to Mirathen. The city he had once called home. He tried to summon memories of Solavere Palace—the spires rising high against the sky, the streets alive with merchants and nobles alike. The court, with its whispered intrigues and forced smiles. But the memories felt *wrong*, blurred at the edges, like a dream half-forgotten upon waking.

Gwenna broke the silence, her voice softer than before. "What do you think it'll be like? Going back, I mean."

Cedric let out a slow breath. "I don't know." He hesitated before admitting, "Part of me is terrified. What if...what if people recognize me? What if—"

"What if *Darius* recognizes you?" Gwenna finished, her tone grim.

Cedric didn't answer. They both knew the truth. Gwenna might be the missing princess, but *he* was supposed to be *dead*. That was what had kept them safe all these years. One missing royal was an inconvenience. Two missing royals? That was a threat. And Darius didn't tolerate threats.

Gwenna sighed, rolling her shoulders as if shaking off the weight of their shared past. "I think *I'm* the bigger problem. The one more likely to be recognized," she muttered. "Those infernal flyers. I swear, as much as I love the printing press, right now it's *really* working against me."

Cedric couldn't help it—he chuckled, a low, tired sound. It had been so long since he'd laughed that it startled even *him*. The moment was brief, but it was *something*. But as soon as it passed, the guilt set in. Finn. Cedric was here, free to laugh, to walk under the stars, while Finn was *suffering*—alone, imprisoned, possibly worse.

They continued on, weaving through the night, avoiding the well-worn roads where travelers might cross their path. The night was deep, and the forest held its usual sounds—the rustling of unseen creatures, the distant hoot of an owl—but to Cedric, it all felt different. Heavy. Like a storm was about to break.

Then, as the eastern sky lightened, the warning prickled along his spine.

"We need to find cover," he said, his voice tight. "The sun will be up soon."

Gwenna nodded, scanning the terrain. "Let's get off the path. There's got to be something nearby." They pushed through the underbrush, the sharp branches clawing at their clothes and skin. Cedric almost wished for his tough scales—but he would have his scales soon enough, whether or not he wanted them.

Then Gwenna gasped. "There's a cabin ahead!" Relief brightened her voice, but she hesitated. They had learned not to trust easy shelter. Still, they had no choice. She squared her shoulders and called out, loud enough to carry through the trees: "Hello to the house!"

They both froze, listening. The wind stirred the trees, rustling through the branches like whispered warnings. Cedric strained his ears, picking up the distant calls of birds and the skittering of squirrels. No voices. No footsteps. No sign of anyone nearby.

Good.

Before Gwenna could stop him, he strode forward and knocked once on the cabin door. The wood groaned under his touch, the hinges giving way with a long, aching creak. The place smelled of old wood and disuse, the scent of long-empty rooms left to decay.

"Abandoned," he called over his shoulder.

Gwenna peered past him into the gloom. "Well, it needs work, but this will do." Without hesitation, she swung her pack off her back and let it drop onto the warped wooden floor. Then she pinned him with a look. "What about you?"

Cedric shook his head. The clearing outside wasn't large, but it would have to be enough. The familiar, insistent pull of the transformation clawed at his bones, growing stronger with each passing second. He swallowed hard. "I'll—" But the words died in his throat. It was too late.

Gwenna flapped a hand at him. "Go." She reached for

the straps of his pack, helping him shrug it off as he staggered back out the door, his fingers already fumbling at the fastenings of his clothes.

The shift hit like a hammer, folding him in on himself. The world blurred, pain drowning out thought. Cedric gritted his teeth against it, against the instinct to *fight*, because that only made it worse. He had learned to endure, to let the agony wash over him like a tide until it passed.

And then, silence.

He exhaled, a long, shuddering breath, steam curling from his nostrils. His wings ached from the force of the change, his body stiff. He gave them a slow shake, stretching them to ease the soreness.

A shadow moved in the doorway. Gwenna stepped outside, arms crossed, her face soft with sympathy. "You okay?"

He nodded once.

She sighed. "I'll bring you some food from our rations in a minute."

The day passed in uneasy stillness. Gwenna slept inside while Cedric dozed in the clearing, his dragon senses ever alert. Even in sleep, he listened—to the rustle of creatures in the brush, the distant murmur of voices from the road beyond the trees. Travelers, perhaps. Or worse.

But none came near.

Later in the afternoon, Gwenna emerged with more rations, offering a piece of dried meat. "Any trouble?"

Cedric shook his head.

That was in their favor, at least. But on foot, it would take several more days to reach the capital. Maybe a week or more—Cedric wasn't certain. He exhaled sharply, frustration burning in his gut. There was another way. A faster way.

Gwenna caught the shift in his posture, the way his wings tensed. "You're thinking of something."

Oh yes.

The sun was sinking fast, tinging the treetops in gilded light. Cedric had minutes left before the change took him, minutes in which he could cover more ground in the air than they could on foot in a day.

He made his decision. Turning, he gestured to his back with his snout.

Gwenna blinked. "What?"

He sighed, curling his tail impatiently. *There isn't time for this.* Mindful of her fragile skin, Cedric reached forward, closing his claws gently around her waist before she could react.

"*Hey!*" Gwenna hissed, but her protest was cut short as he lifted her and deposited her onto his back. She barely had time to adjust before he bent down, snagged both of their packs in his foreclaws, and launched.

The ground fell away in a rush, trees blurring beneath them as his wings caught the air. The wind tore at Gwenna as she clung to the ridges along his back. "*Cedric!*" she whisper-shouted. "You're going to be *seen!*"

No, he *wasn't*.

This might not have been his usual hunting range, but Cedric had spent ten years perfecting the art of moving unseen. He scanned the horizon, searching for signs of danger—plumes of smoke that marked settlements, clearings where farmers might watch the sky.

Nothing.

Gwenna punched his shoulder—uselessly, given the thick layer of his scales. "*You absolute reckless idiot.*"

Cedric huffed out a laugh, the sound rumbling through his chest.

"*It's not funny!*" she snapped, tightening her grip as he banked, adjusting his course. "You *cannot* just—oh, we are *talking* about this when you can properly form words!"

Already, Cedric felt the shift clawing at the edges of his

being, the telltale warning that his body was about to turn traitor again. He swept low, scanning the landscape.

There.

A small meadow, tucked away from prying eyes. A herd of deer scattered as he descended, the soft *thud* of his landing shaking the ground.

Before his feet had even settled, Gwenna was already scrambling off his back. She whirled on him, finger jabbing toward his snout. "You have a lot of explaining to do!"

Cedric snorted in amusement.

She glared. "Oh, you think you're so clever, don't you?"

He grinned a dragon's grin, then held up a claw, glancing toward the horizon. *Soon.*

Cedric quickly made his way to the far edge of the meadow, where a dense stand of trees offered a modicum of privacy. He braced himself against the rough bark of a tree, his breath coming short as the first ripple of magic tore through him.

Pain struck like lightning, blistering and merciless. Cedric clenched his jaw, forcing himself not to fight it, not to struggle against the inevitable. *Breathe. Endure. Let it pass.* His pulse pounded behind his eyes, and he dug trembling fingers into the earth.

"Gwenna?" His voice was raspy. "Could you bring me my clothes, please?"

Silence. Then, at last, her voice rang out, edged with unmistakable exasperation. "Oh, I don't know. I think you owe me an *explanation* first, brother dear."

Cedric let out a long, suffering sigh, pressing his forehead against his knee before running a hand through his damp hair. He was shivering, the night air nipping his bare skin. "Gwenna, please. It's *chilly* out here."

"Then you'd better talk," she called back, far too pleased with herself. He could practically *hear* her smirk.

Realizing he wasn't getting his clothes back without some groveling, Cedric relented. "Fine," he muttered. "I flew because it's going to take too long if we're only on foot. I know how to stay hidden. I'm no stranger to flight." He flexed his shoulders, still feeling the phantom stretch of wings. "And I didn't intend to fly *all* day with you, but dusk seemed like a low-risk time."

His answer was met with the sound of fabric rustling, followed by his bundled clothes sailing over a bush. Cedric caught them before they could hit the dirt, shaking out the layers before tugging them on. As he stepped out, still fastening his trousers, Gwenna was waiting with his boots, arms crossed.

"I forgive you," she said breezily. Then she punched his shoulder, not holding back. "But next time, I'd love *some* advance notice."

Cedric laughed, rubbing the spot where she'd landed the blow. "Noted." He pulled on his boots and straightened. "Now, do you want a hot meal for dinner? There's a town close to here."

Gwenna's expression instantly brightened. "You don't have to tell me twice. Lead the way."

They set off as twilight embraced the land. The town came into view as darkness fully settled in, the warm glow of lanterns spilling onto the dirt road. The streets were alive with the quiet bustle of evening—shopkeepers locking up, travelers seeking shelter, the scent of roasting meat and fresh bread wafting through the air.

"Remember," Gwenna cautioned as they passed beneath the wooden arch marking the town's entrance, "we're just simple travelers passing through. Nothing remarkable about us." She pulled a shawl out, draping it over her head like a grandmother.

Cedric nodded, adjusting his posture, forcing himself to *breathe*. He could do this.

"There." Gwenna jerked her chin toward an inn with a sign depicting a prancing deer. "Looks promising."

Inside, the inn was warm, inviting, and so very normal. A fire crackled in the hearth, casting flickering light over the faces of weary travelers nursing their drinks and meals. The scent of spiced stew made Cedric's stomach cramp with hunger.

He followed Gwenna to a quiet corner table, lowering himself onto the bench. His gaze snagged on the flyers, plastered onto the walls near the bar, posted beside notices of bandits and trade agreements. Gwenna was right. It looked just like her.

The innkeeper brought them bowls of thick stew, dark bread on the side. Cedric didn't care about the ingredients, so long as it was food. They ate in silence, ears tuned to the murmurs of the tavern.

"...taxes are higher than ever," a man at a nearby table grumbled. "King Darius claims it's for the good of the realm, but I don't see how squeezing us dry helps *anyone* but him."

Cedric stilled, his spoon halfway to his mouth.

"Careful," the woman across from him warned. "You know what happens to those who speak against the king."

A sharp pang hit Cedric's heart. He forced himself to keep eating.

But inside? Inside, something *cracked*. This was his kingdom. The land he had *loved*. And now—*this*? Fear. Oppression.

Darius had done this. How had things gone so *wrong*?

Gwenna had heard it too. Cedric could tell by the way her lips pressed together, by the brief but sharp glimmer of emotion in her eyes—annoyance, yes, but also something deeper. A weariness, a frustration that mirrored his own.

But there was nothing they could do about it now. Finn came first.

Then—and it startled Cedric to even *think* about it—*then* they could decide what to do about Darius.

For ten years, he had let himself believe he no longer cared, that Lunareth had been lost to him the moment he had fled Solavere Palace. But hearing the whispers of suffering, of oppression, made something in his core *tighten*, made his pulse quicken with anger. It was the first time in a decade that he had allowed himself to feel anything for the kingdom he'd left behind.

It was a strange sensation. Not entirely unwelcome. But it would have to wait.

"Come on. The night's not getting any younger," Cedric murmured to Gwenna once they had both finished their meals.

She nodded, rising from the table as he dropped a gold coin onto the worn wooden surface, more than enough to cover the cost of their food. They slipped out of the inn, moving like shadows into the quiet streets, careful to avoid lingering gazes.

Gwenna must have sensed the direction of Cedric's thoughts because she filled the silence with chatter. "Remember that time we snuck out of the castle to see the summer fair?" she asked, glancing at him with a knowing smile. "You were *so* worried we'd be caught, but you still came."

Cedric huffed a quiet laugh. "*Because* you begged me to. And because you promised we wouldn't get into trouble."

She grinned. "I *believed* that at the time. Not my fault we underestimated Father's guards."

He shook his head, remembering the look on their father's face when they had been herded back through the palace gates. "He was furious," Cedric admitted. "But it was worth it to see your face when you saw the acrobats."

Gwenna sighed wistfully. "We were so *carefree* then. Everything seemed possible."

Cedric glanced at her, at the way her expression had softened. "And now?"

She was quiet for a long moment, thoughtful in a way she rarely allowed herself to be. Then, finally, she said, "Now... now I think everything still is possible. Just in a different way. We're not the same people we were then, Ced. But maybe that's not a bad thing."

He wasn't sure how to respond. Was he better or worse than the boy he had once been?

As dawn crept into the sky, they reached the outskirts of another small village. Cedric immediately tensed, his instincts kicking in.

"We should wait until nightfall," he suggested.

But Gwenna shook her head, resolute. "No, last night you were right. We don't have time. I'll go through alone and meet you on the other side after you change. We can't afford to lose another day. We'll find a place to rest *after*."

Cedric clenched his jaw, fighting the urge to argue. He hated splitting up, hated letting her walk straight into potential danger. But she was right. They couldn't afford to slow down.

"Be careful," he said, his voice low. "And if anyone recognizes you—"

"Hit them in the head with a rock," Gwenna interrupted, flashing a quick, grim smile. "I know."

He scowled. "That's what got us into this mess."

She snorted. "Yes, well, you *can't* argue with how effective it is."

Then, before he could say anything else, she slung her pack over her shoulder and strode toward the village.

Cedric stood there for a long moment, watching until she disappeared between the buildings. Then, reluctantly, he turned toward the tree line, retreating into the safety of the shadows just as he felt the first pull of the transformation begin.

When it was over, he folded his wings close, picking up his pack and hanging it from one of the spines on his back. He glanced back, pleased that it was secure.

He slunk through the trees, keeping to the sun-dappled shadows, following a long, winding path around the village until he found the road on the other side. There, he crouched low in a shaded glade, waiting, watching.

An hour passed.

Then another.

His claws dug anxiously into the dirt. She should have been here by now.

Finally, just as he considered risking exposure to search for her, Gwenna appeared at the edge of the trees.

"Sorry," she panted, dropping her pack at her feet. "I got held up. There were posters *everywhere* with my face on them. I had to be extra careful."

Cedric growled low in his throat.

But Gwenna just patted his snout. "Don't worry," she assured him. "No one recognized me." Then her expression darkened. "But Ced...things are worse than we thought. Those posters? They've got people talking nonstop. And Finn..."

Cedric froze.

She met his eyes. "They're running their mouths about Finn—saying he's serving the dragon now. That the 'terrifying beast' scrambled his brains." She gave Cedric a pointed look, since they weren't fully wrong about his impact on the knight. "And supposedly Darius himself is telling people that."

Cedric blew out a long breath, forcing the air slowly through his nostrils. It did little to ease the pressure in his chest. Because that rumor confirmed what he believed all along: Finn hadn't given Darius a scrap of information about Cedric or Gwenna. The knight had protected Cedric, despite everything.

Why did that simultaneously make him feel a flicker of joy and growing horror? *Because he chose me. And that choice might be the very thing that damns him.*

They needed to find shelter. With Gwenna at his side, they moved parallel to the road, staying hidden in the thick brush. Cedric's keen senses picked up distant voices—travelers passing by, the occasional clink of a horse's bridle and the clop of hooves—but nothing close enough to be an immediate concern.

Finally, they found a small clearing tucked deep enough into the woods to keep them hidden. Cedric glanced at their surroundings. No signs of travelers or hunters. Far enough from the nearest farmstead that they should be able to rest without worry.

They settled in the clearing, the towering trees stretching high above like silent sentinels. Cedric rested his head on his claws, but he remained alert, listening to the whisper of the wind through the leaves.

When the sun finally dipped below the horizon, Cedric braced himself.

The change tore through him as it always did. He ignored the chill air on his bare skin, shoving himself upright. His desperation for answers was stronger than his still-trembling body.

"What exactly did you hear about Finn?" His voice came out rough.

"Take it easy, Ced. The official line hasn't changed. He's still in the dungeons. Same accusations. But the rumors outside?" Gwenna tossed him the clothes. "They say he knelt to the dragon. That he protected it. That he lost his mind— or let the beast take it."

Cedric caught the clothing and began to dress. "And it's true. I mean, the protecting part."

"I'd argue he lost his mind, too, but that's a conversation for another day," Gwenna said with a snort. Then her expression softened. "But yes, it sounds like he has tried to protect you. To protect *us*." She wet her lips, meeting his gaze. "We'll get him, Ced."

The determination in her voice warmed Cedric. Gwenna didn't back down easily. If she said something was going to happen, she meant it. "We should get moving, then."

They gathered their few belongings. As they eased out of the clearing, Gwenna glanced back at him. "Are you planning on another flight with me later?"

He raised a brow. "Do I detect a *hint* of enthusiasm at the idea?"

Gwenna lifted her chin, staring straight ahead. "Flying has an appeal I can't deny."

A huff of amusement escaped him. "Maybe. It'll depend on where we are by then."

They walked on, the night swallowing them in its vast quiet, the world around them shrinking down to the crunch of leaves beneath their boots and the distant hum of insects. When they crested the last hill, Cedric froze.

Mirathen.

The city stretched before them, its towers and spires glimmering in the darkness. He never thought he'd see it again.

Gwenna reached for his hand, giving it a squeeze. "We're almost there."

They made their way down the hill, sticking to the darkest shadows of night as they approached the city walls.

"How are we going to get in?" Cedric whispered. "We can't exactly approach the gate and ask for them to allow Princess Gwenna and Prince Cedric to enter."

Gwenna's lips twitched. "I mean, we *could*..."

Cedric turned to glare at her.

She grinned. "You should have seen your face!" Then she sobered. "We can try the south gate. It's the least busy of the gates, especially at night, so the guards are usually drunk and not too careful about who enters."

Cedric narrowed his eyes. "I beg your *finest pardon?*" How did his sister, a *princess*, know about the habits of drunk gate guards?

She waved a hand. "That's how it was ten years ago. Hopefully, that hasn't changed."

Cedric inhaled sharply, casting aside his protective curiosity about her knowledge. He considered her suggestion, then his face fell. "It's too close to dawn. I can't—"

He *couldn't.*

He couldn't be in the middle of the city when the sun rose, couldn't let it happen again—his first transformation, the blood on his hands, the way his world had shattered forever.

Gwenna's face paled. "Oh." Her voice was small. "Sorry. I wasn't thinking." She squared her shoulders, recovering quickly. "You're right. Let's find a safe place to rest. Maybe near the south gate, and I can scout it out to see if it's still a good option."

Cedric sucked in a calming breath. A plan. That was good. That was control. He nodded. "South gate it is."

They had thirty minutes.

Thirty minutes to reach the gate. Thirty minutes to disappear before the sun rose.

And then, once the sun sets...

I'm coming, Finn. Just hang on.

Chapter Twenty-Two

As dusk fell, Cedric exhaled slowly, fastening the last button on his shirt with fingers that still trembled from the transformation. The city lay ahead, the last barrier between him and Finn. *So close.*

His sleep had been restless, his dreams fractured and cruel. He had woken in a cold sweat more than once, heart hammering with nightmares of what they might find in the dungeons.

Twice Cedric had almost given in to his deepest, most selfish instinct. The urge to grab Gwenna and fly them both far away. Just *run*. Hide where no one would ever find them. Let the kingdom and its problems rot.

But he couldn't. Because Finn was still here, in Mirathen. Not by his side, not anymore—but even after everything, after the lies, the betrayal, the truth laid bare between them, Finn *hadn't* turned Cedric in. He could have. Maybe he should have. But he hadn't. And now he was suffering for it. That knowledge gutted Cedric. He had lost so much already, but the thought of losing Finn—of finding him broken, bloodied, or worse, dead—made his breath turn to ash in his lungs.

The rustle of leaves pulled Cedric from his thoughts. Gwenna pushed through the underbrush, adjusting the strap of her pack. Her dark clothing blended into the deep blue of twilight, and the glint of steel at her hip told him she was just as prepared for this as he was.

"Ready?" she asked.

Cedric nodded, though the lump in his throat made it impossible to speak. He was afraid that if he opened his mouth, *everything*—his fears, his guilt, his overwhelming desperation—would come spilling out. Instead, he forced himself forward, forging a path through the hidden glade and toward the city gates.

The south gate loomed ahead, torches flickering against the stone walls. Cedric and Gwenna merged into the flow of merchants returning from a neighboring town, their carts rattling, their voices an indistinct murmur. Cedric ducked his head, keenly aware of every glance from the guards standing watch. His pulse pounded in his ears.

The guards paid them no mind. They were more interested in ushering the merchants along than scrutinizing two weary travelers.

Only once they were past the gate and swallowed by the city's narrow streets did Cedric allow himself a shallow breath of relief. They were *inside*, but they were not safe. Not yet.

As they made their way through the winding streets, Cedric was struck by how much had changed. Buildings he had known all his life had been torn down, replaced by cold stone facades he did not recognize. Open-air markets had been swallowed by new construction, the lively chaos of street vendors replaced with neatly ordered storefronts. It was the same city in name, but Cedric felt like he had stepped into a dream—one where everything was just slightly wrong.

Gwenna tugged at his sleeve. "This way." She guided

him down an alley. The cobblestones were damp beneath his boots, slick with something he preferred not to identify.

They emerged onto a broader street just as two women were locking up a shop for the night. Their voices carried easily in the quiet.

"...heard they're still interrogating that knight," one of them said, her tone hushed.

Cedric's breath stilled.

"Poor soul," the other muttered, shaking her head. "But what did he expect, defying the king like that? These are dangerous times."

Cedric's stomach turned violently. His hands curled into fists, nails biting into his palms. What had Darius done to him? How much longer could he hold out? How much longer *until he broke?*

Cedric quickened his pace, Gwenna matching his stride. They turned a corner and...

Guards.

A patrol was heading straight for them, their lantern painting long, wavering shadows across the stone walls. Cedric's mind went blank for half a second, his body freezing like a deer about to be run down by hounds. Gwenna's hand clamped onto his arm.

"Just act normal," she hissed under her breath. "Pretend like we belong, and they're less likely to stop us."

Cedric nearly laughed. *Act normal?* He was a *dragon* for half the day. He hadn't been *normal* in ten years. Cedric wouldn't know normal if it stepped out of the shadows and introduced itself. But he forced himself to move, his body rigid with effort. One step. Another. *Just keep walking. No dragon princes or feral princesses here. Just totally normal citizens.*

"...increased patrols," one guard was saying. "King's orders. He's paranoid about—"

The rest was lost to distance, but Cedric didn't need to

hear more. He could only guess why Darius was paranoid. But he was pretty sure it involved him and Gwenna.

He released a gusty breath, only daring to meet Gwenna's gaze once the guards passed. She looked just as grim as he felt.

They walked in silence, moving deeper into the city. Every street corner held ghosts of memories. There—the bakery where he and Darius had snuck sweets as children, breathless with laughter, hands sticky with honey. There— the fountain where he had stolen his first kiss, only to realize with a sinking sense of disappointment that the experience had done nothing for him. That no kiss from a girl ever would.

Everything felt distant. Blurred, like an old dream that didn't belong to him anymore.

"Cedric." Gwenna's voice cut through the storm of his thoughts.

He exhaled sharply, dragging his gaze from the towering silhouette of the palace to where she stood, half-hidden by a tangle of overgrown bushes.

"We're here." She pushed aside a mass of foliage, revealing a rusted grate set into the stone wall. It was nearly invisible beneath the creeping ivy, its metal corroded from years of neglect. The faint stench of damp earth and stag-nant water clung to the air. "This leads to an old drainage tunnel," she explained, her voice low. "It should take us right under the castle walls."

Cedric eyed the grate warily, his pulse quickening. He hadn't set foot inside these walls since—*since then*. The last time, he had been something *else*, someone *else*. His body had not been his own, his mind lost to the storm of his first transformation.

The thought of walking back into the palace made his skin crawl. Still, he forced himself to focus on the present. "How did you even know about this?"

Gwenna shot him a sideways glance, mischief glinting in her eyes despite the gravity of their situation. "I may have done some exploring in my younger days. Being a princess can be *terribly* boring, you know."

Cedric shook his head, not remotely surprised. Gwenna had *always* been reckless, always testing the edges of her golden cage, looking for ways to slip through the bars.

She crouched and gripped the edges of the grate, straining. The rusted metal groaned but refused to budge. "It's stuck," she muttered through clenched teeth. "Can you...?"

Cedric stepped forward automatically, bracing his hands against the grate...and *froze*.

A memory slammed into him, fast and brutal.

Claws screeching against stone. The tang of blood in the air. The cries of men as they died. His own breathing—ragged, wild—his heart hammering against the inside of his ribs as he lost himself to the hunger, to the heat, to the sheer, uncontrollable terror of what he had become...

"Cedric?" Gwenna's voice pulled him back, the world shifting beneath his feet as he clawed his way out of the past. He was here. *Now*. Not then. She was watching him, brow furrowed with concern. "Are you all right?"

He swallowed hard. His mouth was dry. "I'm fine," he managed, though his voice sounded brittle. *Liar.* "Let's just— let's just get this open."

Together, they pulled at the grate. Rust flaked beneath their fingers, the metal groaning in protest, but it refused to budge. The years had sealed it shut, the elements conspiring against them.

After several frustrating minutes, Gwenna let out a sharp breath and released it. "Great. Now what?"

Cedric ran a hand through his hair. They *needed* another way in. And then—

A memory stirred. A secret tucked away in the depths of

his childhood. A passage he had *never* told Darius about. Never told *anyone* about.

"I know another way," he said slowly. "It's risky, but it might be our only option."

Gwenna turned to him sharply. "Oh? And when were you planning on sharing this information?"

Cedric ignored the jab, his mind already working through the logistics. "There's a hidden entrance to the royal stables. It was used in times of siege to smuggle in supplies. If it's still there, it should get us inside the castle grounds."

Gwenna blinked. Then her eyes narrowed. "And you're just mentioning this *now*?"

"I'd *forgotten* about it," Cedric admitted, rubbing his temples. "It's not like I've spent the last decade reminiscing about childhood escape routes."

Gwenna huffed, but nodded. "Fine. Let's go."

They moved swiftly through the darkened streets, keeping to the narrowest alleys and the deepest shadows. Cedric's pulse spiked as they neared the eastern side of the palace grounds, where the royal stables awaited them. Would the entrance still be there? Had it been discovered in his absence?

He reached the stand of trees shielding the hidden door and ran his hands over the weathered wood, searching. His fingers brushed against something—an indentation, a faint groove. *There.*

With a quiet *click*, the door swung open.

Gwenna arched a brow. "After you, Your Highness," she said with a mock bow.

Cedric shot her a withering look but stepped inside first, his senses stretching into the darkness. The passage was narrow and smelled of mildew and rodents. They moved carefully, feet whispering against the packed dirt.

Memories played like torchlight on the walls. He had *loved* the stables once. Had spent hours here as a boy, learning to ride, brushing down his favorite horse. *Sunset.* A pang shot through him. *Was she still here?*

He *wanted* to check. Just one look. But there was no time.

They reached the end of the passage, slipping out into the stables proper. A lantern hung near the main entrance, illuminating the rows of stalls.

Cedric's breath hitched. This was it. They were inside. The courtyard lay beyond, silent; the castle looming ahead like a specter. Keeping low, Cedric led the way, slipping from shadow to shadow as they made their way toward the entrance to the dungeons.

As they neared their destination, a new problem presented itself. A jailer sat at a small table just inside the dungeon entrance, his boots propped up on the edge, picking at his teeth with a fingernail. A heavy ring of keys dangled from his belt, swaying as he shifted.

Cedric's jaw tightened. They were so *close.* But without those keys, they might as well have been miles away from Finn.

"We need to get those keys," Gwenna whispered.

Cedric nodded, his mind already racing. Brute force wasn't an option. They couldn't risk a struggle, not when guards could patrol just beyond sight. He and Gwenna were vastly outnumbered.

"I have an idea," he murmured, the beginnings of a plan taking shape. "But it's going to require some teamwork." He quickly outlined his plan to Gwenna.

Her eyes gleamed in the dim light. "Now *that* sounds promising." She grinned, already reaching into her pack. "And as it happens, I have just the thing to help." She pulled out a small vial and held it up.

Cedric arched a brow. "And *that* is...?"

"A little something I picked up in the markets of Duskridge," Gwenna said smugly. "A valerian tincture. It should knock him out long enough for us to do what we need to do."

Cedric didn't ask *why* she had such a thing in her possession. He had long ago learned not to question where Gwenna acquired her tricks. Instead, he nodded and moved into position to do his part.

On the far side of the courtyard, he reached for a precarious stack of crates and gave them a shove. They toppled with a tremendous crash, the sound ricocheting off the stone walls.

The jailer jerked upright, his boots hitting the floor with a heavy *thud*.

"Who's there?" he called, already fumbling for the sword at his hip.

Cedric melted into the shadows, hardly daring to breathe.

While the jailer squinted into the darkness, muttering curses about stray cats and incompetent servants, Gwenna slipped behind him.

Silent as a breath, she reached for his mug. Not to take it —but to add to it.

Cedric held his breath, watching as she tilted the vial toward it, letting the liquid pour seamlessly into the ale. Gwenna picked up the mug, giving it a swirl. Then, just as quickly, she retreated, leaving the mug exactly where it had been.

Cedric waited as the man grumbled, rubbing at his eyes.

Then the jailer reached for the mug, lifted it to his lips, and took a deep swig.

They waited, pressed into the shadows, watching. The effect wasn't immediate, but within minutes, the jailer's head bobbed once, twice, before he slumped forward onto the table, snoring softly.

"Good work," Cedric whispered as they approached. Gwenna gave an ironic curtsy, then quickly snatched the keys from the sleeping man's belt. Meanwhile, Cedric rifled through the stack of papers spread haphazardly across the table. The ink was smudged in places, but the names listed in the ledger sent a fresh wave of anger through him.

So many names he recognized. People who had once stood by his parents. Nobles, yes, but many common folk—bakers, cobblers, merchants. Farmers who had dared to voice dissent. His gaze skimmed lower, and his breath caught. Some of these names…they weren't just Lunarethan.

Revendarian.

The realization sent a jolt through him. He had known Darius was turning the kingdom inward, isolating it, but *this?* These weren't just political prisoners. They were *refugees.* People whose only crime was crossing the border.

His stomach twisted. These were people his parents might have once granted sanctuary. People who had fled their own lands, only to find Lunareth's mercy had died with its former king.

Then his gaze snagged on a name.

Finnian Brightmoor.

Cedric's mouth went dry as he stared at the parchment.

"He's in the third level, cell fourteen," he whispered, his gaze skimming further down the page. Then his breath caught in his throat. A single line, written in cold, emotionless ink, sealed their urgency.

Scheduled for execution at dawn.

Gwenna peered over his shoulder. "We don't have much time," she said, voice tight. "Let's go."

They moved swiftly, descending deeper into the bowels of the castle where the air grew colder. The torches lining the walls did little to chase away the oppressive darkness or provide warmth.

The first two levels were eerily silent, most of the cells empty. Those that were occupied held prisoners too broken to react, their gazes vacant, their spirits already gone.

But when they reached the third level, the air was thick with the stench of rot and unwashed bodies. Cedric's stomach churned. Here, the groans of the forgotten echoed through the corridors, accompanied by the distant rattle of chains.

"Fourteen... fourteen..." Gwenna muttered, scanning the doors. "Here!"

Cedric's pulse thundered in his ears.

Iron bands reinforced the heavy wood door, the number etched into the rusted plate above it. His hands shook as he fumbled with the keys, his urgency making him clumsy. The scrape of metal against metal felt deafening as he shoved the key home.

Then—*click*. The lock gave way.

Cedric shoved the door open, the wood slamming against the stone. The cell swallowed him in darkness, the only light bleeding in from a sconce in the corridor.

For a moment, his vision fought against the gloom. Shadows stretched, twisting against the damp walls. The air was thick—damp with sweat and suffering.

And then his gaze landed on a crumpled shape in the corner. Cedric's heart plummeted. It couldn't be him. *Not the knight who made my pulse trip over itself every time he said my name. Not the man I love.*

"Finn?" The name barely escaped him, but it was enough.

The figure stirred, slowly. A head lifted, catching the dim light, and Cedric's breath punched from his lungs.

Aurenis, no.

Bruises marred every inch of Finn's face, his skin swollen and split, hardly recognizable. But those eyes—those storm-grey eyes—remained.

"Cedric?" The voice was a ruin of what it should have been. Finn's lips cracked from thirst, his breathing shallow. "Is it...really you?"

Cedric was at his side in an instant, dropping to his knees. Up close, it was worse. Much worse.

Cuts, bruises, burns—marks of torment carved into Finn's skin. But it was the ugly brands that stopped Cedric cold, stark against pale flesh, as if pain alone could etch ownership into him. Fury clawed up Cedric's throat, but it was nothing compared to the cold terror that followed when his gaze dropped lower. Finn's hand—*his sword hand*—was a ruin. Shattered beyond recognition, crushed fingers swollen and discolored.

"Sweet Sylvara," Gwenna whispered.

Cedric couldn't breathe. Couldn't move.

The sight of Finn like this...so broken, so *far* from the man who had once laughed with him, teased him, kissed him...made something splinter inside his chest.

"It's me," Cedric forced out, his throat tight, the words nearly choking him. He tried to keep his voice calm. Failed.

Who did this to you? The question burned hot and poisonous in his mind, but he swallowed it down. There would be time for vengeance.

Right now, they had to get Finn out.

Finn's eyes fluttered closed, his lashes clumping together, damp from tears. The streaks they left through the grime on his face made Cedric's stomach twist.

"Neither of you should be here," Finn rasped. "It's not safe."

"*I don't care*," Cedric said, too quickly, too fiercely.

How could he? How could he care about *anything* else when Finn looked like a man who had been utterly broken and left to rot?

Finn's head lolled toward him, and his gaze locked onto Cedric's with an intensity that sent icy fingers racing down his spine. "*He knows*," Finn breathed, the words trembling with urgency. "He *knows* about you, Cedric. Knows you're alive."

The world shrank to nothing but Finn's bloodied mouth shaping those words. Darius knew. The ground beneath Cedric felt unsteady, like the entire world had shifted without his permission.

But Finn was still speaking, bloodshot eyes never leaving Cedric's face. "I didn't mean to tell him," the broken knight whispered, his face contorting—not just with pain, but with something deeper. Shame. Guilt.

Whether it was the pain of torture or his own words crushing him, Cedric couldn't tell.

He should have been furious. He should have let himself rage at the unfairness of it. But there was no anger left in him at the moment—only grief.

Only Finn, holding on by a thread.

"I know," Cedric murmured.

He ached to touch him, to comfort him, to make this right. To smooth back his tangled hair, to feel the warmth of Finn's skin beneath his palm—just to know he was still here.

But Finn looked so close to slipping away, so close to passing through the veil to Nivara's domain, that Cedric was afraid to touch him at all. He dragged his gaze to Gwenna.

She swallowed, glancing between them before kneeling beside Finn, pulling something from her satchel. "I have a draught for pain."

Finn nodded, but Cedric saw the way his body sagged forward, as though even holding himself upright had become unbearable. Cedric clenched his jaw so tightly it ached.

Gwenna worked carefully, tilting Finn's head and pressing the vial to his lips. He drank, his throat moving with difficulty, but he finished it. She set the empty vial aside.

Finn looked a little more at ease now. Which, given his condition, meant almost nothing. Cedric took the risk, resting a hand on Finn's shoulder. Beneath his palm, bone and bruised muscle tensed.

"We need to get you out of here." His voice was low but firm. "Can you move?"

Finn's gaze lifted to his. And *gods*—the agony in those eyes. "I don't know."

Three words. They shattered Cedric all over again.

His fingers flexed, as if he could help Finn with touch alone. But they couldn't stay here. Another few hours, and Finn wouldn't survive this dungeon, let alone the executioner's block. "Darius plans to execute you at dawn."

Finn shut his eyes. "I know," he whispered. His brows furrowed, pain twisting his expression. *"You shouldn't be here."*

Cedric pressed his lips together, glancing at Gwenna. Was Finn just disoriented from pain? From exhaustion? Or was there something else?

He was so damn insistent.

But it didn't matter. Cedric wasn't leaving without him. He shook his head. "It's a little late for that. We're here, and we're getting you out."

He shifted to ease one of Finn's arms around his shoulders, then carefully helped the knight rise from the ground, mindful of his mangled hand.

"How are we going to get him out of here without being caught?" Gwenna whispered, moving in to help.

Cedric's lips pursed, already calculating. The draught was helping—Finn's breath was no longer as labored, and some of the tension had left his frame—but he was still weak. Too weak to move fast. And *time*—they needed time.

If Cedric could just get Finn outside the city, somewhere secluded, *he* could fly him to safety at dawn. But that was still at least two hours away. Even if they got Finn out of the dungeons, where could they hide him until then?

His mind worked furiously, piecing through their options until he remembered the ledger he had seen earlier.

"The key," Cedric hissed suddenly. With his free hand, he

slipped it out of his pocket and thrust it at his sister. "Free the other prisoners."

Gwenna's head snapped toward him, eyes wide. "What?"

Cedric's stomach churned, but he was sure of this. "They're *political* prisoners. Many are refugees," he whispered. "Not criminals. They've crossed Darius, somehow. And he's making them suffer."

Gwenna let out a quiet but vicious curse. He felt her hesitation—there was risk in this, *so much risk*—but then her lips pressed into a hard line, and she nodded. "You're probably right. Okay. I'll get to work."

She darted toward the cells lining the corridor, sinking the key into the first lock. Cedric caught the disbelieving gasp as someone whispered, "*Princess.*" He winced. He hadn't accounted for that. If word got out that *both* lost royals were here, they were as good as dead.

But there was no stopping now. The flood had started.

As Gwenna worked, prisoners poured from their cells, silent but desperate—a wave of the forgotten, the wrongly punished, the innocent who had suffered under Darius's rule. Cedric tightened his hold on Finn, bracing the knight against his side as the others streamed past.

None of them stopped. None of them looked too closely at Cedric, and he was fine with that. *Let them think whatever they want. Just let them run far, far away.*

Every few steps, Cedric adjusted his grip on Finn, his own muscles burning under the weight. "We're almost out," he murmured. He wasn't sure if he was reassuring Finn or himself.

Step by step, they climbed. Step by step, they left the dungeon behind. Cedric couldn't think past the single driving command pulsing in his skull.

Get out. Get out. Get out.

And when they did—when the night air hit them and the

shouts of confusion rang through the dungeon below—Cedric knew the escape was far from over.

But for the first time, the world felt just a little wider. The first real breath of hope.

Chapter Twenty-Three

The world was a haze of pain and confusion as Finn stumbled out of the dungeon, his body a ruined thing held together only by Cedric's tender grip. Every step sent daggers of fire through his ribs, his breath shallow and ragged. His legs barely functioned, as though they belonged to someone else entirely. The uneven stone beneath his feet might as well have been shifting sand. He didn't know how he was still moving, only that Cedric was keeping him upright, and that had to be enough.

Through the fog of agony, one truth shone with aching clarity—*Cedric had come for him.*

Finn didn't understand it. Couldn't fathom *why*. Cedric should have let him rot down there. That would have been the *wise* thing, the *safe* thing. Instead, here Cedric was, risking everything.

The cool night air hit Finn's face like a blast, shocking after the stifling warmth of the dungeon. Or maybe he was just feverish from all of his injuries. He gasped, lungs seizing, body rebelling against the sudden shift. The world outside— the *real* world—was overwhelming.

Chaos churned in every direction.

Prisoners spilled from the dungeon entrance, their hoarse shouts splitting the air, some ragged with desperation, others lifted in exultation. Shadows flailed against torchlight as men and women ran, some breaking toward the palace walls, others ducking for cover wherever they could. Guards scrambled, trying to contain the surge of fleeing bodies, but they were *so few* against the tide. Someone tackled a guard to the ground. Another snatched up a fallen sword. The din of combat echoed against the stone walls of the palace courtyard.

Finn swayed, vaguely aware of his own faltering steps. The pain blurred the edges of his vision, turned everything into unfocused shapes and streaks of color. He was slipping —*too much, too fast.*

"Stay with me, Finn," Cedric's voice cut through the haze.

Finn forced himself to nod, teeth gritted against the agony lancing through his skull. *Keep moving.* That was all he had to do. Just *keep moving.* But even as he fought to focus, his senses felt distant and unreliable.

His fevered mind caught on fleeting glimpses of familiar faces—fellow knights, merchants, nobles—people he had once known. Their features blurred together. He had no idea how *any* of them had ended up here. Had Darius done this? Had the kingdom always been rotting from within, and Finn had simply been too blind to see it?

None of it mattered. Not right now.

"Where...where are we going?" Finn didn't recognize the gravelly sound of his own voice.

"The stables," Cedric murmured, his grip tightening around Finn's waist, supporting more of his weight. "Then we'll find a safe place to rest."

Gwenna appeared on Finn's other side, looping his arm over her shoulder to help. Finn let them take the burden without protest, his strength waning fast.

"Should we steal some horses?" Gwenna asked, breathless from running.

Cedric shook his head. "Finn's in no condition to ride. Our best chance is for me to...to transform. I can carry you both to safety."

Finn's gut twisted—not just with pain, but with *fear*.

"Cedric, *no*," he protested. "You'll be seen..." His thoughts spiraled in frantic disarray. Darius *knew*. He *knew* about Cedric, about the dragon. And yet Cedric had come here anyway. *By Kavros's anvil, what were you thinking?*

He wanted to shake Cedric, to demand why he had thrown himself into the fire for someone like Finn. But even as the thought formed, another followed, quieter and sharper—*I'm glad he did.*

"It doesn't matter," Cedric said, his voice fierce. "Getting you two to safety is all that matters now."

Finn squeezed his eyes shut. He wanted to argue, to *fight* him on this. Cedric's well-being *mattered*—of course it did. But he lacked the strength to push back. Right now, all he could do was keep putting one foot in front of the other and hope Cedric knew what he was doing.

They were *so close* now. The stables were only a few paces away. Just a little further, and they'd be under cover. Finn allowed himself the smallest, most fragile sliver of hope. Maybe they would make it. Maybe...

A figure stepped out of the shadows ahead, blocking their path.

Finn's breath seized. Even through the dim torchlight, he recognized that stance instantly. That commanding posture, the lazy arrogance in the set of his shoulders, the gleam of calculation in his cold, dark eyes.

King Darius.

Finn's body reacted before his mind could catch up. His legs froze, his sword hand a limp mess at his side, but he forced himself upright, alert, teeth gritted against the pain.

A pitiful display, but he *refused* to meet Darius as anything less than a knight.

The chaos behind them faded into nothingness, muted by Darius's presence. Finn felt Cedric go rigid beside him, his breath stilling. Gwenna tensed at his other side. But Finn *couldn't* look at either of them, not now.

Because Darius's gaze was locked on Cedric. And King Dickhead was smiling.

"Well, well," Darius drawled, his voice laced with smug satisfaction, each syllable taunting. "What have we here? A convenient jailbreak? How *cute*."

Finn hardly registered the words before he felt Cedric's grip tighten around him. Every muscle in Finn's battered body screamed in protest at the force holding him upright, but the pain was nothing compared to the dread curling in his gut.

"Get out of our way, Darius," Cedric said, his voice surprisingly calm, but Finn could feel the storm raging beneath it.

Darius laughed—a hollow, mirthless sound that sent a chill through Finn's already aching bones. "Oh, I *don't* think so, old friend. You see, I've been waiting for this moment for a *very* long time."

Finn's eyes squeezed shut. He had tried to tell Cedric in the dungeon, but had been in too much pain. *You shouldn't have come.* Finn had suspected Darius's plan to use him as bait. This only confirmed it.

"You *knew*," Finn rasped, the words burning his throat. "You *knew* they would come for me."

Darius's dark eyes gleamed. "Knew? No, Sir Finnian. But I certainly *hoped*." He gestured around them, at the chaos unfolding—guards struggling to control the flood of prisoners, the clash of steel ringing in the distance. "When a loyal knight like yourself returned empty-handed, I had a feeling it was for good reason. And now, thanks to your unwavering sense of honor and your misplaced love, you've led my lost princess and the prince's ghost right to me."

Finn trembled, the knowledge cutting deeper than any wound the royal torturer had carved into him. *This is my fault.*

"You couldn't have known," Cedric whispered

Finn blinked. *Wait.* Had he...? Oh. He'd said that out loud. His stomach twisted, and he let out a rough breath, trying to shove the words back where they belonged. *Too late.*

Cedric's voice was far too gentle, far too forgiving.

Finn clenched his jaw, looking away. Damn it.

Finn hated that understanding tone. He didn't deserve it. Cedric should be furious, should curse Finn for leading them into a trap. Instead, Cedric turned his focus back to Darius, and something changed in his eyes. The raw, open grief Finn had glimpsed in him before was gone, replaced with something darker, *sharper*. Rage.

"What have you done, Darius?" Cedric demanded, voice commanding. *A prince's voice,* Finn thought. "What game are you playing?"

Darius's smirk only deepened. "*Game?*" he repeated, feigning surprise. "Oh, Cedric, this is so much more than a game. This is destiny. *My* destiny. And you're going to help me fulfill it."

With an elegant flick of his wrist, he lifted his hand, letting the moonlight catch the facets of the ring gleaming on his finger. The ruby at its center pulsed—not with reflected light, but with something deeper, something wrong. A slow, rhythmic shimmer of unnatural energy.

Finn had seen magical artifacts before—his own armor, for starters—but *this* was different. This was *wrong*.

Cedric froze. Finn felt the way every part of him locked into place, his breath stalling in his throat. His golden-brown eyes went wide.

"Nice costume jewelry," Gwenna snarled. Gods, Finn had

been so focused on Darius that he'd almost forgotten she was there. "Now go flaunt it to someone who *cares*."

Darius hardly spared her a glance. "I'll get to you in time, my *betrothed*." He said the word like a promise, like a threat. "But for now, I need to have words with your brother."

He took a step forward.

Cedric flinched. A barely perceptible movement, but Finn felt it all the same. His breathing had gone shallow, as if every instinct was screaming at him to move, but he *couldn't*.

What was happening?

Finn's gaze snapped back to the ring. *What does it do? Why is Cedric reacting like this? And more importantly—could I pry it off Darius's hand?* With the way his body currently felt, all signs pointed to *no*. And that was frustrating.

Darius watched Cedric's reaction, satisfaction lighting his expression. He turned the ring slowly on his finger, almost idly, like he was admiring a well-crafted sword. "Strange, isn't it? How something so *small* can wield so much power over you." His eyes gleamed with something danger-ous. "You *feel* it, don't you?"

Cedric's throat bobbed.

"Your body remembers," Darius observed, tilting his head. "Even if *you* don't. A little blood, a little magic, and there you have it—the power to create a monster."

Finn's stomach lurched. The bile burned his tongue.

No.

He turned to Cedric, searching his face, trying to under-stand. But Cedric was staring at the ring like he was about to be sick.

Gwenna, however, had no patience for Darius and his theatrics. "What the *hell* are you talking about?" she snapped. "What monster? What does that *thing* do?"

Darius laughed, delighted, as if she'd set him up perfectly. "Oh, come now. You still don't get it?" His gaze flicked back to Cedric, and his expression turned cruel. "I *made* him."

"What?" Gwenna's voice was sharp, incredulous. "*You*—?"

"I cursed him," Darius said simply, like he was discussing the weather. "I turned him into a beast, made him a creature of nightmares. And the *best* part?" He let out a short laugh, tilting his head. "He never even knew."

Cedric's entire body shook. Finn felt the force of his trembling, heard the ragged way he sucked in air. "You..." Cedric's voice cracked. "*You* did this to me?"

Darius spread his arms. "Of course I did! Who else could have orchestrated such a brilliant plan?" His grin stretched wide, teeth flashing like a predator's. "The beloved prince—transformed into a *beast*. The kingdom, thrown into chaos. And me? Rising to power, ready to save them all."

Finn felt sick. Cedric had never known. Through all the years of suffering, through every agonizing transformation, through all the nights spent alone—he had never known.

Gwenna shook with fury, and before Finn could so much as breathe, she lunged. "You *absolute bastard*—"

Darius tightened his hand into a fist, the ring flaring with light. Cedric collapsed. His knees slammed into the dirt, his breath ripping out of him in a hoarse, guttural sound.

Gwenna pulled up short, her mouth parting in a small, horrified *O* before she clamped it shut.

The breath rushed from Finn's lungs. His body screamed at him to move, to fight, but all he could do was watch. Somehow, he stayed standing—even as every muscle and bone protested.

Cedric convulsed.

His hands hit the ground like something inside him had just snapped. His back arched, his body seizing in violent, unrelenting spasms. A tremor wracked through him, stealing the breath from his lungs.

"*Cedric!*" Gwenna's voice cracked.

Finn hit his knees beside the downed prince, reaching

out, desperate to stop whatever this was. But Cedric only shook, his wild eyes fixed on Darius.

And Darius? King Raging Ego just watched. *Watched.* Like this was entertainment. Like Cedric's suffering was a game.

"What are you doing to him?!" Finn's voice ripped from his throat, raw with fury—but a sick part of him already knew.

"Stop it!" Gwenna's scream was edged with panic. Her hands curled into fists, trembling with helpless rage.

Darius ignored them all. His gaze never left Cedric, fixated.

Cedric screamed. The sound split the world in two. Finn had heard battle cries. The wails of the dying. The broken sobs of men past saving. But this...

This was agony in its purest form.

A soul being *unmade.* Worse than any torture the Duke of Poor Life Choices had visited upon Finn.

A guard grabbed Finn, yanking him back, dragging him away.

"No!" Finn struggled, but he couldn't break free. All he could do was watch.

And what he saw would never leave him. Cedric convulsed again, his body betraying him. Something inhuman clawed through his form, warping muscle, tearing through skin.

His breath hitched in broken gasps, his cries strangled between the horrific cracks of bone and sinew. Cedric's spine lengthened, spikes rising like the crash of a wave. His fingers flexed, claws bursting through flesh.

Fabric ripped, clothing shredded as scales rippled over skin. A ragged, animalistic scream tore from his throat as his jaw extended, jutting forward into a dragon's maw.

Finn had seen Cedric as a dragon before. He had even

seen him directly after a transformation. But this...this was different.

Those intelligent, fiercely *human* eyes were clouded now, hazy with suffering. His massive frame trembled, struggling against the aftermath of a transformation forced upon him. Cedric made an agonized, keening sound, slumping onto his side.

Finn trembled in outrage. He knew pain, knew exhaustion, knew what it meant to have his body pushed beyond its limits. But this? *This* was something worse.

Darius lowered his hand, and the ring's glow dimmed like a dying ember. The air still crackled with residual energy, the taste of magic sharp on Finn's tongue.

A slow, satisfied smile spread across the royal asshat's face. He looked up at Cedric—at the dragon—as if admiring his latest acquisition. "Perfect," he whispered.

Finn's hands clenched into furious fists. "What have you *done*?" he demanded, wishing that he could do something more than stand there, weak and useless. What was he going to do, glare Darius into submission? Threaten to fall over if the king didn't leave them alone? Hopeless.

But still, Finn lifted his chin.

Darius turned his smug gaze on him. "I've solidified my reign," he said smoothly, as if it were the most obvious thing in the world. "With a dragon at my command and my wife at my side, no one will *dare* deny me."

His attention flicked to Gwenna, lingering there, before sliding back to Finn.

The king's gaze made Finn's blood run cold.

"But don't think I've forgotten about *you*, Sir Finnian," Darius added, almost fondly. "It's an important day for you, after all."

Finn's gut twisted. He knew *exactly* what that meant. And he was powerless to stop it.

"*No!*" Gwenna snarled. "He did what you wanted! Leave him alone!"

Darius sighed as if she were a child throwing a tantrum. "I *hope* you don't intend to be this demanding once we're wed, Gwenna. It would be tiresome." He gestured lazily toward his assembled King's Guard, lined up in perfect formation, eyes blank and obedient as hounds awaiting their master's command. "And while I will agree that Sir Finnian's resilience is commendable, I doubt his ethics will allow me to bribe him like this lot."

His gaze flicked to Cedric, still trembling from the forced transformation. Darius smiled. "Beheadings," he said, almost wistfully, "are *so* last year. I think this calls for something more...*sporting*."

Chapter Twenty-Four

Pain splintered Cedric's world into shards.

Sunrise was still hours away. He should have been safe. *Human.*

But this transformation had been ripped from him, a violation so profound it left his body twitching—a puppet with its strings half-severed, limbs jerking, refusing to obey. Every breath scorched his lungs, as if Darius's curse had filled them with smoke and ash.

Move.

He tried. Tried to lift his head, tried to push up from the dirt. But agony shot through his spine. Through blurred vision, he glimpsed...

Finn.

The King's Guard dragged him away. His head lolled, eyes rolling like he might pass out, his body too broken to fight anymore. His legs refused to hold him, and so the guards hauled him like a discarded thing, like something no longer human.

Blood pooled, then smeared, trailing behind him. Their careless treatment had torn open his wounds.

Cedric's claws dug deep into the earth. *Move,* he begged

himself, his mind screaming. *MOVE*.

Finn's eyelids fluttered open just for a moment. His gaze met Cedric's. And—gods help him—there was so much apology in those eyes.

Cedric didn't want to see it.

Couldn't bear to.

A thick, heavy weight clamped around his limbs. Chains.

A ragged sound tore from his throat. Not quite a growl, not quite a whimper. The iron was laced with magic, pulsing in a way that made his scales itch and his bones feel brittle. His wings twitched—useless, trembling, pinned awkwardly against his sides. He could not rise. Could not fight. Could barely breathe without agony spearing through his chest.

Through the haze of pain, his gaze landed on Gwenna. She twisted and thrashed in the grip of a pair of guards who were attempting to placate her with foolish lines that were more likely to get them bashed in the head with a rock.

"It's for your own good, Princess," one of the guards grunted, tightening his grip.

"There's no need to be hysterical!" the other shouted, frustrated.

The bastard never saw her knee coming. The impact sent him staggering back, gasping. For a moment, Cedric wasn't the only one in agony.

"Let him go!" Gwenna shrieked, sounding like a feral creature. A wildcat in human form. Cedric's face dug into the dirt as he watched her with one eye.

No one listened to her.

Footsteps.

The rhythm of a man who had already won. Darius stepped into view, surveying the wreckage before him with the casual amusement of an artist admiring his masterpiece.

His gaze swept across Finn, Gwenna, the trail of blood. Then he turned to Cedric, a smile on his lips.

"Look at you," he crooned, voice dripping with mockery.

"Thought you could come here and reclaim what isn't yours." His lip curled, his gaze flicking to Finn. "Gathering knights who vow themselves to you like a pretender."

Cedric snorted. Dust and blood misted from his nostrils, but it didn't even have the decency to reach Darius's boots.

Disappointing.

He wanted to lunge, to fight, to *rip* the smirk from Darius's face.

Because Darius had hurt Finn.

Had hurt Gwenna.

Had torn apart their home, their lives.

Had stolen, broken, crushed.

Not *just* his family. Not *just* his friends.

His kingdom. *His* people.

Darius wasn't just a monster. He was rot. Decay. The slow death of everything Cedric had ever loved.

And yet, Cedric was the one in chains.

Darius edged closer, resting a hand on Cedric's neck. He wished he could writhe away from the touch, but that was beyond his throbbing body at the moment.

"All that power," Darius mused, running his fingers along Cedric's golden armor. "All that radiance." The ring on his finger gleamed, the ruby glinting in the dim light as he twisted it idly. "And yet, here you are. Chained. Defeated." He tilted his head and sighed. "*The Gilded Nothing.*"

Cedric bared his fangs, but the effort made his vision swim. A tremor shot through him. He couldn't allow this. Gathering all the strength he could, powering past the pain, Cedric surged to his feet.

One blow. One snap of his fangs. That would be all it would take. He lunged.

Pain erupted like fire as Darius lifted his hand, the ring pulsing with a sinister glow. Cedric crashed back down, agony wracking through him like a thousand knives carving him apart from the inside.

"I thought you were smarter than that, Cedric," Darius said, amused. His smirk gleamed like the edge of a dagger. "Don't try to fight me. I'll put you in your place." He rolled his shoulders, feigning boredom, before gesturing to the guards. "See that Princess Gwenna is taken to suitable accommodations in the palace. You already know where to take the traitor knight."

The guards hurried to follow orders. Others stood around Cedric, holding the chains that bound him.

Darius made a show of polishing the ring with his sleeve. "As for you...well, I have a special place for you, dragon."

Gwenna snarled, twisting back to look at him. And in her gaze, Cedric saw everything—the fury, the grief, the silent promise.

This was not over.

But Finn...

Finn was hurt too badly.

And Darius had made one thing crystal clear: The knight didn't have long to live.

Cedric's world crumbled.

If Finn died, it was over.

Chapter Twenty-Five

Finn drifted toward wakefulness. Something was different. The chilly dampness of the dungeon was gone, replaced by warmth. He wasn't lying on stone. His body rested on something *soft*.

I must be dreaming.

A hand ghosted over his arm, feather-light. Finn's eyelids fluttered open, his vision slow to adjust to the shift in brightness. Sunlight. There was sunlight streaming through a narrow slit of a window.

The scent of herbs filled the air, subtle but familiar—marigold and comfrey, clean linen, something faintly lemony beneath it all. The air was warm. Too warm.

This wasn't the dungeon.

Finn's brows furrowed. The agony in his body had dulled, replaced by a deep, distant ache. His last memories came in fragmented flashes—Gwenna's voice, the rush of freedom, leaning heavily on Cedric...and Darius.

His pulse jumped. *Where am I?*

A woman knelt beside him, garbed in the deep blue robes of a royal healer. Finn stiffened, instinct screaming *danger*, but her hands were gentle as she dabbed cool salve along his forearm, where the burns had been. *Had* been. His breath hitched—his skin, raw and blistered before, was pink and *whole*. He hadn't imagined it, had he? The searing agony of the brand, the shattering of bone—

His fingers twitched, and a fresh wave of nausea rolled through him. His right hand was no longer a mangled wreck. The bones, crushed beneath the mallet, had been reset, the deep ache settling into his joints like a phantom pain. It didn't make sense. He should be ruined. He *was* ruined.

His throat worked, but the words caught. He turned his head, sluggish, searching for something—someone—familiar, but the healer only murmured a soothing incantation, her magic whispering against his skin.

For a long moment, Finn simply *breathed*. His body still ached, but it was manageable now. Not the grating, all-consuming fire it had been before.

"Wha—" His voice scraped against his throat like gravel.

The healer glanced up, expression neutral, though something gleamed behind her eyes—*pity*? "Don't talk yet," she instructed. "Drink this."

She pressed a cup to his lips, and Finn swallowed greedily. Water, fresh and sweet, washing away the dryness in his mouth, soothing his ragged throat.

Then the memories returned. The dungeon. Cedric's fierce presence. Gwenna's determination. The sickening crunch of bones reshaping under magic's cruel grip. Darius.

Cedric.

Finn shoved himself up, ignoring the sharp protest of his muscles. "Where are they?" His voice was raw, but forceful. "Where's Cedric? Where's Gwenna?"

The healer's hands were firm but careful as she pushed him back down, stronger than he expected. Or perhaps he was weaker than expected. "I don't have any information for you," she said briskly. "My job is to tend to your wounds, nothing more."

Finn's jaw clenched. He wanted to fight, to *demand* answers, but looking at the healer, he knew it would be futile. She wasn't here to tell him anything. She was here to keep him alive. And if she was under Darius's employ, that meant...

His stomach twisted. He let himself sink back onto the cot, muscles still wound tight with frustration. The healer resumed her work, moving methodically as she changed his bandages.

Finn's brow furrowed. He had been injured badly, but now...healing this quickly? His gaze flicked to the healer. "What are you using?" His voice was quieter this time, edged with suspicion. "I've never felt anything work so fast."

The woman hesitated. Just for a breath. Then she met his eyes, something unreadable in her expression. "A special blend," she said finally, voice softer than before. "Created for...unique circumstances."

A chill crept up Finn's spine. Why would Darius want him healed so quickly? The worst of the pain had fled, and now only hunger and weakness dogged him. Before he could press further, the door creaked open.

Two guards entered, their boots thudding against the stone floor. They moved with the professionalism of trained soldiers, their expressions blank. Finn's pulse kicked up.

"It's time," one of them said.

The healer didn't look up. She began gathering her supplies, never looking at Finn. But as she turned to leave, she paused. Her lips parted. "May Rynvath's ferocity be with you," she murmured. So quiet, Finn almost missed it. Then she was gone.

"Rynvath?" he whispered. The Untamed Spirit, the god of the hunt? Why invoke *his* name?

The guards hauled him to his feet. Finn gritted his teeth as they wrenched him upright, but to his shock, he didn't collapse. His legs held steady, his body moving with only a dull ache instead of searing pain. Whatever the healer had used, it had worked *too* well.

His stomach churned. "Time for what?" he demanded, but neither guard answered.

Their grip on his arms was tight—not quite brutal, but firm enough to leave bruises. He didn't struggle. Not yet. Not until he knew where they were taking him.

The halls blurred past as they dragged him forward. The twists and turns of the castle corridors were disorienting, unfamiliar. He tried to memorize the route, but his head was still fogged, his thoughts slipping like water through his fingers.

Then light. Bright sunlight. Finn winced, squinting against the sudden glare. His eyes adjusted slowly, revealing a small courtyard enclosed by high stone walls. And at its center, a wagon. This wasn't just another interrogation. This wasn't another session with the torturer.

He was being moved. His Majesty, the Royal Prick, had plans for him. And given the king's flair for the dramatic, nothing about them would be good.

As the guards shoved him into the wagon, Finn barely caught himself before he hit the rough wooden planks. Still-healing bruises throbbed, but it could have been far worse, if not for the healing. The wagon lurched forward, the wheels clattering against the cobblestone streets, and through the gaps in the covering, Finn caught snippets of conversation from the crowd outside.

"...biggest event in years..."

"...never seen the arena so full..."

"...wonder if the knight stands a chance..."

Arena? Finn's stomach twisted. His pulse pounded in his ears, drowning out the rhythmic clatter of the wagon wheels. What was Darius planning?

Through the slats, the city blurred past—banners hanging from balconies, vendors calling out, the streets lined with people craning their necks, eager for whatever spectacle they had been promised. Finn saw flashes of painted signs with crude illustrations, though he couldn't quite make them out. Whatever it was, the citizens of Mirathen were expecting blood.

His mouth was dry as he stared at their eager, animated faces. There was no fear here, no solemnity. Only anticipation. A festival atmosphere, a celebration of violence.

When the wagon finally rolled to a stop, Finn's nerves were stretched to the breaking point. The guards yanked him out, dragging him forward. And then they reached the destination. The arena.

Its towering stone walls loomed over him. The very air seemed charged, vibrating with the distant roar of a restless crowd.

A hard shove sent him stumbling forward.

"This way," one of the guards grunted.

Finn had no choice but to comply. They led him down a passageway, deeper into the underbelly of the coliseum. The further they descended, the louder the roar of the spectators became. It rattled through the stone like an approaching storm.

At last, they emerged into a small armory, and Finn's breath hitched.

Racks of weapons lined the walls, swords and spears gleaming in the torchlight. A table bore pieces of armor—not the finest quality, but sturdy enough. Finn's gaze skimmed over them, his unease growing.

And then he saw it.

His armor.

The familiar Revendarian steel was laid out on a nearby table, polished to a shine. All of the dings and scuffs he'd picked up from his ill-conceived battle with Cedric had been repaired. His own gauntlets, his greaves—the gear of a knight of the realm.

Why was it all here?

The realization slammed into him with the force of a charging warhorse.

This wasn't an execution.

This was a *fight*.

Finn turned to the guards, his hands balling into fists. "What is this?" His voice came out hoarse, but the fury behind it was unmistakable. "What are you expecting me to do?"

The guards said nothing. They simply began outfitting him. His own armor, buckled tight against his body. His breastplate, his vambraces, each strap cinched with the swiftness of men who had done this a hundred times before.

Every piece felt heavier than it should.

Finn tensed. His mind screamed at him to resist. But what was the point? Even if he refused, Darius would force his hand another way.

Then, finally, one of the guards retrieved a weapon from the table and turned, extending it toward him.

Sunwrath.

The ruby in the sword's pommel glinted, the blade's edge gleaming even in the dim light. His fingers curled around the hilt instinctively, the weight settling into his palm like an old companion. A shield followed—though this was not his own. Finn seldom used them, finding they only interfered with his preferred fighting style.

But he was so unbalanced all he could do was stare down at the shield as he understood what was coming.

A trial by combat.

Darius meant to make a spectacle of him. Would he face the king's champion? Finn's mind stretched, running through all of the senior knights. There were several who might step up to fight and put Finn in his place.

They marched him forward into an antechamber, a heavy wooden gate barring the way ahead. Finn caught glimpses of the crowd through the slats—thousands of spectators, their voices a deafening roar of excitement.

One guard lingered for just a moment. "Kavros watch over you," he muttered under his breath. Then they were gone.

Finn swallowed hard. A horn blared, loud enough to rattle his skull. The gate rose.

Finn squared his shoulders, forcing his feet onward, stepping into the blinding light of the arena.

The noise hit him like a wave. Thousands of voices rose in a mixture of cheers and jeers, a chaotic rumble of bloodlust. The scent of sand and sweat filled his lungs, the ground beneath his boots uneven and well-trodden.

His gaze swept the arena, taking in the towering walls, the vast stretch of the battlefield—built not for honor, but for spectacle. And close enough to savor every moment was the royal box.

It wasn't set high and distant like in some grand coliseum. No, Darius wanted to *watch* this. His Highness, Lord of Petty Tyranny, wanted to see *every* drop of blood spilled, *every* desperate moment. The royal box was positioned just above the first rows, an open, elevated platform where the nobility could enjoy the best view of the slaughter to come.

And there—so close that Finn could see the tension in her shoulders, the flex of her fingers—sat Gwenna. She was a vision of poise, swathed in embroidered silks, her hair pinned in a crown of intricate braids. But Finn knew her too well to be fooled. Every line of her body was too rigid, her hands too tightly curled in her lap. She wasn't there to watch. She was waiting. And *seething*.

His Royal Dumbassery didn't know of the brewing storm beside him.

The king rose to his feet, arms outstretched, and slowly, the roar of the crowd faded into a tense, expectant hush.

"People of Lunareth!" Darius's voice boomed over the

coliseum, amplified by magic. "Today, we witness a trial by combat! Before you stands Sir Finnian Brightmoor, accused of treason against the crown."

Treason. Finn clenched his jaw so hard it ached. *You're the traitor.* But screaming it here wouldn't matter.

King Dickhead paced the length of the royal box, his posture radiating control, his voice rich with performative mercy. "But I am a fair king. I offer Sir Finnian a chance to prove his innocence and regain his freedom. If he can defeat the monster that has plagued our kingdom for so long—the dragon that slaughtered the royal family—he will be exonerated of all charges."

Finn froze. *No.*

No, he wouldn't. He couldn't.

A thunderous roar erupted from the crowd, but Finn only heard the roar of blood rushing to his head. His fingers turned to ice around the hilt of his sword.

"Let the trial begin!"

The opposite gate groaned open. Finn whipped around, every muscle locking into place.

A massive scaled head emerged from the shadows, followed by the sinuous length of a golden neck. Sunlight struck Cedric's scales, setting them ablaze in a gleaming display of raw power. The dragon did not hesitate. He did not resist. He *charged*, a force of nature given form, his wings flaring as he surged forward, the ground quaking beneath his weight.

The only thing that stopped him were the chains. Eight men strained against them, their bodies braced, their faces twisted with effort as they fought to hold him back. Even so, Cedric *dragged* them, talons carving deep furrows into the sand, his powerful body flexing with unchecked aggression. The iron links groaned, the enchantments woven into them flaring with arcane light to reinforce their hold. Without them, Finn knew Cedric would already be upon him.

Finn's hope shattered as he locked eyes with the dragon before him.

There was nothing there.

No sign of recognition. No intelligence, no warmth. Just a predator with golden glowing eyes staring at its prey.

The Cedric he knew—the man—was gone.

Chapter Twenty-Six

Finn's stomach plummeted as he stared across the sand at Cedric.

The dragon's muscles rippled like a living tapestry beneath shimmering scales, straining against the enchanted chains that held him back. *Cedric.*

His Cedric.

The sight of him, so majestic and yet so cruelly bound, was a dagger in Finn's heart, twisting with each heated breath the dragon took.

Finn's grip on Sunwrath tightened, a jolt of pain lancing through his fingers. Even healed, the bones were stiff, the ache a dull throb beneath Sunwrath's weight. His palms were slick inside his gauntlets, sweat mingling with the ghost of old wounds. How could he do this? How could he raise his weapon against Cedric, even if the prince was currently more beast than man?

But the dragon's golden eyes showed no signs of humanity. Instead, they fixed on him with predatory intensity, pupils narrowing to slits that seemed to pierce straight through him. A low growl thundered from Cedric's chest, building to a deafening roar that shook the very foundations of the arena, a primal challenge that echoed off the stone walls and reverberated in Finn's bones.

His chest constricted. His mind rebelled against it, clawing for some explanation, some reason, but there was none. Why was he like this?

The ache in Finn's chest bloomed, not from his healing injuries, but from the hollow, sickening certainty settling in his bones.

It didn't matter.

The dragon in front of him was going to kill him.

From the royal box, Darius's voice rang out, *"Begin."*

The crowd erupted. Cheers. Jeers. Roaring voices that crashed like waves against Finn's skull. The sheer hunger in the air made his stomach lurch. This was a game to them. A spectacle. They wanted blood, and they didn't care whose.

Darius. This was *his* doing. *All* of it.

I wish you stood before me right now, Darius. I'd drive my sword right through that black heart of yours. Even if it killed me.

But there was no time for that. No time for hate... because with a series of metallic clanks, the chains fell away. The heavy links crashed to the sand as the handlers bolted for the dragon's antechamber.

For a heartbeat, Cedric did not move.

He crouched, muscles coiled, golden scales gleaming like a shattered sun.

Then he launched forward, a detonation of power. A shockwave of dust burst outward, blinding, the force of it nearly knocking Finn off his feet.

Move.

Finn sprinted. His heart thundered, boots carving deep furrows into the sand. No time to think. Only to act.

A blur of gold and fury filled his vision. Cedric lunged. Finn threw up his shield. Talons slammed into steel. A thunderous clang rang out, echoing across the arena.

Pain. A shockwave tore up Finn's arm, rattling his bones,

nearly dislocating his shoulder. He staggered, the world seeming to roll beneath him. Sweat ran into one eye and Finn didn't even have time to wipe it away.

The dragon was already closing in.

Again.

Another strike. Another unrelenting, bone-shaking blow. Finn's boots skidded across the sand, shield trembling beneath the assault. Runes along its rim flickered to life, absorbing some of the impact, but even reinforced magic had limits.

Too strong. Too fast. His arm screamed in protest, muscles threatening to give out.

Claws scraped against metal, shrieking like the wailing of the damned. The shield held—but Finn could feel the enchantments buckling, the magic struggling to disperse the sheer force behind Cedric's strikes.

The dragon's breath was hot against his skin. Finn had never felt more like prey. There was no kindness in those golden eyes. No trace of the man who had once looked at him like he was something worth holding on to.

Just hunger. Just instinct. The realization solidified like iron in Finn's heart. This was not Cedric. Not anymore.

The attacks slowed. Not by much. Not by *enough*. Finn barely had time to register it—just a shift in weight, a fraction of hesitation before another brutal strike.

But hesitation meant nothing. It wasn't human. It wasn't *him*.

Finn's breath came fast and ragged, lungs burning with effort, the reek of scorched sand and his own blood thick in his throat. He had let himself *believe*. Like an idiot.

"Cedric," he rasped, but it wasn't a plea. It was a farewell.

The dragon's head tilted, just slightly. For the barest instant, something almost human flickered in those eyes. Finn's heart lurched—*stupid*—and he crushed the thought before it could root. A trick of the light. A lie. The moment vanished as quickly as it had come, if it had ever been there at all.

Cedric struck. His tail scythed through the air.

Finn jumped. Too slow. A spike scraped his leg, sending him sprawling. Sand blinded him. The world tilted.

Jaws snapped.

A second slower, and his leg would have been gone. Finn dropped his shield and rolled, Sunwrath still in hand. *I don't want to hurt you. I can't.*

But he couldn't keep running forever.

The dragon followed his tumble. Too large, too powerful, *too fast*. Finn dove beneath Cedric's belly, surging up on the other side.

The dragon's head whipped around. Seconds. That's all he had.

Finn's sword lifted, his grip tight. Cedric snarled. Finn swung. Not to kill. Not even to wound. Just enough to survive.

The flat of his blade slammed into Cedric's shoulder, inches below the wing joint. Enough to buy him time.

THE SCENT OF BLOOD. The delicious stench of fear. The sharp tang of sweat.

It filled his nostrils, curling through his sinuses like smoke. He could taste it—metallic, hot, the promise of a fresh kill—coating his tongue, pooling in the back of his throat.

Hunger sharpened his mind to a singular edge.

He moved, sleek and sure, muscles rippling beneath gilded armor. Sand shifted under his talons, grains crunching between his claws as he stalked forward, silent as death. The two-legged creature before him was nothing. Fragile. Slow. Weak. A thing to be torn apart.

The beast circled, eyes slitted, nostrils flaring. Heat radiated from his prey's body in fevered waves, the frantic drumbeat of its heart nearly deafening in the dragon's ears. Its chest heaved, breath coming too fast, too shallow.

The acrid scent of terror. Prey. Prey could not run forever.

It had tried. Brandishing pointless metal, cowering behind a flimsy barrier. But the dragon was faster. *Stronger.* He had already proven this.

A slow, rolling growl gathered in his chest. His prey shifted, weight adjusting, feet bracing in the sand.

Useless. It would fall. They always fell.

He lunged.

Metal shrieked. The shield locked in place, but the force of the impact sent a jolt through the beast, a visceral pleasure. Grit churned beneath his claws, a cloud of dust rising. The vibrations of the blow rolled through his spine, rattled the very air.

Good.

The fight, the chase, the slow, *delicious* destruction of hope.

The shield lifted once more. The dragon struck. Again. Again.

A sharp cry broke from the prey's lips. The sound of an animal pushed past its limits. The scent of blood bloomed like crushed fruit in the air, rich and tantalizing.

A snarl of triumph ripped from the dragon's throat. His pupils flared wide, drinking in the sight of his prey sagging, barely able to hold itself upright. The human's arm trembled, body teetering.

Almost.

The beast coiled, muscles flexing, preparing for another strike.

Then...hesitation. Not his own. Confusion swarmed.

The dragon growled, a deep, rumbling note that vibrated in his chest.

The prey faltered. It made a strange sound, hoarse and shaking, a wounded animal's cry. His head cocked. He had seen this moment before.

Submission. But prey must never submit too soon. The fight had not been won. Had not been fully enjoyed.

The dragon's lips peeled back, fangs gleaming like ivory scythes. He reared up on his hind legs, scales rasping against each other as he loosed a bone-shaking roar that rattled the walls.

Let the prey scramble. *Let it try*.

It was only prolonging the inevitable.

IT WAS RECKLESS. It was stupid. But for a moment, Finn swore he saw it. A flicker in Cedric's golden eyes, the tiniest hesitation.

Finn latched onto it with both hands. "Remember the night atop the tower?" His breath burned in his throat as he dodged, narrowly escaping Cedric's claws. The strike whistled past his head, so close he felt the wind of it.

"You showed me the telescope—you and Gwenna worked on it for months." His breath came in ragged gasps, legs burning as he twisted away from a tail strike. Sand exploded beneath him. "I never got the chance to tell you, but it was one of the most remarkable things I've ever seen."

Cedric didn't stop. Didn't hesitate.

Finn's boots skidded in the dirt as he somehow avoided another swipe. Cedric loomed above him, all furious muscle and lethal instinct. Finn swallowed hard and lifted his chin. "Outside of *you*, that is."

Because if he was going to die here, he was *damn well* going to make it memorable.

A heartbeat of stillness.

Cedric's head twitched. A shift in weight, nostrils flaring as if he'd caught some unfamiliar scent. Finn's breath hitched. Was that real? Or just the calculation of a predator?

The dragon didn't move.

Finn's pulse hammered, his lungs ached, but he didn't dare move. Didn't dare break whatever this was.

"I saw a shooting star that night," Finn rasped, forcing the words past the tightness in his throat. "And I made a wish." He held Sunwrath like a lifeline. Not to strike. Never to strike. Only to hold on.

Cedric snorted, a hot gust of air hitting Finn square in the face.

Finn coughed, half-laughing despite himself. "Yeah, yeah. Seems unlikely to come true at this point. But I wanted to tell you what it was."

The pupils in Cedric's eyes contracted—inhuman, predatory.

"I wished for more nights like that," Finn whispered. "More time with you."

The dragon huffed, a great exhale that stirred Finn's hair. His wings twitched, tail curling—not in a strike, but in something almost thoughtful. Finn swallowed hard, hope rising like a tide. Gods, was this working?

Cedric's muscles coiled, talons flexing against the sand.

The thread between them stretched. One more pull and it would snap.

Finn swallowed hard, his voice little more than a whisper. "So, you know. If you could not roast me alive right now, that'd be a good start."

And just like that, it was gone.

The dragon's pupils narrowed to slits. His fangs bared. A sound—not quite a growl, not quite a snarl—rumbled through his chest, and then he moved.

Finn had just enough time to suck in a breath before the

world came crashing down. With a rumbling bellow that shook the arena, Cedric lunged.

Finn braced himself, every muscle in his body taut. He snatched up his shield and raised it to absorb another impact. The collision was cataclysmic—scales against steel, raw power against fragile flesh. The force sent Finn hurtling backward, his body weightless for half a second before crashing into the sand.

The enchantments woven into his armor flared to life, softening the worst of the impact. Even so, pain erupted everywhere at once, blooming sharp and hot as he skidded across the arena floor. His armor scraped against the coarse grit, metal screeching, bones jarring.

Blood filled his mouth, a nauseating warmth against his tongue. His whole body screamed *stay down*, but Finn had never been great at listening to advice—even from himself.

Get up. Move. Or you're dead.

With a groan that was equal parts agony and defiance, he forced himself upright. His legs shook, his lungs burned, his breath came in short gasps, but he was still standing.

"I know you're in there, Cedric," he panted, swiping a shaking hand across his mouth, smearing blood at the corner of his lips. His body felt like a warhorse had stomped on him. Or, more accurately, a very large, *very* pissed-off dragon.

Another step. Another breath. He had to keep talking. Had to keep pulling Cedric back.

"I know you can hear me," he rasped, wincing as the effort sent another stab of pain through his chest. "Any chance we could go five minutes without you knocking the breath out of me? I know you don't enjoy talking about your big, bad secret, but I think we're past that."

Every word scraped like glass in his throat, but he pushed through it. He had to.

Cedric snorted, another gust of hot breath washing over Finn.

Finn let out a wheezing laugh, barely holding himself upright. "See? You *do* hear me." His vision swam, the world tilting, but he held firm. "Please," his voice cracked, "come back to me."

The dragon froze.

For one agonizing heartbeat, Finn thought he might have won.

THE WORLD WAS RED. Hunger and fury and fire.

The rich scent of blood filled the dragon's lungs, calling him forward. The prey stood before him, chittering like a squirrel. He prowled closer, savoring the scent of sweat, the way his quarry trembled, the way its pulse beat a frantic rhythm—weak, erratic.

Mine.

The fire deep in his throat burned. It was time to finish this.

"You don't want to do this, Cedric. And I sure as hell don't want to fight you." The prey stared up at him, still bleeding. And somehow, defiant.

The name cracked through the dragon's mind like a hammer striking glass. He reared back with wings flared, shaking his head as if to dislodge something burrowing inside his skull.

Cedric.

More than just a name. A *truth*. *His* truth. But the beast did not understand truths. Only hunger. For a moment, the dragon faltered. Huffed a confused, uneasy breath.

"Cedric!" Another voice, this one sharp and commanding. The beast snapped his head around to peer at the crowd, focusing on a single creature.

The female.

The dragon's pupils narrowed. Females were prey. But... *no.* He knew her. Not prey. Not nameless.

Gwenna. The knowledge sent a bolt of lightning through him, shredding the veil of magic that bound him.

The dragon spun back to his prey. No, the knight. *His* knight. Finn. *Mine.*

His gaze locked onto the human standing before him, sword lowered, breath ragged, staring up at him not with terror, but something *worse.*

Trust.

The dragon did not understand. Shaking his head, he huffed out another too-hot breath. The dragon was driven by instinct, but he was not mindless. And he *would* figure this out.

No, I am not a dragon. I'm...a man. A prince. A brother. A lover. I am Cedric.

The knowledge struck with the force of a thunderclap. *I am Cedric. I know this man. I love this man.*

The dragon staggered back a step, claws flexing in the sand. The magic twisted inside him, resisting, snarling. But for the first time, he was fighting it. Truly fighting it.

"Please come back to me," the knight whispered. Finn— *gods, Finn*—he wasn't running. Even when he should be.

Stupid Finn. Stupid, wonderful Finn.

To hold on to hope in the face of certain death. To look upon a beast and believe there was still something worth saving.

It wasn't bravery. It wasn't even love.

It was madness.

The dragon's tail lashed out. Not by will. Not by *choice.* Cedric screamed within himself, a soundless explosion of grief.

Finn's body tumbled across the sand, limbs flailing, his sword spinning away in a glittering arc.

No, no, no! The word was a battering ram in Cedric's skull, but it meant nothing. It changed *nothing*. The dragon advanced, a predator closing in on its quarry, its jaws parting to reveal the deadly promise of its maw.

Fire pooled in his throat. One breath, and his prey would be nothing but smoldering ruin.

No, not prey. Finn. Gods, Finn!

He saw it—the outcome, the destruction—his fire licking over pale skin, blackening it, burning away everything he loved.

Cedric hurled himself at the unyielding walls of his own mind, slamming against them like a caged animal. He fought with the ferocity of a dying thing, tearing at the threads of Darius's enchantment, trying to claw his way back.

But it wasn't enough. The beast did not falter. The beast did not weep. But deep inside, Cedric did.

Please. The word was nothing more than a breathless prayer, a desperate plea hurled into the void. *Aurenis, gods, anyone—don't let me be the end of him.*

Time slowed.

Every heartbeat, every breath stretched thin. Finn lay there, motionless, staring up at the creature poised to end his life.

The roar of the crowd faded, reduced to a meaningless hum. Only one thing mattered.

Cedric.

He saw him—not just as a dragon, not just as a beast commanded to kill, but as *everything* Cedric had ever been.

The shimmer of his golden scales, more than just gold— streaked with amber and bronze, shifting in intricate patterns like veins in autumn leaves. The delicate iridescence of his wing membranes, catching the sunlight like spun glass.

The power in every line of his body, magnificent and terrifying in equal measure.

And then there were his eyes.

Those beautiful, familiar amber-flecked eyes. The eyes Finn had lost himself in. The eyes that had once softened when Cedric smiled, when he laughed, when he looked at Finn like he *mattered*.

"Cedric," Finn choked out, the sound little more than a whisper, devoured by the arena's frenzied hunger. But he didn't care about the thousands of voices baying for his death.

He only spoke to one.

"You are *not* what he's made you." Finn stared up at Cedric.

The dragon shuddered. A tremor that rippled from the very marrow of his being. His scales rattled, his claws flexing against the sand as if trying to root himself—as if resisting a command only his body obeyed.

And Finn saw it.

Another flicker of humanity in those tortured eyes, drowning beneath the weight of something that threatened to crush it entirely. A soul caught in a war it hadn't asked for.

Ignoring the protest of his battered, screaming body, he pushed himself to his feet, vision spinning. "Come on, golden boy," he urged, voice low. Gentle. As if speaking too loudly would shatter this fragile moment. "I've seen you fight harder against Clarence the goat. Don't let King Dickhead win."

Please, gods, let him listen.

Then, with agonizing slowness, Cedric stepped back. A single jerky movement. Then another.

Each step was stilted, like a marionette yanked against its will. But he was moving. Away from Finn. Away from the kill.

Finn's breath caught. This was *real*. Cedric had fought it. Cedric had chosen *him*.

Finn stepped forward, close enough that he could have reached out and touched Cedric's snout, had he dared. "Even like this, I trust you. Gods help me, *I trust you*."

The sword in Finn's grip trembled. Finn glanced down at it, swallowing as the memory rose of his first fight against the golden dragon at the tower. How Cedric had refused to fight, had only met each sword thrust with a parry of claws. The dragon could have killed him then, if he'd wanted to.

But he hadn't.

Finn's grip loosened. He let the sword fall. The crowd's roar dampened the *clang*.

The surrender wasn't for them. It was for Cedric. For everything they had been. For everything they still could be. He peered up at the dragon. At the prince he loved.

A chilling voice shattered the tenuous peace. "*Obey*." Darius, the single word full of command. "You belong to *me*. Now do as you were made to do."

The dragon let out a sound unlike anything Finn had ever heard. A keening cry that spoke of a soul being torn apart. It left Finn blinking against the sting of sudden tears.

"Rynvath's fangs." Finn's breath hitched. "*No*."

The dragon twitched. Claws flexed. His head gave the barest shake.

Please, Finn begged silently. *Please fight it*. He lifted a shaking hand, fingers ghosting against the tiny golden scales on Cedric's snout. The dragon shuddered, and for a single heartbeat, he leaned into it. A press against Finn's palm as fragile as a butterfly's wings.

For one agonizing heartbeat, he thought Cedric had won.

Then the humanity in his eyes faded. *Extinguished*, like a candle snuffed out. Like a man losing the war. Like a beast surrendering to instinct.

And in that instant, Finn knew he should never have dropped his sword. He had been *horribly* wrong.

One moment of hope, *gone*.

A blur of gold and terror crashed into Finn, so fast he had no time to react. Pain exploded through his skull as his back slammed into the earth. His lungs crushed under the dragon's claws.

Finn gasped for air. This was real. This was happening.

He had made a terrible, terrible mistake.

Above him, jaws unhinged. Flames lit the depths of the dragon's throat. And Finn understood, at last, that he was going to die.

He should have been afraid. He should have begged.

Instead, he whispered, "I love you." His voice broke. Finn tasted blood on his tongue. "I love you. And I forgive you."

THE DRAGON LOOMED over its prey.

The weak thing beneath his claws was still breathing, still trembling, still *his*. Molten fire swelled inside him, ready to burn the last fight out of this creature.

He had done this before. Again and again. He had felt bones snap, tasted the tang of a kill. It was instinct, it was hunger, it was *right*.

His prey did not beg. It whispered.

"I love you."

The dragon shuddered. The words were meaningless. They *should* have been meaningless. But something inside him cracked.

A tremor rippled through his scales. The magic snarled at the disturbance, coiling tighter around his mind, pressing its will upon his flesh. *Finish it. Burn him. Kill him.*

The voice came again, soft as a dying breath. "I love you. And I forgive you."

Cedric screamed. But not out loud. Not in a way anyone could hear.

He was there. Inside the dragon's mind. Watching. *Powerless.*

And Finn was about to die.

The dragon did not understand love. It did not understand forgiveness. But Cedric did. And gods, he couldn't *bear* it.

He saw Finn clearly now, not as prey, but as everything.

The man who had stood beside him beneath the stars. Who had shamelessly flirted with him, who had watched him carve wood into something beautiful. The man who had *trusted* him.

And now Finn was trusting him with his death.

No. No, please, gods, no.

The magic lashed at him, a thousand barbed chains yanking him deeper into the beast. His body was not his own. The fire in his throat gathered, ready to reduce Finn to nothing.

Move. Fight. Stop this.

But the dragon was stronger. His body would not listen.

Finn didn't cower beneath Cedric's claws. He didn't look away. He met Cedric's gaze with bloodshot eyes, ready for whatever might come. Then he lifted a filthy, bloodstained hand and rested it on Cedric's claw. Warm and intimate, a sign of love.

The dragon flinched.

It was enough. Cedric took it. He wrenched at the curse that had bound him. He clawed for himself, for Finn, for his own damn soul. The fire in his throat guttered out. His talons lifted.

A ragged snarl tore from his chest, and he staggered

back. The chains of magic screeched against him, yanking him toward obedience.

Beneath him, Finn stirred. "Cedric?" His voice was pained but *alive*.

And gods, Cedric had never wanted anything more than to keep it that way. The magic roared in protest, sinking hooks into his bones. The beast was still there, waiting to take control again.

Cedric shrank back another step.

I have to leave. Now.

Because if he stayed, he would not win this fight twice.

"What's wrong, beast?" Darius again. A pause, then a slow, taunting smirk. "Kill him, or I'll make you watch what I do to him instead."

Cedric's body went rigid, head swinging toward the royal box. For a single heartbeat, Finn thought Cedric might lunge at Darius instead. That the dragon would tear through the stands, raze the king's gilded throne to ruin, end this madness. But he didn't.

Cedric's gaze drifted back to Finn.

Finn shut his eyes. Whatever hold Darius had on Cedric, it was too much. Stronger than Cedric's heart and soul. He had tried.

But Cedric was slipping away again.

The corners of Finn's eyes burned with tears, and he didn't know if they were for himself, Cedric, or losing what they could have been. Maybe all of it.

He remembered the feel of Cedric against him that night in the stable, soft, warm, and *right*. The way the prince had resisted, terrified of *wanting*, and then the way he had finally given himself up. Not because he'd been forced, not because he'd lost, but because he had felt *safe*.

Trembling, Finn's eyes flashed open. His body was wrecked. Every muscle ached. His arms trembled from holding a shield that was long gone. He had no strength left.

Finn was done.

His gaze met Cedric's...and his breath caught. There was true recognition in those eyes again. Pain. Anguish.

And beneath it all, a desperate, clinging love.

Cedric was himself for the moment. But what could they do? A knight and a dragon, outnumbered.

Outmatched.

Already, Finn glimpsed guards preparing to enter the arena at Darius's behest. Then he and Cedric would both die, and this would all be for nothing.

And Darius wasn't going to let them die quickly.

Finn's blood went cold. His head tipped back against the sand, staring up at the sky. If Cedric didn't kill him now, Darius would use him as a knife to carve the prince apart.

He couldn't let that happen.

"You said I was yours," Finn rasped, forcing the words through the raw ruin of his throat. "Then take me, Cedric. But don't let him have me. Not again."

He shut his eyes. If this was the end, let it be Cedric.

Not Darius. Not torture. Just...Cedric. Just him. Just *them*.

When nothing happened, Finn's lashes fluttered open again. Cedric—his dragon—stared at him, then shook his head. *No.* A human gesture. A refusal.

Why? Didn't Cedric see? Didn't he understand?

The arena doors groaned open. Spears glinted as guards raced in. Finn's head thumped back into the sand, resigned.

"Cedric, *please*. If you love me, don't let me go back." Finn squeezed his eyes shut. A sob lodged somewhere deep in his chest. His hands curled into useless fists in the sand.

A sound rumbled from Cedric's chest—a low, broken rumble that rattled through the marrow of Finn's bones. He smiled, though his eyes burned from the grit and unshed tears.

He let go. Relaxed into it. Cedric would make it quick. Painless.

Scales rattled with sudden movement. Claws curled around him. Not piercing. Not crushing. *Holding* him.

Finn's eyes flashed open.

The ground lurched.

Powerful wings snapped open, kicking up a whirlwind of dust as Cedric launched them skyward.

"*What?*" The word tore from his throat, choked and disbelieving.

Screams of panic in the distance. Below them, the arena shrank into nothing. The spears, the guards, Darius's cruelty —everything was left behind.

Cedric's grip was tight around him, his heartbeat a thundering drum beneath Finn's cheek. But he was careful, so very careful, as if Finn was something precious.

Finn turned his face into Cedric's scales, exhaling a shuddering breath.

Cedric hadn't been his end after all.

Chapter Twenty-Seven

If you love me, don't let me go back.

Finn's words roared in Cedric's mind as he shot away from the arena. He trembled, magic burning like cold iron beneath his scales. The beast inside him snarled for release, urging him to tighten his grip. To crush. To kill.

But the knight's plea overpowered it all. Cedric remembered the horrifying condition of Finn in the dungeon. His protective rage battled Darius's magic. No, he would not let Finn go back to that.

Ever.

Finn was a warm weight against his chest, curled into the cage of his foreclaws. Beneath his palm, Cedric felt the knight's heartbeat—a frantic drum against his scales. So fragile. So precious. His other foreclaw held Finn's sword, wrested from the sand in his desperate escape.

But Darius's magic still lingered. It coiled in the marrow of his bones, whispering, *demanding*. No. He would *not* give in.

He forced his mind elsewhere. To Finn's broken voice in the arena. *I love you. And I forgive you.* Gods, *why?* Why had Finn forgiven him? And more importantly, *how?*

His grip on the knight tightened imperceptibly.

Below, the city churned in chaos. The metallic glint of guards scrambling, torches flaring along the streets, the distant clang of alarm bells. Cedric knew they would be pursued soon. His escape was not an end—only a stolen moment.

But it was a moment, nonetheless.

He angled his wings, catching an updraft, lifting them higher. Finn was silent in his grasp, but his breath was uneven. Pain or fear, Cedric couldn't tell. Maybe both.

The city fell away behind them. The buildings blurred into nothing but a smudge on the horizon, replaced by the vast sprawl of the countryside—fields a patchwork quilt under the late afternoon sun, winding rivers like veins of quicksilver, the dark line of forest curling toward the mountains.

Ahead, a lone tower loomed in the distance.

The outpost. The only place that offered any hope of safety, even if just for tonight.

But safety was a fragile thing. Gwenna was still in Darius's grasp. His sister, the one person who had never abandoned him, the one person he had failed time and again. The guilt choked him, thick as smoke.

He would save her. He swore it. But first, he had to make sure Finn survived this night.

As they neared the small valley, Cedric began his descent, the air whistling past his scaled hide. He circled the tower once, scanning the perimeter. The wind ruffled his spines, his nostrils flaring to catch any scent of danger, before landing with a soft thud in the small clearing before the outpost.

Gently, so gently, Cedric set Finn down in the clearing. The knight swayed as his feet met the earth, his balance faltering. He reached out, catching himself against Cedric's side. The dragon went utterly still.

Finn was *touching* him.

He braced for the recoil—for the disgust, for the moment Finn would remember, would see the monster he had been, the monster he still was. Any second now, Finn would pull away.

He would look up with horror, with betrayal.

But he didn't.

Instead, when Finn finally lifted his gaze, relief shone in his bloodshot eyes.

Relief. Not fear. Not hatred.

How? How could Finn still look at him like that, after everything?

A tremor ran through Cedric, his breath rattling out with a shudder. He wanted to say *something*, but his voice was locked away, trapped behind fangs and scales. He lowered his massive head, drawing as close to Finn as he dared. A soft, keening sound slipped past his lips—apology, plea, all the words he couldn't form.

Finn didn't move at first. His hand hovered, fingers shaking, hesitation hanging like a thin barrier between them. But then, with a deep breath, he closed the distance. His palm pressed against Cedric's snout. The knight's fingers traced the rough edges of his scales, the warmth of his touch searing through Cedric's skin like sunlight breaking through storm clouds.

"It's okay," Finn murmured, voice hoarse. "I mean, *not okay*-okay, considering you just tried to flatten me, but—" he exhaled, shoulders sagging. "I know it wasn't your fault."

Cedric shut his eyes. *I don't deserve this. I don't deserve you.*

But gods, he would take it. He would hold on to it with everything he had.

The sun sank lower, the sky painted in hues of amber and crimson. A prickle ran through Cedric's body. The warning of his shift approaching. Pain was coming.

He let out a slow, breathy sigh, nudging Finn with his

snout before turning toward the stable. Cedric heard the distant bleat of a goat as he paused at the stable entrance.

He didn't want to be alone. Not tonight.

When he turned, Finn was already there, watching him. No hesitation, no questions—just a quiet understanding in his gaze.

Without a word, Finn followed him inside, shutting the door behind them.

The last light faded, and the pain began.

FINN WATCHED, jaw tight, as Cedric's transformation began.

The dragon's form convulsed, scales rippling like water, melting into sweat-slicked skin. Bones snapped and groaned, twisting, realigning, a grotesque symphony of suffering.

Finn had seen gruesome battlefield wounds, had held dying men in his arms, but this? This was something else.

This was *slow*. This was agony stretched thin.

Cedric panted, muscles seizing and trembling as his body fought itself. His claws dug into the dirt, talons shrinking into fingers, his wings crumpling in on themselves like paper crushed in a fist. Each shattered breath was a sound Finn never wanted to hear again.

He wanted to *do* something. To reach out. To stop it.

But he couldn't.

Finn stood there, helpless, bearing witness to Cedric's torment—a torment he *never* should have had to endure.

Darius had made him into this. Had twisted and broken him, piece by piece, until Cedric's own body had become his cage.

And Cedric had hidden it. Not out of malice. Not out of deceit. But to *survive*.

Finn had hated him for that lie once—had burned with betrayal at the thought of it.

Now?

Now he would burn Darius's entire kingdom to the ground before letting anyone put chains on Cedric again. Finn's jaw clenched so hard his teeth ached.

At last, after what felt like a lifetime, Cedric collapsed. Where a dragon had been moments before, a man lay curled on the stable floor. His chest rose and fell in unsteady gasps, his skin damp with sweat, trembling.

Finn moved before he could think—too fast, too reckless. Pain lanced through him, a visceral reminder of everything his body had endured. His breath hitched, but he forced himself to his knees, biting back a groan as he braced his still-healing hand against the ground for balance.

Grit scraped his skin as he lowered himself beside Cedric, not gracefully, but with sheer stubborn determination.

His hand found Cedric's forehead, brushing damp strands of hair from his flushed skin. "Cedric?"

"Finn." The word was little more than breath. Then Cedric's eyes squeezed shut, tears sliding from the corners.

Finn's heart ached. Pain? Exhaustion? Or...everything?

"You saved me." Finn's fingers traced over Cedric's wrist, over the pulse still beating there, searching for wounds, for any sign that the magic had left damage deeper than what he could see. Finn had fought back against the dragon, though he'd done what he could to minimize the blows. Had he hurt Cedric?

The prince shook his head, his voice cracked. "No. I almost killed you."

"Shh." Finn pulled him close, wrapping his arms around him. Holding him together. Holding them *both* together. "But you didn't. You fought it. You broke free. That's what matters."

Cedric buried his face against Finn's chest, his body shaking with silent sobs. Finn held him tight, a safe harbor.

Whispering quiet reassurances, fingers combing through damp hair, until the trembling finally eased.

And then Finn moved—just a little shift, just a slight adjustment—and pain shot through his ribs like a red-hot dagger. His breath hitched. His arms locked tighter around Cedric, more out of reflex than comfort, and a low groan slipped through his teeth.

Cedric stiffened immediately. Pulled back. Too fast, too sharp. His red-rimmed eyes darted over Finn, realization dawning. "Finn, you're—"

"Shhh," Finn exhaled through gritted teeth, still half-wincing. "We were having a moment. Let me suffer in peace."

Cedric did *not* look amused.

Finn sighed. "Fine. Yes. I am in horrible, agonizing pain. But that's beside the point." He waved a lazy hand, as if dismissing his own battered state.

A strangled sound slipped from Cedric, something between a disbelieving laugh and a sob. His shoulders sagged and the crease between his brows deepened. "Finn..."

Finn smirked. "I can't have you thinking you're the *only* one who's suffering here."

Cedric huffed out a breath—half-exasperation, half something else. But the guilt still lingered in his expression.

"Hey." Finn reached up, thumbing away a stray tear on Cedric's cheek. "I'd say we're even now. You tried to kill me. I tried to talk you into killing me. Frankly, I think I was the bigger idiot."

Cedric closed his eyes, his lips pressing into a thin line. Then, quietly, "Thank you."

Finn didn't ask for what. He just pulled Cedric back in, ignoring every screaming ache in his body, and held him.

After a moment, Cedric pulled back. He still looked like an emotional wreck, but his voice was stronger when he said, "We should...tend to our wounds." He swallowed. "Especially yours. I don't know how you even walked in the arena after..." He trailed off, lips pressing into a frown.

Finn huffed out a tired laugh. "Pure spite, mostly."

A dry, broken chuckle escaped Cedric. "That...actually explains a lot."

Finn smirked. "It's gotten me this far." Then he shook his head. "King Dickhead couldn't have a half-dead man fighting a dragon. Wouldn't be *sporting*." He let sarcasm coat the words, covering them like armor. "He had a healer tend to me beforehand."

Cedric blinked, then huffed out a derisive snort. "Well, that's a small kindness I hadn't expected. Twisted, but kind." He paused, eyes narrowing. "King Dickhead? You called him that in the arena...I remember."

"Oh, yes. I came up with *many*, *many* creative names for the current ruler of Lunareth while I was enjoying my stay in the dungeon." Finn smiled, though even his face hurt.

Amusement danced in Cedric's eyes. "I'd love to hear more of those in time." Then he cleared his throat and shifted. "Give me a moment. I'm underdressed." He disentangled from Finn, pushing to his feet as he strode the short distance to a peg holding a set of clothing.

Battered and bruised as he was, Finn couldn't help himself. "That's a pity. I was enjoying the view."

Cedric froze, turning to stare at him. His face went utterly blank. "You...*what?*"

Finn laughed, the sound unexpected, scraping up from somewhere deep inside him. Gods, he *needed* that laugh.

"You heard me," he said, grinning at the gaping prince. Which Finn regretted, because smiling hurt.

Cedric's shoulders stiffened as he tugged the clothing off the peg. He faced away from Finn as he dressed, as if he feared what he'd discover in Finn's expression. "I don't understand." His voice was small, almost lost. "Not after what you said before."

Said before? Finn cocked his head, brow creasing. A pang of confusion rippled through him. "What in Kavros's name are you talking about?"

Cedric turned back to him, something painful in the way his fingers clutched at his half-buttoned shirt. "When...when you found out what I was." His voice was almost inaudible. He stood there, hesitant and vulnerable.

Oh.

The shock, the fury, the *betrayal* he had felt in that moment—when he had thought Cedric was just another monster to slay. When he thought everything between them had been a lie.

Finn exhaled slowly. *What I said then doesn't matter*, he wanted to say. But it *did*, and they both knew it. He had thrown those words like stones, and Cedric had felt every strike.

With a soft grunt, he rose and limped closer, buttoning the rest of Cedric's shirt with clumsy fingers. "I didn't know then what I know now."

If Cedric had trusted him sooner, would things have been different? Finn didn't know. He *couldn't* know. He wanted to believe he would have handled it better. That he wouldn't have drawn his sword, wouldn't have recoiled. But what if he had?

Maybe Cedric had been right not to tell him. Maybe Finn had never given him a reason to.

"Finn?" Cedric's voice was soft, hesitant, like a plea.

Finn stepped back, taking him in. Cedric looked hollowed-out, his exhaustion evident in the way his hands trembled. And yet, somehow, he was still infuriatingly, impossibly beautiful. It wasn't fair. "Yes, Your Highness?" The title came out lighter than he meant—teasing, but weary, a half-hearted shield against everything that still ached.

The prince hesitated, as if thrown by Finn's response.

But Cedric's shoulders relaxed, which Finn took as a victory. "I'm glad you're here."

Cedric's soft words were so heartfelt that for a moment, Finn forgot his pain. "Me, too. Let's go to the tower," he suggested, forcing himself to focus, to push past the exhaustion that threatened to overwhelm him. "We can tend to our wounds and...and talk."

Cedric nodded, and they made their way out of the stables. The climb to the tower was slow, every bruise and ache making itself known, but Finn welcomed the pain. It reminded him that he was *alive*. That they *both* were.

Inside the familiar confines of the tower, Finn let out a soft breath. Here, at least for the moment, they were safe. The knowledge didn't halt the bone-deep ache in his body, but it settled something deeper.

They reached the small room where Finn had convalesced. It looked the same. But Finn wasn't the same man who had rested here last.

He watched as Cedric went through a cabinet, pulling out supplies. Clean cloths for bandages, a basin for water, a jar of the healing salve from Finn's Gwenna-related injury.

Cedric laid them out neatly, like he needed the structure to settle his mind. His hands rested atop the salve for a second longer than necessary, then he exhaled, rolling his shoulders as if shaking something off.

After a pause, he gestured to the cot. "Take off everything but your drawers and lie down."

Finn smirked, seizing the opportunity. "I could take *everything* off, if you like." He winked, letting the teasing settle between them, hoping it would keep Cedric from sinking too deep into his own head.

Cedric blinked. *Stared*. As if Finn had just suggested something as outrageous as declaring war in his underclothes. Then, slowly, his shoulders loosened again. "Perhaps another time, when we're not half-dead."

Finn chuckled, but immediately regretted it when pain shot through his ribs. He exhaled slowly and peeled away his shirt, wincing as sore muscles protested the stretch.

Cedric's expression didn't change. But Finn caught the way his gaze skimmed over his body, scanning every bruise, every scrape, every mark. Finn knew that look. It was becoming a frustratingly consistent part of the prince's expressive repertoire.

Guilt.

As Cedric knelt beside him, fingers steady but tense, the silence stretched. The cool touch of the salve should have been a relief, but Cedric's hesitation made it burn.

"I remember *everything*," Cedric whispered as he worked. His voice was so quiet, so *heavy*, that Finn felt it more than heard it. "Every moment in the arena. I could *see* what was happening, but I couldn't stop myself. It was like being trapped inside my own body, *watching* as I—"

His voice broke. He swallowed hard, staring at his hands as if they were blood-covered talons. "As I tried to kill you."

Finn gritted his teeth as Cedric's fingers brushed over a particularly tender bruise, but he forced himself to meet his gaze. "But you *did* stop," he reminded him, his voice gentle. "You broke through Darius's spell. You saved both of us."

Cedric shook his head. Not a defiant motion, but a slow, weary refusal. His eyes, burning with unspoken torment, locked onto Finn's. "Only because of *you*."

His hands trembled as they hovered over Finn's skin, as if afraid to touch.

"Your words..." A painful inhale before Cedric continued, "they *reached* me, even when nothing else could." He hesitated, then whispered, "When you said you loved me, that you *forgave* me..."

Finn reached up, cupping Cedric's face in his hands, feeling the softness of his skin beneath his fingertips, the warmth of his cheek against his palm. "I meant every word," he said firmly, his voice thick with emotion. "I love you, Cedric. And I forgive you, not because I have to, but because there is nothing to forgive. Because I *know* you." He stroked his thumb along Cedric's cheek, feeling the way his jaw clenched, like he was holding back something painful. "What happened wasn't your fault. Unless you're telling me you *wanted* to crush me like a bug."

Cedric huffed a tired, disbelieving breath. "Of course not."

The prince's breath hitched. His shoulders sagged, tension bleeding from his frame as his eyes slid shut. For a moment, he stayed there, pressing just a little closer, like he needed the contact to anchor himself. Like he was holding onto Finn to keep from breaking apart.

Then, slowly, his breath evened. His lashes fluttered, and his eyes opened again, still glassy, still tired. Still carrying that weight.

"I love you too," he whispered. "More than I ever thought possible. And that's the problem." He blew out a long breath, shaking his head. "I—I can't do this. I can't risk this happening again. I *can't*—" His breath stuttered, his voice barely holding together. "I almost lost you. And not just to Darius. *To me*."

The anguish was so raw in his voice, Finn knew Cedric was one heartbeat from shutting him out again. Not allowed. Not after the hell they'd just been through.

"If you think I'm going to let you walk away now, you have another thing coming." Finn paused. "Or fly away. Whatever."

Cedric stared at him with a gaze that held the same fear as when he'd kept his secret from Finn. As if he was terrified their feelings would make the situation worse.

"And you're afraid for me? *Good*. That means everything between us is *real*." Finn didn't rein in the possessive satisfaction lacing his tone. "I'm a *knight*, Ced. I don't give up easily.

I'll chase you if I must, but *gods*, I'd rather just have you here."

His words stirred something in Cedric. The prince snapped out of whatever darkness he'd fallen into. He drew in a long breath, then whispered, "Mine."

"Damn right," Finn muttered. He leaned in, eyes blazing with conviction. "I swore myself to you in front of Darius."

A beat of silence as Cedric's eyebrows shot up.

Finn let out a breath. "Which, in hindsight, was probably a bad survival strategy."

Cedric blinked once. "*Finn*."

Then something cracked in Cedric's expression. He exhaled, shaky, like his body had just remembered how to breathe. "You're an *idiot*."

Finn huffed a soft laugh. "*You're* calling *me* the idiot? That's rich."

"Of all the royals you could pledge yourself to," Cedric went on, shaking his head, "you chose the *supposedly-dead-but-really-a-monster* prince."

"I said what I said." Finn ignored the fire in his ribs and leaned in, pressing a gentle kiss to Cedric's lips. Not a kiss of passion, but a promise. A *vow*.

When they parted, Cedric smiled again. Soft, but *real*. Then his expression turned serious. "Darius has Gwenna."

"With luck, he won't live to regret that." Finn nudged Cedric's hand with his own.

Cedric's brows flew up. "What do you mean?"

Finn grinned. "Your sister hit me with a *rock* to protect you. A woman like that won't be the submissive wife someone like Darius wants."

Cedric considered this for a moment, lips pursed, his brow furrowed in thought. "You're not wrong. And for any other woman stuck with someone like Darius, that might be dangerous for her." He paused, still thinking, his gaze unfocused. "But Darius obviously wants or needs her for something. So Gwenna should be safe, at least for a while."

Maybe long enough for Finn and Cedric to figure out a way to save her.

But Gwenna wasn't the only one who needed saving. And Finn didn't want to say what came next, but...

"Cedric, you have to take the crown." The words felt like lead on his tongue.

Cedric stiffened. His eyes widened, and for a second, he just *looked* at Finn, as if he couldn't quite believe he'd said it. "I don't... I *can't*..." He trailed off, shaking his head as panic brewed.

Finn swallowed. He should have waited for this conversation. Given Cedric time to breathe, to *recover*. But there *wasn't* time. "You think being a dragon half the day disqualifies you?"

Cedric scrubbed a hand through his hair, collecting himself, then let out a humorless snort. "That *does* put a damper on kingly duties, yes. Among other things."

Finn didn't hesitate. "If we break this curse, will you reconsider?"

Cedric sucked in a breath. "*If*," he echoed. He paused. "Finn, you think...it's possible?"

Finn nodded. "I'm *hopeful* that the curse can be removed or broken, yes."

Cedric's throat bobbed. His eyes slid shut, his breath uneven. Then, finally, his eyes snapped open with determination. "Then *yes*." A pause. "*Yes*, but it's just the two of us. I don't know how we stand a chance."

Then something clattered downstairs.

Both men tensed. Their gazes met. Then, they moved.

Pain ignored. Exhaustion forgotten.

Finn hardly noticed the ache in his ribs as he surged to his feet. Adrenaline overrode it. He reached the bottom of the stairs first—and only then did it occur to him that charging into danger in nothing but his drawers was not a strategically sound move.

They reached the kitchen, skidding to a stop. There, standing in the middle of the room, was Clarence. The *goat*.

Clarence stared at them, chewing absently, his slitted pupils holding a strange intensity. Then magic rippled across his hide.

Finn froze.

Before his eyes, the goat shifted—legs stretching, fur vanishing, horns receding, form twisting until, where the goat had once stood, there was now a man.

A man dressed in leather, grinning at them.

"It's not *just* the two of you now, is it?"

Cedric's jaw dropped open. Finn thought he might have to help him close it for a moment, but then Cedric snapped it shut. "*Clarence?*"

The former goat tilted his head, eyes glinting with unmistakable mischief. "*Who else* would it be, *Prince* Cedric?" His grin widened. "It seems we have work to do."

About the Author

Amy Campbell is a former librarian and current wrangler of two boisterous boys. She lives in Texas where she avoids the heat by sitting inside and writing.

You can find out more about her books at amycampbell.info

Also by Amy Campbell

Tales of the Outlaw Mages

Breaker

Effigest

Dreamer

Persuader

Songbinder

Heartseeker

Airship Dragons

Dragon Latitudes

Dragon Meridians

Novellas

Dawn of the Jade Empress (Airship Dragons)

Breaking the Ice (Tales of the Outlaw Mages)

www.ingramcontent.com/pod-product-compliance
Lightning Source LLC
Chambersburg PA
CBHW011129190726
48289CB00012B/2974